We can Work it out

BELLE HENDERSON
& CJ MORROW

Dedication:

For Jamie, Katie, Barbara and Peter for their support and encouragement.

One

Emily

'Hey, how's it going? You all ready for your big day?'

'No, no I'm not. I'm panicking, Sab.' I appraise myself in my wardrobe mirror. I don't feel comfortable at all. 'This outfit is just all wrong!' I stare at my reflection with my phone wedged between my neck and shoulder. The nerves are really setting in now.

'It's a bit late for outfit changes now darling, you have to leave soon,' Sabrina says gently.

'The shirt you lent me, it's bit small. I mean I love it, but it's just a bit...' I pull at the gaping shirt and try to make it stretch better across my boobs. It doesn't and it's now exposing some of my bra.

I'm wearing a black skirt suit with a white, very tight, shirt and some black high heels that are smart but I wouldn't wear them on a night out. I'm not wearing tights, it's autumn but apparently, we are having an Indian summer. It's one of those gorgeous, crisp, sunny days where the sky is a cloudless bright blue and the leaves are starting to turn golden. It's my absolute favourite time of year, and just a few months away from Christmas when I can truly spoil my little girl, Rosie. I

1

smile as I remember her excited squeals last year as she came running into my room on Christmas morning. Rosie is five, that special age where she still believes in all things magical such as Santa, the Easter bunny and talking animals.

'Oh yeah, I bought that shirt back in my Atkins diet days, super skinny back then. What are you wearing it with?' Sabrina asks as I simultaneously take a photo and send it to her.

'Wow, you look gorgeous, love the hair, very professional. The shirt looks fine to me, darling. There's nothing like flaunting what you've got to get what you want.'

Oh hell. Now I feel like a whore.

'I'm not sure. It's a bit inappropriate for an interview, don't you think?' I open up my wardrobe and stare at the alternatives. There is a navy-blue shirt but I can't wear that as it will clash with black. I also own a white shirt but it has too many ruffles and looks too flouncy, not serious enough. I have to make an executive decision and I don't have anything else suitable. I will have to wear this, breathe in all day and just hope I don't burst out of it. Oh, why didn't I check the fit before? I could have bought something new. As I do up my jacket buttons, I reassure – or delude – myself that the jacket should cover most of my modesty.

'It's perfect, trust me. Do you have your stuff ready for your presentation?'

'Yes, I've printed everything out, all stapled and good to go.'

'Why the printing? Is it 1987?'

'Oh, I'm taking my laptop too.' I laugh. If only Sabrina could see the wheelie case I'm taking as well! I used to take it to London when I worked there many years ago and it worked a treat when running for the train, which I often did.

'I can't find my memory stick and I'm assuming they'll want to project my presentation onto a big screen, so I have to take the laptop. If not, I can give out handouts. I thought I'd cover all bases, you know.' Come to think of it, I last saw Rosie playing with the memory stick, perhaps she's taken it to my mum's by accident. I wouldn't be surprised, she once took our TV remote to school.

'You'll be fine, you will dazzle them with your presentation and your personality. You've got this,' Sabrina encourages against my babbling.

'I hope so, I really want this job. It's so nerve wracking, I haven't had a second interview in years.' I chew on my nails as I think of the possibilities, there's a lot resting on this. Holidays for Rosie and I, day trips to Legoland and the cinema, maybe a spa day for me and Sab. And finally, the possibility of buying a house of my own. Oh the endless opportunities that come with securing this job. I yearn to earn my own money on a permanent basis and not rely on income solely from *him* and the government and intermittent temp jobs.

'Emily, you'll be fine. You've got this. It's your time to shine.'

'Thanks, Sab. I'll message you later.'

'You better do! See you soon and good luck, not that you need it. Bye.'

I end the call while rummaging through my drawers, still not satisfied with my outfit, I come across an old neck scarf. Its black and purple vertical stripes will zhush up my ensemble, inject a bit of colour and hide my obscene cleavage. Perfect, I'm finally ready.

Well, ready as I'll ever be.

Realising I have less than ten minutes to go, I reach for the Kalms on my bedside table. These little gems have become slightly addictive since my husband left me. It takes the edge off and I have actually cut down quite a lot on all things recreational in the last couple of years. When he first left, I was smoking a lot, probably around twenty cigarettes a day if I'm honest, and around two or three glasses of wine a night, sometimes a bottle if it was a bad day. I took Kalms during the day to keep me going and help mask what I was going through. I think I've done pretty well since the dark days. I've given up smoking and cut way down on the wine, I'm only having about a glass a night now and sometimes I don't have any, so Kalms are really my only vice and of course I'll give them up eventually. Just once I get this job. Anyway, they're herbal, aren't they?

My thoughts are interrupted by a message from Mum showing a photo of Rosie grinning back at the camera with both hands wrapped around what looks like a massive chocolate doughnut. Mum then messages seconds later. Hmmm interesting breakfast, Mum.

My mum: *Nanna's house, nanna's rules.*

I roll my eyes, chuckling to myself and reply to her choosing to ignore her attempt to wind me up.

Me: *Hehe she looks sweet! Leaving in a minute, give Rosie a kiss from me and wish me luck?!*

She sends a little video back of Rosie with chocolate smeared all over her face. *Good luck Mummy, you are the bestest Mummy.*

My heart melts and I send back three loves hearts. It's just typical that my interview clashes with a teacher training day, otherwise Rosie would have been in school now.

I lock my phone and chuck it into my wheelie case. As I leave my bedroom a thought creeps into my mind that I now resemble an air hostess.

Positive thinking. Yay, I'm about to board the flight to my potential new life!

My neighbour's fat, grey, fluffy cat is crouched under my car staring at me with such disdain I swear it wants me dead so it can live under my car forever. We have this confrontation most days. Rosie is normally the one who is good at getting rid of it by patting its bum and shooing it away. Something about it unnerves me and I won't get too close.

'Hsssssss,' I attempt.

The cat stays put, giving me a contemptuous, defiant look.

'Hssssssssssss,' I attempt again, this time louder while showing my teeth.

It just blinks at me. Time to try a different tactic.

'Ruff ruff. Ruff ruff.' Wow I didn't know I could imitate a dog so well.

The cat just blinks its big, green eyes.

'Ruff ruff.' Unable to crouch due to the combination of tight shirt and fitted skirt, I'm now on all fours, getting down to its level. The rough pavement cuts into my knees and I'm glad I'm not wearing tights.

Our eyes lock in a stare off. The cat's tongue flicks lazily across its nose.

'Ruff ruff ruff ruff ruff.' Louder I bark, more aggressively this time but the cat *still* stares. 'Grrrrrrrrrrr. Ruff ruff,' I snarl, showing my fangs as I feel a dribble of saliva slide out the corner of my mouth. God knows what that's doing to my carefully applied makeup. My throat is beginning to get sore.

'Ooooooowww owwwwww.' Howling to the sky to call upon the rest of my pack.

The cat still stares.

'Ruff ruff, oooooowwwwww.' I must be looking really menacing now. Why isn't it backing away? 'Owwwwwwwwwww, ruff ruff ruff ruff.' I've had enough of this shit. 'MOVE YOUR FAT FURRY ARSE FROM UNDERNEATH MY CAR YOU BIG BALL OF FLUFF!!' I bellow.

The cat nonchalantly licks its paws and I swear it's smirking.

I feel a burning in the back of my head. I turn to see my pensioner neighbour, Margaret, staring at me in horror.

'Pss pssst, come to Mummy, darling Patrick. Come away from the scary lady,' she calls in a shaky voice with her arms stretched out.

'Umm, sorry Margaret but it wouldn't move and I need to get my car out. I'm in a bit of a rush for a job interview,' I hear myself say, sounding pathetic and apologetic.

Margaret pauses and regards me cautiously before replying. 'Yes dear, and he's a *he*, not an *it*. His name's Patrick.'

'Okay. He. Right.'

'Remember dear, he's only an innocent little cat. You can always just come and get me next time if he's causing you any trouble.' Margaret shuffles over to Patrick and scoops the fat ball of fur into her tiny hands.

'I'm sure you're not doing your knees any good, dear,' she says as she retreats up the path to her house. I clamber inelegantly to my feet and dust my knees off.

Bloody Patrick has now made me late.

6

I'm not going to deny that I most definitely break a few speed limits on my way to my job interview at Genevre's. The journey is only ten minutes and I'm grateful that the appointment is at 10am, just missing the worst of rush hour which sometimes more than triples the time of any journey. I drive into the car park, negotiating a space close to the pay and display. Turning off the ignition I pull down the mirror to study my face and reapply my Heather Shimmer lipstick.

My face looks okay, no lines yet and I'm lucky to have olive skin that I'm often told makes me look younger than my thirty-two years. I reach into the back seat to grab my bottle of water for a quick pre-interview whistle wetting and it's then that I freeze.

Shhittttttttt.

There's a sudden satisfying, yet ominous, release across my chest. I force myself to look down and see that the top two shirt buttons have burst open and are each hanging on by a thread, oh hell! I feel thankful that I am wearing the air hostess neck scarf and rearrange it from being tied at the side to down the front, it just about covers my cleavage but it now looks like I'm wearing just a bra underneath as you can see a little bit of skin on either side of the neck scarf. I decide to tuck the corners into my bra creating the image of it being a top, it looks a little wacky but at least I don't look like a stripper. This is not a good look and I am super stressed after this morning's antics; I think someone is trying to tell me that this job isn't meant to be.

Get a grip, I tell myself and I grab my wheelie case from the passenger seat and force my body out of the car and head towards the pay and display to get my ticket. I'm nearly there when my phone beeps and I stop and open my case and rummage inside for it. As soon as I see the display, I realise I should have ignored it because it's Liam – my ex-husband. His timing is just impeccable.

Cheating Bastard: *Hi Emily, we need to talk. I've been thinking and I want to see Rosie a lot more, she loves it here with us. Rosie and Tiger Lily are just like sisters. When are you free to talk this through?*

Bastard. I knew this day would come but I can't think about it now. Must. Stay. Focused.

I glance at the ticket machine.

'Oh, shit.'

'You okay?' A male voice asks.

I look up, and keep on looking up because the voice belongs to a big guy, well over six-foot-tall, big built but not muscly, or fat. He's probably a bit younger than me with what I can only describe as brown smoke for hair, and despite his size there's something gentle about him. His stance reminds me of the character Lennie from *Of Mice and Men*. I want to say no I'm bloody not and burst into tears and clutch onto him and sob but all I manage is, 'It needs coins,' before running off back to my car to search for change and almost falling arse over tit in the process.

I am seriously considering getting into the driving seat, admitting defeat and going home.

But I can't. I *need* this job.

I grab some change from the car and stomp back to the pay and display and he's still there. I ram the coins into the machine as he watches and I wonder why he's being such a gentleman by letting me go first. The final 20p coin keeps rejecting and he suggests I wet it. What is he talking about? He silently hands me a replacement coin when I ask if he could swap one with me. The machine finally spits out a ticket and I snatch it and stomp back to my car.

When I head back past the pay and display, the gentle giant is still there, slowly licking coins and popping them into the coin slots, bless him. I wonder who told him that works? Probably his mum. His coin licking doesn't seem to be working. Will he crack and end up pummelling the pay and display until it breaks? I'm grateful to him but so stressed I don't think I even manage a smile.

Must think positive and get my game face on for this interview.

Must get this job! Must get this job! Must get this job!

I power into the building and march up to its glossy reception desk.

'Hi, I'm Emily Cod. I have an interview today with the underwriting department at 10am.' I hear my tone go up at the end and wonder when I started speaking like an Australian. The receptionist checks his list with his long, bony fingers tapping gently on his computer screen

'Ah yes, Mrs Cod, they're running a little late today. Please help yourself to coffee and take a seat.' I glance to where his ET index finger is pointing, look back at him and give him a winning smile.

Picking up my already tired feet, I trot over to the machine to get myself a much-needed coffee. How ironic that they are running late after all my panics to get here on time. Oh well, at least I get a little breather to calm down and relax beforehand. I didn't correct the receptionist when he said Mrs, although I suppose I should have but every time I correct someone I feel as though I have to explain/justify *why* I am a Miss even though it's ridiculous to think that they care or would even notice. I'm paranoid that people will judge me as a singleton once they find out I have a child, silly I know.

As inelegant as *Cod* is, I have kept Liam's surname. I didn't want to have a different name from my daughter and believe it or not it's actually better than my maiden name, *Longbottom* – you can imagine the innuendo that surname brought. There's also the added bonus that it probably annoys Liam's wife, Tiny, and that's a small triumph.

Jamie

My phone pings as I drive into the car park.

It pings again just as I am negotiating a particularly large crater filled with muddy water; this is a council car park and they should be ashamed of themselves. It pings again – managing to sound anxious and angry this time – at the very instant I manoeuvre into a tight space. I know who it is.

I switch the engine off, pull out my phone.

My dad: *Knock em dead son.*

My dad: *Good luck.*

My dad: *Everything okay???*

He's a born worrier, my dad. I message back to reassure him. Dads eh? He still thinks I'm a kid; I'm nearly thirty.

Today's my big day, my chance to finally nail the job I want; the job I should have, to be in the place I should be by now – according to my dad. Today is final interview day, I'm on a shortlist of two.

I take deep breaths as I head over to the ticket machine, fill my lungs with oxygen to sharpen my brain, calm any last-minute nerves. I remind myself I'm not nervous. I'm not, but I don't want to cock this up.

I haven't parked here before, first time round I parked in Genevre's staff car park, but there isn't space today; some sort of maintenance going on according to their HR department.

My phone pings again; it's reminding me that my interview is in fifteen minutes. Fifteen minutes to lift off. Or let down.

'Oh shit,' a female voice hisses. I look up to see a girl – is that politically correct – no, a woman, standing in front of the ticket machine, her phone in her hand.

'You okay?' I ask as I approach.

She jumps, her super smooth ponytail flicking up in the air.

'It needs coins,' she snaps, turning and trotting back to her car. She's pulling a small, black wheelie case behind her; she cusses as it catches in the ruts on the car park's crappy surface. Anger emanates from her retreating form, the muscles in her legs clench as she puts each foot down. She's wearing smart shoes with blocky heels. Quite high. She would be short without them. A neat black suit completes her look, the skirt just grazing her knee. She's got good legs, gym-toned.

She's reached her car and I'm still staring at her. She yanks open the door, leans in, raises her left leg out behind her for balance. I'm mesmerised.

I drag my eyes back to the ticket machine. She's right, there's no doing this with a phone app. Another reason for the council to be ashamed of this car park; for God's sake, drag yourselves into the 21st century.

I yank my wallet out and start sifting through for the right coins, grateful that I have some, but only because I nipped into the newsagent for some mints before I left.

Flicky ponytail woman is back before I even step up

to the ticket machine. She has coins in her hand and starts thrusting them into the slot, cussing when one is rejected. She tries again, same result. She tuts several times.

'Wet it,' I say, trying to be helpful.

She narrows her eyes at me. 'I don't suppose you have one I could swap with?' She waves 20p in front of me.

I smile and make the swap.

She gets her ticket and dashes off, still trundling her wheelie case behind her.

I step up to the machine and feed my coins in. I give the dodgy 20p a surreptitious lick before I push it in. It bounces straight back out. I try again, this time I'm more generous with my saliva. Ponytail girl whips past me just as I have my tongue on the coin. She frowns but says nothing, just stares with her limpid, brown eyes.

But the machine won't accept the coin and I don't have time for this nonsense now. I press for a ticket, I'm 20p short on the fee.

Ticket on car, and I'm dashing across the car park, rushing towards Genevre's reception but not before I slip and skid. I'm fine, I don't fall, just limp away as my knee throbs. It takes me a few seconds to realise I've trodden in something disgusting; the stench alerting me to its presence. More time wasted wiping it off on the grass verge. It stinks. What is it? Dog muck, fox shit?

I give my name over in a voice that sounds as though I've been running, a lot.

'Ah, Mr Bowe.' The receptionist runs his finger down his screen then glances back up at me. He sniffs the air and a faint frown crosses his brow before he continues. 'They're running late, only about fifteen minutes, please help yourself to a coffee.' He waves in the general direction of a coffee machine, offers a sharp smile, then refocuses on his computer screen before looking past me to his next customer.

Running late, that doesn't bode well. That means that my rival, the other *short-lister*, is doing well, so well they want to hear more.

I forego the coffee and flop down into the low leather seats in the middle of the reception area. I take a quick look at the sole of my shoe but can see no evidence of the shit-stepping.

Flicky ponytail girl is sitting opposite, letting her eyes appraise me. I smile. She doesn't. She adjusts her wheelie case which is now nestling between her feet. What precious cargo hides within?

Two

Emily

I watch as Lennie comes through the reception doors, he pushes through the turnstile before signing in with reception and plonks himself down on the couch opposite me. He looks directly at me and smirks and I feel my cheeks burn as my eyes narrow. Is he laughing at me?

It suddenly registers that he could possibly be my competition and may not be as stupid as he looks. On closer inspection he is carrying a man bag that looks way too small on his cumbersome body. His suit looks good quality, expensive even and his shoes are black, shiny and new. I instantly hate that my potential rival might be this man.

I haven't worked full-time for the last five years for obvious reasons, just part-time temp roles but they've all been relevant to underwriting so I *have* kept my hand in. The recruitment agency was really impressed with my CV and I was thrilled that Genevre had given me the chance of an interview. Now Rosie's in school I'll be able to manage a full-time job with Mum's help with childcare. I'm so desperate to provide the best upbringing I can for her. Before I went on maternity leave my last serious role was as a senior underwriting manager in real-estate but previous to that I had worked in insurance for many years and worked my way up the ladder, quickly whizzing through the exams. I tell myself they can't discriminate. This is the 21st century and companies are really positive about getting women back into work after having kids. Aren't they?

I'm up to this. I am.

Jamie

I'm guessing flicky ponytail girl is a rep, her wares safely in that wheelie case. She has that well-polished, sharp look of a sales rep. I wonder what she's selling? I wonder what Genevre would buy? Could be anything, stationery, furniture, computers. Anything.

Plants. Maybe she's selling plants. There is an abundance of them in this reception area and I know from my brief walk through the offices during my first interview that they are everywhere in this building, or is it a series of buildings?

The Genevre building is a landmark in our town. Some call it the Pentagon, but that's inaccurate. It's a hexagon; six interconnected buildings with a central glass-covered atrium in the middle. The atrium is reminiscent of a shopping mall, complete with gym, hairdresser, cafés and even a convenience store. Rumour has it that a national chain is opening a dentists/opticians here soon, too. The idea is to keep everyone on the office campus as much as possible, especially at lunchtime. They seem to think people work harder if they *live* here.

I've been in the gym; once, two years ago I went as a guest of a girlfriend. I think she wanted to be impressed but evidently wasn't and dumped me a week later.

The campus is impressive externally too, landscaped, a lake with fountains, benches everywhere to eat your lunch on those rare, hot, summer days. Even the car parks are tree lined to create shade for the cars to park in. Ironically, the crappy council car park is a hark back to an abortive attempt to run a park and ride scheme into the town centre. But no one used it. Why would they with everything available here?

You can see the building, called Genevre Lodge – though it couldn't be less like a lodge if it tried – from the motorway. Anyone who travels the M4 knows of it. It's a major employer in our town. Ironically Genevre doesn't occupy all the segments like it used to. Technology has moved on, and a recession, so thirty years after it was purpose built for them, they now only occupy three segments. And *I* want to work in one of those segments. The others are occupied by another insurance company, an accountancy company and some computer organisation I'd never heard of until I did my research.

My phone pings.

Everyone, and I mean everyone, in Reception looks at me; two receptionists, two guys at the vending machine, a woman watering the plants (who I hadn't even noticed previously) and flicky ponytail girl.

I've committed *the* cardinal sin: my phone isn't on silent.

I fish it out of my jacket pocket and quickly rectify my error before it pings again.

It's my dad, again: *How's it going? Got the job yet?*

I don't reply. He knows my interview time, knows that I should be in the room right now impressing them with my presentation on global insurance risks, wowing them with my knowledge and witty insights. If I tell him there's a delay, he'll panic. I suppose I should be grateful to him, at least his message has reminded me to silence my phone and not interrupt my interview. If we'd been running on time, I'd be looking a right idiot now.

I push my phone into my manbag – my dad called it a briefcase but that is pretentious and delusional and so old school – and check the side pocket to make sure my data stick is still there. Can't do the presentation without the slides – although the rules are that only eight are allowed. No death by PowerPoint at Genevre.

Clicking heels echo on the reception area floor and I look up, as does ponytail girl, her hair – as dark brown as her eyes – swishing as she turns her head to see the source of the steps.

Two people approach, both with clipboards. One a guy younger than me, one a woman in her forties. They're heading straight for us and I wonder which one I will get? I can't decide which one looks like a sales type person and which one looks like they work in HR.

'Jamie Bowe?' The woman looks straight at me while holding her clipboard aloft.

I stand up and offer my hand. She shakes it and introduces herself as something that sounds like Burt, but I do catch that she's the head of Human Resources.

Just chill out.

Emily

Lennie has been called by a lady with a clipboard; he gets up and trundles over to her, not picking his feet up properly as he walks.

'Emily Cod,' calls the young man next to her. I get up, smooth my skirt down and paste on my best winning smile. I am now more than convinced that smug, smirky Lennie is my rival, this makes me extra determined and as I go to shake the young man's hand, I dramatically hear a *Hunger Games* quote echoing in my head.

"Let the games commence and may the odds be ever in your favour."

Jamie

'This way.' Burt turns then waits for me to step alongside her. 'Sorry about the delay. Sorry about the car park; they're pruning the trees today so keep sectioning off areas, people have to keep coming out and moving their cars, such a pain, so disruptive. It's why your interview was delayed.' She rolls her eyes. 'Did you manage to park okay?'

'Yes, thank you.' I don't bore her with the 20p fiasco or the dog-shit shoe shuffle.

'Excellent,' she says, not meaning excellent at all. 'Did you have far to come?'

'No, I live local.'

'Excellent.'

She herds me into a tiny, windowless, meeting room. This does not bode well. How the hell am I supposed to do my presentation in here? And who to?

'Take a seat, please,' she says as she sees me hesitate.

I plonk myself down. I wonder if now would be the time to ask if there's any point in my staying any longer. It's becoming increasingly obvious to me that the other candidate, the one who took up extra time, *my* time, has already been given the job. I imagine the message I'll send to my dad; I'll have to make it sound positive as well as let him down gently, prepare the way for my final *unsuccessful* call. And to think I took half a day's leave for this.

'Okay,' she says, sitting across the table from me. 'As you know you were on a shortlist of two.' She smiles, waiting for me to agree. Here it comes, the push off. Just get on with it. 'Well, we've decided, that is the department manager has decided, that your interviews will be in two parts.' She smiles and waits for me to react. I nod and try to look enthusiastic. 'One of you will be meeting the team while the other does their presentation, then you'll swap, then there'll be a sort of group discussion. What do you think?' She sits back and folds her arms as though she's expecting me to congratulate her.

'Okay.' I nod and smile again. Upbeat. 'Which am I doing first?'

'You're meeting the team.' A big smile and she jumps up and trots off at quite a pace with me scurrying to keep up. We head out of the segment and into the atrium. She starts telling me about it, how many panes of glass there are, how it's shaped to maximise sun capture, how the windows open automatically to increase air flow when it's hot and negate the need for air-con. I try to take this all in just in case there are questions later – surely there won't be. She's just telling me this to put me at ease, isn't she?

She's still keeping up quite a pace and I notice that other people are hurrying across the atrium too. All those free gym sessions obviously pay off, if I get the job I'll definitely go. Probably.

Involuntarily I turn and frown as we pass a queue of chatting people outside a coffee shop. She catches my look.

'Mid-morning coffee break,' she says, laughing. 'That place is so popular.'

Mid-morning? According to the clocktower in the

centre of the atrium it's 10.20am. What time do they start here? I thought Genevre's office hours were 9-5. Maybe it's staff from the other segments, the computer place maybe, those geeks like an early start according to my housemate, Tim, who is one, an IT geek, I mean.

We fly through double doors and we're in another Genevre segment. Burt sprints up two flights of stairs and I do my best to match her pace without panting too loudly.

I definitely need those gym sessions.

'Okay?' she asks, waiting for me and seeming to enjoy my barely suppressed puffing.

'Sure,' I smile.

'Don't worry, if you get the job you'll soon be fit; four floors and no lifts.' She grins and my heart sinks at the prospect of more stairs. I'll be sweating like a pig and red in the face by the time I meet the team. But, fortunately, she opens the door and we enter the floor we're already on.

Thank God.

We belt down a corridor and burst into another meeting room. Four smiling faces turn and greet me.

'Hi, I'm Sharon.'

'I'm Karen.'

'I'm Hayden.'

'I'm Jayden.'

I find myself blinking as I run their names through my brain. Is this a joke? Sharon, Karen, Hayden, Jayden.

Their sunny little faces are staring at me, waiting.

'Hi,' I say. 'I'm Jamie.' I wonder if my rival has a name that will fit in with the rest of the team. Is it a prerequisite?

'Cool,' says Karen, or is it Sharon?

'Yeah,' say Hayden and Jayden together.

'Wow,' says Sharon or Karen.

They're easily impressed.

'Coffee?' Jayden asks, standing up as I sit down.

'Please,' I say, because it would be rude to refuse and because everyone else is already hugging their own coffee cups.

'It's just normal coffee.' He glances over at the machine in the corner. 'Or if you want a latte, or a mocha, or a skinny or a cappuccino, I could run down to the atrium for you.'

I imagine him waiting forever in that queue and reply that normal coffee will be just fine.

'Any plans for the weekend?' Sharon/Karen asks, smiling at me.

Oh God, it's Wednesday morning and we're talking about the weekend already. Either they're as bored with their jobs as I am in my current one or they just don't know what to say to me.

'Just the usual.' I'm sure they don't want to know that this weekend I will be helping my Dad finally start to remove all my mum's belongings – we're talking clothes, shoes and handbags mainly – from his loft where he put them nearly five years ago when she died.

'Cool.'

Jayden plonks a murky coffee in front of me and collectively everyone, including me, pick up their cups and drink.

'I'll be back in thirty,' HR Burt says, without waiting for a response.

'Thanks, Berta,' Karen/Sharon says.

And she's gone. Berta, her name's Berta.

All eyes are on me.

No one speaks but a smile goes around the room

like a Mexican wave.

'Are you already working in insurance?' Hayden reads from a prepared list in front of him. I expect he'll tick the question off once I've answered.

'Yeah. I'm over at Kanes in town.'

'Town centre. Parking's expensive,' Karen/Sharon muses.

'It is. Very. And sometimes it's hard to find a space.'

'Yeah. Don't have that problem here.'

'Except today.'

'Yeah,' they all chorus, nodding and rolling their eyes.

This is too awful. Take control. Take control.

'Sharon,' I start, going almost cross-eyed in an attempt to look at both Sharon and Karen at the same time. 'How long have you worked here? What do you do?'

Sharon gives me a little smile and proceeds to tell me everything. Then it's Jayden's turn and pretty soon we've been all around the table. I see Hayden glance down at his list again and I quickly interrupt.

'So, what's the best thing about working at Genevre?'

They all smile and they all nod when Hayden says that it's the atrium facilities and the free gym. Nothing about their jobs or even their boss; no, it's the freebies and perks.

Berta comes and rescues me before I have to ask anything else and the whole team rises and thanks me and smiles and I think, they might like me more now than they did at the beginning. Or, at the very least, they don't hate me. I just wonder how my rival will fair. Will he charm them as much as I hope I have? Probably more.

Emily

The first part of the interview is done and dusted. I think it went extremely well considering I haven't done a presentation for years. I get the feeling I managed to impress the director Alan, and Dirk, the department head who is the rather fit, Greek god type man I'll be replacing.

Dirk was lovely and so encouraging, and it turns out that if I do get the job then he will still be working for Genevre. He mentioned that I can go and drop by and ask him questions whenever I like. I might just have to do that, perhaps we could discuss work over coffee whilst he offers me advice and then I expect we will start chatting about other things such as him taking me out for dinner or a few drinks.

No! Stop.

What am I doing? I haven't even got the job yet and I'm already daydreaming about liaisons with a senior colleague. Mustn't get carried away, must stay focused for the next part of the interview.

'Emily, I've come to collect you for round two. How did round one go?' Young HR man, who has now named himself as George, is standing in the doorway with his head tilted to one side and peering out from underneath his floppy fringe. I'm worried what *round two* may have in store. I walk over and follow him out of the door.

'Yes, really good, I didn't stutter too much and managed to cover everything I wanted to,' I chirp. George just nods as we continue to pad down some stairs.

'We need to go left here,' he signals.

I desperately try to keep up with him as I trot beside

his long strides in my heels which are most definitely now killing me, I can't wait to take these things off and live in orthopaedic shoes forever.

'Wow, this place is enormous, is the gym popular with the staff?' I say this enthusiastically as we pad down more stairs, across the atrium and past a window with eight or nine people running in a row on treadmills. In the next window, there appears to be a yoga class going on and I can envisage myself there already, feeling all zen with my new work pals.

'Oh yes, lots of people are really into their health and fitness here, it's so good for destressing. At Genevre we take mental and physical wellbeing very, very seriously. Healthy body, healthy mind and all that.' George pats his young, toned stomach to highlight the fact that he has no fat there whatsoever and *he* obviously takes it very seriously too.

'And do you go there often George?'

George gives me a sideways glance and slowly replies. 'Yes, most days, I like to keep fit… for my girlfriend.'

Cringe. Now he thinks that I am chatting him up. I am almost old enough to be your mummy, Georgie Porgie! Well, big sister, at least.

'Cool, so how long have you worked here, George?' Porgie.

'About a year, I finished university and applied to Genevre, naturally got the first job I applied for. So where are you currently working?' Well, he's sure of himself.

'Oh, nowhere at the moment. I'm currently on a career break looking after my little one, but she's older now and at school so I'm in a good position to return to full-time work and concentrate a bit more on my career.' Whoa, that was a mouthful of explaining in the hope that he gets the hint I am a mum and not interested in a little boy.

'Oh sure, so how long have you been on a break? I wish I could have had a break.' George sniggers and tosses his head to the side making his floppy hair swing like a curtain.

Little toad! I want to tell him not to be so rude and to respect his elders and that he has probably been on a massive big break for the last three years pissing it up at uni. But I bite my tongue, we've all been young and cocky and I don't want to jeopardise this job or risk sounding like a total granny.

'Oh, it's not really a break with a child, but a little while. Wow, this place is really big isn't it?' I reply breezily, secretly hoping we will be there soon as my feet can't take much more stomping and the same goes for the conversation.

'Yup, the team are just in this next room on the right,' he chirps.

'Oh perfect, I can't wait to meet them all,' I squeaky-chirp back.

George turns the handle and walks into the room and I follow in after him careful not to stomp too loudly in my clodhoppers. There are four people, two men and two women and they all turn to welcome me with cheerful, inquisitive faces. I instantly feel at ease.

'Right Emily, I'll leave you in the capable hands of the team, enjoy and good luck.'

'Thank you, George.' I smile before turning to face the team with my enthusiastic *please like me I'm a nice person and a good boss* face on.

'Hi everyone, well as you probably already know, I'm Emily, last name Cod like the fish but I promise I don't smell like one.' Oh hell, I'm cringing at my own introduction when one of the women speaks.

'Hahaha. Hello Emily, nice to meet you too. My surname is Salmon and I promise I don't smell either, well not much. I'm Sharon, by the way, and this is Karen, Hayden and Jayden. As you can see, we have a bit of a weird thing going on with names in this office.' Sharon guffaws and the whole team chuckle along with her.

Sharon Salmon. Wow. That's far worse than Emily Cod.

'Yeah, Sharon doesn't smell *most* of the time, only when she brings in her stinky tuna and broccoli for lunch,' Hayden says, only, I suspect, half joking.

'Oh, *behave,* Hayden. You don't complain when I bring in my special homemade chocolate brownies do you?' Sharon folds her arms and feigns a mock sulk.

'Hmmm did I say you smelt? I'd never say that, Mum. I love *all* your cooking, especially your yummy cakes.' Hayden paints on a cheeky grin and Sharon offers a pretend forgiving smile.

'Oh, are you two related then?' I smile politely and this time Karen replies.

'No, no they aren't related they just act like mother and son. We're like a little family here. Would you like a coffee or anything?' She appears more reserved than the rest of the team but obviously adores her work family.

'A glass of water, if that's ok? All that talking I did at the presentation has made my throat a bit dry. I don't usually gibber on that much, I promise.' I'm hoping that makes me sound like I won't be on their backs nagging all the time rather than me trying to brag about how much I did in my presentation. I am anything but a micro-manager which I hope people appreciate.

Karen teeters off to get my water and I admire her elegant dress, suddenly feeling a bit boring in my dull old skirt suit.

'So, any plans for the weekend Emily?' Sharon asks, smiling.

'Yes, in fact it's quite a busy one this weekend with my little girl *and* I'll be trying to book tickets to see *The Little Mermaid* at the theatre in London. I hope I'm not on the internet *all* weekend, they've only just released the tickets.' I roll my eyes for effect. The trip will be part of her Christmas present and it's going to make me a little skint in all honesty. Whilst I'm talking Jayden suddenly appears very animated, flapping his arms around and widening his eyes.

'OMG, I am truly obsessed with old school Disney. I didn't even know they were doing *The Little Mermaid* in theatres? So amazing I shall have to look that up straight away and get it booked.'

The team all giggle, smiling at him the way you might smile at an over-excited child. My eyes fall on his Aladdin pencil case. I love him.

'How old is your little girl?' Jayden continues.

'She's just turned five. We have all of Disney on DVD, old and new,' I answer as Jayden gives me a beaming smile of approval.

Karen appears and hands me my water and we exchange polite friendly smiles. This is going rather nicely, so far.

'Karen, how old is your little girl, isn't she around that age?' Sharon chips in.

'Yes, she's also five and turning into quite the little madam. What's your little girl's name? What school does she go to?' The quiet Karen is suddenly rather chatty, she blinks through her glasses in anticipation of my answer.

'Her name's Rosie and she goes to St Peter's Primary School. What about your little one?'

'Oh my gosh, that's Chloe's school. They might even be in the same class. She has Mrs Bee; do you know her?

'This is so strange, Karen.' I pause slightly for dramatic affect. 'Rosie is also in Mrs Bee's class.' Karen puts her hand over her mouth as I continue enjoying this revelation. 'I expect I'll see you at many future children's parties or maybe even a play date.' I hope I don't sound too keen or weird, but Karen is clearly more than pleased by the look on her face.

'Oh, yes I am sure we will, and I look forward to meeting little Rosie.'

'Mrs Bee is also my aunt, Emily,' Jayden interrupts flailing his arms around like an octopus. 'Such a small world isn't it, Karen couldn't quite believe it either, and, get this… Mrs Bee is also Sharon's neighbour, *and* Hayden's best friend's cousin's wife's sister.' Jayden is now super animated and is almost falling backwards off his seat.

'Wow,' is all I can manage in response.

'OMG, this is actually hilarious. We are all linked by Mrs Bee, it's almost as if it was meant to BEEEEEEE hehehehehe.' At this point everyone is giggling including me and Hayden is accompanying Jayden's high pitched beeeeeee with low buzzing bee noises whilst Sharon bats at him with a rolled-up piece of paper. Karen looks on and laughs with me as though we are old friends.

'I really hope it is meant to be.' I smile coyly knowing that I sound pure cheese, just as Georgie

Porgie reappears. 'It's been really wonderful meeting you all, I've really enjoyed myself and hope to see you all again really soon.'

'Oooh, yes,' they chorus cheerfully.

I think I can safely say that meeting the team was a huge success.

Jamie

A quick march across the atrium, a comfort break and I'm in front of a panel of three, including Berta, and loading my presentation onto the plasma screen. No technical hitches and we're ready to go. There's the division director and the guy I'm hoping to replace, the department head. The director, Alan, I've met before, but not the department head, he was on holiday when I came for my first interview.

'We haven't met,' he says, standing up. 'I'm Dirk Whittaker.'

'Jamie Bowe. Pleased to meet you, Dirk.' He's suave and smooth and urbane. Dark hair with just the right amount of hair gel sweeps across his head, he has a square jaw with just the perfect length of dark stubble. I bet women fall all over him.

'Welcome, Jimbo.'

I flinch. Is he trying to unnerve me? Arsehole. 'Jamie,' I correct, smiling and feeling anything but smooth and urbane in the suit I last wore to my cousin's wedding two years ago.

I focus my presentation on Alan, he's the one to impress, he's the one with the power. I hope.

It goes well, very well. I've done my research on Genevre. I know about insurance having spent the last nearly three years working my way up in Kanes, from customer service to insurance underwriter team leader.

I know my stuff, I've got the relevant qualifications and I'm confident, yet Dirk does his best to trap me with stupid questions.

He's just asked me how I would handle a tsunami on the Thames, making it sound as though I should be out there baling out cellars when Berta calls a halt to proceedings.

Saved by the bell.

We trot along to another room where coffee and cakes have been laid on.

'That was a serious question,' Dirk says quietly to me. 'It could happen.'

'It could,' I agree. 'So I hope Genevre's current risk assessments account for that possibility.'

'Well, if you get the job you can look into it.' He's got one of those deep, dark voices that might sound sexy to women but just sounds stupid to men. Especially me.

Berta is ushering Alan and Dirk out and asking me to make myself comfortable while they get ready for the final part of the interview.

I sit down and help myself to another pastry. I hope they won't be too long because I want to go home and get out of this suit before I go back to work.

I've just finished my third cake – a doughnut this time – when Berta comes back for me. I hurriedly wipe the sugar off my hands onto a napkin.

'As I explained earlier, we're going to have a group discussion for this last part.'

'Fine,' I say wondering if it really will be fine. I assume she means Dirk and Alan and the whole team. I hope Hayden, or was it Jayden, doesn't bring his list with him.

Back in the room I take my seat as instructed sitting

opposite the panel, but it's just Alan, Dirk and Berta again.

'We're just waiting for the other candidate,' Dirk says, his voice dripping like syrup.

'Right?'

'You don't mind, do you? We thought we'd see how you interact?'

'Okay.' I don't really know why I need to interact with my rival. Oh God, why don't I just get up and go now. I'm seriously considering it when the door opens.

And in walks Ms Flicky Ponytail, complete with wheelie case. Dirk's face lights up and he licks his lips and I know I've got absolutely no chance of getting this job. Not one.

Three

Jamie

As I trundle across the car park, I don't know what to think. I can't help glancing behind me to see if Emily – that's flicky ponytail girl – is following me, but she isn't. Thank God. Though to be fair she looked as confused as I was.

We sat side by side fake smiling at everyone, but especially at each other. Our chairs were turned slightly so that we could see each other's face without actually staring. It was awkward. And from the way Dirk kept salivating every time Emily spoke, I'm certain she will get the job. It's a done deal.

What a waste of a morning, a long one at that. So long that I won't have time to change out of this suit. Even without the jacket I am going to look overdressed at Kanes where smart-casual is more casual than smart and definitely more comfortable than casual.

As I approach my car, I can see it – a bloody parking penalty ticket. I grab it off the windscreen and rip it open. 20p short. A bloody great big £60 fine for 20p. If I'd known I was helping my rival out I wouldn't have swapped that duff 20p.

I get in my car, slam the door and roar off towards

the exit. I'm so riled and preoccupied I almost don't see her as she steps out from between a line of cars. Emily. Still dragging that bloody wheelie case. We both grimace as I hit the brakes and the car screeches to a grinding halt that is so violent, I wait for the airbag to deploy. Mercifully, it doesn't.

Emily stands blinking in shock. I lower my window.

'Sorry. Didn't see you there.'

She blinks several more times.

'Are you okay?'

She nods slowly but doesn't speak. She's ashen faced.

'Really, are you okay?'

'Yes. Yes. I'm fine.' She clutches the wheelie case handle and stomps off.

Now the dilemma; should I run after her? I sit in my car in the middle of the car park and wonder what to do next. What if she's not okay? What if she faints or something? I'll have to check.

I'm just getting out of my car and gingerly sidestepping yet another enormous waterfilled crater when she roars past me and beeps her horn as she does so.

Evidently, she's fine. My shoes are not; she's speeded through the puddle and created a tidal wave. Even the bottom of my trousers are now wet.

'Bitch.' I wasn't quite expecting to say that.

My dad doesn't quite understand what's going on with the job when I finally ring him about it on the way home from work. I've stalled him with texts all afternoon but I can't put him off any longer.

'What do you mean you had to meet with the other candidate? That isn't fair. Is it even legal?'

I would laugh at that if I didn't have an almighty headache; it's been one hell of a day and on top of this morning's fiasco I've had to put up with endless taunts asking about my *court appearance*, and *interview techniques* from my colleagues at Kanes. They'll soon realise that I *haven't* been for an interview when I don't hand in my notice.

'It's not very ethical,' I say in reply to Dad. 'But I don't think it's illegal.'

'Sounds nasty to me.'

'Yeah.'

'I've never heard the like of it.'

'No. Well, that's what it's like now, Dad.' And I haven't even told him about meeting the team and what a giant dick Dirk is.

'When will you find out?'

'Next week.' Though I already know Emily Ponytail is going to get the job.

'Well, good luck, son,' he says before changing the subject. 'You still coming on Saturday.' His voice has an edge of despondency to it.

'Yeah, course I am. Bright and early.'

When I get home my lodger, Tim – the IT geek – is sitting on the sofa in just his wrinkly boxers.

'Woah.' I put my hand over my eyes.

'Sorry.' Tim offers me a pathetic apology face while at the same time pushing some crappy YouTube video from his phone to the TV. My 4K Ultra HD is suddenly filled with a spotted gecko. I scowl and head for the kitchen.

'It's bloody hot in here.' I fill the kettle and wonder what I'm going to have for tea. I've had nothing to eat since the three cakes at Genevre this morning.

'Yeah, had to put the heating on.'

'But it's not even cold outside.' I march past him and turn the thermostat down, it's on 30°C. 30! His rent stays the same no matter what the fuel bills are but *I* have to fund the extra. 'If you're cold put some bloody clothes on.' For someone who's supposed to be clever he can be incredibly stupid sometimes.

'It's not for me.'

'What?'

'The heating, it's for Delilah.' Delilah is the spotted gecko that he keeps in his bedroom.

'Put another heat lamp in her tank then.' This is what I mean about him being stupid.

He looks at me sheepishly.

'No,' I say, hoping and praying.

'Yeah. Sorry. She's done it again.'

'For fuck's sake. How? I thought you sorted out that tank. I thought you fixed it. You promised me it wouldn't happen again.'

'Yeah. Sorry, mate. Thought I'd fixed it too. Seems Delilah is stronger than she looks, she just pushed the sliding glass door along.' He shrugs and turns his attention back to the TV where the lizard thing is now humping another.

'Do we have to have that shit on?' I've really had enough of today.

'I thought, you know, if she saw it, it would make her feel more comfortable. Might entice her to come closer, then I could grab her.'

'I thought she went missing upstairs. She can't get down here.'

'Stairs.' He laughs at me as though I'm the stupid one.

The last time Delilah went missing she was gone for

two weeks. Every night we spent hours hunting for her, looking in cupboards, the wardrobes, in shoes, even round the back of the toilet. We don't know where she went for those two weeks but one morning Tim woke up and found her sitting on his pillow, her forked tongue flicking around his mouth. He said he'd been dreaming about an old girlfriend French kissing him.

I've got nothing against him having a gecko as a pet just so long as it stays in its tank in his room. I do not want it running around my brand-new house, leaping about on my furniture and practicing Parkour on my blinds. I don't want to even think about what it's doing to my cables and skirting boards.

I bought this house just two years ago and having a lodger is the only way I can afford the mortgage. Dad gave me the deposit which was incredibly generous of him. He said it was a reward for spending two years volunteering overseas. I think it was more a bribe to keep me in the UK. I don't blame him; it can't have been easy for him since Mum died.

'You'd better bloody find it soon. Beth is staying over on Saturday night. She hates crawly things.'

'It's not a crawly thing, it's a gecko.' Tim rolls his eyes at me and smiles. 'Women, eh.'

'Just find the fucker.'

After I've whipped myself up a cheesy pasta – which Tim manages to devour half of, even though he was supposed to be making himself something else – I go to bed. I've still got my headache and I want today to end. But even lying in bed there is no peace; Tim is opening every cupboard door in the kitchen looking for Delilah.

I just hope she *isn't* in the kitchen.

Emily

'Olivia! Look after Billy and Rosie please. Bill, look at me, in the eyes, listen to me, use your ears, yes, those two big holes on either side of your head . . . absolutely no biting, you will be in serious trouble if you do it again and this time, I *will* bite you back. Hard. Okay now go and play nice kids, look after each other, no fighting in the ball pit and have lots of fun, what are you waiting for! Go, play, SKEDADDLE!!'

'Play nice Rosie, have fun sweetheart,' I add to Sabrina's rant, before giving Rosie a kiss and watching them run off towards the slides. 'Oh dear, biting again?' I say as Sabrina rolls her eyes.

'Yup, honestly if he bites someone again, I will lose my mind, he's feral.' Sabrina, my lovely and very best friend turns to me with her long wavy dark locks cascading around her shoulders. How does she manage to look so preened and gorgeous with two kids and a full-time job?! It's sickening!

I'm about to reply when there's a blood curdling, high decibel scream that goes on for quite some time. All parents (including us) freeze, silent for a moment as worried eyes scan the slides and various climbing apparatus to see who is in trouble. It's just a kid going down one of the slides at soft play enjoying himself a bit too much, but boy was that loud! The sound is still ringing in my ears when everyone relaxes and the chatter goes back to normal. Seriously, some kids should have volume control.

'How's Rosie's bite mark? I'm so sorry, Em!' Sabrina looks embarrassed.

'Yeah, she's fine. It didn't pierce the skin this time.'

'Oh God.' Sabrina puts her hand on her head, exasperated.

'It's just a little bruise, don't worry, they all do it at some point,' I lie, though Rosie has never done it, but I don't judge as I know plenty that have.

'Yes, I know but Olivia was never this bad. It's boys I swear, he's such a little animal.'

'Kids are feral in general, you have to train it out of them,' I agree.

'You know the other day I caught him trying to scoop a shit out of the toilet to *inspect it*.' Sabrina mimes using a magnifying glass on an imaginary shit.

'That's brilliant, you have a mini-scientist on your hands,' I say chuckling.

'It's so, so wrong Emily. What makes it even worse is that it wasn't even *his* shit, it was Dave's.'

'Oh no. Gross,' I say putting my hand over my mouth.

'That man really needs to learn to flush the bloody toilet. I love him madly, deeply, truly and he is an amazing father, but he is a beast, a rotten dirty beast. That must be where Bill gets it from.' Sabrina tosses her hair over her shoulder again and I catch one of the dads on the opposite table checking her out. *Or* is he looking at me? Hard to tell, so I smile at Sabrina and then give him eye contact, he grins right back at me. I look away nervously.

'Why doesn't he flush the toilet, Sab? You seriously need to train him better.' I laugh, glancing at the dad to see if he's looking at me, we lock eyes and smile again before my eyes flit back to concentrate on Sabrina.

'Yes, tell me about it. We do have a rule, *if it's brown flush it down and if it's yellow let it mellow.*'

'Good rule, I'm impressed, helping with the environment and all that.'

'Yes, you'd think! The kids can manage it so why

can't he! It doesn't help that his mother basically wiped his bumbum until he left home at the age of twenty-seven. Honestly, she must have been flushing his shits too!'

'Oh Sabrina, stop it. You do make me laugh,' I say almost choking on my crappy soft play coffee. I love Sabrina, she makes me laugh so much; she's half Italian and *everything* is a drama or a reason for a rant – not that I'm stereotyping.

'It's going to take me decades to re-train him Emily. Decades. Anyway, enough about shit! How are things with you my darling?' Sabrina looks at me intently as my eyes catch Rosie behind her playing with Billy in the ball pit, they're throwing balls at each other and laughing as they dive and submerge into the pit to avoid getting hit. Olivia appears to have made friends with some kids her own age and is sat in a corner near some tunnel thing, talking with her new crew.

'Yes, not bad. Managed to book *The Little Mermaid,* spent hours online, click-clicking. But I would not give up and it paid off. Oh, and I'm still waiting to hear back from that job, it's only been a few days but if they were keen, they would have told me by now, surely?'

'Nah, not necessarily, Dave's work took two weeks to tell him he got the job.'

'Really? That makes me feel a bit better.' It doesn't make me feel better in the slightest.

'Good, it should!'

'I felt like I really connected with the team plus my presentation went well. I didn't even need the handouts, they had the right cables that connected my laptop to the projector. Me not having a memory stick didn't faze them at all.'

'Well, that's great! You were saved from looking like

a bloody dinosaur.' Sabrina grins cheekily.

'Yeah, I guess. I think they'll give it to someone else.' Lennie springs to mind. Of course they are going to choose him over me with all his experience and zero commitments.

'Like who?'

'I dunno. Probably a man who hasn't been bringing up a child for the last five years.' I sound like Eeyore from Winnie the Pooh, all down trodden and depressed.

'Don't be such a negative Nancy, it's only been a few days! I'm sure you will have done absolutely amazing and if you don't get the job then it just means it wasn't meant to be and there's something better around the corner.'

'True, I know you're right. It's just torture waiting and I'm impatient.' And I want this job, not just any job, *this* job.

Sabrina's eyes suddenly light up and I know what's coming. 'You need something to keep your mind off this job thing while you wait,' she says gleefully as I hold my palm up in protest. 'You need to go on a date.' Sabrina claps her hands in excitement and I put my hands over hers to stop her clapping like Cilla Black.

'Oh no, not this again. There is no way I am signing up to go on*100 Days to Find Love!* I told you I won't be embarrassed on TV in front of the whole nation.'

'Okay, well what about internet dating, you know that's how I met my Dave. The girls at work are all raving about this new dating app, SwipeySwipey. If I were single, I would give it a go for sure.' She takes a sip of her coffee and waits patiently for my reply.

I haven't been on a date since Liam. In fact, I don't think *we* even did dating, we were just always together from school, Liam and Emily, Emily and Liam. Then he left me, the day after Rosie's first birthday. We'd had a lovely day with the whole family over, everyone watched Rosie toddle about as she opened her presents, giggled and played with the cardboard boxes and wrapping paper. I had no idea what was coming.

Later that evening, we had a few glasses of wine when Rosie was in bed and happily reminisced about what a nice day it had been. We even discussed how great it would be for Rosie to have a sibling one day and when it would be convenient to start trying. The future for our little family was happy and full of exciting possibilities.

The next day was a Friday and he told me that night, he must have planned to do it just before the weekend so he could run away to *her*. It was such a shock, an awful gut-wrenching bullet that caused my stomach to drop, body to shake and bile to rise to my throat when he uttered the most cliché words.

'I'm leaving you, Em. I'm so sorry, I don't love you anymore and I've met someone else.' And he was gone, just like that. Moved out that night, the bastard. I'm just thankful he did it when Rosie was so young that I didn't have to explain anything to her, although she has started asking questions recently.

So here I am, four years later and still single. Sometimes the loneliness is depressing.

'Oooh. Hiii, Emily. Fancy seeing you here. How are things? Liam said he messaged you.' The shrill high-pitched voice of Tiny cuts through my thoughts like a razor. As if by magic, the woman who stole my husband has appeared before my very eyes. She has the same perfect timing as him.

'What?' I hear myself mutter as I stare at her in

disbelief.

'The girls can play together! They are such good sisters! Yay! Off you go Tiger-Lily, go and find Rosie. Mummy is just chatting to Emily.' She puts a hand on Tiger-Lily's back and shoves her in the general direction of Rosie.

'Hi, Tiny,' I say in the false jolly voice that I've perfected when speaking to her. 'I'm good thanks, just catching up with Sabrina.' Hopefully she'll get the hint and go away. Soon.

'Yes, Emily and I have loads to catch up on, Teeny Tiny, so if you don't mind.' Sabrina motions small shooing actions with her hands at Tiny. I open my mouth like a shocked goldfish and swallow down a smirk, I wasn't expecting that. Sabrina hates Tiny, on my behalf, more than I do.

Tiny ignores Sabrina and looks pointedly at me. 'Well, *I* was hoping to bump into *you,* Emily. Liam said he messaged you about the girls?'

Sabrina looks at me and I shoot her a *keep quiet* glare.

'Oh yes, I've got the message and I'll speak to *him* about it when I have time.' Cheeky cow, it's none of her business. I wish she'd just go away. Why does she always have to talk to me like she's trying to prove some sort of point?

'Well, please make sure you do, the girls *are* like sisters you know and it would be such a shame if you stopped them from spending more time together. Think of the children and what's best for them.' Tiny arranges her face to look concerned but I know she is just being an utter bitch. The absolute gall of the woman.

My eyes narrow and I lower my voice before speaking slowly.

'As I've already said, I'll talk to Liam about it, not you. It doesn't concern you, so if you don't mind.' Now it's my turn to shoo her away and her face turns puce clashing nicely with her pillar box red hair.

Sabrina laughs, bobbing around on her seat. 'Yeah, why don't you skedaddle now Teeny Tiny, go on now, go back into your teeny tiny box.' Sabrina chortles making tiny box signs with her hands. We both stare at Tiny as she huffs, defeated, turning on her enormous, ridiculous heels before trotting off to the other side of soft play. We watch on as her big puffy skirt sways clumsily from side to side.

'She reminds me of the backside of a pantomime horse,' Sabrina snorts and we laugh like a couple of hyenas for quite some time while Sabrina does impressions of a horse neighing and galloping.

'More like a pantomime dame with that makeup,' I splutter. We must look like right weirdos to the other parents. Of course, all of this is out of earshot of Tiny. We aren't that horrid to the woman who was shagging my husband.

'Em, have you noticed the *DILF* that's been checking you out the whole time we've been here? You should go and talk to him, he's a tasty one.'

I look over and the dad who smiled at me earlier catches my eye again and this time gives me a cheeky wink. Suddenly I feel brave and flattered but no sooner does he think I've looked away when I see him eyeing up an attractive blonde. I sigh. It's amusing, if not a little depressing. Sabrina notices too, she rolls her eyes while I purse my lips and shake my head. Bloody men.

'No thanks, but I suppose you can sign me up to this SwipeySwipey. Let's do it before I change my mind, I'm feeling brave.'

Sabrina claps her hands, squealing as I bite my nails. What am I letting myself in for?

Four

Jamie

Saturday morning and I'm round Dad's in my scruffy clothes and ready for work. I've decreed that I'll be the one going up and down the ladder to the loft even though, as he has reminded me several times, he put the stuff up there in the first place.

'But that was years ago, Dad,' I say as he attempts to muscle his way past me and up the ladder. 'You were almost five years younger.'

'Don't remind me I'm getting older.' He half laughs and steps aside.

Up in the loft I'm overwhelmed by how many bin bags are lined up. I count twenty, then give up. I hand several down to Dad and go back down the ladder.

'How do you want to do this? Sort a couple at a time or shall I bring the whole lot down?'

He looks at me as though I'm speaking a foreign language. At that moment a ray of sunshine bursts through the landing window and illuminates Dad's face. He looks angelic. And old. I hadn't realised quite how old. He was a lot older than Mum and certainly hadn't expected to outlive her. Life can be so unfair sometimes.

'What do you think?' he asks, belatedly answering my question.

'Few at a time.' I pick the bags up and take them through to the spare room.

We start sifting through and it's soon obvious that he's emptied the entire contents of Mum's wardrobes and drawers straight into the bags without sorting them out at all. There's underwear mixed in with jewellery and makeup. I suppress a sigh; this is going to be a hard, old slog. I look at Dad, his face is creased in sadness. I hope he isn't going to cry.

I feel guilty for not being here when he did this. His reaction to her sudden loss was to bundle everything of hers away and literally close the door – or loft hatch – on it. Mine was to skip off with the VSO to Cambodia and teach English. I should have stayed with him. At the very least I should have come home sooner instead of continually asking for more assignments and moving from one country to another and staying away for a couple of years instead of a couple of months. I was selfish in my grief.

'Why don't you nip down and make us a cup of tea and I'll make a start on getting rid of the perishable stuff.'

'Err, yes, okay.' He turns to leave before turning back. 'Perishable?'

'Makeup and stuff, Dad. I think it's off, it smells rank.'

'Ah, right.'

Once he's down the stairs I quickly go through the bags and pull out the few things that are worth keeping, some good clothes, a pair of expensive boots I never saw Mum wear and three handbags. The rest I consign to the perishable pile.

In the end I do most of it alone while Dad is either making us tea, coffee or lunch.

Dad is in the room when I find her jewellery box. I hand it to him without speaking then occupy myself with the next bag. He takes the box away and after about ten minutes I pad out onto the landing to find him in his bedroom, sitting on his bed, the unopened box is on his lap and he's just staring at it.

'Jamie, son,' he says when he notices me. 'You come and have a look through this.'

I really don't want to. This seems so much more personal than my mum's other belongings, even her underwear.

He pushes the jewellery box at me and I really have no choice. I drop down on the bed next to him, rest it on *my* lap, flick the catch and lift the lid.

We both stare at the contents. Necklaces I remember, earrings I don't. There's a tiny little white envelope in one of the compartments. Dad reaches for it.

'Her wedding and engagement rings,' he says. 'The funeral people gave them to me.'

A sudden, horrible image comes into my head of them removing the rings from my mum's dead hand.

Dad drops the envelope back in the box.

'We don't need to do this now.' I slowly push the lid closed, careful not to let it slam.

'No. No. It can wait.' He stands up, gives me a weak smile. 'More tea? And a doughnut.'

'Yeah. Why not? Give me a shout when it's ready.'

By the time I leave there are piles of good stuff on the bed, stuff we – well, I – can put on eBay. Mum had some expensive handbags and we should be able to sell them okay. Some coats and shoes too. There are a lot of charity bags and a lot of rubbish – perishables. I take the perishables with me in my car. I don't want Dad looking through to see what I've thrown away. I tell him I'll do the charity run in the week. He's perfectly capable of taking the stuff to a charity shop himself and he's retired so he has the time to do it, but I know he won't.

I'm lucky at the tip, it's not long until closing time which means there isn't much of a queue. I drop Mum's old stuff over the side and watch it hit the giant skip below. Landfill. That's where it will end up. Poor Mum.

Tim is sitting on the sofa when I burst through the door, at least this time he is dressed, in fact he's overdressed – shirt, proper trousers, polished shoes. This is a man who wears trainers, jeans and a different colour Led Zeppelin t-shirt every day. He's clean but he is not smart. Even though I'm in a rush to shower before Beth turns up, I have to stop and ask him what's going on.

'Yeah, going to a wedding,' he says, flicking through his phone. 'Well, the evening bit. Just waiting for the taxi.'

'Cool.' This is even better, I had warned him that I wanted the house to myself tonight and he had said he would entertain himself in his bedroom. If this were anyone but Tim that would make me shudder, but I know that what he means is dismantling a computer or writing a few hundred lines of code.

'Whose wedding?'

'Some girl at work. She invited everyone to the evening do.' He shrugs.

'Enjoy.' I start to walk away then remember the gecko. 'Have you found Delilah yet?'

He smiles at me in his patented sheepish way and shakes his head.

I groan aloud.

'Don't worry, I'm doing everything I can to lure her back. She'll soon be back safely in her tank.'

'She'd better not make an appearance tonight; it'll creep Beth right out.'

He doesn't answer me because his phone pings and he jumps up. 'Taxi,' he mutters and leaves without so much as a goodbye.

Thirty minutes later I've changed the bed, had a shower and am waiting in the living room for Beth. We've agreed we'll order food in and I have a selection of menus waiting on the coffee table.

When she arrives, she looks lovely and she smells good enough to eat. As we're kissing each other hello I find myself imagining what we're going to do after we've eaten.

'Good day?' she asks, dropping a capacious handbag on the floor and shrugging off her jacket to reveal a flimsy top and sprayed-on jeans. God, she's got good legs; I do like good legs.

'Not bad, been helping my dad, you know.' I roll my eyes to indicate what a nuisance he is then immediately feel guilty.

'Urgh, tell me about it. My dad's on one again, about me moving out. Says I ought to find a place of my own at my age, especially now I've got a proper job.' At twenty-two, Beth is nearly eight years younger than me and barely a year out of university.

'Dad's eh?' I say because this isn't a conversation I want to get into. I'm hardly qualified either. At her age I still lived with my parents and only left after Mum died

– and that was running away.

'I've told him I can't afford anywhere on my own. He says I should share, that's what people normally do, don't they?'

'Yeah. I suppose so.'

'You share, don't you? You've got that weirdy Tom man living here, haven't you?'

'Tim. Yeah, he's my lodger.'

'Yeah, that's what I thought.' She smiles at me and winks. 'Where is he tonight, anyway?'

'He's at a wedding. He'll be back late, he said.'

'Good. We wouldn't want him disturbing us.' She winks at me again.

I quickly pick up the pile of menus and flap them about. 'What would you like?'

'Thai,' she says without even looking. 'Have you got White Orchid's menu?'

'Um.' I pretend to look through the menus knowing full well I haven't.

'No probs, I'll get it on my phone.' She yanks her phone out of her jeans pocket, which is a feat in itself given how tight they are and starts swiping the screen. 'What do you fancy?'

'You,' I say in my best seductive voice then suddenly have a vision of creepy Dirk from Genevre, but she laughs and gives me a quick hug.

Thai food is not my favourite but I manage to force down a sizeable meal, we've also drunk a whole bottle of red and started on a second. We're soon kissing on the sofa.

'What colour's this room?' Beth suddenly asks, pulling away from me.

'What? The walls?'

'Well, yes.' She squints at me.

'Magnolia?'

'Don't you know?'

'Magnolia,' I say with conviction.

'Is it what the builders did?'

'Yes.'

'You never thought of repainting it? Choosing a different colour?'

'No. Not really. It's still new. The house is less than two years old.'

'That doesn't mean you have to keep it this nothing colour.' She laughs and nudges me with her elbow. 'It's a bit bland, isn't it?'

'Yeah.' I've never thought about it but now I am I find I quite like its blandness. It's clean and tidy and goes with the beige carpet, also chosen by the builders. It's the complete opposite to my dad's place which, thanks to my mum, is a riot of tasteful and colourful décor, and it's a thousand steps up from anywhere I lived when I was with the VSO in Cambodia or The Philippines.

'Is your bedroom this colour too?' She smiles at me and actually flutters her eyelashes.

'You know it is.' I laugh as she plonks a big kiss on my lips.

'We could take our wine up there.' She giggles and grabs the bottle.

'We could.' I grab our glasses.

We don't exactly rip each other's clothes off, this is, after all, not the first time we've slept together. It's more sedate, more dignified, I like to think. Beth sits on the bed and watches me as I take my jeans off and fold them up before laying them over the chair. She gives me a smile of encouragement and pulls off her socks before flinging them at me. Then she giggles.

'This is so funny,' she says.

'What?' What the hell is funny? I'm trying to be sexy and seductive and she is laughing.

'I can see your front, and your back in the wardrobe mirror doors and I can see my own reflection too. It's weird.'

'It's just a mirror.' I feign a laugh and shake my arse.

She laughs again. 'See. It's funny.' Then she winks. 'Take your shirt off.'

I slowly unbutton my shirt and jig about a bit like a stripper. I feel a bit stupid but it brings a big smile to Beth's face.

When I've finished, I fold the shirt neatly and lay it over the chair on top of my jeans. That makes her roll her eyes a little before smiling again.

'Your turn,' I say, standing with my hands on my hips.

She gives me a lovely smile and lifts her flimsy top up and over her head. She's about to fling it in my direction, just like she had her socks, when her eyes widen in horror and her mouth forms a silent O.

'What?' I glance down at myself, even twist and look at my rear reflection.

'Cockroach,' she screeches, clutching her top to her chest and pulling her feet up onto the bed.

'What? No. Where?'

She points to the floor just to my left.

'It's not a cockroach,' I say as my eyes alight on the cricket admiring itself in the mirrored wardrobe doors, either that or it thinks it's found a mate.

'What is it then?'

'It's a cricket.'

'It's a big bug. You've got bugs in your house.' She pulls her top back over her head in one speedy movement. 'Can you pass my socks please?'

'Why?' Stupid question.

'I can't stay here. You're infested.'

'No. It's just a cricket.'

'It's disgusting. What's it doing there?'

'It's what Tim feeds his gecko...' I let my voice trail off. This is what he meant when he said he was doing everything he could to entice Delilah back. I shudder as I wonder how many crickets he has left around the house. Has he laid a trail all the way back to the cage?

'Socks please.' She holds out her hand for her socks.

Five minutes later and we're back downstairs. She's fully dressed including her jacket and handbag. I'm just in my jeans – ever deluded that we can resolve this. She's clutching her phone and waiting for the taxi to arrive. I can't even drive her home because I'm over the limit.

'Look it won't hurt you. It's fine now I've caught it.'

'You've put a glass over it.' She frowns at me and sneers. 'At the very least you should have killed it.'

Before I get a chance to answer her phone pings and she's out the door with me calling after her that I'll ring her tomorrow when she's calmed down. If she even hears me, she doesn't answer.

I turn the lights off and pad back upstairs; it's late, I'm tired and the night has become a complete disaster. I might as well go to bed now.

My bedroom door is still ajar and before I enter, I hear scratching. I don't barge in, but angle myself so I can see the cricket in the mirror. It's still safely under the glass and Delilah is there, scratching the carpet and nudging the glass.

I creep back along the landing and retrieve the plastic bin from the bathroom, emptying the contents onto the floor before I creep back to my room. Delilah is still there, still nudging the glass.

Will she run when I lunge for her?

Nothing ventured, nothing gained. She's free roaming anyway.

I step into the room and freeze. Delilah glances over at me and tastes the air with her tongue. I edge towards her. She nudges the glass again as the cricket climbs up inside it. I lunge.

'Yessss.' In one perfect move I have placed the bin over both Delilah and the cricket.

So now the night has not been a total waste.

Not quite.

Emily

Swipe left, swipe left, swipe left swipe left, swipe left. Swipe right.

This online dating malarkey has become a little addictive and I find myself trawling through the endless list of singletons within a five-mile radius most nights. I am being picky with the distance because quite frankly I can't be bothered to traipse around the UK to go on dates. Mr Right has to be Mr Right Around the Corner, which doesn't sound very romantic but you have to be practical when you have kids. Unfortunately, this does limit the number of available suitors massively. I haven't spoken to anyone yet because I hadn't actually swiped right until five seconds ago!

YOU HAVE A MATCH ON SWIPEYSWIPEY!!

'Hi, how's it going?' Eeeeek he's messaged me already. What the hell do I say?

'Hi, yes good thanks, how are you?' I type my

mundane reply before taking a sip of red wine and eagerly await his response.

All the better for matching with you. How long have you been on Swipey? He's smooth.

About a week, you're my first match. What about you?

Yeah about the same. I haven't matched with anyone else either. Look this is a bit forward but do you fancy grabbing a drink sometime? I'd prefer to get to know you in person than on here, I'm kind of old fashioned like that, I hope that doesn't scare you away!

Oh hell! He has asked me out on a date already. A date! Sabrina told me you talk to them for at least a week before meeting unless they are desperate weirdos or only after one thing, but he doesn't seem like a weirdo or a sleaze, quite genuine in fact. I stare at his profile and his gorgeous smile beams back at me. What the hell, let's give this a go. I take another sip of my wine before responding.

It just so happens that I'm old fashioned too and think it would be a great idea to meet for a drink, when are you thinking?

Tonight?

Oh sorry, I can't do tonight. I have my little girl so I have to plan, I can do Tuesday or Friday next week? Tonight? Is he serious? People have lives!

I pad out to the kitchen leaving my phone on the sofa to make myself some toast and pour myself another glass of wine whilst I let Swipey man think about which day is best for him. What do I wear? I'll have to call Sabrina to get her advice.

I plonk myself down and check my phone excitedly, my heart sinks a little bit because he still hasn't replied, maybe he has done the same as me and got himself something to drink or gone to the toilet. Ten minutes go by, then an hour, then three hours and it's time for bed. It dawns on me that he probably isn't going to reply. Well that's a new one, I've been ignored. Ghosted on social media.

Online dating is harsh.

'Rosie! Remember your bag please, honey. Do you want to take any toys to nanny's?'

Rosie shakes her head in response.

'Ok, put your coat on, there we go, lovely.' It's the morning after the night before and my head is killing after one too many red wines. I'm ashamed to say I drowned my sorrows a bit after being ignored by my match on Swipey. I seriously need to get a life.

'Mummy can we go and get ice cream later?' She looks at me all expectant with big brown eyes that match my own, cute as a button in her dungarees and flowery top. There's a lovely American style ice cream parlour in town and we've got into the habit of visiting – probably too often.

'Ice cream? Yes, why not. In fact, I think that's a very good idea sweetie.' She deserves a treat, after all today is the day I'll be meeting with her father to discuss her staying over there more. After bumping into Tiny yesterday, I finally messaged Liam. I still don't know what I'm going to say to him.

'Right, are you ready then? Let's go. I need you to scare off Patrick for me.' I wink at her.

'Mummy, you're so silly, Patrick is just a nice old cat. His second home is under your car, he told me.' How do children always make you feel like a bad human? They always see the good in people and animals. I wonder when that ends? I'm sure it does for most adults.

'I know, sweetheart, but he likes you more, so he will

listen to you.'

'Yes, I know he's not your friend, Mummy, is he? He doesn't like you. He told me, but I like you, Mummy. I love you lots and lots.' She looks up at me and her smile melts my heart. I suddenly feel guilty about scaring Patrick off so aggressively the other day. She wouldn't have been impressed.

'I love you too Rosie, more than anyone in the world and no we can't all be friends, can we? As long as we aren't mean to each other that's all that matters, isn't it? Come on then.' An image of Tiny smiling with her red frizzy hair in one of her ridiculous pantomime dame frocks pops into my mind. I blink, forcing it away. Was it guilt that made me think of her? I hate that I feel bad for being rude to her at soft play. Doesn't she deserve everything she gets?

We make the journey across town to my mum's and arrive just in time for elevenses. Rosie skips off to sit on grandad's knee and enjoy a croissant. I really want to stay, but force myself to get back in the car and drive to meet her father, the cheating bastard.

Five

Emily

I drive slowly across town to meet with Liam, taking my time as I know lateness winds him up. I doubt he had much else on anyway and to be honest I don't really care if he does. I park up and meander along to the coffee shop, spying him sitting by the window. He's playing with his stupid hipster moustache that twizzles up at the ends. His Rumpelstiltskin boots peak out underneath the table, the immenseness of them enhanced by super skinny jeans on his scrawny legs. He's wearing a long-unbuttoned rain jacket and reading a huge oversized newspaper.

He's so pretentious I could vomit.

I do wonder what I ever saw in him.

'Hello Em. Coffee?' He looks up from his newspaper but doesn't put it down.

'Hi, oh yes please. Can I have a tall skinny latte, extra hot and extra wet please?' I stare at him, deadpan.

He puts his newspaper down. 'Are you joking? I'm not asking for that.'

Hook line and sinker. Oh yes you are.

'Why? It's a perfectly normal drink and that's what I'd like.' I smile, daring him to complain again. 'I come here all the time and it's what I always have,' I insist feigning innocence.

'Well perhaps you can go and order it then.' He digs deep into his pockets and offers me his loose change; I blink at him without looking at the change and he huffs.

'Okay. Fine. What was it again?'

'A tall skinny latte, extra hot and extra wet,' I reply curtly.

He glides off to get it, his stupid long rain jacket flapping behind him. He queues up while I get my phone out to message Sabrina.

Me: *Hey Sab, he's asking for it. Haha. You were right, he isn't going to challenge me today.*

Sabrina: *Oh my fucking god, I wish I was there, can you video it?*

Me: *No. That would look weird. The staff probably won't even bat an eyelid. I'm sure they've heard it all before but I just love that he will be awkward and they will think he's a wanker, just like I do.*

Sabrina: *You go girl and remember. . . don't take no shit!*

Oh, I definitely won't be taking any shit, my friend. I lock my phone and put it back in my handbag before looking around the coffee shop. The franchise, with its bog-standard burgundy sofas, tables and chairs, is in the middle of a busy shopping centre. It's fairly empty inside for a Sunday morning, but I suppose it is fairly early yet.

In the lull some staff are milling around, to my left side there are a couple of staff in their early twenties cleaning cutlery. One, a Mexican looking guy with long hair in a ponytail, has quite an impressive monobrow; I decide he's a fan of heavy metal. Next to him, chatting away is a slim man with amazing dewy skin and slicked back, dyed-blonde hair. I find myself being drawn to them and begin eavesdropping. The blonde one talks.

'So get this Troy, Troy, Troy. I've like won some money on my PPI claim like. I'm so bloody excited like because it's actually like enough money to be able to get everything like I've ever wanted. I'm going to get a nose job, lip fillers, Botox *and* a forehead reduction. I'm so bloody chuffed like, do you know what I mean like? I just can't wait. I tell you what, Troy, I'm going to be a new man.'

Blonde man looks super excited whilst Troy doesn't even respond and merely rolls his eyes while continuing to polish a spoon.

Well, you learn something new every day; I didn't even know there was such a thing as a forehead reduction. Casually, I turn my head to pretend I'm looking out of the other window so I can get a better look at this forehead. It's just an average sized forehead. Puzzled and somewhat disappointed I slowly turn back to face Liam standing there twitching with the drinks. Now *here's* someone who could definitely do with a forehead reduction.

'Here's your latte. They looked at me like I was a complete idiot when I ordered that.' He sounds like a spoilt brat with his stupid moustache bouncing around as he talks.

'Did they? Why? Thanks anyway.' I take a sip and smirk into my cup, it's actually quite nice. He sits down and sips out of his huge coffee before taking a deep breath.

'So, have you had any thoughts on my message?' he says, but before I can answer he cuts across me. 'Listen

I'll be straight okay, let's cut to the chase, I'm just going put it out there. I want to spend more time with Rosie. I was thinking fifty/fifty.'

'What?' I almost spit my coffee out. Is he having a laugh?

'Yup, it's only fair, she's half mine, plus Rosie and Tiger-Lily get on so well, just like their sisters. Well, they are actually stepsisters. It would be a shame to deny Rosie more time with her best friend.' He sounds strange, like he has rehearsed it.

I can't hide that I am shocked but I can't be a total bitch either because he is right, she is half his but I can't help thinking that Tiny is behind this.

'I'll have to think about it,' I say carefully.

'Right,' he replies, his voice echoing around the café.

'You only see her twice a week at the moment which is what you wanted so it would be a big change for everyone, especially Rosie. I'm happy for you to have her more but I don't know about that much more.' I think my reply is fair enough but a flash of irritation crosses his face and his tone changes to clipped and angry.

'Listen Emily, you really need to fucking get over it and stop using Rosie as a weapon. It was four long years ago. Haven't you got a boyfriend yet? You really need to move on and stop being such a bitch to Tiny, it wasn't her fault, I wanted to leave you, she didn't make me.' The words fall out of his mouth like hot lava, spitting and stinging my heart. We haven't spoken about it properly since he left. I lower my voice to limit any potential eavesdroppers.

'How dare you? We were *married* and you were having an affair with the *art teacher* for over a year. I must have still been *pregnant* when it started. You're

61

disgusting. I bet you had a right laugh flirting in the staff room and banging in the stationery cupboards whilst I was at home getting everything ready for our baby. So don't you dare tell me to get over it, which by the way, I very much have.'

'Pah, yeah right,' he spits, making my blood boil.

'If your wife wasn't such an interfering busy body and in my face all the time, I wouldn't need to be short with her. She just needs to leave me alone and not get involved.'

'She's just trying to be nice, for fuck's sake. Can't you just let it go now?' He sounds so impatient and his words sting like venom.

I shake my head, unable to answer, swallowing a lump in my throat before getting up to leave.

Liam grabs my wrist and looks at me, pleading. 'Just think about it please, I need to see her more, she is *my* daughter too.'

Jamie

'What time did you get in?'

'Who are you? My mother?' Tim gives me a long sideways look as he empties the remaining half-box of Cheerios into his cereal bowl and follows it with the remains of the milk.

'I didn't hear you come in, that's all.' I pick up the empty milk bottle and cereal box and put them in recycling box. I'll have to go out for more milk if *I* want cereal.

'I've just come in.' He smirks at me.

'Good night, then?' I don't smirk back at him.

'You could say that. What about you?' He smirks again.

'Shit night, actually.'

'Ah. Right.' He picks up his cereal bowl, the milk sloshing as he moves, and heads for the living room and sofa.

'Ask me why?' I challenge him, following in his wake.

'None of my business.' He flicks the TV on.

'It is actually.'

He blinks at me and grimaces.

'Since you're not going to ask, I'm going to tell you anyway. We had gecko-gate here last night…'

'Hey, is Delilah back? Cool.' He dumps his cereal bowl on the coffee table, slopping milk onto it in the process, and leaps up. 'Did you get her back in her cage?'

'No. She's trapped in my bedroom,' I say to Tim's retreating form as he thunders up the stairs and I follow him.

'Where?'

'Over there.' I point to the bathroom bin still covering Delilah and the cricket. In the night I've piled a couple of heavy books on top of it to make sure she doesn't escape again.

'How long's she been in there?' He doesn't sound very happy; ungrateful arse.

'Dunno. Since last night.'

'What? Like that? You've probably killed her.' He moves gingerly towards Delilah's trap.

'How?'

'Suffocation,' he says, his voice drawn out. He swipes the books away.

Suffocation, ah, I hadn't thought of that.

He lies on the floor, lifts the bin a little and peaks under it. Then he hurls the bin and grabs his gecko.

'Look, she's all floppy.'

'But still alive,' I say, trying to sound upbeat.

'No thanks to you.'

Delilah licks an eyeball with her tongue.

'She managed to get the cricket though.' I point to the upturned glass. 'She's probably just exhausted from all the effort, or, maybe she's having a post breakfast snooze.'

'She's cold.' Tim snuggles the gecko to his chest.

'Sooner you get her back in that tank with the heat lamp on, the better, eh?' I smile and attempt to ease him out of my bedroom.

'She'd better not die.' He narrows his eyes at me as he slopes slowly away.

'No, and she'd better not escape again either.' I watch him disappear into his room and close the door. 'Oh, and you're welcome,' I yell. Ungrateful sod. It seems I can't do right by anyone this weekend.

I ring Beth at lunchtime, hoping that she's had a chance to forget the cricket ordeal. It goes straight to voicemail. I leave a suitably unctuous message. When she doesn't call back a few hours later, I message her several times. She doesn't reply but I can see that she's read my messages.

One final call on Sunday evening and she's still not answering me, so I don't even bother leaving a voicemail message. I can't believe she's still angry over a cricket. Maybe she's ill. I send her a quick message to say I hope she's okay, then realise I could have worded it better.

Six

Jamie

Monday morning looms and it's raining which is not a good start to the working week. It's further dampened by an email which rattles round Kanes at 10am sharp. It's from the CEO. It's the usual doom mongering about times being hard – not that anyone buys that in the insurance business – and costs must be cut, budgets controlled. We've seen these before but this one has a final sting in its tail – no pay rises this year.

The mood in the building drops even lower than normal for a Monday morning. Everyone is glum. Rumours soon start to circulate. There is talk of redundancies even though there is no mention of that possibility in the email. Apparently, although no one knows if it is true, several on the board of directors have already gone. I don't believe it, they would definitely announce that. The trouble with Kanes is that it's a small company compared to the likes of Genevre. It doesn't have the international clout or the resources; it's part of the reason I want to move. Kanes is small fry compared to Genevre, it's not somewhere you can climb up the ladder easily, it's dead man's shoes. But I think my dreams of working in Genevre are just that:

dreams.

To cheer myself up I drop Beth another message. She reads it but doesn't reply. Am I going to have to turn up at her place with a bunch of flowers and box of chocs? Maybe I could send them to her. I could order them online now for delivery tonight. Maybe I should offer a weekend away in a swanky hotel. Would that impress her? It would, at least, be bug free. I'm just grateful that she didn't see Delilah.

After lunch everyone has calmed down, the rumours have stopped and heads are occupied with work rather than doom laden gossip. That is, until, another email blasts around the company. It's confirmation of the retirement – read sacking – of no less than four directors on Kanes' board. After that there is very little work done.

I feel sick to my stomach that I won't get out of here, because I'm fairly certain I won't get the job at Genevre.

And Beth still hasn't messaged me back. I have ordered the flowers and chocs though; they'll be delivered about six, which is just after she gets home from work.

There's a mass frenzy at ten-to-five, no one actually turns their computer off or anything obvious like that, but everyone starts going to the toilet, packing away their paperwork – we operate a clean desk policy at Kanes – and grabbing their coats in readiness to leave. It's not normally this bad but everyone is so demoralised now.

The email arrives at five-to-five. It stuns us all.

'Aren't you going to ask about Delilah?' Tim asks as I let myself into my home and drop my work stuff on the sofa. He's sitting in his usual place, swiping his phone and frowning to himself. I really can do without this shit after what I've just read.

'She better not have escaped again.' I flop into an armchair.

'She's dehydrated.' He nods his head and shakes his shoulders as though I'm supposed to say sorry.

'And?'

'Probably from being trapped in the bin in your bedroom all Saturday night.'

'How do you know she's dehydrated? Can geckos even get dehydrated? Don't they live in deserts? Wasn't the cricket juicy enough?'

'There's no need to get snarky.' He glares at me. I fight hard not to roll my eyes in response. 'I've looked it up on the world wide web.' Tim always insists on calling the internet the world wide web, it's as though that's its proper name and only he is privy to it. 'And she has all the symptoms of dehydration.'

'Well, she'll soon recover now, won't she? Now you're feeding and watering her.' I sigh. I really can't be bothered with this. 'Anyway, I doubt it was one night in my bedroom that did it, it was probably days and days of cavorting around this house.' I get up and go to the kitchen to put the kettle on. Tim follows me.

'You're in a right mood today. Hasn't Beth called you yet?' Tim cuts himself a large chunk of bread and lays a thick slab of butter onto it.

I laugh out loud. I'd quite forgotten about my problems with Beth. The contents of the work email are still rattling around in my brain.

'We've just been told there's going to be fifteen percent redundancies at work.'

Tim stops chewing, the bread and butter now fills

his mouth, and blinks.

'Fucking hell, mate,' he says, buttery dribbles slide down his chin.

'Yeah.'

'What are they offering?'

'What?'

'Well, if you get that job at Genevre you'll be laughing. What redundancy package are they offering?' He grins at me and shows his butter-caked teeth.

'I won't be laughing and they haven't said. Anyway, I haven't been there that long.' I take two large mugs of coffee into the lounge and plonk them on the coffee table. 'And I won't be getting that job.'

'You might.' Tim, still chewing on his bread and butter, follows me.

I think of Emily flicky-hair and Dirk's wide-eyed grin. 'No. I won't.'

'Right. At least your CV is up to date. That's a positive.' He turns his attention back to his phone and pushes another godawful YouTube video about lizards to the TV.

I can't even be bothered to groan.

Emily

Swipe left, swipe left, swipe left, swipe left, swipe left. Swipe right.

Liam's words about me getting over him are ringing in my ears. I've realised I'm probably not over it completely, it, his leaving me, not him. So I've taken charge and put myself out there giving SwipeySwipey another go. And it's paid off, as this evening I have a date. Eeeeek.

As I'm getting ready my phone beeps and I reach to take a look at it. I have a missed call and a voicemail from Genevre. Feeling my heart sink, I have a horrible feeling they've called to tell me I haven't got the job. I'm not going to listen to it now, I don't want anything to knock my confidence before this date, I'll listen to it later, when I get home.

After fifteen outfit changes and three phone calls to Sabrina, I'm finally here. I'm nervous as I walk into the pub and look around to see if I can pick Simon out. I've made sure I'm a bit late as there was no way I was getting here first. My stomach jumps as I spot him in the corner by the window and am instantly relieved that he looks every bit like his photo but, even more nervous that he looks every bit like his photo.

He is absolutely drop dead gorgeous.

Wearing dark jeans and a red jumper which really accentuates his lovely big arms, he's drinking a pint of beer as he scrolls through his phone. Still scrolling when I appear at the table.

'Umm hi, Simon?' I say in a mouse voice as he looks up from his phone and proceeds to stuff it into his back pocket.

'It's me, Emily.' The mouse. I smile, trying to give my best Swipey smile with no gums, the one that matches my photo.

'Oh hi, Emily, nice to meet you. You're looking stunning, radiant even.' He doesn't hide the fact that he is looking me up and down and gives me a big lopsided grin. I notice he has the most amazing eye lashes.

'Thank you,' I reply shyly, annoyed I am blushing but he is *so* good looking.

'I hope you don't mind but I took the liberty of already getting you a drink.' He points to a large glass of white wine and I cringe. I hate white wine, I'm a red girl only plus for all I know he could have put Rohypnol in it. I've only been talking to him for four days; can I trust him? I could force the white wine down but what if it's drugged? Don't be stupid, he's not going to drug you woman.

'Lovely thanks, I love white wine.' Oh no! Why did I lie? Now he will always buy me white wine and I will have to pretend I like it. Forever. Everything will be based on a big fat lie. Plus, it's a bit presumptuous to pre-order my drink when he doesn't even know me, but I'll let him off this once.

'Fantastic, so tell me about yourself, what do you do for fun?'

My heart sinks, I feel like I'm in an interview, what do I do for fun? I'm a mum for god's sake, I don't have time for anything other than that right now.

'Umm well for fun...' I start as he looks at me, with his lopsided smile. 'I like to do a bit of crocheting and yoga when I get the chance.' Which is hardly ever, the last thing I crocheted was over five years ago but it was an amazing little baby hat and cardigan for Rosie. I last went to a yoga class about two years ago, I think I can still count that.

'Great. Sounds interesting maybe you can crochet something for me, but what I mean is, what do you really do for fun?'

Is this a trick? I'm confused.

'That's what I do. For fun. Of course, most of my time is taken up looking after my daughter.' After the last match ghosted me, I updated my profile on Swipey, so there's no secrets, Simon knows I have a child.

'Hahaha you're so sweet and innocent for a sexy old MILF, I mean fun fun, like real fun.'

I don't know if I'm more offended by old or MILF so I stay silent and wait for him to elaborate.

'Okay, I'll go first you shy thing. Anal, S&M,

roleplay, threesomes, voyeurism, public. What's your preference? I'm not fussy, I like all of it if I'm honest but my favourite is roleplay, student and teacher.'

Oh my god! I go to take a sip of my wine to stall for time but think better of it. I'm more convinced than ever that there's Rohypnol in there and probably enough to tranquilise a horse. Forever.

'Um I'll let you know in a minute, just popping to the loo to powder my nose.' I fake smile at him and take my bag with me, scuttling off feeling like the biggest prude on earth. Why did I say powder my nose like it's 1942? I'm pretty sure it's code for going to do a line of coke. He probably thinks that's what I'm doing now, to get in the mood. I get into the toilets and call Sabrina.

'Hey, hey. How's it going my lovely lady, is he the man of your dreams?' Sabrina asks.

'Oh my God, it's awful. He wants to hold me hostage in his sex dungeon, and that's just not me!' I squeal.

'What?'

He asked me what I do for fun, I said crochet and yoga and he said no *fun fun* and listed all things to do with sex. That's not romantic.'

I hear Sabrina crack up laughing down the other end of the phone but I'm too horrified to laugh with her.

'Crochet and yoga, you liar. You need to get the fuck out of there. He's obviously a creep after a one-night stand or even worse, a Christian Gray contract.'

'Yes, but his messages were so sweet in the four days that we spoke. In reality he's like a different person, though he looks just as good as his photo.'

'That's how they lure you in my darling. Listen, if Dave was here I'd come and get you but he's gone to rugby. What are you going to do? Can you get out of the pub without him seeing you?'

'The toilet is opposite our table so he will most likely see me. But I need to leave, I'll just make a run for it, it's not like I have to see him again.'

'Okay, phone me afterwards so I know you are safe.'

'Will do.'

I put my phone in my bag and take a deep breath, I'm going to look like a mad woman but needs must. I open the toilet door and sneak a peek to where we were sitting, I spot Simon, conveniently looking at his phone again. It's now or never.

And I'm running, I'm running the fastest I have ever run in heels in my life and it's hard work as they wobble over the uneven wooden floor. Just a few steps more and I am out of the danger zone. I'm almost out of his line of vision when I run full-on into a guy carrying two beers, causing both pints to be poured *all* over me. I want to die.

'Oh shit, shit, shit.' I can actually taste the beer as some of it splashed onto my face.

I'm absolutely soaked.

'Oh God, are you okay? I'm so sorry. Why were you running?' The guy looks at me with concern etched onto his face and rushes to put his empty glasses on a nearby table. I can feel people looking at me sniggering.

'Here let me get something to clean you up.' He's back in seconds with paper napkins and hands them to me to mop myself up. But all I can think is that I'm anxious Simon has seen and will make his way over. I must get out of here now.

'Sorry, I'm trying to escape, I had to make a run for it, I'm *still* making a run for it.' Honestly, I sound insane.

'Sounds serious, what are you escaping from exactly?' The guy hands me some more paper napkins and I pat myself down with them, it's really making no difference at all.

'A man!' I exclaim as I spot Simon getting up from his seat. He's looking at me, frowning and waving his arms at me to get my attention. The guy sees the terror on my face and takes my arm.

'Come with me, let's get you out of here.' He takes me outside round the back of the pub and calls a taxi. As he waves me off, he tells me to text him when I am home so that he knows I am safe and not in someone's sex dungeon. In the few minutes we waited for the taxi, I told this stranger all about my depressing date – which he found rather amusing. I'm glad someone did. I plonk myself down in the taxi and close my eyes feeling utterly rubbish about my failed attempt at dating. Maybe internet dating isn't for me.

Jamie

It's nine-thirty before Beth manages to message me. I've resisted the temptation to message her and ask if the flowers arrived okay.

Beth: *Just got in. Thank you for the gorgeous flowers. And the chocolates.* She follows this with two smiley faces not the usual half a dozen kisses she usually adds to her messages.

Me: *You're welcome. You're late home xx*

Beth: *Zumba. Off for a shower now.*

I thought Zumba was a different night but I'm hardly going to argue with her.

Me: *I'm really sorry about the cricket thing on Saturday.*

Beth: *No probs. Off for a shower now. Talk tomorrow.* A thumbs-up and two smiley faces follow her message then she goes offline.

Talk tomorrow. Well, that's something, I suppose.

Seven

Jamie

The email giving more detail about the redundancies is waiting in our inboxes when we all arrive for work a few days later. It's timed at 7am; they've been busy. Tim is right, they are offering a package, enhanced for those who volunteer. I peer around at my colleagues, wondering if any will offer themselves up. There are eleven of us in our department so the odds of someone going, even if no one volunteers, are high.

The mood is grim and everyone is shocked. It's going to be another great day at work.

Midmorning my phone starts to vibrate in my pocket. I quickly yank it out. Unknown number, but it's a local one. Maybe it's Beth ringing from her office. I swipe to answer and get up from my desk and head for the corridor – hardly private but better than in here.

'Jamie?' the voice says. It doesn't sound like Beth.

'Y-e-s.'

'Hello, this is Berta, Head of HR at Genevre. We met the other day.'

'Oh, hello.' This is where they let me down nicely. At least it isn't creepy Dirk ringing me to gloat.

'Yes, we've got a proposition for you.' She waits for

me to react. I don't know how to react.

'Okay. What's that?'

'Well, everyone was very impressed with your interview last week.' She pauses to let me take this in. It's sounding very positive. Too positive. Can she be about to offer me the job? 'And the team really liked you.' I can't believe that, I thought they found our meeting as excruciating as I did. 'And what we'd like to do is offer you the position…'

Oh fucking hell, she's offering me the job. She's offering me the job. I can volunteer to go here and probably save someone else's job – how noble of me. I can hardly believe my luck.

'…but obviously that might be a bit of a risk for you.' She's still talking and I've missed some of what she's said because I've been so busy being excited – and noble. Shit. 'So, what do you think?'

'Umm…' I don't know what to think, I've missed half of it. 'Could you run that by me again? Please.' Now I sound pathetic. Or worse, dim.

'Yes, it is rather a lot to take in.' She laughs lightly and gives me the details again, ending with, 'As I said, we were so impressed with both of you that we really can't choose between you. So, we wondered if you'd be prepared to come and work with us for three months, together with Emily of course, and at the end of the three months, we'll make a decision.'

'Right, I thought that's what you said.' I play for time.

'Obviously, we don't expect you to say yes or no right now. Shall we say you ring us Friday morning with a decision. We're just putting the offer in the post, so you should have it tomorrow. That'll be enough time to know whether this is for you.' I can almost hear her smile. I wonder if she can hear my expression: complete bewilderment.

'Okay, fine. Shall I ring you on this number?'

'Yes, please. It's my direct line.'

When I end the call, I notice that I've missed a call from Beth. I message her back to apologise and say I'm in a meeting. Much as I want to talk to Beth, I need some time to assimilate what I've just heard.

I'll be on a three-month trial alongside my rival, Emily flicky-hair. The salary is a lot more than I'm currently getting – and there's no chance of that going up here now. If I don't get the job at the end of the trial, they'll offer outplacement services and a one-month bonus to help me on my way.

I don't know what to do.

If Kanes hadn't announced these redundancies I think I'd tell Genevre to stick their stupid idea where the sun doesn't shine. But, but… can I beat Emily flicky-hair when Dirk is obviously so smitten with her? Is it entirely his decision?

I stop in my tracks. Of course, it's not entirely his decision, because if it was, she would have already got the job.

There's hope. I could just be the best, the very best. I'm good at my job here, it's just there's nowhere for me to progress to. And that's even more the case now. It could just work, or it could be the most stupid thing I've ever done.

I don't have to decide now. I've got until Friday.

I imagine my Dad's reaction when I tell him. It won't be good, he already thinks Genevre have behaved badly over the dual interview process. Maybe I won't tell him the whole truth. If I get the job it won't matter. But what if I don't? I've no idea what Emily is like, how good she is, what her experience is. No idea at all. She might be brilliant, she might make me look a right idiot.

When I go back into the office the atmosphere is still glum and it's nearly lunch time. At twelve everyone gets up and goes – and who can blame them. I decide that I'll take a later lunch; I've got some work I need to catch up on anyway since I've been away from my desk for so long. I hang on another forty-five minutes then leave. Once outside I ring Beth back.

'Hey,' I say when she finally answers. 'Is it a good time.'

There's a silence from her end, too long a silence. 'Of course,' she says finally.

'You'll never guess what. Genevre have only offered me that job. Well sort of.' I wait for her to ask what I mean by sort of, because I think explaining it to Beth might help me get a better perspective on it. I'm also interested to hear what she thinks because I think I might have talked myself into accepting the job and she might think that's madness. Although, she's not had much experience in the proper world of work herself yet.

'Cool. Well done,' she says flatly.

'Yeah, but did you hear what I said, they've only sort of offered it to me. It comes with conditions. They…'

'Jamie,' she says, cutting across me and sighing.

'Yeah?'

'The thing is… I mean, you're a great guy and all that, but the thing is, I need some space of my own…' She stalls. She's waiting for me to say something.

She's dumping me?

I'm not going to do it for her. I wait, silent.

'Yeah, well,' she finally continues. 'As I said, I'm young and I need to find myself, discover who I really am. I don't think we should see each other again.'

'You're dumping me? Over a cricket? Really?'

'Well, um, well, not just the bug.'

'What then?'

'Well…'

'Well, what?'

'The thing is… you're a great guy and all that…but I need to explore myself…' her voice peters out again. Can she actually hear what she's saying? Explore herself, what the hell is that supposed to mean?

'You've already said that.'

'Yep. Well. It's over.'

'Just like that?'

'Yep.' There's a hard edge to her voice now. Hard and cold.

'Right. Well thanks.'

'Good luck with the job and all that.'

'Yeah. Bye.' I end the call first, because I'm not going to be the one staring at my phone in shock.

Except, of course, I do.

Emily

I called Genevre back and they made me a very strange offer. I can't quite believe it so I'm calling Sabrina for a chat on the way to get Rosie from school. Handsfree is a wonderful thing.

'Hey, hey my darling, how was the date? Did you escape?' Shit. I forgot to text her when I got home.

'Oh god. Awful. Sorry I didn't reply, I was shattered, needed to sleep.' Is it bad that I'd almost forgotten about that? Perhaps it was so bad that my memory has tried to erase it, like a trauma.

'Poor you. What happened?' asks Sabrina.

I sigh, already bored of talking about my sad excuse

for a love life, then beep my horn as some idiot cuts me up.

'Well, I managed to escape but, in the process, went hurtling into some poor guy who was carrying a beer in each hand. You can probably guess the rest.'

'Oh no, my darling.' Sabrina is trying to sound sympathetic but I can hear the amusement in her voice.

'Yep, all over me. I was soaked.'

'Oh my God. You poor thing.' She laughs.

'I know, what an idiot. Only me.' I laugh with her because if I don't laugh, I'll cry at how pathetic it is. 'There was something good that came of it though,' I add, suddenly feeling brighter.

'What's that?'

'The guy I ran into took pity on me and ended up helping me get a taxi. He gave me his number to message him that I had got home safely. I think he was kind of hot.'

'And did you message him?

'No not yet, but I might.' I think back to try and remember his face. It all happened so fast that the image of him is a bit fuzzy but I think he was hot.

'You must message him,' Sabrina insists.

'Yeah, I probably will.' Probably won't. I'd guess he was just genuinely checking I was okay and isn't interested romantically in the slightest. 'But listen I wasn't calling you about that. I've heard from Genevre.'

'Yes, yes. Good news?'

'Well, yes, it is.'

'Yes. I knew it. When do you start?'

'I start soon but I'll be on trial for three months alongside someone else. They couldn't choose between us.'

'What does that mean?'

'They choose the person best suited to the role at the end of the three months and the other one is let go,' I explain glumly, as I hear Sabrina gasp.

'What!? That is so harsh. Are you going to accept?'

'I don't know.' I'm thinking I won't after her reaction. Is it that bad an offer?

'It's a tough one, potentially a lot of stress, but you'll do it. You'll win the trial,' Sabrina encourages yet the word trial makes me shiver. I'm going to be on trial for three months. Everything I say and do will be under the microscope, being compared to someone else.

'Do you think? But the other guy has tons more experience.' An image of Lenny pops into my head, licking a 20p coin. Maybe I can do this.

'So, what? They obviously can't decide between you, which is why they've done this. You'll win them over. You're a great boss and a hard worker.' I pull up to the school and spy Rosie with her friends.

'Thanks Sab, I need to think about it, don't I? I've got to go now. At the school.'

'Okay darling, speak soon and let me know what you decide, ciao.'

Rosie and her friends are busy doing a silly dance involving wiggling their bums whilst slapping each other's hands. As I approach, they begin poking their tongues out, making raspberry sounds before twirling around and high fiving each other. YouTube has a lot to answer for. I smile to myself, maybe I should give it a go, for Rosie. I could give her so much more, if only for a few months.

Jamie

'Yeah, well, not like you'd been with her very long, is it?' Tim offers me support, of a sort when I tell him about Beth.

After the dumping phone call, I'd made up my mind that I wouldn't be telling anyone, least of all Tim. Yet, the minute I walked through the door I blurted it out. I'm kicking myself now of course.

'Two months.' I sound pathetic.

'Plenty more fish.' He shrugs. 'Especially online.' He sniggers.

'Thanks for that. Are you staying in this evening or seeing your *lady friend*?' Now it's my turn to snigger.

'What lady friend?'

'Saturday? Your dirty stop out night?' Has he forgotten? Already?

'No, not my girlfriend, just a friend.' He smirks and whispers the rest of the sentence to himself. 'With benefits. I'm not out tonight.'

'So you're in. What shall we have for tea?'

'Takeaway and beer. I fancy Indian. Do you want your usual?' He picks up his phone to send our order which is always the same and he has saved in his favourites.

'Yes, okay.'

This is me, an evening in with my housemate. What a pair we are; fat Tim, the IT geek and sad Jamie, the dumped.

Eight

Jamie

My first day at Genevre.

My dad has sent the inevitable good luck text. I haven't told him the whole truth about the job; the three-month competition where the winner takes it all. I'm hoping I never have to. He's so old school, job for life and all that, that he won't be able to cope with it. Tim has been supportive – his version of supportive, anyway – pointing out that everyone is usually on a three-month trial. Most companies don't let you into the pension and benefits club until then anyway. I'm trying to be philosophical and viewing it that way. Be positive. And, as Tim has pointed out several times, at least I've got my redundancy money from Kanes to fall back on, though it's not nearly as much as Tim seems to think it is.

He's also suggested sabotage. Sabotage, as in I try my hardest to mess it up for my rival. I slapped him down immediately. It's just too low. He laughed at me, called me a sucker, said my rival would definitely be doing it – I hope he's wrong. Sometimes I think Tim watches too many movies.

The traffic is good and I arrive with plenty of time,

feeling confident and calm as I pull into Genevre's car park. Whoa. I wasn't expecting that; the car park is full. I mean, full. Obviously early starts are the norm here. I drive around slowly looking for a space. The car park operates a one-way system so if you go down an aisle you have to circle round to go again. But that's okay, I've got plenty of time.

I spot a space and pull well forward so I can back into it. I prefer to do that because my car is large – my dad jokingly calls it a tank – and it's easier that way. I've just got the car in reverse ready to make my manoeuvre, a quick glance in the rear-view mirror and I'm stunned. A little white car has nipped into my space. MY space. Bloody cheek.

My instinct is to get out and have a go at the space thief. I grip the wheel to restrain myself. I don't know who that is; I could be working with them, sat next to them. I don't want to start the day, a new job, with a fight. I slam my car out of reverse and start to edge forward, flicking my eyes between ahead of me and the rear-view mirror to see who the driver is.

It's her.

Emily flicky-hair.

My rival.

Maybe this is what Tim meant by sabotage.

I pull away and hare off around the corner. It takes me two sweeps of the entire car park before I finally squeeze my car into a tight space I'd missed on the first two passes. I narrowly avoid stepping in a deep puddle when I get out of the door. No wonder this crap space was free.

Emily flicky-hair is sitting in Reception when I arrive. I soon join her, sitting opposite. I nod and smile, though I really want to have a go about the parking space. Then I remind myself that it really doesn't matter. Maybe she didn't see me.

She smiles over at me and blinks slowly. She did bloody see me. So, this is how it's going to be.

A little lad from HR accompanies us to our office.

'Did you both have a good weekend?' His tone is up and down. And irritating.

'*I* did,' I reply, because the way he's phrased the question seems to suggest that we've spent the weekend together.

'Great,' he says, guiding us towards the correct segment of the building and running up the stairs in front of us. Emily flicky-hair doesn't even bother to answer his inane question.

I step aside to let Emily go ahead of me. I'm doing this out of politeness; it's only as I'm following her up the stairs that I realise it might not be very PC and I've almost got my nose up her bum. I fall back. What's a man to do? Be rude?

In the office it's all smiles and greetings. Dirk gives us both a big handshake. I'm sure he doesn't squeeze Emily's hand as hard as he does mine. I try not to respond in kind, but at the same time I don't want him to think I'm weak. Inwardly, I snigger at Tim's comment about Dirk only being one C away from Dick.

The whole team is there except Hayden. He comes bustling in a few minutes after us. Everyone is pleasant and greets him except Dirk, who flashes a quick frown in his general direction but doesn't say anything. Hayden gets the message, whatever it might be.

'Hi everyone, sorry I'm late. Sorry Dirk. Car trouble.'

Dirk nods, his face carefully impassive. Is there a bit

of tension there?

Dirk spends most of the morning giving us a tour of the building, or at least the parts that Genevre uses. We go through so many departments with Dirk giving us information and insights as we go, that it's hard to take it all in. I just hope he doesn't test us later. He marches with purpose across the atrium and up the stairs, Emily seems to have no trouble keeping up with him. I, on the other, resolve to make use of the free onsite gym asap. I used to be much fitter, and, if I'm honest, much thinner, than I am now. In the VSO food wasn't my top priority, but sitting at a desk for the past couple of years and having Tim as my housemate has increased my girth. Tim does like his food, especially takeaways, and it's so easy to eat along with him.

'Okay, yeah. I thought we'd do a bit of a team lunch today. I've booked a meeting room and ordered in.' Dirk juts his jaw in Emily's direction. 'What do you think?'

'Sounds great,' Emily says, with a little flick of her hair, which today is down, loose and waving around her shoulders. Occasionally she pushes it behind her ears then lets it fall forward again.

Dirk looks at me for a response.

'Good way to mix with everyone,' I say, sounding feeble. Man up for God's sake.

'Cool,' Dirk says, managing to make the word sound like *cuel*. His voice is so deep that sometimes, when he speaks, my eardrums vibrate.

We're in the meeting room for lunch before everyone else. There's a selection of salads, meats, fish and dips. There's also a large bowl of fruit. I'd prefer a sandwich, or a sausage roll myself, but there's none of those in evidence. Maybe today is a good day to start eating healthier.

The team drips in slowly and I watch as each person's eyes alight on the food. No one grabs for anything and there doesn't seem to be any urgency to eat. Finally, Dirk grabs the plates and starts dishing them out.

'Did they forget to bring the sandwiches again, Dirk?' Karen asks.

'Nooo,' he says, his voice deep and drawn out. 'I didn't order any. We don't need those wasted carbs. Do we?'

I see Karen and Sharon exchange furtive glances before Sharon picks up a carrot stick and dips it into some pasty liquid offering.

'Don't double dip, Sharon,' Dirk says, affecting a laugh.

'Don't worry, Dirk, I wasn't,' Sharon simpers back.

After we've stuffed ourselves with carrot sticks and hummus – which Emily seems to genuinely enjoy – it's back to work; a one to one meeting with Dirk.

Emily goes first and comes out smiling.

'Okay?' I ask, attempting to be friendly.

'Sure,' she says. 'You'll be fine.'

Now I look like a weak idiot.

I'm in a meeting room with Dirk, it's small and windowless and Dirk's testosterone is floating in the air and clinging to the walls. Even though, physically I'm taller than Dirk, he makes me feel emasculated. I breathe in deeply, trying not to register the stench of his machismo and sit down as instructed, opposite him.

'Hi, and thanks for coming.' His voice is so deep and slow it reminds me of a foghorn.

I nod and smile. What the hell else response is there to that? It's not like I had a choice.

'I thought this would be a good opportunity for us to get to know each other a little.' When he speaks his eyebrows dance in time to his words. 'So, tell me about yourself. Something I don't already know.'

What is there to say that he hasn't already heard about at my *two* interviews? I'm wracking my brain for something new to tell him.

'I used to be quite into my gym,' I lie. 'I'm looking to getting back into it. I'm very sporty and ran a half marathon a few years ago – for charity, obviously. You look fit. Do you use the gym here?' What the hell am I saying? I did run a half marathon – when I was twenty and it nearly killed me. I hate the gym, although I think I need to do some exercise soon.

'Cool,' he says, doing the *cuel* thing again. 'I'm not into running myself, but I do admire those who are.' He raises a solitary eyebrow. 'I do use the gym here, but only during the week. At weekends,' he pauses, 'I go to a proper gym for serious training.' He smiles broadly at me, showing very white teeth which, I realise, I haven't noticed previously because he hasn't smiled properly at me before.

'Oh, what are you training for?'

'Comps,' he says, with a wiggle of his head. 'Body comps.'

'Cool,' I echo.

By the end of my allotted hour with Dirk I know all about his body comps, or what I would call body building competitions. Dirk, on the other hand, knows very little about me. Which is just fine.

I've also agreed to go on a gym session with Dirk later in the week. I felt cornered into agreeing, especially after he told me he already had a session planned with Emily.

When the meeting finishes I sidle off to the office kitchen and make myself a very strong black coffee. I hold the cup up to my nose and inhale the caffeine. I'm enjoying the sensation as I face the window, looking out over the green fields beyond Genevre's car park when a voice suddenly interrupts me.

'Good meeting with Dirk?' It's Emily.

'Yeah, thanks. Yours go okay?' I've already asked that.

'Yeah. Coffee good?' She's clocked me enjoying the caffeine hit.

'It is.' And, for want of something better to say. 'I hear you're doing a gym session with Dirk tomorrow.'

'Yoga,' she corrects, smiling. 'I'm quite into it. Have you ever tried it?' Well, that explains her toned legs and pert backside, not that I've noticed, of course.

'No. But I did try Tai-Chi when I was abroad. It's sort of similar?' I phrase my answer as a question, just in case I'm wildly wrong. In truth I tried Tai-Chi just once.

'Yeah. Sort of. Where was that?'

'Cambodia, when I was with the VSO.'

'Wow. My brother did that, though he only lasted about three months, I think he missed my mum's cooking. Where else did you go? How long were you in it?'

So, I find myself telling Emily about my two years volunteering overseas, about building a school and teaching in it afterwards, about digging wells and helping the fight against the farm poaching which is ruining people's livelihoods. I don't, of course, tell her that I basically ran away from home soon after my mum died leaving my dad to cope with his grief on his own. She listens with genuine interest, asking questions and expressing admiration.

She seems really nice, does Emily. Sod it. I'd prefer to hate my rival.

'Anyway, that's a few years ago now.' I finish my coffee. 'What about you? How did you get into yoga?'

'I took it up for stress relief,' she says, quietly, blinking. 'It's great for that. And toning muscles too.' She laughs lightly as if to pull herself back together.

'Yeah,' I say slowly and realise I really shouldn't have said it like that. I sound as lecherous as I think Dirk is.

'Better get back,' Emily says, taking her coffee with her as I follow alongside her.

Emily

Day one at Genevre went really well.

Much better than expected.

I even managed to secure a car park space without the desperate driving around. Everyone seems so lovely at Genevre, and Dirk my mentor/possible predecessor is *such* a character. Lenny, aka Jamie, seems super switched on and the team seem to like him. This worries me as he's also a lot more experienced than I am. I must prove I'm worthier of this job, so a lot of effort will be required to pip Lenny at the post.

'Hi Emily, Jamie, very pleased to see you both again. Nice to see we didn't scare you off after your first day then?' Dirk approaches us smoothly, wearing stylish navy suit trousers with a light pink very tight fitted shirt, coupled with a colourful tie. His hair is extremely thick and there's no hint of any receding hairline, the envy of lots of men I'm sure.

'Hi Dirk, no, no.' I chuckle cheerily. 'It was actually very pleasant, I had a great first day.' I shake Dirk's hand and smile kindly at Lenny, because he must be looking forward to this three-month stress fest as much as I am. Must stop inwardly referring to him as Lenny in case it slips out. I must be super professional.

'Yeah, I'm good thanks, also had a great first day,' Jamie replies confidently. I watch as Dirk vigorously shakes Jamie's hand and notice his giant arms flexing through his shirt as he does so, I'm thankful he didn't shake my hand that hard. It looks like it could cause some serious damage.

'There's a few things to run through with HR before we get started today, so I'll leave you both in the capable hands of Sue for about thirty-minutes, then you'll be with the team again, okay Emily? Jimbo?' Dirk looks up at us both raising one of his thick yet plucked eyebrows, pursing his lips.

'Sorry Dirk, not meaning to be pedantic, but I *really* do prefer Jamie, not Jimbo.' I feel for Jamie but admire his persistence. I probably would have accepted Jimbo just for now, at least until I'd definitely got the job.

'Sure, sorry, my bad, Jimbo, I mean Jamie, no, so sorry. I must explain. My brother was called Jamie and we always affectionately called him Jimbo, sadly he died.' Dirk looks into the distance and we all stand there in a thick, uncomfortable silence before he runs his fingers through his glossy dark hair and continues.

'It was a car crash, he was only nineteen,' Dirk divulges. 'Hit and run, they never found who did it'

'So sorry to hear that,' Jamie and I say in unison.

'No problem guys, it was hard on the family of course but you take each day as it comes. Jimbo and I were so close, *very* alike. I'm afraid I'm guilty of shortening any Jamie I meet to Jimbo. It helps me to feel closer to my brother. I'm sure you can understand?' Dirk looks at Jamie.

'Ah right, that makes sense,' Jamie mumbles.

'If it makes you feel any better, Jamie in HR is Jimbo, as is Jamie down in the gym, they are all *my* Jimbo's.' Poor Dirk, that's so sad. I can't imagine what I'd do if something awful happened to my brother. It seems like my rival, Jamie, will just have to put up with being called Jimbo.

Dirk walks us into a spacious office where people are busy working in their private pods. We walk what seems like half a mile to the other corner of the office by a big window looking out onto some fields. There's a table underneath the window with some refreshments laid out and a couple of chairs up against the wall. It looks like we are about to have a mini office party. I wonder if they're going to ask us to perform our best dance moves? Do we get scores out of ten?

I sneak a peek at Jamie, he's already slouching over the table, eyeing up the goodies. I bet he doesn't dance. As I stare out of the window, I see a deer gallop out of some trees and scuttle off into the distance. Sighing, I imagine how lovely it must be to work in this segment.

'Ok guys so here we are in HR. Take a seat just by that desk and Sue will be with you in ten. Just help yourself to some coffee, enjoy a croissant and I will see you both in a while, ciao for now.' And off he goes, leaving me alone with my competition.

Jimbo.

I help myself to a coffee and offer Jamie one before eyeing up the croissants and deciding to pass. I'm hoping to have a date in the pipeline soon so I want to look my very best and fit into a certain dress I have in mind. Jamie takes two chocolate croissants and my stomach rumbles in protest.

Nine

Emily

'Hey, are you looking forward to your gym session with Dirk this week?' I ask Jamie in an attempt to make polite conversation. I can't stand awkward silences.

'Ah, yeah. I've not been yet. It's planned for the end of the week and I can't say I'm ecstatic about it. I'm not that sporty, as you can see.' Jamie pats his padded belly, picks up his croissant and puts it down again, frowning. 'Do you know Dirk does body building competitions? He calls them his comps.'

'No, I didn't know. Wow that would explain his build then.' Suddenly I realise that it might sound as though I fancy Dirk. I really don't fancy Dirk. He has a good bod but so not my type with that big ego to match. I prefer a typical dad bod, it shows that they aren't totally self-obsessed and there's a chance they might prefer *me* to the gym.

'Yeah?' Jamie questions, raising an eyebrow. I bet he thinks I'm pathetic now for fancying the boss.

'I'm doing a yoga class with him today. I'm feeling a bit awkward about it. Is it normal to do this type of thing? Work out with the boss? I haven't worked for a corporate company like this for such a long time, so things might be different now?' I question in the hope that I'm making it clear I don't fancy Dirk.

'Ha. No, it's definitely not normal and good luck with yoga.' Jamie guffaws and takes a huge bite of his croissant before talking again with his mouth full. 'I wonder if he'll be wearing Lycra for your class.' He sniggers and a little bit of croissant sprays out. I laugh too, as an image of Dirk in a pink leotard flashes through my mind.

'Thanks, I'll try my very best to remain professional whatever attire he chooses to wear.' I giggle and so does Jamie. He has a kind face. I can't imagine many people dislike him.

'Yeah, let's hope Dirk does too.' He frowns and looks away.

Before I have a chance to ask him what he means, Sue arrives and we are given various HR sheets to fill out. She explains the bonus scheme and perks of the job. Apparently, you can actually buy holiday if you want some more, sounds great to me. I get all excited but apparently it's normal practice in corporate companies, which makes me feel a bit silly and out of touch. Oh well, I am out of touch.

Afterwards, we have a coffee break before meeting with the team again. Time flies and before we know it it's lunch time and I'm dying to check my phone.

A message from Ben, the guy that saved me from Simon the sex dungeon maniac, brings a smile to my face. We've been messaging back and forth since that night and he's actually a very sweet, funny guy. Every cloud and all that.

Ben: *Hi Emily, how's the job going? Bet you're smashing it!*
Me: *Hi, yeah, all good. I've got to go to yoga with the boss in*

a bit though, super awkward, save me!

Ben: *Ha ha oh dear, well if you need rescuing and beer poured all over your head, or his, then I'm your man.*

Me: *I'll be sure to call you if I get stuck in any uncompromising positions.* Oh no, does that sound crude? It was meant to be witty but as soon as I'd sent it, I fear it's just smutty. I'm as bad as sex dungeon maniac Simon.

Ben: *Please do, I'm particularly in favour of the downward dog.*

Cheeky Ben. I feel my face turn hot.

'Hello Emily, so are you ready for some serious namaste ommmmmmmmm?' A deep booming voice bellows down on me. I look up from my phone to see Dirk with his eyes closed and fingers in a meditating position. 'Ommmmmmm,' Dirk does another deep hum, still with his eyes closed and the sound reverberates in my ears. I'm not sure he knows what yoga is.

'Umm hi, Dirk, yes I'm looking forward to trying out the class. Have you been before then?'

'No, not to yoga. I usually weight train but I think this will be good to stretch out all these extra muscles I gain while training for my comps.' He flexes his arms and if I'm not mistaken also his pecs.

Cringe.

'I do meditate though, ommmmmm namaste. It's good for the soul.'

We walk side by side to the gym while Dirk tells me all about his comps and I'm grateful that I don't have to fill any silences. I can just relax, making the right noises in the right places, which suits me fine.

I'm nervous about this class, I haven't been for ages

so I've taken a couple of Kalms today to take the edge off.

We arrive at the gym and each go into our separate changing rooms. I really hope Dirk isn't wearing a pink leotard or *any* type of leotard. I'm wearing black and green Lycra leggings with a Lycra green top over my maximum support sports bra. It's great, the boobs don't move at all and it makes them look a lot smaller, which believe me, is a good thing. One thing I've learnt about yoga as a woman is, you don't want to wear any loose, baggy t-shirts as the whole world will see your belly and bra.

I step out of the changing room to greet Dirk, he's in tiny white shorts paired with a long sleeved, tight white and red training top. Sadly, his tiny legs don't match his bulky body. They remind me of a book Rosie had as a toddler where you match up the top half of the animal to the bottom. This time the animals got mismatched, the top half's a gorilla and the bottom half's a chicken.

'Emily, looking good, gym gear really suits you.' He growls before tipping his head back and taking a gulp out of his water bottle, Man Rox written in red and white all over it. Man Rox, yuk.

'Thanks, Dirk, you too.' God this is already cringe. Never mind it's only forty-five minutes, then I never have to go with him again. Or do I?

'Yoga's this way, come with me.'

I follow Dirk into the room and the class is empty; it appears we are early. The instructor is busy stretching when she looks up to greet us.

'Hi guys, this your first time?' she asks, all smiles and spandex.

'It is indeed my first time but I believe the lovely

Emily has done yoga before,' Dirk replies for himself and for me and the instructor nods.

'Okay, no problem, just take your time and make sure you stop if anything starts to hurt. You're only meant to feel a satisfying stretch, not pain, okay?' The instructor looks at us, studying our faces and we consent to stretching and not causing ourselves pain.

Dirk stays at the front of the class, in front of the mirror. I stay where I am next to him, subtly trying to shuffle a bit more to the side to give myself more space. Would it be rude to go to the back of the class? I guess it's not the best idea if I'm trying to get on the boss's good side. *God* this is going to be painful and not just in the physical sense.

'Okay everyone, please help yourselves to some mats and make sure you have plenty of room around you.' The instructor talks into her headset and it crackles with feedback as she adjusts it. I surreptitiously shuffle a little further away from Dirk then he signals at me to stay put before sauntering off to get our yoga mats. When he returns, he sits considerably closer to me than before and my efforts to gain some personal space are lost.

The class fills up quickly, Dirk is the only man. A trio of women, all super slim-toned yoga pros, come to the front but most people remain at the back. Right at the back. There's a big empty space around me and Dirk. I feel very on display.

'Welcome back and to those that are new in the class, very keen at the front here, that's great. I love enthusiasm. Right let's start with our sun salutations to warm up.' The instructor looks at Dirk and he gives her a massive grin and thumbs up. What a cheese ball.

She puts on some calming whale music and we begin our sun salutations, rotating round to the right after each set. I soon remember what I should be doing. It feels good to be exercising again. I glance over at Dirk to witness him moving rigidly from one position to the next. He's so stiff he can barely reach his toes which really aren't that far away from his hands. With every movement we make Dirk makes a big thud as he places his feet and hands in different places. My eyes are drawn to his feet which are very wide and flat and I notice his toes are so hairy you could probably plait them.

Hobbit feet; he has hobbit feet.

'Okay everyone, now doooown into downward doggggg and really feeeeel that stretch,' sings the instructor.

I bend down into downward dog as does Dirk, whose arse is now in front of my head.

'Grrr, oh God, this is tougher than I thought. You okay there, Emily?'

'Yes, thanks Dirk.' I wish he wouldn't talk to me through his legs, I could do without his eyes peering at me through his bum cheeks.

'Now bring your left leg up as high as you can and point your toes to the skyyyyy. I want you to hold for a count of ten.'

We all lift our legs in unison and in my peripheral vision I notice Dirk's leg only come up about two inches off the floor. He must be really stiff.

'One, two, three, four,' the instructor counts slowly and the time feels much longer than it should.

'Umph, my leg just doesn't want to go up anymore, the muscle must weigh too much,' Dirk mutters. I pretend not to hear but I can hear Dirk panting and huffing loudly. A couple of women giggle at the back.

'Five, six, seven,' the instructor continues.

'Oooff, arrgghhhh,' Dirk grunts.

The instructor talks to the class but it is clearly aimed at Dirk. 'Remember you're only meant to be feeling a stretch and not pain. So, if you *are* in pain then please release your leg and put it *down*.'

Thank god she said it! But Dirk's leg is still well and truly off the floor. He isn't listening to the instructor because he's too busy concentrating on keeping his leg up.

'Eight, nine, ten annnnd release back down into downward dogggg.'

'Arrghhhh ump humph, bloody hell,' Dirk splutters, dropping to his knees, puffing and panting like he's just run a marathon.

'Okay everyone, now take your riiiight leggggg and point that as highhhhh as you can towards the skyyyy, remember we want to feel it pulling and stretching *not* hurting,' advises the instructor. I spy her assessing Dirk but he is still on his knees, so maybe he will stay there this time and take a rest. Probably best.

But no. He heaves himself up into downward dog again.

'One, two three, four,' the instructor counts.

'Arrghhharghhhh,' Dirk groans, stretching his leg.

I hear giggling from the back again.

'Arrghhhohhh goooddarrghhh,' Dirk carries on groaning. I can't stand this any longer so I come out of downward dog onto my knees and face Dirk through his legs.

'Dirk, are you okay?'

His eyes are screwed shut and his face is red, almost purple.

'Arrgharrghhhummphhh, I think I've got cramp.'

The instructor is looking worried and the rest of the class have stopped what they are doing to watch. She approaches Dirk, taking off her headset, she talks to him in a quiet voice.

'Okay there, what you need to do, my lovely, is slowly come out of downward dog onto your knees. I'll support you just here and then you need some water. Don't worry, it's quite common for this to happen, some water and a little rest will sort you out.' The instructor smiles sympathetically and leans forward holding Dirk's leg and helping him bring it down before patting him on the head.

'Yes, I know I've had cramp before!' Dirk snaps as the instructor places his Man Rox water bottle next to him and continues with the class.

'Okay everyone riiiight leg up, one, two, three, four.'

'Arrrghhhhhhhghhhh,' Dirk roars, slowly bringing his right leg up.

What the hell is he doing? What's he trying to prove? I thought he had cramp. I hear more giggles from the back of the room. Dirk is still insisting on continuing with forcing his leg up. I am going red for him.

'Five, six, seven, eight.'

'Arrghh, umph, aaarrghhh.' Dirk sounds like a cow giving birth.

'Nine, ten annnnnnd release.'

I look up to see if Dirk is okay and see his leg violently shaking to stay up longer than everyone else's. We all bring down our right legs and I hear Dirk groaning again before his leg goes down with a massive thud.

'Parrrrrppppppppppp.' He lets out an almighty, loud fart.

Right in my face.

Dirk collapses on the floor in a giant heap of muscle, sweat and stink.

'Parrrrrrrrp.' He's done another one, is he even aware?

I am horrified and so should he be.

'Well, that's one way of releasing it,' screeches a lady from the back of the class and several laugh along with her. I would be laughing too but the smells making me retch. It's a mixture of eggs and cabbage.

'Sorry ladies, it's all those protein shakes, these muscles need feeding.' Dirk turns around red faced yet flexing his arms to the class. Several women flutter their eyelashes and giggle at him.

Really? That stink is enough to put anyone off surely.

The class continues and amongst others we do the swan position which Dirk ends up getting stuck in and the instructor has to help him again.

'Annnnd nowww to finish everyone pleassssse relax into the child's possssse,' the instructor sings.

I glance over at Dirk and see him face down on his knees, panting and trying to recover from all his efforts. He's really enjoying the child's pose and I don't blame him; his back arches and his hands reach forward as with a groan he brings his bum up even more.

And there it is.

I pinch my hand hard.

So hard as I desperately try to cause myself enough pain not to laugh. *I must not* laugh at the small, brown mark on his white shorts.

He's sharted.

After yoga, Dirk scurries off into the changing rooms to get changed and, I hope, put on some fresh pants. I don't see him for the rest of the day, something tells me he might be slightly embarrassed.

Jamie
The week progresses, the team seem nice and the work is interesting. Fortunately, Dirk seems to attend a lot of meetings, but, as he explains to us, he is, effectively doing two jobs. His new one, and ours.

Tuesday lunchtime comes and goes and Emily and Dirk go for their yoga session. They don't come back together, which irrationally, makes me feel better. In fact, Dirk doesn't appear in our office all afternoon, he's obviously off doing his *other* job.

When I come back from a coffee break mid-afternoon, I find Emily, Karen and Sharon huddled together giggling. Hayden and Jayden are in a meeting elsewhere so aren't part of this bonding. All three women stop laughing when they realise I am there and turn back to their work. I don't want to be paranoid but I feel as though I am the butt of their jokes.

'How did your yoga session go?' I ask Emily.

A little smile plays across her lips before she answers. 'Yeah, really well. I'll be going regularly.'

'Good,' I say and notice that Karen and Sharon are watching our exchange. 'No Dirk this afternoon?'

'Um, no. He's busy elsewhere,' Emily says looking down and definitely smiling to herself.

Right, so that's how it's going to be. She's going to be in the know and I'm not. He's probably charmed and smarmed her already, and her, him. I'm going to have to work doubly hard to counter their obvious attraction. I fight to suppress a sigh but it still escapes through my nostrils and comes out as a snort. Karen, Sharon and Emily turn and look at me.

'Sorry,' I say.

'No probs,' Karen says. 'As long as you're not asleep, it did sound like a snore.' They all giggle.

Fuck's sake.

It's my turn in the gym with Dirk today. I can't wait.

I've spent fifty quid on gym gear and that doesn't include trainers because I've borrowed a pair – as new, unused in the box – from Tim. I don't know who I'm trying to impress.

Yes, I do. Dirk.

We get in there and I'm told I'll have to undergo an assessment and training session before I can use any of the equipment. I'll have to book it, and there are no spaces until next week.

Phew, what a relief.

'Hey, cut us some slack here,' Dirk demands. 'I'll just show Jimbo around.'

'Jamie,' I correct.

'Okay. But no exertion for you.' The guy behind the desk – super fit, as you would expect – says, eyeing my stomach.

'Thank you,' I mutter, wishing he hadn't been so easily persuaded.

Dirk ushers me towards the changing rooms. They're communal with lockers around the walls. Oh shit. There are small, individual cubicles in a corner but they have neither doors nor curtains.

'Oh, we don't use them,' Dirk says seeing me glancing over at a little bit of potential privacy. 'They're for pussies and pervs.'

Did he really just say that? Have I misheard him?

'I wasn't going to bother changing since I can't use the equipment.'

'Oh yeah, but you need to get a feel for it. Anyway, you'll put others off if you're wandering around in your office garb.'

Dirk starts stripping off his clothes with abandon and I, with considerably less abandon, do the same. Once I'm in my new gym gear – at least I had the foresight to remove the tags – I feel less conspicuous.

Dirk is dressed top to toe in white. His shorts are very short, his wifebeater vest very tight. He is admirably muscled and the white shows off his tan. I am in black, and glad of it – it makes me feel invisible, especially compared to Dirk. Dirk whips out a thick, black leather belt and wraps it around his body, buckling it up and cinching in his waist. There's red and white writing across the back. As I follow him out of the changing rooms, I read the words: Man Rox.

In the main gym area Dirk shows me around, pointing out the machines he likes to use. 'Weights, of course.' He drops down and does a few impromptu squats in front of the mirror, admiring himself as he does so. Then he points out the machines I should use. 'Running and cycling, for you. Get a bit of cardio going. After they've approved you, of course.' He low chuckles to himself.

I nod my agreement at the same time wanting to punch his stupid, square jaw with its perfect black stubble.

He raises his arms to grab at a machine, loading up more weights onto it, and I notice heavy staining around the armpit of his vest. I have to say something, if only to get my own back.

'Um, Dirk,' I feign embarrassment on his behalf. 'Your vest is badly stained. Really shows when you put your arms up.' I nod at his armpit, pretending to be discreet as several other gym bunnies look over and frown.

He glances down at his armpits, but doesn't lower his arms.

'Oh that, not to worry. It's fake tan from my comps. Everybody here knows me and what it is.' He glances around for agreement and several nod back at him. 'It stains. What can I do?' He laughs his deep throaty laugh and I want to punch his taut gut. Bastard.

Forty of the longest minutes of my life pass by in a blur of Dirk on the weight machines, Dirk on the bench press, Dirk on every bloody machine he can show off on while I stand around in my new gym kit and watch.

When will this hell be over?

In the changing rooms Dirk rips off his top and shorts and stands in skimpy, white budgie smugglers, flexing his muscles and rippling his eight pack.

'Shower,' he declares. 'Come on.'

'I don't think I need to. I've hardly moved a muscle.'

He frowns at me, his disapproval clearly evident.

'Come on,' he says again, patting me on the back. 'I think you've probably absorbed a bit of my sweat when you were watching me.'

How I wish I could punch his stupid, smug, square jaw.

At least the showers are in separate cubicles but the partitions are only opaque glass so hardly private. I grudgingly take a shower, dry myself and dress as quickly as I can, all the while seething at Dirk's arrogance.

'Hey.' Emily smiles at me when I go back into the

office. Mercifully, Dirk isn't with me; he's off doing something or other, he did say but I couldn't be bothered to listen. He's such a dick.

I nod at Emily.

'Good time with Dirk in the gym?' There's an air of mischief about her question. Has someone already reported back to her about me having to follow Dirk around like an adoring fan?

'Yeah, fine, thanks,' I manage.

I've no sooner sat down and stuffed a large sausage roll in my mouth than a meeting request comes through from Dirk for me and Emily. It's later this afternoon and my stomach sinks at the prospect.

Ten

Jamie

'Hey, hi. Thanks for coming.' Dirk trots out his usual inane greeting which neither of us responds to. 'I expect you're wondering what this is about?' His eyes sweep over me in a quick, dismissive gesture then he turns to Emily and grins. No, leers.

'Yes,' we both chorus.

Oh, great, this is the part where he tells me it's all over, we don't need to bother with the three-month probation and Emily is the victor. Don't be so negative, I tell myself.

'Well, I'd like you both to organise a team building event, an awayday.'

'Cool,' Emily says.

'Right,' I say, still recovering from the news not being *all* bad.

'Emily, I'd like you to do this one.' He pushes a leaflet with "Chocolate Testing" emblazoned across it, towards Emily.

'Oh wow,' she says, sounding excited. 'This should be fun.'

'And for you, Jimbo.'

'Jamie,' I correct; it may be his dead brother's name

but it's not mine. Dirk isn't listening as he pushes my leaflet towards me. I snatch it up. 'Paintballing. Wow.' I don't sound as enthusiastic as Emily did.

I bloody hate paintballing.

Emily

Ben finally asked me out on a date . . . well sort of.

I told him about the chocolate team tasting event I had to organise and after weeks of flirty messaging back and forth, he came up with the great idea of us going to try it out together.

It's a bit of a drive into the countryside and we are going in separate cars and I'm grateful; it might have felt awkward in the car for that long with Ben. I don't know him that well, yet. And, I wanted to make my entrance of course. Sabrina also agreed I need my own car so that I can make a quick getaway if it turns out to be another disaster date.

Thanks for the positivity, Sab.

So here I am, waiting in the car park, my eyes scanning every car to see if it's him. The radio blasts out *Your Song* by Elton John and I enthusiastically sing along to it, could this be a sign? Will it be wonderful now that Ben is in *my* world? I have certainly felt the happiest I've been in a long time.

Last night we were on the phone for two hours just like a couple of teenagers each afraid to hang up first. We discovered that we have loads in common. Same bad taste in music; *Celine Dione* being our guilty pleasure growing up, an interest in yoga, a fear of cats and we both have kids so he totally gets everything that comes along with having children, including the annoying exes. Also, he split up with his wife two years ago after she *also* had an affair.

I like him even more.

I'm wearing my floral satin mini-dress with 100 denier tights, brown suede boots, a leather jacket and a thick red snuggly, yet stylish, scarf. I'm feeling pretty good about my appearance but hope I don't look too dressed up for a day event. My stomach flips as I spot Ben driving into the carpark, a lady has just reversed out of a space right by the back entrance of the pub and I watch him hang back and wait patiently before manoeuvring into it with ease. Even the way he drives is sexy.

I check my red lipstick to see if it's migrated to my teeth and practice my best non-gummy smile in the mirror while spying on Ben. He still hasn't seen me so I indulge in watching him get out of the car and walking into the pub. He has a nice bum. Brushing my hair, I decide to wait here for five more minutes before making my grand entrance.

The pub really is stunning, it's white stone with a traditional thatched cottage roof, an old English country pub with class. Many centuries ago, I imagine it was someone's home and they would go to bed by candle light. The building really is special and I can't wait to show the team.

The pub boasts its very own chocolatier on site which is rather unusual, yet charming. I've managed to bag us a free tasting today which I'm pretty chuffed about.

The wooden door creaks loudly as I push hard against it. After what seems like ages, I finally manage to open the door with a lot of effort and unattractive grunting. I've now got a sweat on so I take off my scarf and coat. I'm glad Ben's not witnessing this. Dusting off my hands on my scarf, my nostrils twitch as the heavy smell hits me like heat does when you step fresh off the plane in a hot country.

Chocolate. Heaven.

'Hey, hello, hi. So, you must be Emily. Ben is already here, come with me my lovely.' A round, older woman, who introduces herself as Julie, welcomes me with her friendly, doughy face and farmer's accent.

We walk past the main bar with its ancient high beams into a cosy smaller room with a log fire burning and a much smaller bar. The smell of chocolate is so rich in here that I start to salivate. Ben is sitting on a bar stool smiling at me, holding a glass of – what looks like – water.

'Hey.' He waves.

'Hey.' I give a little wave back.

'Let me get you a glass of water too, my love. The chocolatier only allows water to be drunk for the classes in case it muddies the taste of the chocolate. I hope that's okay?' Julie asks before handing me a glass of water. She has dimples in her cheeks that are so deep they look like they've been engraved.

'Yes sure, no problem, I'm fine with water. I wouldn't want anything to distract me from the taste of chocolate, believe me. It smells amazing in here, has he already started?' I smile at Julie and look at Ben, who winks at me. He's so hot.

'Oh, *he* is a *she* my lovely and yes she has. She likes to make sure everything is just right so she makes a few samples beforehand.' Julie hands me a quaint wooden bowl containing six chocolates, all individually and beautifully wrapped in gold and coloured paper. 'Here, have three each and see if you can tell what they are. I'll be right back,' she adds as she scuttles away.

'No worries,' I say to Julie and steal a glance at Ben. He's wearing jeans and a checked lumberjack shirt, it seems he got the memo about dressing for the countryside. He looks scrummy. Suddenly I feel nervous and instantly crave a huge glass of wine and to my surprise, a cigarette. Yuk!

'Found it okay then? You look nice.' Ben leans over on his bar stool to kiss me. The impression of his kiss lingers on my cheek.

I wonder what he looks like naked. Calm down.

'Thank you. Yeah, it's beautiful isn't it, so far so good, apart from the water. A wine would go down very well in this setting right now.'

'Or a couple of pints of beer on your head?' Ben teases.

I frown and giggle.

'Sorry for the shit joke, I'm a bit nervous. You look amazing, I forgot how stunning you are,' Ben confesses.

I feel so attracted to him and I can't believe how much we have in common, it's almost too good to be true.

'Right my lovelies, what did you think of the chocolates?' Julie returns wearing a white apron and a tall, white chef hat. Underneath her hair has been scraped into a bun and is covered by a hair net.

'Ah, we haven't eaten them yet,' Ben replies.

'Not a problem, you can both eat them now. By the way, *I'm* your chocolatier.' She grins at us and spins around on the spot holding out her apron. Ben and I both giggle and lock eyes. This is going to be fun.

'Okay, I guess I'll try this one first, it looks delicious,' I say picking up one of the chocolates wrapped in brown foil and a purple ribbon. I'm guessing it's a nut one, not my favourite. I open it and a milk chocolate truffle is revealed. Biting it in half a mini explosion takes place in my mouth; I close my eyes and enjoy the sumptuous flavours. Delicious. Heaven.

'Good?' queries Julie.

'Hmmm this is amazing,' I say between scoffs. I let the chocolate melt in my mouth and close my eyes. 'Hmm I can taste caramel, no, salted caramel and is it strawberry?'

'Why, what an educated palate you have young lady, it is indeed all of those things plus just a smidgen of almond.' Julie gives us a big dimply, rosy-cheeked smile.

'You're good at this, I have a lot to live up to,' Ben compliments and gives me a cheeky wink before taking a chocolate. He pops the whole thing in his mouth before closing his eyes. He's mocking me and I love it. 'Hmmm, hmmm this is fudge isn't it?'

Julie stays silent and nods quickly, encouraging him to continue.

'Hmmm, hmmm with a bit of cinnamon and wait, is that pepper I can taste?' Ben asks.

'You are one hundred percent correct, sir.' Julie grins.

'It appears you have an educated palate too,' I comment, grinning at Ben. He closes his eyes and purses his lips, taking the piss out of me again. I give his arm a gentle shove and he pretends to fall off his stool.

'Right then my beauties, you've had a little sample, you can take the rest of the chocolates home and enjoy them. We now need to get down to the nitty gritty. Making the chocolate.' Julie rubs her hands together.

Ben and I look at each other with wide eyes, excited.

'Follow me and I'll get you both an apron.' Julie takes us out into the kitchen, it's huge and pristine, stainless steel as far as the eye can see, with everything neatly put away in its place. Not what you'd imagine in an old country pub, they must have had a refurb recently. She gives us both a white apron and a smaller chef hat to wear. Ben and I laugh at each other before taking a selfie to show the team.

'Okay then my young lovers, you two are going to be making a giant chocolate button together but before we do let me tell you a little about the history of chocolate.' Julie goes into detail about the timeline of chocolate and you can tell that it really is her passion. My mouth is salivating for my next chocolatey treat as she speaks.

'So that's where chocolate originated from my lovelies. The first actual *chocolate bar* was made in Britain by Joseph Fry and his son in 1847. They made it by pressing a paste made of cocoa powder and sugar into a bar shape. The chocolate bar was later developed in 1849 when John *Cadbury* introduced *his* brand of chocolate which we still all know and love today.' Julie smiles her big dimply smile before continuing.

'Okay then, now we make our chocolate button.' Julie hands us our gloves and a giant wooden spoon. Ben takes the spoon from Julie and sneakily smacks me on the bum with it. It takes me by surprise and I let out my own sneaky surprise, luckily it's silent and not smelly.

Thank God.

'You need to choose your chocolate and then we melt it. It's melted in a bowl over hot water in the pan, not directly in the pan as it would burn, my lovelies. When your team make the chocolate button the pair with the most creative and tasty design wins. And of course, tis I, the chocolatier, who will be the judge of them.' Julie nods her head and places her chubby hands on her wide hips.

'Okay fab, that sounds perfect Julie,' I chirp.

'Fantastic, I'll leave you both to select and melt the chocolate while I go and let the dog out. See you in a little while.' She leaves the instructions and recipe on the side and bounces off to see to her dog. It's just Ben and I left alone in the kitchen. His shoulder touching mine. There's a tingle of electricity between us and I have the urge to grab and kiss him, but I don't. If he pushes me away, I could never come back from the shame. A bell dings and keeps on dinging in my head, the bell of shame from *Game of Thrones*. I watch way too much TV.

'So, what do you want to go for then Ben? Milk? Dark? White?' I say to him in a hopefully seductive sounding voice.' He's so close I can feel his breath on me when he talks. I'm glad he has nice fresh breath. There's nothing worse than halitosis.

'Umm, I don't mind, how about white, it's super sweet, just like you.' Ben winks at me again and laughs but I can tell he's embarrassed by his cheesy line. It's so endearing and I love his cute little winks. He does it a lot.

We break the correct amount of white chocolate into the bowl and then proceed to heat a pan of boiling water.

'Let's take the bowl over,' I suggest as I walk back to the work top to get it.

'Okay, are you going to help me stir?' he asks. I turn around to face him and he's smiling shyly from under his eyelashes. His eyes are so blue under the light, they glow.

'I'd love to.' I smile.

The radio is playing. Celine Dione has just come on, *The Power of Love*. No way. Is this another sign?

The whispers in the morning
Of lovers sleeping tight
Are rolling by like thunder now
As I look in your eyes

I walk over to the stove with a provocative swagger taking my time to get there in the seven steps it takes. Enjoying him watching me as I mouth the words to our favourite singer. Ben steps away letting me take the lead in the stirring. His arms wrap around me and his hands cover mine on the handle of the thick wooden spoon. Together we stir the chocolate in big circular motions watching it slowly melt as Celine belts out her ballad.

I hold on to your body
And feel each move you make
Your voice is warm and tender
A love that I could not forsake

Feeling all warm and fuzzy inside my arms tingle with the touch of him. I can feel his breath on my neck and I'm willing him to kiss me. An image of Sebastian – the crab from *The Little Mermaid* – pops into my mind singing, *'Kiss the Girl'*

I'm Ariel. I'm Ariel and Ben is Eric!

Kiss me Eric so I can have my voice back!!

Cause I'm your lady
And you are my man
Whenever you reach for me
I'll do all that I can

We continue to stir the chocolate in time to the music even though there is nothing left to melt. Ben picks up the spoon and lets the white chocolate drip slowly off the end back into the pan. I giggle but it's strangely erotic. I tilt my head up towards him to encourage him to touch me.

Finally, he kisses me on the neck.

Soft, slow and tender kisses burn into my skin and it's not long before I feel him grow hard, pressed against my back.

We continue to stir and drip the chocolate and before I know it the white chocolate is being dripped into my mouth from the wooden spoon. I wonder if they'll be any left to make the button. Ben continues to kiss my neck as I devour the sweet, white liquid.

He lets out a pleasurable groan as I reach back and tentatively feel his hardness through his jeans. Things are getting really hot in this kitchen.

He's coughing now. Why is he coughing?

'Ahem.'

Oh God, it wasn't Ben coughing. Julie is back. Clearing her throat. And she is staring right at me with my hand on Ben's jeans. She doesn't look impressed.

I'm dying.

'Sorry I was a little longer than expected, the dog ran off when he went out for a wee. But I can see you were quite happy here.' She snorts, clearly annoyed at our unprofessionalism.

'No problem,' I splutter before turning off the stove and moving the bowl. I feel like a naughty school child. This is utter humiliation.

Ben smiles at Julie sweetly like butter wouldn't melt and we all stand in an awkward silence.

Julie's face softens and she shrugs her shoulders.

'Okay, okay.' She chuckles. 'No, no, none of my business, young lovers, I'm glad I came in when I did though. Let's forget it hey, the less said the better.' She gives Ben a knowing look and smiles at me, deep dimples forming in her cheeks. Did her eyes just twinkle? How did he do that?

We leave the pub with our homemade chocolate button and a new friend in Julie, it turns out older women have a soft spot for Ben. Who knew he could work such magic?

'You've saved me once again, Ben.' I go to give him a friendly albeit awkward punch on the arm in the car park and he grabs my hand and kisses it. I look into his eyes. 'Thank you for that, I mean really thank you. You managed to charm Julie and dig us out of that embarrassing hole. I'm so glad that we can go back with the team because they will love it. I'll just have to live with my shame and hope that Julie really does say no more.' I laugh nervously, hearing the shame bell once again. Ding ding.

'Yep, don't worry, she won't. Whilst you were in the loo, I charmed her a little more and she told me the story of how she met her husband. She's a lovely lady and it's not like we were doing anything that bad. It could have been a lot worse.'

'Yes, I suppose so,' I reply. What I don't say is that I hope we can do a lot worse. And very soon.

'I do have something to ask you though,' Ben admits.

'What?' He's going to ask me to be his girlfriend. He's going to ask me to be his girlfriend. Already? Remain cool. Remain calm.

'Do you know you still have white chocolate all around here?' He points to my mouth and chin area and I look at him horrified. Ding ding. The shame bell is ringing in my ears, again.

'Oh hell, how embarrassing, I'm sure I checked it in the loo mirror.' I reach into my handbag to get my compact mirror out to take a look and notice Ben laughing.

He's winding me up.

'You git.' I push him and he pulls me into a massive bearhug before giving me the most earth shattering, knee weakening kiss I think I've ever had.

Pure bliss.

Eleven

Jamie

The end of the working week is always welcome but to be fair I'm enjoying working at Genevre, especially when Dirk isn't in the office. I'm getting on well with the rest of the team – though probably not as well as Emily, who seems to have struck up a close relationship with Karen and Sharon already.

I'm spending the weekend doing little more than seeing my dad and doing domestic things.

'Not going out tonight?' Tim is getting ready, dressed in his version of smart-going-out, which is a clean t-shirt and jeans instead of cargos.

'No. I think I'll catch a movie later,' I say, even though I haven't given it any thought at all.

Tim flicks through his phone then flings it at me. 'Have a look, make a choice and I'll push it to your screen before I go out.'

'Is this legal?' I ask, picking up the phone.

He grins, which means it isn't.

'Where are you off to, anyway?' I'm half considering asking if I can tag along with him.

'Ah, well. You know.' He grins again and wanders

off into the kitchen.

'Does that mean you're on a date?' I can't believe that, although, allegedly he did strike gold a few weeks ago.

He comes back from the kitchen scoffing from a giant bag of crisps and plonks himself down.

'Well?'

'Double date.' Another grin, this time accompanied by crisp crumbs. 'Otherwise you could come with me.'

'Double date? More detail. Is this the girl you hooked up with recently?' The night he struck gold when Beth ran out on me after squawking about *his* gecko's cricket.

'Yeah. Gotta go now.' He drops the empty crisp bag on the coffee table, stands up and half-heartedly brushes the crumbs off his clothes and glances at his phone, still in my hand. 'Chosen yet?'

'Nah. You're all right. I'll find something,' I pause, 'Legal.'

'Suit yourself.' He takes his phone and stuffs it in his back pocket.

'Have fun.'

'Yeah. Intend to.' He grabs his jacket and heads for the door, but stops just before he leaves. 'You want to get yourself a girlfriend,' he says. 'Better than sitting in on a Saturday night alone.'

'I had one,' I counter, without even looking at him. 'But she wasn't lizard friendly.'

'Gecko,' he corrects just before he slams the door behind him.

Lizard, Gecko. Jimbo, Jamie. Names matter.

Monday morning in the office is a calm and pleasant time: there's no Dirk. In the afternoon, however, he appears, grinning and – to my eyes at least – perving all over Emily. I don't like the way he gets so close when he speaks to her. She doesn't react badly though, either she doesn't notice – I can't believe that – or she likes it.

The job's hers. I don't know why I'm bothering.

Except apart from this bizarre situation I like it here, I like the people and the work.

I get an email from the gym telling me my induction session is tomorrow. I've half a mind to cancel it then imagine being intimidated into going again with Dirk, so I force myself to confirm. I could do with getting fit, and, if I'm honest, dropping a few pounds.

Late afternoon and we're in a team meeting. Everyone sits around with their notebooks ready to deliver their updates. Even Emily has something to update the team on. I don't. I evidently didn't get *that* email. I do, however, manage an impromptu blather about something I am working on and it's no more boring than anyone else's update.

Finally, we're into the wind up of the meeting when Dirk asks Emily to tell everyone what she's planning for her team awayday.

'Oh cool,' says Jayden, rubbing his hands with glee. 'I sooo love chocolate. I've been to one of these things before, I felt sooo sick by the end of it, but sooo happy.'

The others laugh. There are smiles all round. Everyone is more than happy to go on a chocolate tasting team event. Even those who profess to be watching what they eat – that is, Dirk – are licking their lips in anticipation.

'I love team days like this,' Karen says while the others nod enthusiastically.

Dirk smiles and nods, then turns to me. 'Your turn.'

'Okay. I'm organising a team awayday that is probably the polar opposite of chocolate tasting.'

No one speaks but all eyes are on me – and not necessarily in a good way. There's a brief, eerie silence.

'Don't tease us, Jimbo.'

'Jamie,' I correct. 'Okay, we're going on a paintballing adventure.'

There's none of the delight displayed when Emily made her announcement. No one says anything for thirty or more seconds. If the proverbial tumbleweed skidded in through the door and rolled across the floor I wouldn't be surprised. I want to apologise and say it wasn't my idea, but of course, I can't.

'Sounds like fun,' Emily says, smiling brightly. 'All that running around will be a good way to compensate for the choco-binge the day before.'

I could almost kiss her for that.

'Yeah, it will.' Jadyen nods his head in agreement even though his face doesn't really join in.

Sharon and Karen are less enthusiastic but they nod and say yeah in a gamely manner, as does Hayden.

I think the whole team are looking forward to this as much as I am. Not.

'Cuel,' growls Dirk. 'It'll be exhilarating.'

Emily

'So, the team building event I've organised for you all will be *chocolate* making with *lots* of tasting too.' I pause to gauge the team's reaction and, thank God, they all love it. Who wouldn't? I'm so pleased to see the team genuinely excited about this. I hope I didn't go red at the memory of Ben and I stirring the chocolate. Ding ding ding. I wish that bloody bell would go away.

'Oooh how exciting,' Karen says.

'Yum yum,' says Hayden.

Jayden claps his hands.

Sharon grins and Dirk licks his lips.

Jamie smiles vacantly and I continue.

'I'll be putting you in pairs and each couple will be making a giant chocolate button. The button will then be judged on taste, presentation and originality. Julie, the chocolatier, will choose the winner and the winning team gets a little trophy, and a box of chocolates to share. Of course, you each get to keep your giant button. Here are a few photos of the venue and the button that I made with my friend when I went on my site visit.' I pass round some printed photos to the team and to my delight there are lots of ooohs and aaaahs. I can't wait.

An image of Ben dripping white chocolate into my mouth flashes before my eyes, followed by an image of him naked, which I haven't yet seen. We messaged all weekend but he was busy with his football and kids so we have arranged to meet again on Wednesday. Ben is coming to mine when Rosie is at her dad's. Eeeek.

'The pairs shall be Sharon and Hayden, Jayden and Karen and Dirk with Jamie and I. Hope that's okay guys? We do have a three but Jamie and I will count as one person as I'll hang back, what with it being my event.' Plus, there is only one job so we really *do* count as one person. No one objects to the unfair number, all nodding their agreement and chatting excitedly about the event. I really can't wait to get to know the team better.

'Your turn,' Dirk commands. He takes a swig of his coffee, raising one eyebrow and tilting his head as he stares at Jamie.

'Okay, I'm organising a team awayday that is

probably the polar opposite of chocolate tasting.' He smiles but it doesn't reach his eyes.

'Don't tease us, Jimbo,' Dirk goads him.

'Jamie. Okay. We're going on a paintballing adventure.' Jamie waves his hands around in a jazz like fashion. I'm guessing in an attempt to gee up the team. There are a few false smiles, definitely not the reaction the chocolate event got.

Poor Jamie, I feel for him.

That really is a bit shit.

I went paintballing years ago with Liam under duress and came out *covered* in bruises. My worry would be that it isn't that suitable for a couple of middle-aged women and Jayden, who states on a daily basis how he hates any form of exercise and as soon as he can afford it, he's getting liposuction. Oh well, Hayden and Dirk will probably enjoy it. I say something lame to Jamie to try and make him feel better in front of the team. He grimaces and I feel bad, was that a bit patronising of me?

Jamie

I'm in the kitchen having a crafty coffee before work finishes when Emily comes in. She gives me a little smile then and, with her own coffee in her hand, joins me at the window as I stare out across the countryside.

'Great view,' she says.

'It is.'

'I'm sorry Dirk dumped the paintballing thing on you. It was mean of him.'

I turn to look at her, puzzled, wondering if she's gloating or taking the piss. I don't think it's either.

'You did all right though.'

'I know. I'm sorry.'

125

'Really?' I turn to look at her, half expecting her to burst out laughing, but her face is deadly serious.

We stand in semi-companionable silence.

'Bit awkward all this, isn't it?'

'What?' I ask.

'This pitting us against each other. Not very ethical in my opinion.'

'No. It's not.'

'I'm being philosophical about it; at least it's three months paid work plus the outplacement and a bonus. It'll look good on my CV.' She shrugs, turns away and takes her coffee back to the office.

I'm left puzzled. Does she really think she's not going to get the job? Or, is she just playing nice?

It's Tuesday lunchtime and I'm just leaving the office to go down to the gym for my induction. I can't pretend I'm looking forward to it.

'Going my way?' Emily asks, suddenly keeping step with me.

'Um, not sure.' How the hell do I know where she's going? 'I'm off to the gym.'

'Me too. Well, yoga. I'm really not up to all those heavy-duty machines.' She laughs then and her whole face lights up.

'Me neither,' I admit.

'Dirk's well into it, isn't he,' she half whispers as we head down the stairs.

'Very.' I shudder at the memory.

We arrive at the gym and Emily has already disappeared when I give my name at the reception desk. I'm sent off to change and told where to wait for my instructor to join me.

'Hi, Jamie.' A female hand snakes towards mine. 'I'm Michelle, your personal trainer. Call me Chelle. How are you?'

'Good, thanks.' I can't help smiling at her. She's lovely. Toned, of course, as you would expect, and she has skin like dark chocolate and caramel coloured eyes. She's too lovely; I feel woefully inadequate, fat and lumpy.

She pulls me away to a little side desk and we sit down. She grabs an iPad from a drawer and starts to type on it.

'Okay.' She smiles at me. What perfect teeth. 'Just a few questions. I've set it up so maybe you'd like to just whip through it yourself instead of having me read everything out.' She hands over the iPad. 'It shouldn't take you long, I'll be back in a min.'

She disappears and I start on the questionnaire. It's the usual stuff, medical disclaimer, any illnesses and finally my version of my fitness levels. I start off marking myself quite highly, then get real. If I say I'm fitter than I am then the programme Chelle creates will probably kill me. So I own up to having a sedentary lifestyle and not always eating healthily.

A quick flick through it and Chelle smiles at me.

'Want to start gentle?' she purrs and I feel my loins stir. Stop it.

'Yes,' I say and wish she was a man.

'Great, let's get started.'

She puts me through my paces, assessing my levels and abilities and I'm so glad that I didn't lie on the iPad form. By the end of the session I'm sweaty and exhausted and looking forward to having a shower. But, unexpectedly, I've enjoyed it and surprise even myself when I book another session with Chelle for the end of the week.

She's on the reception desk as I pass on my way out and I thank her for her time.

'Just doin' my job,' she jokes. 'See you Friday.'

Friday can't come fast enough for me.

I've just started the slog up the stairs, when Emily bobs up behind me.

'Good time?'

'Yes, it was. You?'

'Yeah, but I'm aching now. It's been a while since I did yoga on a regular basis and my body is telling me about it.'

Twelve

Jamie

The next day I have lunch with Emily. I didn't intend for it to happen and I'm sure she didn't. We're victims of circumstance.

I'm sitting at the table in the atrium café being very virtuous eating salad and drinking tap water from the giant chilled dispenser in the corner. The place is popular and full but I've managed to grab myself a table for four. I realise it's only a matter of time before someone joins me and when the inevitable happens, I'm quite happy that it's Karen, Sharon and Emily. They ask to join me – it would be weird if they didn't – and it would be weirder still if I turned them away.

'Is that the quinoa and spinach?' Sharon asks, inspecting my plate.

'Yes, it is.'

'I had that the other day. So nice.'

'Are you being good after all your gym sessions?' Emily asks as she tucks into a giant toasted panini. It looks so good, I can smell the melted cheese.

'Yes. Am I so obvious?' I smile to show I don't mind her commenting, even though a little part of me does.

'I should have a salad really, but I'm a bit of a piggy and I'm starving.'

'You'll never eat it all,' Karen says. 'They're far too big, the paninis in here.'

'I will.' Emily laughs. 'I just said, I'm a piggy.'

'How can you be a piggy? Look at you,' Sharon observes. 'There's nothing of you.'

'I am. I eat a lot.'

'Urgh, you're one of those aren't you. Skinny and greedy,' Karen says the words with humour but there's a slight edge to them.

''It's all the running around after my daughter.' Now Emily feels the need to justify her trim figure, her toned glutes. I shake the image out of my head. At least when everyone is focussing on Emily's food, they're not watching what I'm eating.

Emily, to her credit does plough on through the enormous panini. I wonder if she would have given up sooner if she hadn't made the statement about finishing it. Karen and Sharon both leave when they've finished and I've not even started on the zero-fat yogurt I've bought.

So, it's just me and Emily and an uncomfortable silence.

'How old is your little girl?' I ask to break the silence.

'Rosie is five.' Emily's eyes shine as she speaks. 'Do you have children?'

'No. No.' I almost laugh. 'I haven't even got a girlfriend.' What? Why did I just say that?

'Me neither. Boyfriend.' A little nervous laugh escapes her lips. 'Not girlfriend, obviously. Not that, well you know…'

'Yeah, I know,' I say, smiling and hopefully saving

her the whole *I'm not judging* speech.

'So, where have you been working between the VSO and here?' Emily is changing the subject nicely.

I tell her about Kanes, even the part about the redundancies and ask about her work history.

'Bit sketchy, really,' she confides. 'On account of Rosie. Her father left me when she was tiny, so I wanted to spend as much time as possible with her, but she's well settled at school now. I've temped here and there and kept up to date. This could be my big chance, if things work out…' Her voice trails away.

And we're back to another uncomfortable silence.

'I expect *you'll* get it,' Emily says suddenly. 'What with your experience and everything.'

I stare at her, perhaps for a bit too long.

'I don't think that's a foregone conclusion. Not at all. And Dirk likes you a lot more than he does me.'

'Does he?'

I raise my eyebrows; now she's playing me.

'He gave you chocolate tasting. Need I say more?'

'Paintballing could be fun,' Emily says in a voice that sounds more hopeful than convinced.

'Yeah, right. If you'll excuse me, I need to get back.' I tidy up my plate and glass and pick up my tray.

'See you later,' Emily says before finally taking her last bite of panini.

I've almost reached the top of the stairs when Dirk bursts through the door.

'Hey, Jimbo,' he growls and grins.

'Hi, Dick.' Two can play at that game.

He starts to skip down the stairs as I yank open the door.

'Hey, Jimbo,' he calls back up the stairs. 'I was

thinking it would be good for you, me and Emily to meet for drinks sometime, out of work, I mean.'

'Yeah, sounds good,' I lie.

'Cuel, I'll sort out a date.' He skips on down the stairs without waiting for me to reply.

I can't wait for that little treat; Dirk perving over Emily, Emily pretending she doesn't notice and me, piggy in the middle.

I've been at my desk barely minutes when Emily pops up in front of me.

'Hey, did Dirk mention the drinks out of work thing?'

'Yes, just now.'

'Me too. Caught me in the atrium. Couldn't really say no.' She pulls her mouth into a straight line that suggests suppressed horror.

'No. Quite.' I don't really know what she wants me to say. I don't want to go either.

'Anyway, at least we'll both be there.' She smiles and bobs off back to her desk.

Is she afraid of being on her own with Dirk?

The week seems to fly by and before I know it, I'm down in the gym ready for my next session with Chelle. I'm early and eager.

'Ready to build those muscles, Jamie?' Chelle says as she approaches me. She's looking stunning today, clad in some white Lycra catsuit thing that shows off every toned muscle in her body yet manages to look classy, not tacky.

'Yes,' I say, a little too eagerly.

'Let's get at it.'

Afterwards I wish I hadn't sounded so keen because

she really has put me through my paces. I just keep imagining a six pack every time my muscles scream in protest.

Even though it's hard I enjoy it and, on my way out, I catch Chelle waiting for her next victim.

'Thanks for today's session. I'm starting to feel the benefit already.' I laugh and so does she.

'We'll soon have you fighting fit.'

'Yeah. Bit of a way to go.' I laugh again, it's embarrassment.

'Oh, I don't know. I think you're doing okay. You're not in bad shape for someone who hasn't bothered much.' She steps back and casts her eyes over me. 'Not in bad shape at all.' Her smile is so wide and so bright it stirs my loins. I think she's flirting with me. I wish.

'I'm healthy eating too.' Listen to me.

'Good. It's important to do both. Have you tried the salads at the atrium café?'

'I have. Spinach and quinoa.'

'My favourite. Hey, maybe I'll catch you over there for lunch one day.'

'I go most days,' I say, which isn't strictly true, but it could be. And hopefully Emily won't plonk herself at my table as she's done a second time this week.

'Mmm.' She frowns. 'I think I'll be over there on Monday at one. I don't have anyone booked in then.'

'Me too, probably.'

'Save me a seat,' she says, looking over my shoulder and smiling at someone. 'I'll give you some nutrition tips.'

'See you Monday.' I step aside as her next victim arrives.

I think we have a date. Get in!

Emily

The days go by and I sit with Jamie a couple of times for lunch. He's definitely more qualified for the job than I am, probably deserves it more than I do too. Surprisingly this competing for the job lark isn't as bad as I thought it would be. I envisioned us each trying to sabotage the other in order to win but Jamie doesn't seem like the arsehole I feared he might be, and I would never do anything like that.

Ben had to cancel on Wednesday as one of his kids was sick, which was a shame but we are hopefully meeting up this weekend.

Fingers crossed.

It's Friday. Thank God, as this week has dragged. I can't wait to pick Rosie up and snuggle up with some Disney. I'd let her pick but it would be *Frozen* every time; think we'll have a bit of Cinderella tonight, classic. When she's gone to bed, I'm going to treat myself to a few glasses of red and phone Sabrina.

I think back to the time I was on SwipeySwipey and met the sex dungeon Rohypnol creep before bumping into Ben. I'm so relieved I've met someone the organic way. Having said that, I still haven't heard back from him. I won't message first.

Don't want to look desperate.

Feeling suddenly like a love-sick teenager, I pack up my things to leave for the day. Just as I'm about to turn off my PC an email pops up from Dirk titled 'Catch up'. Normally I'd leave it until Monday but something makes me click on the ominous sounding title.

Hi Guys,
I think it would be great to meet up for a couple of drinkies to see how you are both getting on. . .

I'm happy for you to pick my brains if you have any questions but equally happy to just have a few drinks and get to know you both better. I believe it's important to form a close bond with your colleagues and all work and no play makes Dirky a dull boy.

Obviously, the drinks are on me. I suggest we start at TP's for happy hour cocktails.

Regards
Dirk

He gives a date and I wonder if I can use Rosie as an excuse not to go. The email makes me feel a little anxious. I don't want to get drunk in front of either of Dirk or Jamie and his email implies a night out on the town, despite his *couple of drinks, few drinks* statements. I strongly believe you shouldn't mix business with pleasure. Also, now it's in an email it's a formal thing so it's more likely to actually happen. Oh hell. I guess I'll just have to go, have a few drinks then make my excuses and leave before Dirky gets drunky.

Jamie

I arrive at the atrium café before Chelle and wonder whether to find a seat or get my food first. I scan the menu wall above the counter looking for inspiration before deciding that I'll probably go for the quinoa and spinach again.

'Hey,' Chelle's soft voice comes from behind me. 'There's just too much choice.'

I turn and smile. 'I know, but I'm opting for the same again.' I give my order at the counter and Chelle does the same, she grabs the wooden spoon that shows our order number.

'Let's nab a table before it gets too busy.' She edges

135

me outside before calling back to the waitress where we'll be.

I hover, scanning the tables and start to make for a table for four near the front, reasoning that it makes me look non-threatening and not desperate.

'Hey, this is better,' Chelle counters, indicating a cosy table for two tucked away on the side.

'Okay. Yeah.' This is going better than I hoped.

We plonk ourselves down and Chelle displays the numbered wooden spoon so that it's prominent.

'I don't like to sit too out in the open cos people spot me and want to discuss their training schedules.' Chelle rolls her eyes in a dramatic but jokey fashion. 'I do love my clients, but I also love my food.' She laughs and her face crinkles up in a most attractive way.

'Shall I get us water?' I ask, needing something to do to stop me staring at Chelle's perfect face.

'Sure. That'll be good.'

When I return, our identical salads are just being delivered.

'Snap,' Chelle says, laughing. 'Great minds…'

'Yeah. I had this the other day, really enjoyed it.'

'You veggie?'

For a moment I don't know what to say. Is she? If I say I'm not will she take offence? Mentally, I shake myself. Just be honest.

'No. Are you?'

She grins. 'Lord no, I need as much protein as I can get and I can't really get enough without some meat.'

'Right.'

'I do love this though, always choose this salad when I eat here.'

'It is good.' I don't want to spend the rest of my lunch break talking about quinoa and spinach, so change tack, slightly. 'When you don't eat here, what do you do for lunch?'

'Most days I'm working through lunch time because that's when most people want to train with me. But Mondays are a bit easier, I think everyone's recovering from the weekend. Most days I usually bring my own sandwiches.' She glances from side to side, theatrically, her large brown eyes scanning the people around us. 'Usually meat sandwiches.' She giggles.

'Does it matter? If you eat meat, I mean.'

'Lord no, but some people can be funny. So, I don't advertise that I'm not a veggie. Many assume I am.'

'Sounds complicated.'

'Tell me about it.' She tucks into her food with gusto. I like that.

'What do you do after work?'

She frowns at me, then smiles. 'Go home.'

'No, what I meant was,' I say, sounding like a jabbering idiot, 'What do you do for fun, recreation. A lot of people go to the gym to unwind but …'

'Oh yes, I see. No, I have enough gym all day. I just do normal things like everyone else. Shopping, eating – lots of that.' She laughs again. 'Watching TV, going out. Just normal stuff. What about you?'

'Same.' I smile and decide that I'm not going to tell her about the ongoing project of clearing my dad's loft of my mum's things. 'How long have you worked here?'

'Genevre Gym, five years or more. Before that I worked in finance.'

'Really?'

'Yeah. Dull and tiring. I'm actually a qualified accountant.' She rolls her eyes again and I just love the way she does that. 'Not really for me, all that sitting at a desk, messing about on computers. So, I retrained and here I am. I used to work for Clayrights Chartered Accountants.' She nods over in the direction of one of the building segments off the atrium where Clayrights logo is boldly displayed. 'Two years.' She shakes her head and her hair; a thick glossy afro moves seductively. God, she's gorgeous. 'That was enough for me to know I couldn't do that day in, day out.'

'No, you don't look like an accountant.'

She laughs. 'I'm going to take that as a compliment.'

'It was meant as one.'

We both concentrate on eating our food before Chelle asks me about myself. I tell her the VSO story, I tell her about Kanes, but I miss out the redundancy part. I don't tell her about the three-month competition with Emily, my rival; but I do tell her about the forthcoming paintball fiasco.

'Hey, that's fun. I've been on a few of those. As long as you keep moving and don't get hit, it's a laugh. But, Lord, it hurts if you get paintballed.'

'So I hear.'

'What, you never been before? You're organising a team awayday and you've never done it yourself?' She looks at me with eyes wide open in amused amazement.

'No. To be honest it wasn't really my choice. Dirk suggested it, well, insisted on it.'

'Dirk. Figures. He likes those macho things.' She picks up her glass and drains it. 'Another?'

I watch her lithe figure move panther-like as she walks across to the water dispenser.

'I'm going in for a pudding,' she says, placing our full glasses back on the table. 'I need those calories. What about you?'

I'd love a pudding. 'No, thank you. I've had enough.' I haven't, not at all.

She comes back carrying the largest piece of cherry cheesecake I've ever seen and I feel immense food envy as she sits down and tucks into it.

'I've been thinking,' she says, between mouthfuls. 'We need to get your stamina up so you can run away from those pesky paintballs.' She giggles. 'I'll work out a programme for you.'

'Better be quick, it's Friday.'

'This week?' She roars her amusement, and I join in her laughter. I just hope I'll still be laughing by the weekend.

True to her word Chelle has me on an intense training plan. Tuesday lunchtime sees me pounding the treadmill, as does Wednesday. I don't feel energised or as if my stamina is increasing afterwards, I just feel knackered. Stupidly – though I'd do anything to spend time with Chelle – I've agreed to a session on Thursday after work. Thursday is also Emily's team awayday, so I'm hoping we'll finish a bit early. Chelle finishes at six so I have to arrive at five pm sharp.

Despite spending so much time with Chelle in the gym, or maybe because of it, our relationship hasn't progressed beyond gym buddies. And Chelle, as my trainer, has the upper hand there. I've promised myself that I'm going to ask her out. Properly. On a proper date. In the evening.

But, before I can do that, I've got two intense days to get through – chocolate tasting – or, as it's become known in the office, chocolate heaven, and paintballing. Behind my back they're calling *that* hell day. I overheard Jaydon bitching about it to Karen.

I wanted to interrupt. I wanted to join in. I wanted to tell them I didn't want to fucking go either.

Thirteen

Emily

'Oh wow this looks fancy Emily.' Jayden's jaw drops as we pull up to the venue, all aboard the company minibus.

'I hope you all enjoy it as much as I did guys.' I think of Ben and wonder what he's up to, we've had a great few weeks meeting up here and there in between having the kids. It's hard with children because it restricts how much we can see each other, but it's good not rushing into anything. Both of us have decided not to introduce the kids until we've been together at least three months and I am completely happy with that. It's a big thing to introduce Rosie to a potential stepdad. Can't believe I just said *stepdad*, even in my head.

Get a grip woman.

'I haven't even had breakfast as I intend to eat my bodyweight in chocolate,' Sharon announces and there's a mix of agreements and giggles.

'Well that would be an *immense* amount of chocolate, Sharon,' Dirk growls, folding his arms and tilting his big, square jaw to the ceiling. Sharon's mouth opens, aghast, and it looks as though she is going to speak but instead looks out of the window. That was really low and unnecessary, what's his problem with Sharon? I've noticed him taking a few swipes at her before.

'Don't worry, Sharon, if we're talking about chocolate allowance in terms of bodyweight,' Jamie offers, 'I think I win the competition on who can eat the most chocolate. Compared to you, I'd be allowed more than three times the amount.' Jamie reassures Sharon and pats his stomach. I notice he's lost weight, a lot of weight. Meanwhile, he chooses to ignore Dirk who is laughing and agreeing with Jamie's chocolate portion allowance. Jamie is so sweet trying to make Sharon feel better but it appears to fall on deaf ears. Sharon merely glances at him, gives a tight-lipped smile before continuing to stare out of the window.

Everyone disembarks the bus and I make sure I'm at the front to lead the way. It's only November but already the Christmas decorations are up and it looks simply stunning. There's a huge oak tree outside and I notice it has been decorated with gold baubles and coloured lights, I bet it looks so pretty at night. Suddenly I feel all Christmassy even though we still have quite a while to go. We reach the pub's enormous door and, again, I struggle to open it.

'Allow me, damsel in distress.' Dirk swaggers over and shoulder barges the door rather aggressively. It opens in one push and the door swings open banging against the inside wall. Dirk stumbles over himself, falling into the pub but quickly regains his balance before flexing his guns to the team. No one comments but Jamie rolls his eyes at me. I pinch the skin on my hand to stop a laugh escaping. It's going to be interesting with these two in my chocolate team.

Julie runs over to greet us, out of breath and

flustered.

'Hello, Emily, my lovely. Hi everyone, I'm Julie.' She's panting between smiles and her big doughy cheeks are puffing in and out. I just want to squeeze them and put my fingers in her dimples to see how deep they are – a weird thought I know, but I've never seen dimples like Julie's.

'So sorry I hadn't opened the door yet, you guys are quite early.' She looks at her watch and I see the realisation sweep across her face that actually, we are only five minutes early. 'That loud bang gave me quite a fright. I thought we had burglars but so glad it's just you lovely lot. Come with me.' Julie chuckles, red-faced as we follow her through the big bar then the little bar and into the kitchen for the chocolate tasting.

She gives us all aprons and chefs hats and we all laugh at Jamie who looks ridiculous with his big frame wrapped in a tiny apron. We all pose with our brightest smiles while Julie takes a team photo of us before we get into our groups, Karen and Jayden, Sharon and Hayden, and me, Dirk and Jamie.

'A rose between two thorns,' Jayden whispers in my ear as we go to collect our wooden spoons, bowls and pans. 'It's like beauty and the beast but this time there are two beasts.' His eyes twinkle with malicious humour.

'Nah, not my thing, I much prefer *Eric* out of *The Little Mermaid*.' I wink and he high fives me for our shared appreciation of Disney.

Julie dishes out the homemade chocolates and each team takes turns in guessing the flavours.

'I think this is a citrus one,' Hayden says making a sour face to go with it. He reaches out to take another chocolate before Sharon bats his hand away.

'Not so fast, it's their turn now. Was that right Julie?' Sharon asks.

'I'll let you have that, it was in fact, lime.' Julie signals towards Karen and Jayden to take their go and Karen reaches across to take a chocolate with a red case.

'Ooo I hope it's strawberry, I love those ones. My favourite in the chocolate tin and it's great because in our house because it's only me that likes them.' Karen pops the little truffle into her mouth and we all watch in anticipation.

'Yuk,' she says. Her expression changing from excited to disgusted. 'What is this?' She splutters. 'Oh yuk, no.' She is coughing now and her face is turning red.

'Help, yuk, urgh, urgh.' Oh hell. Is she choking? Her face is looking more and more red.

'Quick someone get her a water,' I yell to those closer to the sink. Jamie, I notice, has already sprinted off and is returning with one.

'Here, have this.' He thrusts the glass into Karen's hand but she continues to cough, chucking most of the water on the table and herself. She can't seem to control her arms and is now holding her throat.

'Help!' Karen splutters between coughs.

The water is not helping.

'It's burning,' she splutters.

Out of nowhere, Dirk pushes Jamie out of the way. Marching over to Karen, he puts his arms around her waist and starts thrusting. Vigorously. Poor Karen is now bent over the table in a very uncompromising position – with Dirk – as she chokes on a chocolate.

It almost feels like we shouldn't be watching.

I glance over at Jayden who is clearly battling

concern and amusement. I wouldn't be surprised if he started laughing hysterically.

Please don't, I think.

Now is *not* the time.

'Burning,' Karen gasps.

'Don't worry, Karen, I'll get this out of you,' Dirk pants between his over exaggerated thrusts as beads of sweat fall off the end of his nose.

We all look on helpless. Horrified.

'Should I call an ambulance, she could be in…' Jayden screeches.

'Julie, she says its burning, could it be chilli?' Jamie interrupts. 'If it is, please get me some sugar.'

Julie obeys his order and scurries off to get it.

'Dirk move, let me try something.'

Dirk ignores Jamie and continues to thrust whilst Karen looks pleadingly at Jamie. Tears are streaming down her face. She's stopped coughing but is poking her tongue out whilst scraping it with her finger nails.

'MOVE. DIRK!' Jamie bellows, making Jayden jump. Dirk carries on thrusting. Jamie strides over and yanks Dirk off Karen, tossing him aside like a rag doll. Jamie gives Karen a spoonful of sugar and we watch while she swallows it down. Almost immediately her red face fades, she stops coughing, and her shoulders relax while a bewildered Dirk looks on.

Thank the Lord.

'Oh God, it's worked. But how?' blurts Hayden.

'Yeah, that like totally saved her life!' Jayden cries, his voice shrill with excitement.

'The sugar neutralizes the heat from the chilli. You should never drink water with hot food as it just spreads the heat around the mouth and makes it worse.'

Everyone looks at Jamie; we're so impressed.

'My flat mate eats a lot of spicy food,' he explains.

I feel so stupid for suggesting water. Oh well, at least Karen is still alive and I've learnt something new. I'm glad Jamie stepped in and played the hero. Dirk, not so much. I look over at him and he's in the corner whispering with Sharon about something, she looks distressed.

The rest of the day thankfully goes smoothly. Karen and Jayden win the best chocolate button award with their *cookie crumble gooey galaxy deluxe* chocolate button. Sharon and Haydon come second with their *marble white and dark buttons inside a giant milk chocolate button*. Dirk, Jamie and I come last with our *sea salt, caramel and liquorish twist chocolate button*. Dirk was insistent on the liquorish which I think is utterly disgusting but I didn't argue with him; I'm choosing my battles wisely.

I'm glad we lost. Fair and square.

We board the minibus for the return journey back to work and everyone looks super tired and all *chocolated* out. Jayden is clutching on to his award with one hand, whilst messaging on his phone with the other. He's already done his Oscar winning speech which made everyone laugh. Hayden is quietly chatting on his phone at the back of the minibus and Dirk and Sharon are asleep. Karen, who has now fully recovered, is listening to some music with her earphones in.

'Pssttt, Jamie,' I say quietly over Karen's head so as not to disturb anyone, 'Thanks for coming to the rescue earlier, you really saved the day.'

'Ahh, it was nothing really, but I'll be expecting the same from you at paintballing tomorrow.' He grins at me and I feel *so* pleased he's here. My rival could be a lot worse than him. I smile back and check my phone. Wow, I'm popular, I have a message from Ben *and*

Sabrina.

Ben: *Hey gorgeous, what are you doing later? I have a free evening now; my brother is happy to have the kids stay for a sleepover.*

My heat skips a beat and a big smile spreads across my face. I don't have Rosie tonight so Ben could be in luck. Before replying to him, I scroll down and check Sabrina's message.

Sab: *Hi Em, don't forget tonight! Psychic night at the Royal Cherry Tree. Meet me there at 7pm for pre-show drinks xx*

Oh hell. As much as I would love to see Ben, I can't let her down. Sabrina's mum passed away a few years ago and she really believes in the afterlife. It's not really my thing if I'm honest but I agreed to go for her. She would do the same for me.

Me: *Hey Sab, yes of course, I wouldn't miss it for the world. See you at 7pm.*

She replies almost instantly.

Sab: *Yay! Can't wait to see you later, fingers crossed Mum comes through.*

Me: *Same, fingers and toes double crossed for you xx*

Jamie

We arrive at the chocolate place and pile inside. It's a small, independent, chocolate makers that's part of a lovely country pub. The surroundings are lovely, the pub is just super great and I wonder how fucking paintballing will compare to this. Everyone is smiley, the staff and our team, including me.

The tasting takes place in a large kitchen full of stainless-steel tables and we're each given an apron – which we can keep – paper hats for our hair and a short health, safety and hygiene talk. After we've all washed our hands thoroughly, we're ready to begin.

I thought we were just going to eat chocolate, but, apparently, we have to make it too. Everyone gets excited about that.

The only bad thing is Karen nearly choking, bad enough in itself but worsened by Dirk's attempts to hump her to save her. Fortunately, it all turns out fine in the end, I buy myself some brownie points with the team because of the sugar trick. I suspect I'm going to need them tomorrow.

I'm in the gym changed and ready, early and waiting for Chelle. I really don't know if I can bear another treadmill session because I've eaten so much chocolate that I feel physically sick. It was fun though. It's a long time since I laughed so much. In retrospect even Dirk humping Karen was funny, though I doubt she thinks so.

I'm dreading tomorrow.

'Hi Jamie. You ready for an intense hour?' Chelle is all bouncy and smiley.

'To be honest, no.'

She widens her eyes and frowns in question.

'Too much chocolate.'

'I bet it was fun though. Come on, we'll soon have you re-energised.'

I actually feel energetic enough due to all the calories and sugar, just a bit laden too.

Twenty minutes of pounding the treadmill feels like hell. Chelle finally concedes defeat and suggests we slop – she actually says slop, which I think is her way of describing me today – over to the café and grab a coffee before it closes.

I don't even bother changing and neither does she,

we just sit in our gym gear watching the world go by in the atrium, although most of the world is heading for home.

'Are you all geared up for tomorrow?'

Inwardly, I shudder, outwardly I force a smile. 'Trying to be.'

'That's the spirit. Just keep running. Are you going to be the captain?'

'The what?'

'Of your team? What are you doing? Men versus women?' She pauses to think. 'Aren't you an odd number if Dirk is going? How will that work?'

'I don't know.' I really don't want to think about it. Chelle's questions have added a whole level of worry to the paintballing nightmare that I hadn't even considered. So, I change the subject by asking Chelle if she is free any day for lunch next week.

Happily, she is, and we agree to meet on Monday.

Emily

I arrive at the Royal Cherry Tree and head for the bar. I'm really in the mood for a drink after today's escapades. It turned out well in the end and Julie was great but it's quite stressful trying to please everyone at these things. And, so it seems, keep them alive. I think of Jamie and his spoonful of sugar and licking the 20p coin, where does he learn all these life hacks?

Paintballing's tomorrow, I bet he can't wait for that to be over, poor Jamie. The weather has turned awful so I can't say I'm looking forward to it and neither is anyone else. Of course, I pretend I am.

'Two porn star martinis please,' I hear myself order from the barman.

'Ohhh, on the old porn stars, now are we?' I know

that cheerful voice.

'Well, it is two-for-one, Sab.' Pleased to see her, I give her a huge hug before we sit on the only two bar stools in the place. Her hair looks amazing and she reminds me of a Disney princess. Suddenly, I feel quite bland by comparison.

'You look amazing,' I say to her. 'I want your hair.'

'And I want your figure but we can't have it all, darling.' She tosses her hair to one side showing off her incredible locks. I take a sip of my martini and find myself daydreaming about Ben. I wonder what he's up to?

'Psssst Em, it's bloody Tiny. She's here.' Sabrina waves to Tiny and I politely do the same.

I hope it's a wave that conveys *yes hello I'm polite but please don't come over*. I turn back to Sabrina.

'She's coming over,' Sabrina says through gritted teeth still waving at her.

'For God sake, stop waving at her then, she thinks you're inviting her over.'

But it's too late. Tiny has already frogmarched over with her entourage - which seem to be several other versions of Tiny. There's a tall Tiny with shorter, straight white hair; a skinny, slightly taller Tiny with frizzy brown hair; two older Tinies and an ancient Tiny with bright purple hair. They're all dressed in big, brightly coloured 1950s dresses and a few of them have rolls in their hair. *All* of them are wearing bright red lipstick. Did I take too many Kalms?

'Hiiii Emily, fancy seeing you here. You're not here for the psychic night, are you?' Tiny has appeared next to me, much too close for my liking and she's grinning from ear to ear. I look at her annoying features. Her eyes crinkle up so much I wonder if she can still see me properly. It pisses me off when I notice she has perfect teeth and is showing them off with her fake whole-face smile.

Husband stealer.

I knew I should have seen Ben tonight instead.

'Yeah we are,' I say nonchalantly and take a sip of my cocktail.

'Oh, that's just fab. I didn't know you believed in all this. Liam never said. Who are you hoping will come through?' Tiny simpers, whilst the other Tinies look on smiling and blinking.

'Emily's come for me, we're hoping my mum comes through,' Sabrina replies coolly.

'Wow, that's just lovely, I hope she comes through for you, I'll see you ladies later, good luck. Toodle pip,' Tiny shrieks.

'Yeah, see you,' Sabrina and I sing.

'Toodle fucking pip,' Sabrina spits when Tiny is out of earshot.

'Who hired the Tiny freak show crew, and why did they have to come here? Tonight. She is everywhere,' I complain as Sab winces.

'Sorry Em, if I'd have known I wouldn't have made you come along, I know it's awkward but let's just ignore her and have a good time. Bollocks to her.'

She's right. Bollocks to them all.

'Two more porn star martinis please,' I say to the barman as I drain my glass.

We take our drinks and walk over to the room where the psychic night is taking place. A woman standing outside the room ticks our names off on her clipboard as we enter. I notice the list is very short and there must only be about thirty names on it. This is going to be an intimate event.

With Tiny's whole family.

Oh hell.

The chairs in the room are small. They actually look like children's seats. There's a really fat man sat at the back of the room and I think he might be sitting on two chairs. I want to sit at the back near the fat man but Sabrina insists we sit at the front so that the *psychic can pick up on her vibrations*; she's wearing her mum's necklace and rubs it as if trying to conjure up her spirit.

Tiny and her entourage enter the room and sit at the back with the fat man; they seem to know him. Tiny's eyes burn into the back of my skull, I hate that she is behind me.

The room slowly fills up until there are no seats left and we are all waiting for the psychic. Finally, an elegant lady of around forty glides into the room, she looks like the psychic sort or what you would imagine one to be anyway. She has long, straight black hair with a sharp fringe and piercing, spooky blue eyes, which I assume must be contacts. She's dressed head to toe in purple and is wearing a big pink stone on a heavy chain around her neck.

'Good evening, ladies and gents, and welcome to my psychic night.' She speaks in a hypnotic, velvety voice which makes me feel a bit sleepy, either that or it's the alcohol.

'As many of you know this is my *last* local psychic floor night as I have been signed to work for Psychic TV.' There's a series of whoops around the room before she continues. 'Thank you. Thank you. Tonight, I shall be connecting to the spirit world, channelling the spirits through *me* to give *you* messages. If I describe a spirit and you think it could be someone you know then please don't be shy and do speak up, there's nothing worse than a trapped spirit.'

A trapped spirit? Oh God, get me out of here. I jump, feeling something on my hand, it's just Sabrina reassuring me.

The psychic closes her eyes and the room falls silent in anticipation. The fat man hacks out a cough and a few heads, including mine, turn around. I accidentally lock eyes with Tiny and she smiles at me. That woman has no shame.

'Okay, I have a small older man with me, he's reading a newspaper in a big, brown leather arm chair and his glasses are perched at the end of his nose. He has white hair. Is this making sense to anyone?' The psychic opens her eyes and scans the room. This really could be a description of anyone's grandad. 'I'm feeling drawn to this area of the room.' She points towards the left side of the room waving her hand above our heads. Everyone remains silent. 'Please speak now if this man means anything to you,' she says firmly, but no one responds. Sabrina and I exchange a sideways glance.

'You!' The psychic lady continues. 'This man is for you.' She's pointing at me with a long finger and glaring down with her pale blue eyes.

'Who me?' I say in a mouse-like voice.

'Yes, you. Are you sure this isn't making sense to you?' She looks annoyed.

'Umm, no, I don't think so.' This is so embarrassing. Should I just play along?

'He has a message. Open your eyes and let the past be the past. True romance awaits once you give L a chance.' Well this really could be for anyone. How vague. The psychic lady stares at me for a response.

'Umm, thank you.'

'Making sense now?'

'Umm, no I don't think so, sorry.' Sorry psychic lady, I can't play along this time. Let's hope you do better on Psychic TV.

'Okay, it may not make sense now but just take it with you as it will make sense in the end, I promise.' She looks at me smiling and her eyes change to a much darker blue. Can contacts change colour? Probably. 'Thank you, yes I know, I've told her. Okay thank you.' She appears to be talking to the spirit now and is saying goodbye to him. Or, at least she is putting on a good show.

'Okay now I have a petite, elegant lady with me, she's wearing red lipstick and I want to say she is before her time, a fashionista. I'm hearing the letter A and she's clutching at her heart.' The psychic holds her heart like she is *personally* in pain. 'I feel like this has something to do with how she died, it's hurting all around *here* and I feel like I am struggling to speak,' she continues and there are several shrieks from the back of the room. I don't even have to turn around to know that they belong to Tiny and her entourage. 'Does this woman mean something to you?' The psychic asks and what could be Tiny's mum, speaks up.

'Yes, that's my mother. Her name was Annabelle and she died of a massive heart attack, previous to that she had voice box problems.' Several gasps can be heard from around the room. Really, people are so gullible. This time Tiny pipes up.

'We all style ourselves on her fashion, she was a very elegant lady and definitely ahead of her time.' She spreads her hands out, palms up to show off her ridiculous dress and shoes that don't match. Several of the other Tinies do the same, paying homage to their elegant relation.

'She *really* is a beautiful lady,' says the psychic. 'You know she watches each and every one of you and she is very proud.'

All the Tinies gasp and a couple of the older ones wipe away tears. Oh please, what is this? The Tiny show!

'I have a message for one of you but I don't know whom.'

Of course you don't, because they are all basically the same person.

'But the message is to keep being you and keep trying. She will come around eventually and then life will be much easier. Does that make sense?' The Tinies all blink at her and it looks like the original Tiny is welling up.

'She wants you to know that it isn't your fault, you didn't know as he always took off the ring. But that doesn't make him a bad man. He does all he can for you and the girls. He was out of that relationship way before he met you. Does that still make sense?'

Tiny is nodding vigorously now and sobbing deep sobs with big fat tears rolling down her face as all the other Tinies comfort her. I want to turn back and not look at her, but I can't. Tiny speaks again. This time to me.

'I never meant to hurt you, Emily. I didn't know he was married. I just want us to get along for the sake of the girls. Please.' She's looking directly at me and despite myself, tears run down my cheeks.

Fourteen

Jamie

According to the website outdoor clothes are the norm for paintballing. Outdoor clothes – what the hell does that mean? I don't think my usual jeans and a jacket will be suitable.

When I get up just after six and look outside it's still dark but I can see that it's raining. Heavily. A lifeline, maybe we'll be cancelled. I skim through the website again on my phone, but no such luck, the horror will still go ahead, no matter what the weather. They advertise it as a plus point. Ha ha.

In the end I opt for an old pair of cargos – last worn when loft clearing – a long sleeved t-shirt and walking boots I haven't worn for years. When I push my feet into them, they are hard and unyielding.

'Can I borrow this?' I hold up a substantial weatherproof jacket that belongs to Tim, even though I've never seen him wear it. We're both in the kitchen, me fully dressed and breakfasted, Tim in just his too-short bathrobe and a pair of once white, now grey, socks.

'What for?'

'Paintballing.'

He laughs. 'Today? Rather you than me, mate.'

'Thanks. Well?'

'I don't want paint on it.'

'It's not real paint, just gloop with food dye in it.'

'Okay. But you have to wash it if you get shit on it.'

I'm about to argue the toss about getting shit on it, as, when I pull it on, it already smells like shit, but think better of it. I zip it up and push my hands into the pockets to pull it down and feel something that is both soggy and crinkly in the right-hand pocket. I pull out a half-eaten bag of pickled onion Monster Munch.

'Urgh. God. These stink.'

Tim stares at me over the rim of his brimming cereal bowl. 'Oh yeah. I remember those. That would have been the last time I wore it. To a festival.' He goes all glassy-eyed as he recalls the occasion. I dump the crinkly goo-bag into the bin and head for the door before he starts to regale me with his memories.

I can smell the stench of stale corn snack all the way to work in my car. We're not due at the paintballing fiasco until eleven so it's work as usual before we leave, important given that we lost most of yesterday on the chocolate awayday.

'Hi,' Emily says, looking impossibly perky and tiny in combats and flat boots. I'm six-foot-two and judging where she comes up to on me, she can't be more than five-two. 'All set for later?'

'Sure,' I say, not wanting to discuss it. I wonder if she's taking the piss but the look on her face, so sweet and kind, suggests she's not. Maybe she is just genuinely nice. And my rival. My nice rival. Or maybe she has a good poker face.

Karen and Sharon burst in through the door together. Sharon is dressed similarly to Emily, but

Karen is wearing paint splattered jeans and carrying a pair of flowery pink wellies.

'What?' she snaps in an accusatory tone when she sees me looking at her.

'Nothing.' I look away sharpish.

'Well, I wasn't going to wear anything decent for this shit,' she mutters to Emily.

To her credit, Emily just smiles benignly.

'What's that stink?' Sharon says as she hangs her coat up next to mine.

I know what it is, it's the stale Monster Munch but I'm not admitting it.

I change the subject by talking about how we're going to get to the paintballing; there's no point in everyone taking their own cars, so with a bit of complicated shuffling and serious negotiating, we've agreed to go in two cars. Mine and Emily's. I'm grateful to Emily for offering, because it seems that no one else wanted to volunteer their cars, and I suspect it's because they don't want them full of wet mud and paintball smears on the way home.

I mouth a quiet 'thank you' to her across the office.

She gives me a sweet smile back.

At half-ten Dirk bursts through the door smiling. He's wearing full camouflage combat gear and looks as though he's off to fight in a war. He even has an army style utility belt complete with water bottle and zipped pockets. His boots are super shiny too. I hear Jayden snort, but if Dirk hears it, he doesn't react.

'I've got the company minibus,' he announces. 'So we can all go together.'

'Great, but I thought it was booked out.' I had checked, but couldn't get any sense out of anyone as to

157

who had booked it.

Dirk just smiles at me. Of course, *he* was the one who booked it. Bastard could have told me.

When we arrive at the venue it soon becomes obvious that Dirk is well known here. I watch as the instructors greet him like an old friend, I also watch as Hayden, Jayden, Sharon and Karen exchange knowing looks with each other. Everyone looks as pissed off as I feel.

'This should be fun,' Emily says, pulling up her hood and zipping her waterproof jacket right up so that only her eyes are visible before pulling on the khaki camouflage jumpsuit we've all been given. By the time she puts the body armour on, her little body is completely swamped. She struggles to bend down to roll the trouser legs up. I want to help her but feel I can't, it's just too personal, rolling up someone's trouser legs.

Once we're all ready and we've had our safety talk, we're ushered out into the rain to learn how to use the guns on the target practice range. No one moves with any enthusiasm, except Dirk.

That said, I have to admit that I quite like splatting the target with paint especially when I picture Dirk's stupid face on it. I'm going to get him at the first opportunity. Bastard.

Because we're such a small group and because no one else is mad enough to be here today, they've laid on a special little skirmish – their word, not mine – just for us.

We split into two teams, men versus women – Dirk's idea – although Jayden elects to go on the girls' team which, according to him will make it fairer. Four against three.

It still doesn't look very fair to me.

Our aim is to capture the castle, which is somewhere up some muddy trail, prevent the other team from getting there first and take the prize. Apparently, it should only take an hour, then we can have a break in one of the basecamps before embarking on our next mission.

I can't wait.

Full-face helmets on and Dirk is already haring away and yelling for me and Hayden to follow.

Within seconds I feel something whack into my right arse cheek, followed by a load of raucous screaming. I suspect I am going to be everyone's primary target. They all feel about me and this fucking event the way I feel about Dirk – and this fucking event.

Half an hour later and we're lost, even though, as suspected, Dirk admits he has been here several times before. The icy rain running in rivers down our face masks is making visibility hard. Although, everyone on the opposing team seems to have no problem finding me with their paintballs. I'm covered. Hayden has been hit twice but Dirk is still spotless, even I haven't managed to hit him. I've got a few shots off, but frankly, I'm shooting in the dark, just returning fire in the direction I think I'm being hit from. If I've managed to hit anyone it'll be a miracle. Dirk, however, has definitely hit a target or two because when he let off a rapid volley, there were screams and yelps.

'Yay!' yells Dirk as we finally find the castle and wade in to retrieve the prize. But we've been beaten to it. 'Fuck it,' he growls.

Hayden and I exchange glances and I know I'm smirking inside my mask and from the way Hayden's shoulders go up and down, I think he's laughing too.

'How comes you're so clean?' Karen asks Dirk when we reach the basecamp for coffee and cakes.

'Hey, what can I say?'

All the girls and Jayden are paint splattered but none of them as much as me.

'Are you okay?' I ask Emily when we find ourselves sipping our coffee side by side.

'Yeah, just a few bruises coming,' she says, smiling. 'You?'

'Yeah. I think everyone preferred yesterday to today.' I try to sound as though I'm not pissed off about it.

Emily doesn't answer. What can she say?

'You got to the target quickly, well done.' I'm genuinely impressed that they beat us, given Dirk's familiarity with the place.

'Yes, I don't know how that happened. What's next?'

'Zombie crypt. We have to hit the zombie targets and stuff…' I can't even be bothered to think about it, let alone say anymore. Anyway, Emily was there for the briefing the same as me.

We spend another hour chasing zombies and, this time, *we* claim the prize. I'm almost dripping with paint where I've been hit so many times. People are really taking it out on me. I think even Dirk has hit me. I'm covered in so many paint splats that, combined with the rain, it's hard to tell whose hit me by the team colours. I'm going to get that bastard Dirk back for this, at some point.

We have another basecamp break, grateful for another warming coffee. As well as paint splattered, everyone is also covered in mud now, we've all slipped over several times and the rain is showing no signs of letting up, in fact, it's getting heavier.

'This is bloody ridiculous,' Hayden mutters to me. 'I think we should call it a day.'

'No, let's play on. To the death,' Dirk bellows.

If looks could kill Dirk would be dead judging by the way Karen, Sharon and Emily glare at him now.

'Yeah, we should give it up,' Jayden joins it. 'I'm black and blue. These balls hurt.' If he's making a joke, no one laughs.

'No, we need to work this through. It's about team building, remember. Anyway, no one has won yet. We're one-one. We need a winner.' Dirk's voice echoes around the camp as we all stare out into the torrential rain. Then all eyes turn to me.

Me. Because it's MY team building event.

Emily widens her eyes at me. I wish she wasn't doing that. It's an appeal for mercy.

Dirk narrows his eyes at me. It's a dare.

Oh shit.

All eyes on me. Do I lose face with Dirk and lessen my chances of getting the job or do I spare us all from further torture?

Oh shit.

Across the basecamp I see the instructor get off his phone. He looks over at me and draws his hand across his throat. It seems the decision is being taken away from me.

Man up, I tell myself. Take the lead. Before it's too late.

'I think we should stop. It's too dangerous. We can hardly see where we're going.'

'No,' Dirk roars. Bastard.

The instructor heads towards us now.

'Sorry guys, we're going to have to call a halt. It's a health and safety issue. Our insurance won't pay out if anything happens to any of you and we've let you go on in this.'

'Thank God for that,' Jayden says.

'Don't worry,' the instructor continues. 'We'll give you a credit for half a day.'

'Cuel,' Dirk growls amid a volley of dirty looks.

Emily

This weekend I am doing absolutely nothing. Mum has offered to cook a roast for me and Rosie on Sunday. Perfect. There's nothing quite like your mum's cooking and I'm looking forward to laying around drinking cups of tea and watching my dad teach Rosie how to draw cartoons. Today, we will be watching back-to-back Disney films, perhaps bake some cakes and Rosie has convinced me that I need a makeover. She tells me I'll be getting a new hair style, face and clothes because I'm looking *a bit tired.*

Out of the mouths of babes.

I am actually very tired after this week's team building events, especially yesterday. My whole body is covered in bruises, it feels like I've been beaten up. Weirdly, Sharon seemed to be making a beeline for me, even though we were on the same team. I'm not sure if she was confused? It was pretty clear I thought: men against women. Come to think of it she has been acting a little oddly lately, I'm not sure what's got into her.

My phone beeps and my frown disappears as a huge smile spreads across my face.

Ben: *Hey gorgeous, you free Tuesday night?*

Me: *Hey you, I might be . . .*

I am totally free but I can't appear too desperate, can

I? Rosie will be at her dad's.

Ben: *Dinner?*

Me: *Sounds lovely*

Ben: *Excellent, I'll pick you up at 7pm xx*

Me: *Look forward to it xx*

Wow, this is our first outing since the chocolate tasting site visit and I'm excited. Usually he just comes over to my place because it's easier when Rosie's in bed. What should I wear?

Meanwhile, for my makeover, Rosie has selected a black pencil skirt, and a silver shiny top I wore when I went to a fancy-dress party as Lady Gaga. It doesn't look too bad actually.

Jamie

Monday morning comes around again too quickly. I'm almost dreading going into work, facing up to everyone after the disaster that was the paintballing fiasco.

I attempt to slink into the office and my desk without making too much noise; I really don't want to be noticed.

'Hey,' Emily calls. 'Good weekend?'

'Yeah, you?' I keep my voice down.

'Yeah, not bad. Bit bruised from Friday.' She grimaces, but I'm grateful that she doesn't speak too loudly, even though at the moment there's only me, her and Jayden in the office.

'Bruises. Don't talk to me about bruises. My arse is black and blue.' Jayden obviously isn't attempting subtle and I don't know how to respond. 'Still,' he continues, 'Could be worse.' He turns and arches his eyebrows at me before nodding towards the door.

Emily and I turn and follow his gaze to see Karen limping in on crutches and wearing a surgical boot.

'That's not from Friday,' I say, sounding desperate. 'Is it?' I genuinely cannot recall anything happening that would have caused that much damage.

Karen pulls her lips into a straight line and I think she would put her hands on her hips if it wouldn't hinder her balance.

'Yes, it is.' She clomps towards her desk and flops into her chair. 'I'm worn out now, this weighs a ton.'

'How?' I get up from my desk and approach hers. 'When?'

'When we were leaving. Car park was like a swamp. Slipped and twisted my ankle. I spent most of Friday night up A&E. I've got to go back to the hospital again this afternoon.'

How could I have missed that? I was in the minibus the same as everyone else. Although I did secrete myself in the back and pull my hood up and plug my headphones in and listen to music and effectively hide in case anyone wanted to have a go at me.

'Oh.' So not actually during the paintballing then. 'Should you be here?'

Karen narrows her eyes at me before replying. 'Well, I am now, aren't I? Might as well stay. I got a lift in with a friend, but I'll have to get a taxi to and from the hospital. I think the company should pay.' She stares at me defiantly.

'Um. Right. I'll look into that.' Oh shit. I'll have to check with Dirk.

I never do speak to Dirk about it, I just give Karen fifteen pounds out of my own wallet and hope it's enough. I don't tell her it's my own money or that I've sneaked down to the cashpoint in the atrium because I didn't have enough cash.

The only saving grace about today is lunch with Chelle. We have a lovely chat and I try a different salad this time. Chelle even compliments me on my physique; she thinks I'm definitely toning up. Even I have to admit I'm noticing a difference, mainly because my waistband isn't cutting into me anymore. She asks about the paintballing, I give her a very brief description and change the subject. I'm glad it's in the past.

We get chatting about films and it soon becomes apparent that we both enjoy a good sci-fi movie. Apparently, Chelle can never find anyone else to go with. Suddenly, I find myself asking her if she'd like to go and see the latest blockbuster and she agrees. We're even going for an early dinner beforehand.

'That'll be great,' she says, a wide smile spreading across her face. 'We can really make an evening of it. What night can you do? This week?' She's pulling her phone out of her pocket and thumbing through her diary.

'Any.' I try not to sound grateful or desperate. If I were a dog, I'd be panting with glee now, my tail wagging frantically. In fact, I have to clamp my mouth shut to stop my tongue from lolling out.

We agree Thursday evening and it can't come soon enough for me. I would have preferred Friday evening because then we wouldn't have to worry about getting up for work the next day, but I have to go out for drinks with Dirk and Emily.

Tuesday morning looms and there's no sign of Karen, and no word from her either. By nine-thirty I'm starting to fear the worse. I never saw Dirk yesterday but I did email him about Karen's injury and even though it wasn't strictly caused by the paintballing, I have implied that it was. Let's face it, it wouldn't have happened if he hadn't forced me to book a shit paintballing team awayday. It's not something I would choose for team bonding. Team bonding – that's a joke. Team alienation, more like.

Dirk hasn't replied but suddenly he's in front of me, his crotch nudging against my desk. Does he know he's doing that?

'Hey,' he growls.

'Morning,' I say, barely looking up from my computer screen.

'No sign of Karen yet?'

'No. Afraid not.'

'Mmm,' he says, moving away from my desk. 'Hey guys, did everyone have a good time on Friday?'

There's a little silence before Emily pipes up. 'It was definitely different. Shame about the weather.'

'Y-e-a-h. Not to worry. We can go again. For free.'

'I'm never going again,' Karen says, suddenly bursting through the door. She's still wearing the surgical boot but has only a walking stick today instead of crutches.

'Hey, Karen. Been in the wars?' Dirk growls as he nods at Karen's foot.

'No. Not really. I slipped in the swampy car park at that crappy thing on Friday. Remember? You were there, revving the engine and in a hurry to go.'

Dirk gives Karen a cold stare before turning on his heel and leaving.

'How did it go, Karen,' I ask, quickly. I'm embarrassed for Dirk's apparent lack of concern, especially as she seems to be blaming him. I'm not ashamed to admit I'm pleased about that.

'You'll be relieved to know it's only a very bad sprain

166

and not a ruptured Achilles. Just have to wear this for the rest of the week as a precaution.'

'That's good. You must be pleased.'

'I am.' Karen switches her computer on.

'Are you sure you should be here?'

'Yes, but I might be a bit late this week as I have to get a lift. Can't drive.' She waits for a reaction as if willing me to object.

'Okay, if there's anything you need, just let me know.' I scamper back to my desk and immerse myself in my work, grateful for small mercies. Sometimes, I have my doubts about the dynamics of being trapped in an office with the same people all day, every day.

Emily

So far this week, work has been a lot less chaotic and I've been able to catch up on almost all of my emails. I glance over at Karen, she's trying to get comfortable at her desk with her big robot foot. Poor cow had the worse luck ever, choking on a chocolate one day and injuring her ankle at paintballing the next. I bet she never wants to go on another team building event again. Ever. I wouldn't. Jamie must feel awful about it too, I did return the favour though. When she fell, I ran to help her up and onto the minibus. Dirk was beeping the horn like an impatient taxi driver. Embarrassing.

Ben had to cancel Tuesday. One of his kids got taken into hospital with suspected meningitis, poor little love. We are going to rearrange when his son is on the mend, as they still don't know what's wrong with him, though thankfully it wasn't meningitis. Rosie was three when she caught scarlett fever and that was bad enough. I remember feeling so helpless and scared, I can't imagine how Ben must be feeling with a *very* sick child, not knowing what's wrong. I wish I could be there for him – but we aren't quite at that stage yet.

Fifteen

Jamie

By the time Thursday arrives I'm ready for some serious R&R with Chelle. As soon as the clock hits five I'm out of the office and haring home. After a quick shower and fresh clothes, I'm in the kitchen having a coffee when Tim comes lumbering in.

'You smell sweet,' he says, dumping his work bag on the kitchen worktop. 'Like a flower meadow.' He sniffs the air and laughs.

'Shut up. Better than smelling like a cowpat. I'm off out. I've got me a date.' I swagger just to make the point.

'Beth?'

'No. She's old news. I'm over her.'

Tim nods at me approvingly. 'She was weird anyway. Want to grab a takeaway before you go?'

'Nope. This is a dinner date, followed by a movie.'

'Get you. What you seeing?'

When I tell him, his eyes light up like a kid's. 'I want to see that. I don't suppose…' his voice trails away.

I don't even answer, just shake my head, grab my keys and go. Sometimes, I can't quite believe Tim.

I pull up outside Chelle's house – yes, she's given me her address, that's how close we are. Okay, we haven't kissed or anything like that, but it would hardly be appropriate at work, would it? Tonight, everything is going to change.

I stroll up her garden path towards the front door. I have to admit I'm impressed, the house is large, detached and definitely desirable – just like Chelle. I know she's buying it because we've had the inevitable shared moan-come-joke about mortgages. I knock on the door, it's opened swiftly.

'Hey.'

My mouth drops open because it's not Chelle who greets me but another stunning woman, she's the complete opposite of Chelle; tiny and blonde with immense blue eyes. They must be housemates.

'Um, hello…' I start.

'You must be Jamie. I'm Kara. Come in. She's nearly ready.'

I step into the hallway, all pale wood furniture and dark oak flooring. Chelle's housemate wanders into the kitchen.

'Just coming,' Chelle shouts. From the murmurs it's obvious that Chelle is in the kitchen too.

When she bounces into the hall, she is a vision of loveliness. Normally she's in her gym gear and, though super fit, she's nowhere near as glamorous as the Chelle who stands before me now. And, she's only wearing jeans and a casual top.

'You look lovely,' I hear myself mumble.

'Thank you. You do too.' She gives me such a great big smile. 'Shall we go? I'm starving.' She grabs her jacket, opens the door and, as we step through it, she calls a goodbye to her housemate.

'Kara seems nice,' I say as we get into the car.

'Oh, she is.'

In the restaurant we both choose steak and we both enjoy every mouthful. We chat easily and happily about everything and nothing. It's great spending time with Chelle, she's so open and honest and seems so adventurous. She regales me with stories of her gap year in Thailand and, unusually, Japan. I tell her all about my experiences with the VSO. We laugh and joke and get along so well.

I can't help comparing her to Beth who now seems very immature against Chelle.

After the movie, which we both thoroughly enjoy, I drive Chelle home and she invites me in.

I can't believe my luck.

The aroma of coffee fills the kitchen as we both stand over the coffee machine on the worktop in Chelle's immaculate kitchen. It's all black granite and high gloss. Even the floor shines like a mirror.

'This is impressive.' Especially compared to my little kitchen in my two-bed starter home.

'It came with the house,' Chelle says, almost dismissively. 'Though it was a big part of why we bought it. Well, most really.' She laughs lightly, pours our coffees and, carrying both cups, leads the way to the lounge.

Another spectacular room, big TV, large comfy sofas, all so very tasteful. Perfect.

Except for Kara, the housemate, laid full out and dozing on one of the sofas. Chelle smiles at her sleeping friend and sits down on the opposite sofa. Since I can't really sit on Kara, I sit next to Chelle. Silver linings…

We sip our coffee and talk softly, mostly about the film.

'Oh, hello.' Kara awakes. I have to say that even with a sleepy-crease line down one side of her face she still looks beautiful. 'What was the film like?'

'We enjoyed it. You wouldn't.'

Kara laughs and turns to me. 'Thank you so much for going with Chelle, otherwise she would have forced me to go with her.'

'Anytime. I really enjoyed it.'

I wait for Kara to get the hint and disappear and am thrilled and excited when, after a few minutes of small talk, she does.

Then she returns, carrying her own steaming mug and plonks herself back down on *her* sofa.

'Are you drinking coffee?' she asks Chelle, pointedly. 'Y-e-s.'

Kara shakes her head. 'You'll be up half the night. Too much caffeine. I've got camomile.'

Chelle just smiles at her friend before telling me how much she wants to see the new superhero film that's due out next month.

'Oh, please go with her,' Kara cuts in. 'I hate them more than the sci-fi ones.'

'I'd love to.' I smile broadly at Chelle then over at Kara and will her to take her camomile tea and bugger off to bed.

She doesn't.

'Anyone fancy a biscuit?' Kara looks straight at me.

'No, thank you.' Just go to bed.

Half an hour later and we're still sitting there – the three of us. It's nearly midnight and I'm going to have to go.

'I'd better get off. Work tomorrow.' I stand up and

head for the kitchen where I've left my jacket draped over one of the high stools tucked under the island. Chelle follows me.

We're at the front door saying goodbye. Just goodbye. I lean in to kiss Chelle. She turns her face just at the wrong moment and my lips graze her cheek. Damn it, but it could be worse and she does smell delicious.

'Bye,' I say again as Chelle turns the front door handle. 'And thank you for a lovely evening.'

'Me too.' She leans over and kisses *me* on the cheek. 'We don't have a session tomorrow, do we?'

'No.'

'Okay, well, all things being equal, I'll see you for lunch on Monday?' Her question hangs in the air.

'Definitely. It's a date.' And I don't even feel a dick saying *date*.

At work the next day there's a definite buzz of Friday-feeling in the air. Everyone's looking forward to the weekend and, I suspect most, including me, are relieved it's not last Friday.

At lunchtime I get a nice quiet table in the atrium café and settle down to enjoy my salad alone and read today's news on my phone. Who knows, maybe Chelle will find herself free and join me – a happy coincidence; like it's meant to be.

I almost jump when seconds after this thought has crossed my mind a shadow is cast across my table. I look up, excited.

'Hi.' Emily smiles at me.

'Hi.'

'Can I join you?'

I want to say no. There are plenty of empty tables

available. Sit at one of those. 'Course you can.'

Emily sits down with a nervous smile and a humongous meal.

'I eat my main meal at lunchtime,' she explains, seeing my eyes widen.

I want to say it's none of my business, which it isn't, of course, but I've made an issue of it now by staring.

'My little girl,' she continues, 'Has hers at school.'

'Cool.' Is that really the best I can do?

'How are you feeling about tonight?'

'Tonight?' What's she talking about? Ah, drinks, with Dirk. I'd almost forgotten. 'Oh that. Yeah. You?'

She leans in and glances about before speaking. 'Could do without it really. Only agreed because my mum is looking after my little girl for a few hours. I can think of better ways to spend my time.'

'Right.' So can I. Like doing nothing.

'Rather not do a work thing on the weekend, which Friday is really, isn't it?'

'Yeah. It is.' I have to agree with her on that. 'Not sure what the point is. After all, you and I don't really need to get on long term, do we?' That was a bit blunt, Jamie.

'No. Except for that thing we're supposed to be starting together next week.'

'What thing?' Even I can hear the alarm in my voice. This is news to me.

'That tricky case that they haven't been able to resolve. Apparently, the client has been round every big insurer looking for a policy. Now they want us to have a go at underwriting it. I'm so glad I'm working with you on it now. I shouldn't really say this, but I don't have enough knowledge or experience to tackle it on my own. And God knows I've tried.' She's keeping her voice low, and no wonder. I have no idea what she's talking about. Do I play it cool and pretend I do? Or do I let my annoyance show?

'Oh that, yeah.' Cool then.

'Still, that's next week's problem.' She forces a little smile before tucking into her food. She suddenly looks very small and vulnerable. And young. But I know she's older than me; Dirk told me she's thirty-two to my twenty-nine. 'Have you got anything planned for the weekend?'

'Nothing major,' I say, casually. Actually, nothing at all. I might take my car to the car wash. I might see if my dad needs any more help. 'What about you?'

'Well, apart from tonight, I'm hoping this guy I'm seeing will take me somewhere nice.' She has a soppy, dreamy look in her eyes. I bet she's a lovely girlfriend. Why am I thinking that?

Suddenly, I catch sight of Chelle in the distance; she's marching with purpose across the atrium. I stare in her direction and hope she sees me. She does. A big grin spreads across her face and she waves and mouths, 'Hey.'

'She's great, isn't she, Chelle?' Emily says, having watched me drool over Chelle.

'She is.' I can't keep the self-satisfied, smug grin from spreading across my face. 'She really is.'

Emily watches me. Scrutinises me, even. A little frown plays across her forehead. Then she shakes her head and gets back to her food. I don't like that.

'What?' I hear myself ask.

'Nothing. Nothing.' She shakes her head but I'm not convinced.

'Have you got a problem with me and Chelle?' What the hell is going on here?

'No. No.' She shakes her head and I watch a blush rush up from her neck to her forehead.

'We're not doing anything wrong.' I don't know why I'm explaining myself to Emily.

'Yeah, but you're just friends.' It's half question and half statement.

'More than, actually. Not that I'm sure what it's got to do with you.' I'm really annoyed now. What a fucking nerve Emily has telling me who I can see. 'It doesn't interfere with our jobs, it's not like we work together. It's not like it's you and me.' Why did I say that?

Emily doesn't answer, just stares over my shoulder. It's a hard, concentrated stare, so much so that in the end I turn to see what she's looking at.

Across the atrium, Chelle and Kara have their heads together and appear deep in conversation.

Emily turns her attention back to me.

'You do know they're… together…' She lets the words hang in the air.

'Yes. They're housemates. I do know that.'

Emily slowly shakes her head and glances back over at them. 'No, they're a couple.'

I laugh. How ludicrous. 'I don't know what to say to that.' I pick up my plate and glass, dump them on the counter and leave.

What the hell is Emily saying that for? What's her problem?

I don't relish the prospect of spending a whole evening with her and Dirk. I hope she doesn't mention Chelle in front of Dirk.

Late afternoon an email arrives from Dirk, he's finally giving me the information about this case that Emily already knows all about. Thanks for that, Dirk, you dick.

I've just got in my car when a text comes through. It's from Dirk:

Sorry, having to cancel this evening due to sickness. Another time. Ciao.

Ciao. What a knob.

Thank God. No Dirk and no Emily this evening.

I wonder if Chelle is free?

Emily

The last thing I want is a drink tonight. I'm still recovering from the psychic night last week. Sabrina and I ended up getting rather drunk which subsequently led to dissecting the psychic's message. We came to the conclusion or rather *Sabrina* did, that the spirits were trying to tell me to (in the words of *Frozen*) *let it go*.

She was also pretty upset that her mum didn't come through, I on the other hand got someone's random grandad telling me that my true romance was for L. Well, the only L I can think of is Liam, so the spirits must have been having a right laugh. It's utter rubbish anyway, I've got my lovely Ben and most people need to let go of their past a bit and move on, don't they? That message for me really could apply to anyone.

The message for Tiny however was a bit more specific. It did creep me out a little at the time but when I look back at it, you could pretty much *still* apply it to many people. Despite my cynical self, I do believe I should be letting the past go with Liam and Tiny. The past is in the past and I can't change it, I'm moving on. If Tiny didn't know Liam was married then I really can't be blaming *her* anymore. Liam was the villain of the piece.

Only I can make a difference to my present and my future so I should just concentrate on that and live in the moment. That's what children do, don't they? I think of my *Rosie* and the way she is, always making the most out of each day. When she does get upset, she gets over it pretty darn quickly, quick to forgive and forget. Not like us adults who can take years to grow an ugly, festering bitterness, sometimes never getting over it.

Well, that's enough.

I'm not going to let the bitterness engulf me anymore. Today, I'm going to do what all my self-help books suggest and truly live in the present.

This is the new and improved Emily and she is completely and utterly over Liam Cod's betrayal.

Dad's just dropped me off at a local pub to meet Dirk and Jamie for the dreaded work drinks. I'm going to have one or two then make my excuses and leave. Mum has Rosie; I can get back to her just before bedtime as Dad's picking me up in just over an hour. Dirk is sitting at a table as I walk in, he's all dressed up like he's going on a lads' night out, his hair slicked back with extra gel. I'm wearing jeans and a big woolly jumper, nothing about me says I'm up for a night out.

'Hey Emily, what can I get you to drink?' Dirk gets up to greet me, raising his eyebrows as if appraising my choice of outfit, but he's wise enough not to say anything. He kisses both of my cheeks and I notice his fingers are touching the tips of mine, he's never done that before and it feels weird. We aren't on a date.

'Thank you. I'll just have an orange juice, please. I'm not feeling too good.' I do a cough in the hope that it doesn't sound fake. Dirk makes a face resembling disgust and takes a few steps back from me.

'Ooh shame, I thought we were going to get to know each other better. Shall I make that a vodka and orange?' He steps closer to me, with one cocked eyebrow. He's in my personal space. Out of awkwardness I glance down, clocking his extra shiny, pointy shoes.

'No thanks, Dirk, I'm *really* not feeling good. Jamie not here yet?' I ask, looking around. It's not like him to be late.

'Oh no, I forgot to tell you, he isn't coming.'.

'Isn't coming?' I check.

'No, he's not well, must be something going around,' Dirk replies, sounding bored.

Oh great. Jamie has left me here alone. With Dirk. He saunters off to get the drinks, clip clopping in his shiny shoes. They have quite a generous heel on them which must make him a good few inches taller. False advertising, but I guess it's no different to women wearing *suck me in* pants. Everyone in here is dressed up in their best clothes, nice hair and full makeup. I feel like a complete frumpy dump but I can't wait to go home, get in my pyjamas, and snuggle up with Rosie. I'll let her stay up a little later tonight. It is the weekend after all.

'Here's your *orange*.' Dirk plonks the drink down in front of me, smirking. I stare at the two straws and lumps of ice knowing instantly what he's done. Prick.

'Dirk, is there vodka in this?' I ask innocently.

'Maybe...' He smirks again.

'Oh well, one can't hurt can it, it might even help with this cold.' I'll let this slide, little does he know I'll be going soon anyway. It's less than an hour now until Dad picks me up. And counting.

'That's the spirit and there's *definitely* some in your drink.' Dirk leans in and, very effeminately, takes a sip of his cocktail. His skin looks very clear. I think he might be wearing makeup.

'Want to try mine? It's sex on the beach.' He raises his eyebrows and wobbles his head from side to side. Is he drunk?

'No, I'm good thanks, I know what that tastes like,' I say, glancing at my watch.

'I'm sure you do.' He laughs, spitting out some of his drink so that I'm forced to look away. I take a sip of mine in embarrassment and it makes me heave.

'God, Dirk, how many vodkas did you put in this?'

'Just a couple to cheer you up, you're looking a little drab this evening.' He glares at my jumper, barely suppressing a sneer.

'I'm fine Dirk, I don't need cheering up.' Aware of how this is going I try to change the subject. 'So, do you have any more bodybuilding competitions lined up?'

'Why? Do you want to come and watch? I'd be delighted. I have one coming up in June, so this is one of the last blow outs before I get my head down and focus on these.' He lifts his arms up and flexes his muscles, making his pecs dance up and down. He really does look an idiot and I'm so not joining him on this blow out.

'And will you be going to any more yoga classes, to improve flexibility?' I ask. His face colours slightly, probably remembering his cabbage and egg fart. I feel a little bad for embarrassing him.

'Only if I get to stare at your lovely bottom again.'

I don't feel so bad now.

'Urrm, only if I don't get to smell yours.' Oops that

just came out, but he deserved it. Cabbage and egg. Yuk.

'Oooh feisty one you are, I like it. I'm only joking Emily, I may do, yes. I'll let you know, we could go together again, couldn't we? You know it would be really good if we could start getting to know each other better. Good for you in many ways.' He stares at me intently and I hope I've got the wrong end of the stick. This is hell.

The next forty-five minutes consists of Dirk making a few more cringey innuendos before I make my excuses and leave without upsetting him. I think he believed I was ill as I kept up the fake coughing. So I've got away with it. This time.

Jamie

While I'm really pleased that I don't have to put up with Dirk tonight, or Emily for that matter, I'm at a loose end. I messaged Chelle to see if she was free, I kept it casual because I was beginning to think that what Emily told me *could* be true. Equally it could not.

Chelle came back quickly and her message soon enlightened me. Sod it.

Chelle: *Ah, soz. Just leaving on a romantic mini-break!*

Me: *Cool. Where to?* I didn't ask her who with, she obviously thinks I know; I don't think she's being coy.

Chelle: *Kara won't tell me. She's even packed my case with the appropriate clothes. Gotta go. Have a good weekend.*

I manage a sad *you too*, before resigning myself to the inevitable. I can't even say I've been friend-zoned because that's where I've always been as far as Chelle is concerned.

Sadly, it all makes perfect sense now, the way Kara sat with us when we returned from the cinema, the way she expressed her gratitude so profusely to me for going with Chelle to see a movie Kara would hate.

I need to tune up my gaydar.

Emily

I arrive at my parents, disappointed to hear that Rosie is already asleep.

'She was shattered,' exclaims Mum. 'The poor thing could barely keep her eyes open at dinner. I hope you aren't putting her to bed too late.' Mum looks at me disapprovingly, with her hands on her hips.

'Yes, Mum, don't worry, I don't put her to bed late. She is only five and five-year olds get tired if they've been busy.'

'I suppose so, maybe Liam puts her to bed too late then. Have you sorted out what you're going to do about his request for fifty percent custody?' Mum looks worried. I guess my parents will miss out on time with her too. I hadn't thought of that.

'I haven't spoken to him yet, no, but I think I know what I'm going to do.' Mum puts her arm around me and pushes the biscuit tin towards me. I open it and take out a couple of custard creams and push it back to her, otherwise I'll eat the whole tin.

Sixteen

Emily

I think back to Friday night as I walk through the office door and dump my bag down by my desk. It's Monday and I'm in work early. Mum and I had a big chat about everything, the psychic night, Ben, work with pervy Dirk, everything. I feel a lot clearer and better for speaking to her. Tonight, before Ben comes over, I shall be calling Liam to discuss his increased access to Rosie. Dirk, on the other hand, I need to be extremely careful about, and I haven't quite worked out what I'm going to do, if anything.

'Hi Emily, nice weekend?' Jamie struts through the door looking fresh. I know he's been looking after himself and it shows. He's much slimmer and is standing up straighter instead of slumping and trying to go unnoticed. The new *shoulders back* Jamie suits him, he's even verging on attractive.

'It wasn't bad, how about you? You feeling better?' I ask.

'Yeah, mine was okay, didn't do much, trying to be healthy. I'm feeling good, much better not eating all that crap and Chelle is an excellent trainer.' Jamie grins but it quickly fades. I feel bad for telling him about her, he would have found out eventually anyway, why did I need to spoil it? Swiftly, I change the subject.

'So, I went out for drinks with Dirk on Friday, he told me you were ill,' I state, challenging him to tell me the truth. He definitely wasn't sick, faking it more like. To be honest I just wish I had come up with the idea first. Jamie opens his mouth like a goldfish, before narrowing his eyes.

'The bastard,' he whispers, looking around in case anyone is listening. '*He* cancelled *me*. I thought he cancelled us both. I mean, he told me the drinks weren't happening anymore,' Jamie says. 'The sly arse. He did this on purpose to have drinks with you alone.' Jamie laughs. I hadn't found it that funny but I suppose the cheek of Dirk is faintly amusing when you think about it.

'It was painful, I was there an hour and then left,' I protest, forcing a smile. Jamie is still laughing.

'I knew it! I knew it, the sly arse. Sorry for laughing but I just can't believe him. I knew you were going to get the job over me but this has just confirmed it.' His words shock me; surely he doesn't really think I'm going to get the job.

'Well actually, he's put me in rather an awkward position, he kind of made lewd suggestions that I need to get to know him better, if you catch my drift.' I raise an eyebrow hoping it conveys what I'm meaning to say, I don't want to have to say it because if I say it, I might be sick.

'Did he? Oh my God. What a dirty bastard. That's sexual harassment you know, you could get him done for it.' Jamie slams his fist down on his desk and I watch everything on it shake like a mini-earthquake, he must be good at arm wrestling, I bet he could beat

Dirk.

'I know, it's awful, I'm not sure what to do about it. He has a lot of power here.' I glance at the door for any potential eavesdroppers.

'Complain to HR. He's a bully to all the staff and now he is also a sex pest. He shouldn't be making you feel like this, it's completely out of order.' Jamie looks angry now.

'Do you really think they will believe me or even care? I've been here five minutes, he has been with the company over ten years and he *knows people*.' It's true he does; all the directors love him. I wouldn't stand a chance.

'Yeah it's a tough one, but I'll be a witness for you, the lie about me being ill so he can be alone with you looks bad enough,' Jamie says.

I'm suddenly paranoid and wonder if this is just a quick way for Jamie to get rid of me so the job will be his. Encourage me to report Dirk to HR, they investigate, Dirk lies and then I'm gone. It's too easy.

'Emily,' Jamie says seriously. 'I've got your back on this, don't worry. He won't get away with this.'

I don't know what do.

Jamie

Well, Emily told me she went for the drink with Dirk. She was visibly shocked when I told her that he cancelled me, not the other way around.

I laughed. I didn't mean to. It was hardly the right reaction. I was furious. Furious that he should take advantage of her like that, and from what she says make pervy suggestions and even imply that if she plays along the job will be hers. Furious also because it just confirms what I've always thought – the job is hers.

I felt stupid for laughing, her face told me that she didn't think it was at all funny, though to give her credit she did join in, in the end.

I got the impression that she blamed me for not turning up on Friday, but how could that be my fault?

I have offered to back her up if she wants to make a complaint to HR. In truth, I don't know how well that will go down, the two newbies, the rivals, complaining about their boss. Dirk has been with Genevre for years. Who are they going to believe? Who have they already invested in? Who are they going to side with?

I hope she doesn't make a complaint.

I don't know what to do about Dirk.

One thing I do know; I need to take back control of *my* future.

Just before lunchtime I upload my CV to several job search sites – though not the one that found me this job. I have to take positive action otherwise I will be out of job after Christmas. If I'm lucky and manage to secure something maybe I can persuade Genevre to up my goodbye bonus in lieu of not taking up the outplacement advice. I should find something, there are plenty of office jobs about. If that's what I really want.

By lunchtime I've been through the preliminary details of mine and Emily's joint case and I send her an email to arrange a meeting where we can discuss our next actions.

I'm not sure how I feel about helping my rival secure the best job I'll never have.

In the meantime, it's my usual Monday lunch with Chelle.

Maybe she won't turn up.

'Hey,' Chelle says, dropping down into the seat next to me with her tray.

'Hi.' I manage the biggest fake smile of my life. I thought I'd been clever hiding away in a dim corner inside the café.

'Nearly didn't see you here. Was it busy outside when you arrived?'

'Yeah.' I nod to confirm my lie.

'It's empty now. Fancy moving.'

I don't answer but she reads the reluctance on my face.

'Nah,' she says. 'Hardly worth it.' She picks up her glass and drinks half of it down in one go. 'Oh, I needed that. Were you early or am I late?'

'I was a bit early, I need to leave early, I have a meeting soon.' Another lie, my meeting with Emily isn't for another hour.

'Shame.' Chelle starts to tuck into her salad.

'Yeah.' I smile and so does Chelle. I take a deep breath before I speak again. 'How was your weekend?'

'Fab. Absolutely bloody fab. We went to London. Shopping. Dinner. Theatre. The works. Fab hotel. It was the best.' The grin on her face, the sparkle in her eyes says it all.

'Special occasion?' I don't really want to know, but Chelle's my friend. *Only* my friend.

'Well,' she leans in grinning. 'Only this.' She flashes her left hand at me. A jumbo solitaire sparkles even in the dimness of the dark corner I've attempted to hide in.

'Wow. Congratulations.'

Chelle holds her hand out towards me, I think she expects me to grab her hand to inspect the ring more.

I'm not doing that. I'm not one of her *girl* friends.

'How long have you and Kara been together?' I ask this, not because I want to know but because I want her to know I'm cool with it.

'Apparently, not that I realised, it was exactly five years ago on Saturday that our eyes met over a complex spreadsheet. Kara's good at remembering dates and stuff.' She smiles to herself. 'I mean, I remember the occasion, you do, don't you, things like that. But I didn't know the date.'

'That's great.' I sound almost absent minded, maybe I am. I glance at my watch. 'Look, I've got to go and get ready for this meeting. Congratulations again.' I stand up and grab my tray.

'Wedding's in May. You'll be getting an invite.' She grins at me. 'Kara wants to keep you onside for all the sci-fi and superhero movies.'

'Cheers.'

I cast a quick glance back at Chelle as I walk away; she's beautiful, just flawless. The fittest girlfriend I never had.

My meeting with Emily starts promptly and we're crowded into a tiny meeting room that can barely contain the two of us, yet there are three chairs. Three people in here would be too intimate; two is bad enough.

Emily soon confesses that she's out of her depth with this one. She also confesses that Dirk gave it to her two weeks ago and she had to go to him, finally, and admit she was out of her depth. Dumping it, and her, on me was his solution.

'I'm sorry,' she says, when she's finished. 'I know it's not fair.' Her eyes are moist and in this close, windowless, overlit space I can see her pulse throbbing in her neck.

'No worries.' I'm trying to play this cool, trying not to make her feel any worse that she already does. 'I've looked through it and it may be that Genevre has to pass on it too. Didn't you say it had been to several other insurance companies already?'

'Yes,' Emily says, quietly. Too quietly.

'What?' Her tone has raised my hackles, there's more to this.

'Well, Dirk has sort of promised the CEO that we can do it. Dirk wants to impress him and the CEO has a personal interest in it, he's mates with the CEO of the company that wants the cover.' Emily looks away. 'I'm so sorry. I feel like I'm handing you the poisoned chalice. The one that Dirk handed to me.'

I frown. 'I thought we were working on this together.'

'We are. We are.' Emily stops and takes a deep breath. 'But since I've tried and can't solve it, it'll be down to you.' She flushes pink and I see her eyes moisten again.

I hope she isn't going to cry.

I wait for a moment, partly to let her get over her angst and partly to regroup my thinking.

'Let me get this straight. Are you implying that if I fail the failure is all mine, but if I succeed, you and Dirk will share the glory with me?'

'I think so. I'm sorry.'

'We'd better get on with it then, hadn't we?'

Emily

I rush to Rosie's after school club to pick her up and take her home, dinner is done, homework complete,

189

four bedtime stories later and my little angel is fast asleep. It's 7.30pm. I have an hour to phone Liam and get ready for Ben, who's arriving at 8.30pm. It turns out his son just had a funny turn and it's nothing serious; thank goodness he's okay. Why do I put myself under so much time pressure? I almost hope Ben's late. Sitting on my sofa with EastEnders on in the background I scroll down and find Liam's name. It feels weird calling him as we do everything via message.

'Hello, Emily.' It's Tiny. Answering Liam's phone.

'Hi Tiny, how are you?'

'Yes, I'm well, thank you for asking.' She sounds cheerful. 'How are you?'

'I'm good thanks, umm is Liam about? I just wanted to chat to him about Rosie.'

'Yes, sure, I'll just grab him, he's in his games room…oh Emily?'

'Yeah.'

'It was nice to see you the other night, at the psychic night I mean.'

'Yeah it was good to see you too,' I say cringing, as an image of us crying at each other plays on my mind. Please don't bring it up. Please don't bring it up.

'It was, really good in fact.' I can hear her smiling down the phone as she pads to the games room.

Let's not pretend it isn't still awkward, Tiny. I don't hate you but we definitely aren't bezzies yet, though I do feel a lot more disposed to you than I previously did.

'Liam, I've got Emily on the phone for you.' There's muffled talking for quite some time, somebody must have put their hand over the speaker. I imagine Liam doesn't want to talk to me, especially if Tiny has told him that the psychic outed him as taking off his wedding ring. I feel a bit cross all of a sudden and have an urge to confront him but then I think better of it, it's not worth it. Ben will be here soon and I haven't got time for that shit.

'What's up? Rosie okay? He sounds pissed off.

'Hi, yeah she's fine. I was just ringing to chat to you about custody, I thought it would be better to do it over the phone rather than in a message.' And I don't want to have to look at you so this is the next best thing.

'Go on then, say it.' God, what's got into him? He's super snappy today, more so than usual. Probably because I've interrupted his game.

'Say what?' I ask as he sighs dramatically down the phone. The noise kind of makes me want to reach down the phone and punch him. 'Okay?' I say, because I am not quite sure what *I've* done wrong. I'll ignore him and carry on with what I was going to say, that's what I'll do. In my best business voice, I reply slowly. 'Well, I was ringing to say that I've given it lots of thought and I agree it would be a good idea for you to have Rosie fifty percent of the time.' I stop to hear his reaction. There's a big pause and then another loud sigh.

'Oh really,' he replies, sounding sarcastic.

'Yes, aren't you pleased?' I almost shriek because he is, quite frankly, acting like a massive tool.

'Of course, and I bet Ben is over the moon about this, isn't he?' Liam snaps and I imagine him aggressively playing with the ends of his tosser moustache.

'Excuse me?' I laugh. The pure cheek of the man.

'Yes, I bet Ben can't wait to spend more time with you. And now he can,' he spits. Ah, so this is what it's all about.

'That's none of your business, thanks,' I say flatly. How dare he?

'Oh, I think it is if you've introduced him to *my* daughter, she's already talking about him like he's her new dad.'

'That's none of your business,' I repeat. 'Ben and I are just friends, and they haven't met yet, though I have told her about him, of course. And when I do introduce him to Rosie, I will do so whenever I choose and I certainly won't be asking your permission.'

Ha. Take that, Liam.

'Oh, is that so.' I can tell that he's speaking through gritted teeth.

'Yes, that's exactly so. Just like you didn't ask my permission to introduce Tiny to Rosie, I won't be asking yours, is that clear?' He doesn't reply, just breathes heavily. Yes, I know Rosie was little more than a baby, but that's not the point. How dare he. 'I'll be in touch regarding Rosie's time with you, in the meantime I suggest you grow up and get over it.' This feels *so* good.

'Fine, next time, send a message.'

'Don't worry, I won't phone again, in fact maybe I will and next time I'll speak to Tiny instead, she's much more pleasant. Goodbye Liam.' Burn.

If I didn't know him any better, I'd think he was jealous. With the phone call taking less time than expected, I now have over 30 minutes to sort my face out and get out of these grim work clothes.

Perfect.

I race up the stairs with light feet, careful not to wake Rosie and creep over to my bedroom. Hmm what to wear? Should I change my underwear? No, no, not with Rosie in the house. I opt for tight dark blue skinny jeans and a tight black top with silver beaded embellishment. My hair was down already for work so I give it a quick brush before boofing it up with some volume spray. I apply some fresh highlighter to my cheeks and some concealer to the mum bags under my eyes, finishing off with some rose coloured lipstick. I assess myself in the mirror and decide that I don't look too bad at all. Padding down the stairs, the doorbell rings. Just in time.

'Hey.' I open the door to Ben's big smiley face and my stomach lurches with excitement.

'Hey, come in.' I stand aside and let him in. He takes my face in his hands and gives me a big sensual kiss that makes me go weak at the knees. Before things get too frisky, I pull away and lead him through the living room to my kitchen. He sits at the kitchen table and I hover by the fridge.

'Beer?' I say casually as I open up the fridge like his own personal barmaid.

'Ah yeah, I'd love one.'

I grab two beers from the fridge and pass one to Ben.

'So how was work? Any more beef with Birk?'

'Birk, I love. Suits him too. No. I'm still deciding what to do about that, just sort of keeping a low profile and avoiding him as much as I can at the moment, well as much as I can avoid my boss that is.' I bite my nails again, drinks with Dirk has ramped up my anxiety.

'Yeah, that's sucks.' Ben puts his hand on mine, he has lovely soft hands yet still manly and very wide, with wide fingers.

'Doesn't it. How was your day?' I ask.

'Yeah, good. We employed a new barber today, he's young and fresh so is up to date with all the latest haircuts. We need that, everyone else is old and past it.' He laughs and his eyes crinkle up perfectly symmetrical. He's one of those that just gets better with age. He's pushing forty but looks fab.

'I'll have to come and check out your barbers, I'd love to see where you work. What's it called?'

'I wouldn't, you'd probably leave with a short back and sides.' He laughs. 'It's called Ben's Barbers. Original I know.' He looks a bit embarrassed, it's quite endearing.

'I think it's amazing that you have your own business. I really admire that.' I take a sip of my beer; the taste makes me flinch. I don't even like beer, I think I'll settle for a squash next.

Ben stares at me attentively with his hypnotic blue eyes and I have an overwhelming urge to know everything about him.

We have a lovely night and stay up laughing and talking until gone midnight. I'd love to rip his clothes off and unwrap him like a present but I'm not comfortable doing that with my daughter in the house and Ben respects that, which makes me like him even more. The night ends even better than I could have imagined with Ben inviting me on a weekend away to Dublin. Now that Liam will be having Rosie half of the time, this could be possible.

I can't wait!

Jamie

Emily and I have been working solidly together for three days. We've been going around in circles but this afternoon I feel as though we're finally getting somewhere.

'Coffee?' Emily says, as she watches me lean back in

my chair and rub my temples; I've had a tension headache on and off all week.

'Great idea.'

We trot off to the kitchen and when Emily offers to make my coffee, I let her.

'Biscuit?' She waves a packet in front of me.

'Better not.' I half laugh and think of my gruelling lunchtime session in the gym. I no longer need Chelle's instruction or positive encouragement and I don't want to undo all the good work by starting packing away biscuits again.

'Are you still doing your sessions with Chelle?'

'Yes. No.' I laugh. 'I'm on my own mostly. She just gives me pointers if she's passing. You know, *bend your knees, straighten your back*, that sort of thing.'

'Cool,' Emily says as we stand side by side looking out of the window at the green fields beyond. Again. 'That was lovely news about her and Kara, wasn't it?' This is Emily tactfully testing me.

'Yeah. Lovely ring too. Kara is a nice person.'

'You've met her?'

'Yeah. When I took Chelle to the cinema, Kara was waiting for us with hot chocolate and biscuits, and grateful thanks that I can go with Chelle so Kara doesn't have to. She hates Sci-fi films.' Maybe it wasn't quite like that, but almost.

'That's, err, really good, though I'm sure Chelle could go on her own. She's a big girl,' Emily says with a frown.

'Yeah, but not so much fun.'

Emily takes a large gulp of her coffee before helping herself to her second biscuit. 'Your gym sessions are certainly making a difference to your...' she falters for the right word, 'Physique.'

'Thanks.' I smile to myself.

'Yeah, you're really trim now.'

'Thanks.'

'Not that you were fat before, obviously.'

I pause to let her suffer a little and watch her blush pink.

'I was heading that way.' I grab her empty cup and take it with mine to the sink. 'Shall we get back to it?'

'Yeah, we should.' She smiles, then I notice her mouth is quivering a little. Is that nerves? 'About Dirk,' she lowers her voice. 'I've decided to just leave it for now. Not complain to HR, I mean.'

'Okay,' I say, trying to sound neutral. 'Probably wise, for now.'

'Yeah,' she says.

What a relief; we don't have to go up against Dirk.

We've soon got our heads together again, deep into our underwriting problem when Emily's mobile rings. She glances at me, mouths a sorry and takes the call, getting up and walking away as she's talking.

Five minutes pass and I'm starting to worry when she comes back smiling.

'Sorry about that, it was my mum. You know what mums are like.' She rolls her eyes. 'She was just checking about Rosie's ballet, what time it is. She's taking her for me, I warned her I might be late.'

'Late? Did you? How late?'

Emily shrugs and smiles and sits back down, leaning over to study what we've been working on. I can smell her perfume, even this late in the afternoon it's still quite strong, and rather nice. I wonder if she's just reapplied it.

'Don't know,' she says softly, answering my

question. 'Just that we've worked late every night so far.'

'Have we?' I'm genuinely shocked. Now I stop to think about it, she's right. I suppose I did notice that everyone else had gone but I wasn't that conscious of the time. I glance around the office now and see that it's just us from our team and one or two people in the distance.

'God, I'm sorry. I forgot you had your daughter to look after. I just didn't notice the time. You should have said.' I feel a right shit now. I start clearing away our work.

'It's not a problem. Really. It's just my mum, she likes to know where I am. Mum's worry, don't they? I know I do. I bet your mum still does about you.'

'Not anymore.' I suddenly feel an ache deep inside.

'I'm sure she does,' Emily says and she nudges me, it's both playful and intimate and we both immediately pull away. What just happened? 'Sorry,' she mutters.

'It's all right.' Then I find myself telling her all about my mum, her death, my escape into the VSO and how my dad is only now managing to clear my mum's stuff out. I don't actually cry, but I feel as though I could. Why am I telling her? She doesn't need to know this stuff about me.

It's only when I've finished unburdening myself that I look down and see that Emily is grasping my hand. I'm grateful that hand is on the desk and not under it or it could be even weirder.

She smiles and lets go. She isn't embarrassed. I am.

'I'm sorry about your mum. That must be hard.'

'Yeah. Come on, let's get out of here. I think we've nearly cracked this and if we sleep on it, we might find the solution tomorrow.' I hurriedly tidy everything away and stand up. Then I hear myself being stupid again. 'I'd suggest a drink to wind down but I think you need to get home to your little girl.'

'Yeah, thanks.'

On the way home, I go over the last half hour's conversation. Sitting in the traffic I'm shaking my head in disbelief. Whatever possessed me to unburden myself on Emily like that? I hardly know her and we're rivals. Well, not rivals. She's a shoo in for the job, especially if she sucks up to Dirk enough.

I should probably think of her as my enemy.

Yes, that's what I should do.

Seventeen

Emily

It seems like an eternity since Ben invited me to Dublin but finally the day has come and I couldn't be more excited! Rosie is at her dad's, he's taking her to see Santa this weekend at the local garden centre. Her little face was so excited, I'm so pleased she is going to be doing something nice. Often, he does things like drag her round supermarkets or take her to watch him get his haircut, strange man. My phone flashes with a message from Sabrina.

Sab: *You all ready for Dublin? Super jealous.*

Me: *Yes, think so, just double checking everything now, so nervous.*

Sab: *Nothing to be nervous about my darling, just enjoy yourself and be you.*

Me: *I know, I'm nervous about the flight more than anything. You know what I'm like.* I think back to the time we went to Ibiza on a hen do and I clung onto my friend Claire's hand so tight I managed to break two of her fingers. She spent most of the hen do at the hospital. Needless to say, I didn't see her much after we got back home.

Sab: *Oh come on, you're a grown ass woman Em, just have a few shots of vodka before to numb the nerves and you'll be fine.*

Me: *Lol thanks for the support mate.* I reach for my Kalms and consider taking a couple. I've done so well without them recently and I don't want to have to use something as a crutch, I'll be fine. I have big strong Ben to look after me – and possibly a few shots of vodka.

My taxi arrives with Ben already in it. The taxi driver hops out and helps me with my case and I smile through the window at Ben as he winks back at me from inside the cab. I love his winking.

'Hey, you're looking lovely, come here.' Ben gives me a big kiss and rests his hand on my leg, gently circling his fingers on my tights. Instantly my thoughts turn to the hotel room and the bed, my mind flashes with images of us on it and I feel myself blush.

'You don't look so bad yourself.' I go in for a kiss and hope I'm wearing enough makeup to cover my flushed face, he carries on kissing me with his hands everywhere like an octopus. I pull away, it feels a bit weird with the poor taxi driver having to listen to our lips smacking together. That, in itself, sounds gross. We can save ourselves for later.

We pull up to the airport and I feel the dreaded pang of anxiety; I was okay until I started to see the planes flying low over us. Ben doesn't know I'm scared of flying. I feel a bit stupid telling him because I don't want to appear pathetic or ungrateful, he has paid for the flights and hotel after all. Why didn't I bring my Kalms? God dammit. I need my Kalms! We get through security and head straight for a bar, I love that I don't even have to suggest it. Ben likes a beer and I'm definitely in need of something strong.

'What do you fancy then? Coke?' Ben offers.

'No thanks, I think I'll have a cocktail actually,' I

reply.

'A cocktail this early? Go you.' Ben laughs. Great. Now I feel like an alcoholic.

'Yeah, well I am on holiday after all, I'll let you choose.' Anything I will him. Anything with lots of alcohol in it. I grin at Ben and he shakes his head laughing.

'Okay, I was only going to have a coke myself but I guess I'll join you, I'll be back in a bit.' I watch Ben as he walks off to the bar and catch one of the barmaids eyeing him up. I feel proud he's with me. He is certainly a catch; owns his own business, nice manners, kind, funny *and* gorgeous. The full package.

Three very strong cocktails later and I am feeling a bit squiffy to say the least. Our flight has been delayed by two hours, giving me the chance to down more alcohol. I cringed when Ben brought back *Sex on the Beach* and he laughed when I told him it was the drink that Dirk (or Birk as Ben likes to call him) was drinking on our work's night out.

'That's our flight, Emily,' Ben says and I blink at him slowly.

'Huh? What fight?'

'Hehe come on drunky, they've just announced our flight, we need to get to the gate,' he explains and gets up to leave.

'Okay, hang on a minute.' I go to down the rest of my cocktail but Ben pulls it out of my reach.

'I've got you some water, have this instead.' He thrusts the bottle at me.

'No, I want my cocktail.' I need my cocktail.

'Emily, please, they won't let us on the flight if you're this drunk.' Ben looks amused yet he speaks with an edge of sternness. I better do as he says and not get us banned from the plane before we are even on it. Although that might not be a bad idea.

'Hic! Okay *big* Ben.' I take a sip of water and then link my arm into his as he drags me to the gate.

'Woohoo this is funnnnn,' I scream as he skates me along on the slippery floor and over many an escalator.

'Shhhhh, honestly you need to act sober now.' He pulls my arm in close to him. He's very strong.

'Oh shit, I didn't know I was acting drunk.'

'Shhhhh, Emily.' Ben gives me a stern look as we go to take a seat in the lounge. Is he cross? He seems a bit cross. He's not smiling anymore.

'Where's the wink, you aren't winking like the old big Ben I know. Hic!'

Ben just looks at me and smiles a polite smile to the room whilst I sit there concentrating on not hiccupping and not being drunk. It's good in a way because it gives me something to focus on other than the flight.

Oh hell.

The flight.

By the time we get on the plane I'm starting to feel less drunk *and* rather sick. Panic and an instant hangover have set in. The air hostess does her spiel while signalling to all the emergency exits and my mind wanders, fantasising about running out of the nearest one.

'Ben,' I whisper as I touch his knee tentatively.

'Yep, you okay, sober?' He eyes me up and down, he doesn't seem pissed off now but he could be hiding it. He winks.

'I don't think I can do this,' I blurt out with my eyes closed.

'Do what? What do you mean?' He takes my hand

in his.

'This.' I do a circling motion with my finger to signal that I mean the plane.

'We're just taking things slow, Em. It's just fun, we don't have to get all serious now,' he reassures, getting the wrong end of the stick.

'No, I mean…' Ben looks confused but I can't say the words because now I'm *really* going to vomit. The seatbelt sign has just come on so I can't move. Frantically I check the front seat pockets for a brown paper bag to be sick into, there aren't any, just crumbs and crumpled up magazines from the flight before. Shitty, economy *Windswept Airlines*. I suppose you get what you pay for and in my case, nothing.

'Bag. Sick,' I mumble and Ben begins searching as frantically as I am for something for me to be sick into; there isn't anything and there's no sign of an air hostess.

'Urgh fuck,' Ben says in disgust as I reach for my handbag and begin emptying everything out to be sick into it, heaving whilst doing so. I can hear him shouting down the aisle for an air hostess. She quickly scurries back with a brown paper bag. Too late. As she approaches, I'm puking into my handbag.

Oh, the shame. Ding.

'It's okay, it's okay.' Ben's rubbing my back as I vomit violently into my bag, there's so much of it. I'm sure I haven't eaten that much today. I'm just glad I had the common sense to empty its contents out beforehand. My student days have taught me that much.

'Here you go.' The air hostess comes back with a plastic cup of water and hands it to me. Now I'm just retching. Her nose twitches and she grimaces before plastering on a big fake smile.

'I have to get back now, we have to be seated for take-off. Is there anything else I can get you sir?' she asks Ben and he looks at me.

'Umm, maybe some more brown paper bags, just in case,' he says.

'No problem. Back later.' She smiles at him, a big genuine, sincere smile just for him.

I watch her saunter off again and turn to face Ben, I can barely look him in the eye.

So embarrassed.

'I'm so sorry Ben, this is so embarrassing,' I whine, feeling pathetic. All the puking means I'm now stone cold sober.

'Hey, no need to be sorry, we've all been there. Let's just take it easy in Dublin, yeah?' He smiles and rubs my back and I feel as if I am about to cry.

'I'm terrified of flying. I'm sorry. I can't do this.' Big tears start to roll down my cheeks. I can't stop the sobbing. This is utter humiliation.

'You can do this, you'll be just fine. Just take my hand and squeeze it as hard as you like. The flight's only an hour and we'll be there before we know it, I promise.' He winks and smiles kindly at me, looking down on me with his twinkly, blue eyes.

'The last person's hand I squeezed ended up with broken fingers,' I explain between sobs. Ben laughs his warm laugh and rubs my arm.

'You better not break these or I'll sue you for loss of business.' He's teasing me but I can't find the strength to laugh. I'm sobbing like a big baby. Boohoo.

'You'll be fine, just take a deep breath and hold my hand, squeeze it as hard as you like, I mean it. These fat fingers can take it.' He wiggles his wide fingers at me and I close my eyes and take his hand. As the loud rumble of the engine begins, he holds me tight and whispers reassuring words in my ear. I squeeze his hand as we take off and hold my breath at the same time. This is the worst bit. As we reach the climax, I keep my eyes closed and remain quiet for the rest for the flight, holding my breath again as we land.

'Emily, Emily.'

I open one eye and peer at him, I feel like absolute shit and probably look it.

'Hey,' I manage.

'We're here, in Dublin.' He does a fake Irish accent on the word Dublin in an attempt to make me laugh. 'We've landed to be sure,' he continues in his Irish accent, in another attempt to make me laugh.

'Yay,' I say meekly and Ben chuckles.

'Let's get you sorted out, you probably want to get rid of that.' He points and makes a face at my completely ruined Louis Vuitton handbag. A gift from Liam's mum, my one and only designer item. I can't believe we have been sat the whole flight with it there, I feel sick again looking at it and the smell is nauseating. I pity the other passengers. The contents of my handbag are now bursting out of a sick bag.

Two hours later and I am a completely different person, it's amazing what ibuprofen and a new, clean handbag can do. Aside from that, I've had a shower and am sorting my face out in the swanky hotel whilst Ben's gone out to source us some much-needed coffees. I take my phone out to text Sab to let her know I got here in one piece. Just about.

Me: *Hey, got here ok but was sick in my handbag on the flight. Was terrible. Ben was such a sweetie, he looked after me and even offered to buy me a new handbag.*

Sab: *Hahaha oh my god! You poor thing, but sick in your handbag . . . please don't tell me it was the Louis Vuitton?!'*

Me: *Sadly, yes.*

Sab: *Oh dear, so he bought you a new Louis Vuitton handbag? WTF! He's a keeper!*

Me: *No, I didn't let him, got myself one from New Look.*

Sab: *You're so strange girl, haha! What are you doing tonight?*

Me: *We're going out for a meal down Temple Bar, just going to chill out in the hotel this afternoon and get over my vomit trauma.*

Sab: *You mean "shag" in the hotel this afternoon, ok my darling, have fun and don't do anything I wouldn't do...which isn't much.*

Sabrina wasn't wrong, we did spend the rest of the afternoon in bed and it was just lovely. Ben certainly knows how to please in that department. After a long, much needed nap, we get ready for the evening and leave our swanky hotel. We step outside in the freezing Irish November air and I spy a black, fancy horse and carriage trotting by. It's beautifully painted with flowers and swirls and the driver is dressed smartly, wearing a tall, black top hat.

'Oh Ben, look at that, how romantic. I've always wanted to go on one of those. I wonder if...'

Before I've even finished my sentence, Ben has sprinted halfway down the road to catch the horse and carriage. He chats with the driver for a few minutes before he comes sprinting back with a big grin on his face.

'Your carriage awaits me lady,' Ben says with a sparkle in his blue eyes as the horse and carriage trots up alongside him.

'Oh my God. Can you actually go on them? I mean it doesn't belong to someone?' I want to say *belong to a gypsy* but I think better of it. That doesn't sound very PC, Emily.

'No of course not, they belong to a company. They're a tourist attraction. We can get a ride down the road to our restaurant, come on, hop on.' Ben takes my hand and I climb up into the carriage. It's beautifully lined in crimson velvet. I take my glove off and smooth over the glorious material with my fingers, then sit back to admire the streets and people of Dublin. I feel like I'm in a 1920s film, playing the main character with her potential love interest. The horse begins to gently clip clop as we bob along the city to our restaurant. I put my glove back on and nuzzle into my thick cosy scarf, it's freezing, some five degrees colder than sunny Wiltshire.

'Let me know, where's good for ya, fella?' the driver says in a thick Dublin accent.

'Yep, just anywhere around here, whatever's easier for you mate. That's spot on, cheers.'

'Sure, that's grand, I'll drop you off on the corner just here. Have a great evening,' the driver chirps, taking off his hat to us after Ben leaves a generous tip.

We step out onto Temple Bar, it's a busy Saturday night and there are lots of hen and stag parties about. One stag passes us dressed as a giant inflatable penis with an entourage of about twenty men, followed closely by another stag party, this stag is dressed in a wedding dress. There's a hen party approaching on the opposite side of the road; around ten women, all with amazing figures, dressed in sequin dresses and glitter makeup. They all look amazing and several stags wolf whistle as the hens strut past.

I let Ben lead me down a side street, grateful to get away from the hen and stag groups and we pass a lovely, traditional, Irish bar playing live, acoustic music.

'Oh Ben, please can we go in?' I burst, sounding like an excited kid wanting more sweeties.

'Yeah, sure. We've got half an hour to kill.' He swings his arm around my shoulders.

We step inside and the pub is everything you imagine a Dublin bar to be. There's a quirky painting on the wall of a huge pint of Guinness. A few old men are dotted about drinking on their own. It's dark and dingy, and in the corner the singer is strumming a *Christy Moore* song on his guitar.

'Riiiiide on, seeee youuu, I could never go with you no matter how I wanted toooo.'

He has a fantastic voice, singing with everything he has as though he's performing to a crowd at Wembley. Ben and I watch mesmerised, drinking in the atmosphere as we wait at the bar. I'm enjoying it so much that I surprise myself when I suddenly feel an unlikely pang of guilt. My thoughts turn to *Jamie* of all people. He helped me out of a pretty tricky situation last week at work and though we still aren't completely out of the woods, it's going to be okay.

I hope he's okay.

'Runnnnn your claw along my gut, one last time, I turn to face an empty space where once you used to lie. . .'

'Emily, you okay? We can go if it's not what you thought it was going to be,' Ben shouts over the music and several of the old men turn around.

'Oh no, no, I love it, let's stay.' We stay for two more songs before strolling off to our restaurant. I'm absolutely starving and the thought of food is making me salivate.

'It's Irish food, I hope you don't mind?' Ben says as we enter the restaurant.

'No, that's great. To be expected in Ireland isn't it?' I beam at Ben as I wonder what Irish food actually is. I'm not particularly fussy but I can't say I've tried Irish food. I'm guessing it must be all stews and potatoes, which is fine by me. The waiter takes us to a cosy table for two in a little cubby hole, there's a candle in a large glass jar and a single red rose placed next to a bottle of champagne with two glasses.

Very cosy, very romantic.

'Oh Ben, how sweet, for me?' I say as I pick up the red rose, examining it like I've never seen one before.

'Of course.' He winks, grabbing it out of my hand and putting it between his teeth. He looks like a puppy dog and suddenly much younger than his years.

'You're so silly, come here.' I grab the rose out of his mouth, gently tossing it onto the table, taking his face with both hands, I pull him towards me. Those lips, I could be attached to them forever.

'Ahem. Do you two need a couple more minutes?' The young waiter grins as we pull away from our dreamy kiss.

'Yeah, if that's alright mate. We haven't had a chance to choose yet.' Ben winks at the waiter.

'No problem, sir. I'd be doing the same if I had this pretty lady on my arm like you, very lucky man there.' He winks at Ben and Ben winks back.

'Indeed mate, indeed.' Ben winks at the waiter again as he walks off to give us more time.

'So, there's something I have to do tomorrow,' Ben reveals, taking my hands in his.

'Oh okay, what's that then?'

'I have a hair competition I have to attend.' He rubs

the back of my hands.

'That's great,' I chirp, excited at the prospect of watching him at work.

'It can go on for the whole day but I should be able to sneak off after a few hours, pretend I'm sick or something,' he explains, biting his lip before continuing. 'Yeah, they're pretty boring really, but it's something I signed up for ages ago so I have to show my face, lead by example and all that.' He smiles with a straight mouth and awaits my response.

'Oh wow, Ben that's amazing, I can't wait to watch you at work. How exciting.' I squeal, probably a bit too enthusiastically. Maybe there'll be someone there who can fix my hair, I fancy a new do.

'See, the thing is I'm not allowed to bring anyone.'

'Oh.' I pull my hands away from his.

'Yeah, they get funny about guests at this particular competition so I have to go it alone. Sorry, Em. Sorry I didn't tell you before.'

'Okay,' I murmur.

'I thought you might not want to come to Dublin if you knew I was doing this.' He shuffles his feet around under the table.

'It's a shame I can't watch,' I reply, not over the moon about it as he could be out for the whole day but what can I say? He's paid for the flights and hotel so do I really have a right to complain?

'I know,' Ben admits, biting his lip and searching my face for approval.

'Don't worry, I'm a big girl and I can entertain myself, really it's fine.' Shopping springs to mind.

'You sure?' he says, still searching my face as he moves a strand of hair away from my eye.

'Yeah, of course. You go and do your thing and I'll

go and do mine. It's no big deal.' I'm so relaxed or so it appears. In fact, I am pissed off, who wouldn't be? But shopping will be fun, I'm sure I can find some lovely Christmas presents for Rosie.

'You're so amazing, Emily. You're so laid back and you never moan on like most women, that's what I love about you.' Shit. He said the L word.

'Haha did you see me on the plane?' I say bashfully choosing to ignore the L word. Perhaps it was a slip of the tongue, even so it sounded nice on his lips as he said it to me.

'Yes, well apart from that. No one's perfect after all and it wasn't that bad, it was actually quite funny. A great story to tell our grandkids,' Ben gushes.

'Haha definitely not a story for the grandkids,' I protest. Shit. Grandkids?! Maybe he was serious.

Maybe he actually loves me.

The rest of the trip goes by in a quick, lovely, romantic blur. I pretty much finish my Christmas shopping, including some beautiful wooden toys for Rosie. Ben came third in the competition and we end up having *the chat* and make our relationship official. He is now my man, my boyfriend, my other half, my partner and I couldn't be feeling more wonderful.

Emily Cod, has finally moved on.

Jamie

Emily's all super smiley today.

'Hey, did you have a good weekend?' I ask.

'Oh, I did, I did.' She laughs. 'Went to Dublin for the weekend with my boyfriend.' She says boyfriend in that gooey way girls sometimes do when they talk about their boyfriends. I wonder how they would react if men went all gooey when they said girlfriend. Outright laugh, no doubt.

'Cool,' I say, immediately regretting it because I sound like Dirk. 'I've never been to Dublin.'

'You should go, it's fab.' Emily smiles and her eyes almost cross as her brain goes off elsewhere.

'Did you go to the Temple Bar?' Hayden calls and Emily turns around to talk to him.

I busy myself with my work because very soon Sharon, Karen and Jayden are all talking about the times they went to Dublin and I have nothing to add to their conversation. Emily is the centre of attention and everyone is enjoying themselves.

Emily fits in very well.

'You get up to anything good?' Hayden calls over to me when he realises I'm not involved. That's good of him.

'Oh, the usual,' I say with a smile and hope that will stop it right there. I'm sure no one wants to hear about the highlight of my weekend; a trip to the tip with my dad with the final car load of my mum's stuff that's either too tatty or too personal to go to a charity shop.

We queued up for over an hour. Most of the time we chatted but every so often Dad would remind me that if we'd come sooner, we wouldn't be in such a big queue. I didn't care; I had nothing better to do. And, as I eventually pointed out to him, neither did he.

'Who says I haven't.' He sounded indignant.

'Okay. Well, have you?'

'I'm meeting a friend at the gym later.' He folded his arms and it looked so out of character, so comical, I laughed.

'What, you don't think I should go to the gym? You think that's just for you young men?'

'No. I…I didn't mean that.'

'Well, what did you mean?'

Oh God. I didn't mean anything. It just sounded funny but I could hardly say that to my dad.

'Well?' Dad said again when I didn't answer.

'I don't know. Sorry. I shouldn't have laughed.'

'No, you shouldn't. And, just so you know,' Dad continued, 'The friend I'm seeing later is a lady.'

I swallowed hard. I didn't know what to say, except maybe it would be better if he referred to her as a woman, rather than a lady.

'Okay.'

'It's been over four years now since your mum died. I won't ever forget her, course I won't, but, well, you know…'

'Of course,' I said, but I didn't know.

Traitor.

'You look glum,' Tim said when I got back. He was hovering in the kitchen.

'Do I?'

'Yes. You. Do.' He enunciated the words as though I were a child or deaf, or both.

'What the…?' It was only then that I looked at him properly I saw that he was wearing a pair of oven gloves. I couldn't smell anything cooking.

'Delilah,' Tim said, by way of an explanation.

I began to wonder if the day could get any worse.

'Yeah? Do I really want to know?'

'She's wedged between the cooker and the side of the cupboard. It's good you're back cos you can chase her out with this.' He held up the feather – well not feather, nylon – duster that we occasionally flick round the house, mostly when we have guests coming. 'And

I'll catch her. Just poke it down there. Easier with two of us.'

'Why the gloves?'

'Yeah.' He sighed. 'She's been in there a while and is a bit agitated now, so these will make it…,' he paused, 'nicer for her,' he said after thinking about it.

'What, you think she might bite you?'

'I'm sure she won't.'

I hoped she would. I held out my hand out for the duster, ready to ram it down the gap next to the cooker.

Forty minutes later and Delilah was still trapped, or obstinate, and we were both sweaty – Tim has turned the heating up again so *she* didn't get cold – and pissed off.

'I'm turning the heating down.' I threw the duster on the worktop on my way to the hall to adjust the thermostat.

'But Delilah,' Tim's plaintive voice called after me.

'Maybe she'll come out if she's not so cosy.' When I came back, I put the kettle on and made us both a coffee. Then I got out the biscuits, the ones I'd bought on the way back from dropping my dad home so he could get off to his date at the gym. Then I told Tim about it. Stupid that, because Tim thinks he knows about people and what he calls *the human condition*.

'If your dad's moved on,' Tim began and I wanted to slap him. 'Maybe it's time you did. There she is.' Tim jumped up and grabbed the oven gloves again. He dive-bombed across the kitchen and landed Delilah like a try in rugby.

I wondered if she'd survive.

But she did.

'I was thinking,' Tim said on Sunday morning. 'I might

get rid of Delilah.'

I had to stop myself from punching the air, from shouting and yelling my approval, instead I managed a sedate, 'Why? I thought you loved her.'

Tim snorted. 'Not love, mate. That's a bit, you know…'

'Okay.' I meant okay, whatever and good riddance.

'Yeah, Ian at work has a python. I might swap with him.

'What the…'

But Tim never heard the mouthful of expletives because he was out the door and gone.

He better bloody NOT get a python.

So that was my weekend, doesn't really compare to a lovey-dovey mini-break in Dublin, does it?

Eighteen

Jamie

'Hey,' Emily says later in the week when we find ourselves alone in the kitchen, sipping coffee and staring out of the window. 'What a day.'

It's raining hard and the trees in the car park are bending over in the wind.

'Hi. We seem to be making a habit of this. Standing here, I mean.'

'Yeah.' She sips her coffee and I sense that she wants to say something but also doesn't.

'You okay?' I ask.

'Yeah, good. Thanks. Um...' There it is, hesitancy. 'I've been called to a meeting with Alan.'

'Yeah?' Alan, our Director, who I haven't seen since my interview.

'Yeah, me and Dirk.'

'Right.' I don't even attempt to keep the irritation from my voice. I've not been called to a meeting with Alan, so this can only mean one thing – they're not even waiting until Christmas to give her the job.

'I think it's about that underwriting problem we solved last week.'

'Yeah?' I bet it is.

'I'm pretty sure it is. I owe you big time for helping me out with that. I know I do. I know I couldn't do it, no, didn't do it, on my own. I know you did and could.' She waits for me to react, so I turn and stare at her.

'Yeah. That's right.' My tone is deliberately flat.

'I know. I'm grateful. Really grateful. And, if… Well, I'm going to make sure that Alan knows exactly who solved that tricky case, and that it wasn't me and it certainly wasn't Dirk.'

'Good.' I stare back out across the rain-soaked car park, over the distant countryside and swallow back that I'm pissed off at having not been invited.

'You should be there too. Why don't you come along?'

Is she joking? 'Because,' I say, turning back to face her, 'I haven't been invited.'

'But you should be there.'

I knock the rest of my coffee back, dump the cup in the sink and walk away. Emily remains in the kitchen on her own.

Back at my desk I check her diary to see when her meeting is. I'm almost tempted to gate crash it. I'm so bloody angry. This is Dirk's doing, not that he would admit it to my face. I haven't seen him for days. He's made himself scarce, hiding in his office which is out of sight of ours, or attending meetings in the bowels of the building.

When Emily trots off to her meeting, pausing briefly at my desk I half stand up, then sit back down again. She doesn't say anything, neither do I. Then she's gone.

An hour later she's back. Again, she says nothing. There's an atmosphere in the office now, between us, at least. I'm wondering if anyone else can sense it. I'm wondering if working here can get any worse. It's just as well I'll be on my way in January.

An email pings through from Alan.

My hand shakes as I hover over the mouse to open it. Fucking ridiculous.

He's giving me praise. He's acknowledging my key part. He's telling me that he's going to make sure the CEO knows it was me.

He hasn't invited me to any meetings to discuss it.

I look up and Emily is watching me. I look back down, get on with my work.

Big bloody deal.

Emily

It's Liam's week with Rosie again. We've done it like that, one week each. We decided it was more stable for Rosie, rather than passing her about every few days. Who knows, it might not work and things could change but at this moment in time, this is what's best. The downside is I really miss her when she isn't here and it seems like forever. The upside is, I get to have a guilt free adult life every other week without having to rely on Mum and Dad to babysit.

It's Saturday night and tonight I'm going *out* out with Sabrina. We've got the music turned up and we're getting ready for a much-needed girls' night.

'Let's have a look at your clothes then, I might have to borrow something to wear tonight. I have nothing nice, it's been a hundred years since I've been *out* out,' confesses Sabrina. She hands me her wine glass and opens up my wardrobe, peering inside, examining my clothes.

'Hmmm, what's this little number?' She raises an eyebrow as she pulls out the new black dress that I bought recently.

'Oh, I bought it for Dublin but it was way too cold to wear it. I haven't worn it yet but you go head.' I smile before taking a sip of my wine. I haven't taken this long to get ready for years and I feel like I'm in my early twenties again. I feel good.

'Oh no, I couldn't do that, are you sure?' Her eyebrow is raised in question. I wouldn't let anyone else wear a dress I hadn't worn yet but it's Sabrina and she's done me a favour tonight.

'Yeah sure, but if it looks better on you, you're taking it off.' I wink at her and scold myself for taking on Ben's wink. I love it, but he does it so much I seem to have caught it. Are mannerisms contagious?

Ben should be here tonight, but he let me down. Something about his brother not being able to have the kids, so Sabrina stepped in to cheer me up. I open up my makeup bag and begin to apply my foundation generously; the older you get the more you need.

'Was that the door?' Sabrina says as she pulls herself into my dress.

'Was it?' I wasn't listening, too busy day dreaming about Ben. The doorbell rings again followed by an eager rap at the door.

'Coming!' I shout as I pull on my old dressing gown and stomp down the stairs. There's a few of Rosie's old bogeys stuck to the sleeve from when she had a cold, yuk. Why do kids have to wipe their noses on your clothes? Annoyed at whoever it is for disturbing my getting ready time, I stomp closer to the door, I bet it's my neighbour complaining about the noisy music.

I make out a familiar silhouette. It's bloody Ben. What the hell is he doing here? I have a face full of unblended foundation and fluffy hair. Not to mention the snot, I desperately try to pick it off but it's like

219

cement. He's never seen me like this as I'm always careful about my appearance, sneaking out of bed early to apply makeup and going to bed with a full face. Oh well, I can't hide from him now. He has to love me at my worse too. I take a deep breath and open the door.

'Hey, oh wow! You look. . .' Ben's standing there with a massive bouquet of flowers, wearing an amused expression.

'Yeah...I know,' I mumble, embarrassed. 'I'm getting ready to go out with Sabrina.'

'Oh, right, sorry. I didn't know you'd made plans. I had a spare hour so thought I'd pop over.' He looks from side to side and I realise I haven't invited him in yet.

'Ahh that's sweet, come in, you can meet Sabrina,' I say excitedly as he steps inside and kisses me whilst snaking his spare hand underneath my dressing gown. I'm pretty sure I know what he had planned for his spare hour.

'These for me?' A mixture of purple, white and pink flowers including roses, lilies and chrysanthemums press up against me, they really are beautiful and must have cost a fortune.

'Indeed, they're to say sorry for not being able to make tonight, my bloody brother, he's a bit unreliable sometimes.' Ben looks at the floor and I feel bad for him, it must be hard. He doesn't say much about his ex but from the sounds of it, she doesn't appear to see the kids very often.

'It's okay,' I croak.

'No, it's not, you deserve to be treated like a queen. My queen.' He says stroking my foundation face with his spare hand. I smile and put one arm behind my back to hide the cement bogeys.

'Come on silly,' I say as I take his spare hand purposefully making sure he still has the flowers so Sabrina can see them. 'Come and meet Sabrina.' I lead him up the stairs and knock on my bedroom door.

'Hey, Sab, are you decent? Ben's just popped by to say hello.' I hear her shriek from inside and stomp over to the door.

'Oooooh woohoo the famous Ben. Yes, I'm dressed.' She opens the door. There's a loud gasp. Was that me or Ben or both? She looks absolutely stunning.

In *my* dress.

Her hair and makeup are perfect, she looks the opposite of me right now. For a second, I wish she was just a *bit* ugly. Just for tonight.

'Wow you look amazing, Sab,' I gush, hiding my envy.

'Thank you, darling. Dave would shit a brick if he saw me going out in this, he gets so jealous.' Sabrina smooths down her dress, showing off *all* her curves.

'And I can see why, you MILF. This is Ben, Ben, this is my best mate Sabrina,' I say, in my bogey dressing gown.

'Hey.' Ben steps forward and kisses both of Sabrina's cheeks.

'Hi Ben. Love the flowers, Emily is one lucky girl, but I'm luckier for spending this evening with her.' Sabrina giggles.

'Yeah, I know, I let her down.'

Sabrina stares at him with her hands on her hips and a mock, unimpressed look. I know she's joking but I can see how it might be intimidating if you didn't know her.

'Don't be silly it's fine, these things happen, especially with kids.' I squeeze Ben's hand to reassure

221

him. At least the poor guy is trying, he didn't have to come over.

'Where are your kids now?' Sabrina asks.

'They're at their mum's, I'm just going to get them now.'

'You look familiar,' Sabrina says appraising him.

'Ben owns his own barbers,' I say, half trying to change the subject because I feel like she's acting a bit like my mum, giving him the third degree.

'Oh really, maybe my husband goes there, I'll have to ask him.'

'Yeah, tell him to come in, I'll give him a free haircut. Although it is chocca at the moment in the lead up to Christmas,' Ben offers.

'I will, thank you. What's the name of your barbers again?' Sabrina asks.

'Ben's Barnets.'

'Fabulous, Ben's Barnets,' she repeats. Only *she* could bag a free haircut in the space of two minutes.

'Well, I better get going and leave you two ladies to it,' Ben announces, looking uncomfortable.

'Don't you want to stay for a drink?' I ask, probably a bit too desperately.

'No, no, I can see you still need to get ready. It could take hours.' He winks at me and I bash him gently with the flowers. The git.

'Cheeky sod. Come on then, I'll see you out.' I chuckle and put my hand on his back.

'Bye, Sabrina, nice to meet you. Look after my girl will you.' Ben winks.

'Oh don't worry about that Ben, she's a big girl, she doesn't need looking after. I'll take these and put them in some water for you, Em. So lovely, must have cost a bomb.' Smiling, she takes the flowers and then shakes

Ben's hand.

I hope they are going to get on, it would be great to have some actual couple friends. Liam didn't like Sabrina's Dave so we never hung out like that. Liam didn't like anyone.

Jamie

'You got plans for tonight?' Tim asks on his way from the kitchen to his bedroom. He's finishing off a taco as he passes.

'Thought I might watch the X Factor final.'

Tim, now halfway up the stairs, stops and slithers back down the banister. He better not fucking break it again. He stands between me and the TV.

'What did you just say?'

'You heard.' I'm half joking, but, on the other hand, I don't actually have anything better to do.

'Aren't you going out? It's Saturday. Where's that Beth girl?' What a short memory Tim has. He may be shit-hot with computers but in everything else he's pretty useless.

'Chased off by your gecko,' I remind him.

'Not exactly,' he says, perhaps remembering it was Delilah's dinner that scared Beth off, not actually Delilah.

He snatches the TV remote from its place on the sofa next to me and switches the TV off.

'Come on. You're coming out with me.'

'No. Thanks, mate. For the offer. But you're all right.' I don't want to go out with Tim and his girlfriend-not-girlfriend. I'm not that much of a sad loser.

'Come on.' He adopts a hands-on-hips stance. 'There's a whole bunch of us going out, we're

223

celebrating.'

'Why's that?' I ask, really not wanting to know.

'We've just finished the latest upgrade to the finance software that is our biggest seller and since I wrote most of the code, I don't expect I'll be buying many drinks.' He laughs more to himself than me. 'Anyway, you can tag along and bask in my reflected glory.'

'No. You go and enjoy yourself.' I make a grab for the remote control but he holds it above his head. Inwardly, I groan. Really? If I stand up, I can snatch it out of his hand.

'No. You're coming with me. Get your sorry arse up those stairs. You can go in the shower first. I won't take no for an answer.'

This time I do groan out loud. While he's been talking, he's removed the batteries from the remote and is now legging it up the stairs, dropping the remote back next to me as he goes.

'I'm putting 'em in Delilah's cage,' he shouts, knowing I won't attempt to retrieve them.

'They'll kill her if she eats them. Anyway, I can just get some more out of the drawer.'

'All gone,' he shouts.

He's right. The battery box in the drawer is empty. Bastard. I look around for something to steal the batteries from.

'Give it up,' he shouts down the stairs. 'Don't be a saddo. You haven't even watched the X Factor. You don't even know who's in it.'

'I have. I do. I'm following it.' Listen to me.

'Lying bloody saddo,' he shouts again.

An hour later I'm in the pub with Tim and his colleagues. There are about ten of them, mostly men, milling about with pints of cider. I'm drinking beer, but I might move onto whisky soon.

'This is Ian,' Tim says, introducing me to a guy who could be Tim's long-lost brother from a tiny mother. 'Ian wants to swap his python for Delilah.'

As this gem drops out of Tim's mouth a peal of laughter sounds behind me and a tall woman pushes her way into the middle of us.

'Hey, Lex.' Tim wraps an arm around her and hugs her to him. 'Meet Jamie, my landlord.'

'Housemate,' I correct, although, I suppose, landlord is technically correct and Tim does like to be technically correct. I extend a hand towards Lex who gives me a fierce handshake back.

'What you doing later?' Tim whispers, not particularly subtly, to Lex.

Lex rolls her eyes. 'Busy tonight,' she says. 'Maybe tomorrow?'

'Cool.'

'My place. Come for dinner. Seven.'

'Yeah.' I hear Tim growl and it reminds me of Dirk. Dirk. God help us.

'Drink?' Lex waves a twenty-pound note around. 'I'm getting one in for Codemaster.'

'Codemaster?' I ask, stupidly. 'Tim? Right.'

'That's what we call him. He's been nominated for the annual innovation and excellence prize. Did he tell you? I think he'll get it.' She gives Tim a great big smile and kisses him on the cheek. 'Cider, or something stronger? Ian? Jamie?'

Two hours later there's just me, Tim and Ian left in the pub. We've all had too much to drink, especially Tim who has fallen into the Christmas tree in the corner at least twice. Fortunately, it's sufficiently plastic to withstand his clumsiness.

'I am ready to partaaay!' Tim announces.

'Don't say that,' I mutter. 'Please.'

'Where shall we go?'

'Home.'

'Don't be such a partaaay pooper.' He knocks back his drink and nudges my elbow to do the same. I'm on whisky now and in no mood to knock it back. 'You're up for it, aren't you, Ian?'

'Yeah.'

'Haven't you got a python to get home to?'

Ian narrows his eyes at me and knocks back his own drink.

'Let's go to Vengeance.' Tim pulls on his coat and thrusts mine at me.

'Must we? Where is that anyway?'

'In town.' Tim rolls his eyes at me. 'You've lived here all your life; how can you not know.'

It's bloody freezing outside as we stomp along the pavements for ten chilling minutes until we get to Vengeance.

'This used to be Pharaoh's,' I say as we shuffle inside. The name may have changed but the décor is exactly the same as it was when I last came here five years ago, sticky brown carpet and an excess of chrome. I had my *leaving to join the VSO* party here. I'm told it was a memorable night but I can't remember much about it other than the banging hangover I had for two days. Getting on a long-haul flight feeling like that is not to be recommended.

Tim stumps up the excessive charge for us to get in, insisting on paying for me as he's spent no money all evening because everyone kept buying him drinks. I don't argue. I don't want to pay anything for the privilege of being overcharged for drinks and having my ears assaulted by thumping *partaaay* music.

'Where's Ian?'

'Gone home.'

'When?' I didn't even notice him escaping. 'How is it that he can piss off home and I can't.'

'Oh, you.' Tim grins at me. 'He's coming back, he just had to sort out his snake. He's bringing Kev back with him. We'll do shots later. Line 'em up.'

I hope *Kev* isn't the python.

Shots, I can't wait. I hope Tim has a banging hangover in the morning, he's earning it.

Emily

Sabrina and I are finally *out* out and knocking back the porn star martinis like there's no tomorrow.

'These go down *way* too well,' Sabrina announces as she finishes the last few swigs of her cocktail before picking up the passionfruit to slurp up every last drop. There's really no need. It's two for the price of one and we have another cocktail, premade and waiting.

'You're gross, woman,' I gibe jovially. 'We need to pace ourselves or we'll be home before eleven,' I add, giggling. Sabrina puts her finger up to volunteer an idea.

'Ahha, perhaps we change to the gin,' she says sounding a bit slurry already. Is this a good time to address the big elephant in the room perhaps? Ben.

'Sounds good to me. So, what did you think of Ben, honestly?' I can't believe it's taken me this long to ask her. Normally she is very forthcoming with her opinion but she hasn't said *anything* yet. I've even filled her in about Dublin and the official relationship conversation which I thought would prompt her, but still, nothing.

'Yeah, he seems okay,' she replies a bit too breezily. Hmm that sounds ominous. My heart sinks, I can't have my best friend not liking my man. That wasn't the plan.

'Just okay?'

'Yeah, on first impressions he seems okay. I mean he seems nice enough.' Just nice enough? That's disappointing. She's being very diplomatic for her, which worries me even more. 'But . . .'

Uh oh, here comes the truth…

'He's let you down quite a few times Ems, tonight included.' She taps her finger on the table to make a point.

'I know what you're saying, but it's difficult for him, he has kids and the mum is a bit absent. He's really lovely and I'm happy, Sab, happier than I've been in a long time,' I protest before slurping on my cocktail.

'Yes, I know my darling and I'm happy for you. I'm just over protective. You know me.' She chinks my glass as we both pick up the second of our two-for-one cocktails.

'I mean, he seemed quite sweet, but what's that thing with his eye?' Sabrina asks, screwing up her face disapprovingly.

'You mean his wink? Yeah, he always does that, it's so sexy but I think he does it more when he's nervous, bless him.' Poor Ben.

'I did wonder if he had a twitch or something. He was winky-wink-wink during the whole five minutes I met him.' Sabrina does a funny impression of him winking with bog eyes and I laugh, despite myself.

Poor guy. His wink was on overload tonight. Much more so than usual. Was he winking at Sabrina in *my* Dublin dress? She does look stunning, almost every guy in the bar is drooling over her. I sigh inwardly, then realise it escaped.

'Oh Em, I'm sure he is lovely, all I'm saying is be careful, you don't have to fall in love with the first guy you date. And do you really want someone who already has kids, because that just makes it so much more complicated, surely. Do you really want to play stepmother to two snotty brats who are instantly going to hate you? Because let's face it, they will, they all do at first,' Sabrina lectures and I feel my face burn in irritation.

'Yes, well we can't all have a perfect family like you,' I say, a little too bluntly. 'Anyway, *I've* got a kid.'

'Oh darling, please don't be cross, you wanted my opinion.'

'Yeah, I did. I just didn't expect it to be so harsh.'

We sit awkwardly in silence whilst we sip our cocktails. I'm hurt by her comments and her negativity towards Ben.

'You know, a friend should be pleased when her mate is happy, not try to shit all over it,' I say, staring into her beautifully made-up eyes.

'Ems, I'm not shitting on anything, I just want what's best for you.'

'Listen, you aren't my mother, Sabrina, so maybe as a friend you could just assume that I know what's best for me. I am a grown ass woman after all.'

'Right then, I have to tell you…' Sabrina starts.

'Hey gorgeous ladies, can I buy you both a drink?' A male voice chirps up, interrupting Sabrina mid-sentence.

'No thanks,' I say staring at Sabrina, not even looking to see who it is, we aren't interested, she's married and I'm with Ben.

'Sorry about him, Emily. Fancy seeing you here.' I look up and I'm surprised to see Jamie, of all people.

'Oh hi, Jamie, hi umm.' I look at his friend and smile.

'This is Tim, my housemate,' he nods towards his mate.

'Hi Tim,' I say, 'This is Sabrina.' The Tim guy isn't even listening to me, he's too busy drooling over her. Typical. I must have rolled my eyes because Jamie laughs.

'Just ignore him, dog on heat that one.' Jamie chuckles and Sabrina gives her award-winning smile whilst I try to do mine without showing my gums.

'What brings you out tonight then?' Jamie asks.

'Just had some free . . .' I begin before Sabrina interrupts.

'Her boyfriend let her down, again. So, we decided to come out on a girls' night, and you?' Bitch. I can't believe she's just said that.

'Too bad. We're out celebrating my innovation and excellence nomination. And where's your boyfriend then?' Tim boasts as he puffs his chest out at Sabrina.

'I'm married, hun.' Sabrina points to her ring and Tim smacks his palm against his forehead.

'DOH. Too bad. Well, we best get going, I've got to meet the rest of the gang for celebratory shots.' Tim nudges Jamie away.

'Yeah, sure mate.' It's Jamie's turn to roll his eyes now. I've heard about Tim and his gecko and he sounds like a character.

'Bye, bye.' Sabrina waves them away.

'See you later then, Emily. Have a goodnight, girls,' Jamie says sweetly.

'Yeah, you too Jamie, see you Monday.

Congratulations, Tim,' I reply.

'Cheers.' Jamie smiles.

It appears Tim can't wait to leave now Sabrina is not an option; he's now looking over our heads, scanning the distance. Jamie notices and smirks.

'Come on mate, let's get those shots down you. Bye girls.' Jamie puts his arm around Tim's shoulder and takes him off. I'm still watching when he looks back and waves. I wave back and consider calling a taxi.

'You have got to be joking me,' Sabrina says.

'What?'

'That's Lenny? *The* Lenny?'

'Yes Jamie, Jamie is Lenny. Why?' I frown.

'Now, *that* is lovely,' she states.

Jamie? Lovely?

'Really?' I ask, still angry with her and yet intrigued.

'Yes, *he* is lovely, gorgeous in fact and wow does he only have eyes for you, missy.' She means, he didn't fall over himself to talk to her.

'Oh, don't be stupid.' I scoff, feeling *so* ready to go home.

'No, really Em. You should have seen the way he looked at you, did you not see?' She looks at me like I'm an idiot, eyes wide.

'What? No!' I shake my head.

'Oh. My. God.' Sabrina puts her hand over her mouth as her eyes widen further.

'What, what is it?' I ask, suddenly worried.

'Lenny! *He* is the L!' Sabrina shrieks.

'What?' What is she going on about?

'Em, don't you see, Jamie is Lenny, Lenny is the L.'

'I don't follow,' I say flatly.

'From the psychic night, L for Lenny. *Jamie* is your true love,' Sabrina says slowly folding her arms, looking pleased with herself. Utter bullshit. What planet is she on? 'Two more porn star martinis please. Is it still happy hour?' Sabrina grins at me as she talks to the barman.

'Mate, no,' I plead.

'No what?' Sabrina says looking bewildered.

'I think I've had enough, I want to go home.'

I check the time when I get home and it's not even eleven. I was right, I knew this would happen. But I'm not drunk; I couldn't be more sober considering the amount I've drunk. I make myself a cup of tea and search for a load of chocolate biscuits to go with it before thinking back on this evening. Sabrina can be so harsh at times. I'm upset with her for criticising Ben. Even if she had those thoughts, she shouldn't have said them, at least not yet. Poor Ben, I look at the beautiful flowers he bought me and close my eyes, exhausted.

I wish he was here.

Jamie

We've only been in Vengeance five minutes, have just made it to the bar and ordered our drinks when Tim starts hitting on someone.

'Look at her. Yum,' he slurs.

'What. No.' I can't even be bothered to turn around and look.

'Don't worry, there's a cute one for you too.'

'Shut up.'

'Hey, gorgeous ladies, can I buy you both a drink?'

'Fuck's sake.' Why did I let myself be bullied into coming out with him? Now he's going to drunk-slobber all over some random woman. I turn around to apologise on his behalf and come face to face with

Emily.

She greets me, she's smiling. She looks lovely. I'm already forgiving her for the Dirk/Alan thing. It's not her fault. She's told Alan how it really was. I give her a big, friendly smile back.

Tim is leering at her friend, Sabrina, I think Emily introduced her as. She is a stunner but Tim is batting way out of his league. It's laughable. And, just as I feared he's drunk-slobbering all over her. Has he already forgotten his Lex?

Sabrina's polite in her brush off, tells him she's married and Emily has a boyfriend. That's us told.

Tim comes up with some lame line about us having to catch up with the gang. Gang. Ha. Mini-me Ian and Kev the python.

'You got to be joking, mate,' Tim babbles.

'What?' I haven't been listening to him but I think he's been wittering on all the time we've been moving away from Emily and her friend.

'That little girl you work with. Wow.'

'She's not a little girl, she's older than me. And she's my rival.'

'She's lovely. Just what you need.' He thrusts his elbow into my ribs and I push him away. He stumbles forward but manages to right himself and his drink. 'Hit a nerve, hit a nerve.'

'Fuck off.'

'If you don't want her, I'll have her.'

'Shut up now, you're embarrassing yourself.'

'No. Really.'

I don't answer, he's way too drunk to be reasonable.

'Well, the offer's there. If you don't want her, I'd be interested.'

'You're bloody delusional. Anyway, I thought you

fancied her friend. And what about your girlfriend?'

'Friend's married.' He nods at me as though he's just uncovered a secret. 'And me and Lex are just very good friends.' He winks. I could punch him.

'Yeah and Emily has a boyfriend.'

'Nah, not a problem. Not a problem. Not even a tiny little, weeny problem.'

'Shut up.'

I hope he has the biggest hangover in history.

Nineteen

Emily

'So, girls. Which one do you think? Black or Silver?' I ask Rosie and the babysitter. I'm holding up the black dress I bought for Dublin (and didn't wear, although Sabrina subsequently has) and an old silver dress I found at the back of my wardrobe. Sequins are in this season and they also must also have been in around seven years ago because that's when I would have bought it. I've already tried both of them on and performed the obligatory fashion show.

Now it's decision time.

'Hmmm I love the black, but the silver is *way* more Christmassy, I'd say silver for tonight. You look fab in both though.' I'm glad the babysitter said silver. There's a slightly bitter taste in my mouth about wearing the black one as that's the one Sabrina wore on our night *out* out. She looked way better in it than I ever could. She actually messaged me earlier to meet up soon. I'm stalling on my reply as I'm still a bit pissed off with her about her Ben comments. I feel a bit sad and sense I could do with a little break from Sabrina right now. She's my best mate so she should be happy for me, not trying to bring me down.

'Yes, yes, silver, Mummy. You will look like a princess at your Christmas party.' Rosie's eyes twinkle with love and admiration as she looks up at me, smiling from the sofa in her unicorn pyjamas. Seeing her little face like that makes me even more determined to be the best role model I can be for her.

And I think *tonight* is setting an extra special example.

'Ahh stop, you two are both too cute. Silver it is then. Never thought I'd be asking *you* for advice on dresses, life is funny hey,' I say to the babysitter. Tiny.

'It sure is,' she says brightly with a huge smile as she hugs Rosie to her.

That's right *Tiny*. Yes. Tiny is babysitting tonight in my house whilst I attend my work Christmas party.

Never in my wildest nightmares would I have imagined the woman my husband was having an affair with would be babysitting for me in my house years later, however it now makes perfect sense. She knows Rosie and Rosie adores her. Mum also couldn't do it, she's out on a date night with Dad so I asked Tiny and she jumped at the chance as she doesn't have Tiger Lily tonight and Liam's out on *his* work do. It's so nice of her to babysit here as it means I don't have to worry about picking Rosie up from anywhere in my hungover state tomorrow morning.

Tiny and I actually get on well, she is really rather nice and I never thought I'd hear myself say this, but I can see what Liam sees in her. She's kind, caring and very sweet. In the way of stepmothers, Rosie could do a lot worse, so I'm feeling grateful. Even Liam's attitude has changed towards me recently and he has almost welcomed mine and Tiny's newfound friendship. It's much easier when everyone gets along and more importantly, much nicer for Rosie, my angel.

'That's my taxi. Rosie be good for Tiny, will you. I'll see you in the morning,' I say as I grab my bag and shimmy into my coat by the front door.

'Oh, she's always good, aren't you sweetheart,' coos Tiny as I bend down and give Rosie a kiss goodbye.

'Cheers, Tiny, thanks again. I'll be home way before midnight I should think.' The taxi driver impatiently beeps his horn as I'm finishing saying my goodbyes, no doubt eager to pick up his next Christmas party fare.

'No rush, Cinderella, have an amazing time, see you later.' Tiny chuckles as she squeezes Rosie in close, Rosie rubs her eyes, clutches her cuddly bear. My angel is so tired, I bet she'll be asleep before I've even arrived at the venue.

'Bye, Mummy, love you,' she says sleepily.

'Love you too poppet, bye bye.' They wave goodbye and I look back to see Tiny close the front door before I rush over to the taxi, climbing in and plonking myself down in the backseat. I feel weirdly excited and slightly nervous. I look out of the window at the pretty Christmas lights that people have decorated their houses with. I truly love this time of year but something's missing.

Ben.

He should be here tonight as my guest but he has his own Christmas work do to attend. Sod's law it's the same night as mine. Never mind, let's not let that dampen my Christmas spirit. It could be the couple of glasses of prosecco I've had that have made me all giddy but I can't stop a smile creeping across my face. I wonder what tonight has in store? There is always *so* much shit going down at Christmas work parties, especially in big companies like Genevre.

Jamie

'I'm really not looking forward to tonight. Really not.'

I'm standing in the kitchen buffing up my smart black shoes while Tim whips himself up some mashed potato and cream cheese concoction to go with his tinned spaghetti hoops. I think I prefer it when he orders in. There are pans and bowls everywhere and the microwave seems to have been on full pelt for the whole ten minutes I've been in the kitchen.

'Don't go then,' Tim says, as though it's that easy.

'I have to. It would look odd.'

Tim shrugs. Looking odd never comes into anything he does or says. He *is* odd, he either doesn't know, or care, or just embraces it.

'I have to.'

'Then go.' He adds another shrug before dolloping an immense blob of butter into his bubbling hot spaghetti hoops. I could make a comment about fat and cholesterol but he's already told me I'm turning into a health freak bore. 'It's free, isn't it?'

'Yeah.' Genevre's staff Christmas party is free to all staff and all staff are expected to go, not that anyone actually says that. It's not obligatory, but it sort of is. If you want to take a guest you have to pay for them. I'd ordered a ticket for Beth but fortunately, before I paid for it, I was able to cancel it after she dumped me. After I'd cancelled it, Tim informed me he would have gone in her place. He's heard *good things* about Genevre's Christmas parties. Good things in Tim's world means excess. Too much free booze and food. That's why I'm not participating in Tim's culinary delight now.

He starts to slop it out onto a plate. There's too much and he catches me watching as the cheesy potato collapses under its own weight and spreads to the edge of the plate.

'Sure you don't want some? There's plenty. Line your stomach.'

'No, thanks. There's a three-course meal.'

'Yeah, probably better than my efforts.' He laughs. He doesn't give a shit. 'What you wearing?'

'What?'

'What are you wearing, to the do?'

'Suit.' I fish around in my bag for the ticket. 'Dinner or lounge suit,' I read out. 'So, my suit.' I've even ironed a white shirt and borrowed a darkish tie from my dad. Not black, not his funeral tie.

'I've got a dinner suit you can borrow. Probably fit you now.'

I'm not sure how to reply to that, Tim and I are both tall but there the similarities end. He's skinny with a BIG pot belly and double chin – quite a weird combination. I'm broad all over, although I am thinner than I was. I can't imagine any world where's Tim's dinner suit would fit me.

'Thanks,' I mutter.

'Offer's there if you want it. It's all still in the dry cleaner's bag, shirt too. And dickie. Doesn't fit me anymore.' He laughs and I join in before heading off upstairs to the shower.

Twenty minutes later and I'm scrutinising my reflection in the mirror. It's only a few months since I last wore this suit; I had it on for my interviews at Genevre. It was a good fit. Now it bags around the backside and the shoulders slope off down towards my elbows, I do up all three buttons. I still look like I'm wearing someone else's suit.

Downstairs I find Tim digging into a second plate of

his sloppy food as I walk past him to retrieve my shoes.

'What the fuck are you?' He roars with laughter.

'What?' I snap. I'm already feeling shit about tonight, about my suit, about the whole *no job after Christmas* scenario so I don't need any crap from him.

'You look like…' he stops when I turn and stare at him. 'Just saying…' he mutters before stuffing another forkful of mash into his mouth.

'Just saying what?' I stand and wait for him to reply.

'Suit's a bit big.' He doesn't even look at me.

'Not that bad.' I turn, walk away to find my shoes.

'Have you seen your arse?'

'What?' He's really pissing me off now.

'I mean, you look like you haven't got one. It's lost in the folds.'

'Ha, bloody ha.'

'Try mine on.' He plonks his half full plate on the coffee table, gets up and urges me up the stairs. 'It's a good one.'

Knowing how Tim lives in grunge t-shirts and washed out, crumpled cargos, I doubt that very much.

Nevertheless, I find myself in his bedroom, the wardrobe door flung open while he locates the suit, and all under the watchful eye of a tongue-flicking Delilah.

'Just try the jacket first.' He rips the dry cleaner's plastic off and holds the jacket up.

I slip my own off, though to be more accurate it falls off once I undo the buttons.

It looks good. It looks amazing. It fits. It's smart and modern and fashionable. I turn to admire myself in the mirror, the slim fit jacket just emphasising the bagging of my own trousers.

'Here.' Tim flings the pants at me.

Under his, and Delilah's scrutiny I change into them.

'They're too long,' I say, sounding sulky and feeling shit about myself, about Tim, about the suit. But, mostly about having to go tonight. What's the point when I won't even be there after Christmas.

'Put your shoes on.'

I follow his order and I have to admit I look good. The shoes lift the trousers perfectly.

'Shirt and tie,' he says, handing them over. The shirt is still in a box with the name of the dry cleaners emblazoned across it.

'You sent your shirt to the cleaners?' I can't quite believe this.

'Yeah. They didn't dry clean it, they washed it.'

'You sent your shirt to the cleaners so they could wash it?' This is even more unbelievable.

'Yeah. Long story. I didn't pay, someone else did.' He gives a dismissive shrug and I decide not to pursue that one. 'Is that fit Emily going to be there?' He grins at me.

'Dunno.' I know full well that she will be.

'Well, offer still stands, if you don't want her…' He lets the words trail away because he can see the look of disgust on my face. 'Do you want a lift?'

'No. Thanks. I'm going to drive.'

'What? With all that free booze?'

'Yeah, I'm not planning on drinking.' My plan is eat, smile, stay for the speeches – yes there are speeches from the CEO and the FD – then I'll slip away once the entertainment starts.

Tim snorts. 'Mate, I'll give you a lift. You don't want to lose your driving licence.'

Emily

I turn up and realise I'm a little early, the nerves have

well and truly set in now *but* I haven't taken any Kalms. The old Emily would most definitely be hiding in the loos gobbling down a few Kalms or even more likely . . . not even turn up to the party.

Not the new Emily.

I'm going to force myself to seek out someone to socialise with. I'm just debating on which direction to go in and who to talk to when I'm saved by a familiar voice.

'Emily, *omg* you look fabulous! Like a modern-day Cinderella. You *shall* go to the ball!' Jayden takes my hand and kisses it like a Disney prince before twirling me around.

I love him.

'Aww thanks, Jayden, I must say you look ever so dashing too, good enough to be a prince, I'd say'

'Thank you so much, sweets,' Jayden chirps graciously before he takes a bow.

'And are you going to introduce me . . .' I ask, smiling as I motion to the young man standing next to him.

'Oh, of course, let me introduce you to Sasha, my boyfriend.' Jayden proudly puffs out his chest as he swings an arm around his boyfriend. Sasha beams back at him before turning to me, showing his impressive big white shiny teeth.

'Hello, very pleased to meet you Emily, you do look beautiful,' Sasha agrees, still beaming.

'Thank you very much, that's very kind,' I say as I look down bashfully, a little embarrassed by all the compliments but also secretly enjoying them.

'And what are *we* in the Disney world darling? Don't you dare say the ugly sisters. I just won't have it!' Sasha puts his hands on his hips and pouts like a professional before shaking his head and waggling his finger from side to side. Jayden and I both giggle at Sasha and I catch a look in Jayden's eye that makes my heart melt.

He really likes this guy.

'No, no we most definitely won't be the ugly sisters darling but we...' Jayden pauses mid-sentence, distracted, staring over my head. 'But I tell you what, *there* is the *real* prince,' he continues. Sasha and I watch Jayden's jaw drop further as our eyes follow the direction of his pointed finger.

It's Jamie and he looks just as Jayden described, a handsome prince. Jayden covers his mouth with his hand and squeezes Sasha in tight with the other. They both air kiss me goodbye, making their excuses about having to make the most of the free booze before sauntering off together.

Well, I guess I should go and say hello then.

Jamie

'Hey,' Emily calls, waving at me across the busy hotel foyer. I've just checked my coat in and I'm stuffing the ticket into one of the many pockets in Tim's rather impressive suit.

I smile in her direction before taking a hasty glance behind me in case it's not me she's calling to. I've been caught like that before.

'You look smart,' she says, running a hand over my sleeve. 'Smart suit.' I think she's already started on the free booze because she seems far more familiar than usual, then I realise she can't have yet, so she must have had some Dutch courage before she came out.

'Thanks. You look lovely too.' It sounds so fake and forced, but she does look lovely. She's wearing a little silver dress that shows off her curves. It has long sleeves but her shoulders are exposed.

'Yeah?' She sounds unsure, but she could just be fishing for compliments. 'I couldn't decide between this dress and another.' She rolls her eyes theatrically. 'I'm glad I saw you. Didn't want to go up on my own.'

'No,' I agree, then, unexpectedly I offer her my arm, and she takes it.

We trot along to the lift and head up to the third floor where the ballroom is.

'I've never been in this hotel before,' Emily confides. 'Nice, isn't it?'

'Yeah.' We're alone in the lift, which, given how many people were in the foyer is surprising. It feels odd and intimate.

'Have you been here before?' Emily has definitely been at the booze.

'Err, yeah. I came to a wedding a while back.' I'm about to say that I wore the same suit but catch sight of myself in the lift mirror wearing Tim's suit before I do.

'Sounds nice.'

'It was. From what I can remember.'

'Ooo, did you drink too much?'

'I might have,' I admit just as the lift stops and a disembodied voice tells us the doors are opening.

'I have to confess I had a couple before I came out. Did you?'

I don't answer straightaway because I'm considering my response. If I say yes, that'll be a lie, if I say no, Emily is going to feel foolish.

'Come on, let's get ourselves a glass of fizz,' I say instead. We head for the welcoming drinks tables and I congratulate myself on not having to lie or embarrass Emily. I'm also surprised to find that she is still attached to me, clutching my arm as though we are together.

Drinks in hand we drift off to the noticeboard where the table plans are displayed. We've already seen them in the office and know that we're sitting with the rest of our team but, judging by the number of people milling around the easels we're not alone in checking.

'We're on that one, right down the bloody front.' A finger, nail painted a glossy blood-red, stabs at the plan. A little drink sloshes from the glass she's holding. Emily and I turn to see Sharon's slightly angry face; she's holding a drink in her other hand too. 'And, yes, these are both for me,' she says, knocking one back in one go.

'Hi Sharon,' Emily says, ignoring Sharon's anger.

'Yeah. Hi.' She knocks back the other drink then looks around for somewhere to discard her empty glasses. 'I bet Dirk put us there. Arse.' She narrows her eyes at our still linked arms and then, without another word heads off in the direction of the welcoming drinks table.

'Surely she's not going to get another one,' Emily giggles into my ear.

'Who knows.' I don't really care. I check the table plan, confirming that Emily will be sat directly across from me. Part of me is pleased about that, part of me, oddly, is not. And I'm definitely not happy about her sitting next to Dirk. If Sharon is to be believed he had influence over the table plans, even though he told us he didn't, which means he put himself next to Emily.

Another nail in my coffin regarding my career prospects at Genevre. And I'm sat next to Sharon, who I can already see has two fresh drinks in her hands.

Emily and I are the last to arrive at the table, I don't

even know why. We haven't had any more drinks, we haven't been anywhere else, I really don't know what we've been doing other than chatting. Emily confessed to me that she felt nervous about tonight. And excited. I've assured her she doesn't need to worry. She also said she was anxious about sitting next to Dirk, worried she might say something unpleasant if he gets a bit too forward. She doesn't trust him after the drinks evening scam, where he cancelled me at the last minute.

More to reassure her than because I think Dirk would be stupid enough to do anything at the company Christmas party, we've agreed a distress signal. If she asks me to pass the water that means she wants me to rescue her from Dirk. I'm not sure what form the rescue will take but the plan seems to reassure Emily.

The table is impressive, a mass of white linen, silver cutlery and sparkling glass. I escort Emily to her seat before finding my own.

'Hi again,' Sharon says as I sit down next to her. She has a half empty bottle of white wine in front of her and a full glass in her hand. 'What?' she says, seeing me notice. 'There's plenty for everyone and if we run out, they'll bring more.' She takes a swig just to make her point.

'I didn't say anything,' I say defensively, even if I was thinking it.

'Yeah, well, it was written all over your face.'

Great, I'm sitting next to an angry, heavy drinking Sharon, who doesn't particularly mince her words when sober. On my other side is Jayden, he's brought his boyfriend Sasha with him. After a very brief introduction Jayden turns his back on me and puts his head close to Sasha's. Apparently, they haven't been together long and are very much in love. I look up and catch Emily's eye. She gives me a complicit smile.

The food is good and since I'm now very hungry I concentrate on eating it. I notice Sharon plays with hers but manages to empty the wine bottle and reaches for another from the centre of the table. She waves the empty bottle in the air and within seconds it's removed and two full ones appear.

'See,' she says to me. 'Told you.'

'I never said anything,' I mutter.

It's going to be a long evening.

By the time we get to the dessert course everyone has had enough wine to be happy, except Sharon, who despite the copious amount of wine she's knocked back definitely isn't happy.

Karen has brought her husband, and Hayden has brought his girlfriend. So the only singletons on the table are Dirk, Emily, Sharon and me.

Once the dessert course is cleared away the waiters rush around filling our glasses.

'Urgh, it's speech time,' Sharon groans. 'But it's also toast time.' She raises her glass.

'Shush, Sharon,' Jayden says. 'Someone will hear you.'

'That's not my fault, is it? I didn't put us on a table at the front.' Sharon glares over at Dirk who returns her look with one of steely defiance, before turning and smiling sweetly at Emily. If I didn't know better, I'd think he was making a point.

Hang on, I don't know better.

'What's going on?' I ask Sharon, thinking she's had enough to drink to either enlighten me or tell me where to go.

'Don't ask me. Ask him.' She nods her head at Dirk who's now deep in conversation with Emily. 'Or your girlfriend. Huh.' She follows this with a large swig.

'She's not my girlfriend,' I mutter. This really isn't a conversation I want to have.

Across the table I see Emily reach for her own wine glass; she's drinking red. So am I. She's listening to Dirk who seems to be whispering in her ear.

The CEO's voice is piped through loudspeakers as he delivers a rabble-rousing speech and at the end, we're all invited to toast a good year and future success. I can hardly bring myself to repeat the toast. It makes no difference to me what Genevre's future plans are, does it?

The financial director comes on and talks numbers for five solid minutes. Sharon yawns and makes no attempt to stifle it. Across the table Dirk glowers at her. She grins back at him.

I wonder how long it will be before I can make my escape. Soon, I hope.

I catch Emily's eye and we exchange glances. She hasn't had to use our secret code so that, at least, is something.

The music strikes up and acrobats come on, juggling and bouncing around.

'Wow,' Sasha says. 'I love this stuff.'

'Gawd,' Sharon slurs. 'I want vodka. I'm going to the bar.'

The whole table breathes a sigh of relief as Sharon stumbles off in search of vodka.

'Someone's not very happy,' Sasha says.

'Well, some might say she has good reason to be miserable this Christmas', Karen cuts in.

I don't know what they're talking about and I don't think I want to. I'll check Sharon's okay tomorrow at work; she should be sober by then.

On come the aerial acrobats, tumbling from the ceiling on unfurling red ribbons, spinning and twirling high above our heads. It's quite a spectacle. They're followed by a pair of male fire-eaters clad in nothing but silver budgie smugglers, they have six packs solid enough to intimidate even Dirk.

A woman comes on with a metal breastplate and an angle grinder; as the sparks fly, I wonder what the purpose of her act is. It's scary and dangerous but I don't get it.

Suddenly Emily is sitting in Sharon's seat.

'Hey,' I say, surprised.

'Dirk's gone to the loo so I thought I'd take the opportunity to escape him.' She's brought her wine glass and a full bottle of red.

'Everything okay?'

'Yeah, he was just prattling on about his body building.' She drops her voice to imitate Dirk's low growl. 'This is my very last blowout before I get back to serious training.'

I can't help laughing.

'I don't get this act, do you?' Emily nods at the angle grinder just as sparks shower the air.

'No, I don't,' I agree. 'Looks dangerous though.'

'There's dancing after this.'

'Yeah. I think I'm going to make my escape then.'

'Really. You're not going to boogie all night?'

'Not really me.'

'But weren't you shaking your stuff last weekend when I saw you out with your mate?'

'Not really.' Surely she hadn't seen me. 'I'd had way too much to drink that night.'

'Oh dear.' Emily tops up her glass then leans over and tops up mine. I can smell her perfume, feel the warmth of her body. I slowly pull myself away. 'Everything okay?' Emily asks, frowning.

'Yeah. Fine. Good.'

'Before you go, at least have one dance with me. Save me from Dirk. He says he wants to mark my dance card, whatever that means.'

'I think he's been watching too many period dramas. My mum used to love them, I've seen bits. Women had little cards and men would ask to put their names against dances.'

Emily laughs. 'Listen to you.'

'Yeah. Sorry. I don't get out much.'

'Must be especially tough at this time of year.' She doesn't say anymore but I know she's talking about my mum.

I nod silently.

'Please stay and have a couple of dances with me so that Dirk doesn't.'

In the distance I can see Dirk weaving his way back across the ballroom. I can see him mouthing 'Heys,' to people, waving and even saluting as he passes the directors' table. What a tosser.

'Okay. Just a couple.'

In the end I stay much longer than I intend to. I dance several times with Emily and I drink far, far too much, as does Emily. Sharon, however, surpasses us all and dances a few merry jigs on her own in the middle of the dance floor.

Emily and I finish dancing a fast one which is followed by a slow one, we look at each other and head back to our table.

Sharon is asleep – or she could be dead, it's hard to tell – slumped in her chair.

'She all right?' I ask Karen.

'Not really. She's drunk and with good cause. I just hope she hasn't done anything silly.'

'What like dancing?' I joke.

Karen gives me a quick, mock smile that slides into a sneer.

'What's wrong with Sharon?' Emily asks, following Karen's cue.

'Well, let's just say that she's been used and abused and discarded.'

'Oh, right.' Emily leans over and pats unconscious Sharon's hand.

'And now she's looking for revenge. I just hope it's not too late.'

'Too late?' I ask, because even I can tell that Karen is bursting to tell us.

'Yes.'

'In what way?' Emily asks, feeding Karen the line she needs to tell us more.

'Let's just say that she's in possession of a video that could ruin someone's career and reputation if they don't start treating her properly. As I said, I just hope it's not too late.'

'What video? Who?' Emily looks as though she's enjoying the gossip.

Karen taps her nose and smiles, then draws her pinched fingers across her mouth, suggesting her lips are sealed.

'Let's dance,' Karen's husband says, and grabs his wife's hand to pull her up.

Emily tops up our glasses and we both take large gulps. I feel I am going to pay for this in the morning, but I'm actually quite enjoying myself, even if I am spending too much time with my rival.

Seconds later Sharon lets out a long groan and

slumps down, her head falling forward and onto the table.

'Do you think she's okay?' Emily shakes Sharon's shoulder. 'Sharon, Sharon, are you okay.'

A long groan escapes Sharon's mouth.

'I think I'll take her home. I know where she lives.' Emily starts looking around for Sharon's handbag. 'Could you help me get her downstairs then the hotel can order a taxi.'

'Course I can. In fact, if you don't mind, I might join you in the taxi. I've had enough of this.'

Emily narrows her eyes.

'No. I mean, it's been fun dancing with you and everything…' Oh just shut up.

Emily starts to laugh and nudges me.

'Come on, let's get this sleeping beauty home.'

And that's how I come to be alone in the back of a taxi with Emily after we manhandled Sharon into her house and into bed and left her with a glass of water and a bucket which Emily found under the kitchen sink.

'I hope she's okay,' Emily says.

'Me too.'

'Not how I expected the evening to go. To be honest I didn't really want to go, just felt I had to.'

'Me too,' I agree. 'And when my suit didn't fit, I really didn't want to go.'

'Your suit looks fantastic. You look really fit. Oh.' Emily puts her hand over her mouth and giggles.

'Not this suit.' I giggle now. It's as though now we've discharged out duty of looking after Sharon, all the alcohol we've slowly consumed is catching up with us. 'This is Tim's.'

'What, Tim you were out with last weekend?'

'Yeah.'

'No.' She shakes her head and giggles some more.

'Yes.' I nod my head vigorously just as we go over a speed bump.

Suddenly we're jostled together, face to face, eye to eye, mouth to mouth.

Oh God, I am so going to pay for this in the morning, but for now I am enjoying every tiny little second.

Twenty

Emily

It's Friday morning, the morning after the night before. The Christmas Party was truly amazing, and it ended in the most unexpected way.

Jamie and I kissed.

We must have been swept along and caught up in the mood of it all. Although it was oddly nice, I'm feeling gut wrenchingly guilty. Right now, I really want to call Sabrina but I fear she'd tell me to get rid of Ben which is not what I *need* or want to hear. An image of her imitating Ben winking pops into my mind, and I frown to make it go away.

His winking is endearing, not annoying.

Padding into the office, I sit myself down at my desk, nursing a takeaway coffee and a couple of painkillers. No Kalms today. I'm going cold turkey. This is going to be a *long* day. Why oh why do they hold Christmas parties on a Thursday?

'Hey, Emily, good night at the party?' Karen eyes me shiftily from behind her computer. Does she know about the kiss? Do they all know? How could they?

'Hi Karen, yes, it was great, wasn't it? Jamie and I

ended up taking Sharon home. Bless her, she was a little worse for wear. How about you?' I ask, feeling bad for gossiping about Sharon to distract the attention away from me. Although it was no secret that Sharon was definitely a little worse for wear, and that's putting it politely.

She was utterly shit faced.

'Yes, poor Sharon, it's all going to come out in the wash eventually, probably sooner rather than later,' warns Karen, tapping her nose.

'What's that?' I ask, eager to know what she's talking about, yet trying my best to sound casual.

'It'll come out soon I'm sure, I just hope she didn't do anything too stupid,' Karen says more to herself than me as she pushes her glasses up her nose. She jumps, suddenly getting distracted by something on her screen and begins to type frantically.

'Bacon sarnnniesssss, Bacon sarrrniiesssss!' Jayden sings as he bustles through the door. His eyes are blood shot, he still looks pissed. 'Bacon sarnies for everyone! Merrrry Christmasss.'

My mouth waters as Jayden begins to dish them out around the office.

'Not for me lovely, I can't eat the next day, makes me sick.' Karen turns green as he sticks it under her nose. Jayden sticks his bottom lip out and bats his eyelids.

'Wow, thanks mate, just what the doctor ordered. I'm hanging, I'll have Karen's.' Hayden chuckles, helping himself to Karen's, much to her relief. 'Got any tommy k mate?'

'What am I? The bloody office waiter?'

Hayden nods his head smiling like an expectant puppy dog as he enthusiastically takes a bite of his bacon roll.

'Of course I do sir, I wouldn't forget *that* now, would I?' Jayden smiles before throwing several tomato ketchup sachets at Hayden, one of them hits him in the eye. Everyone laughs and Karen spits her coffee out. Jayden knows how to brighten the office, especially one with a communal hangover.

'Ah, Jamie, just the man.' Jayden trots over to him as he walks through the door. My stomach drops at the sound of his name and then again at the sight of him. 'Just in time, I got you two because you're a big guy, I mean they're only little and you're tall, not big, oh you know what I mean,' splutters Jayden, digging himself deeper and deeper. Jamie catches my eye and gives me the sweetest of smiles.

'Yes, Jayden, I know what you mean. I'm not a fat git anymore but I'm still a unit so I might be needing two.' He grins, patting Jayden on the shoulder with one of his large hands.

'You're not big, Jamie, sorry. You look fabulous,' Jayden simpers.

'These look amazing. Thank you.'

'My pleasure.' Jayden smiles from under his eyelashes.

'*Get in my belly,*' roars Jamie in a fake Scottish accent, causing the whole office to giggle, before feasting silently on their much-needed hangover grease.

'Did you see Susan from accounts getting off with the apprentice? I mean, I knew she was a maneater but a boy eater too?' Jayden claps his hand over his mouth as though he didn't mean that piece of information to escape. The gossip master.

'Yes, I know, so bad,' agrees Karen, still looking a little green but perkier than before.

'I wonder who Dirk went home with, he always pulls at the Christmas party,' Hayden joins in, smirking and unaware that he has tomato ketchup on his lip.

'Hang on a minute, where's Sharon?' I interrupt. 'Has anyone heard from her?' I'm met with blank stares.

'Don't worry, I'll text her, see if she's okay.' Karen pulls out her phone.

'Okay, let me know once you hear from her, Karen. Maybe I'll give her a ring if we don't hear from her within the next hour,' I say, exchanging furtive looks with Jamie. I hope she's okay.

An hour goes by and still no word from Sharon. I pad over to the meeting room, making sure I close the door before I make the call. She picks up almost immediately, which I'm both surprised at and relieved by.

'Hello.' Her voice sounds exceptionally hoarse, which I guess is normal for a monster hangover.

'Hi Sharon, I just wanted to check you were okay as you're not here and I haven't heard from you. Everyone is worried.'

'It's not Sharon, it's her sister. Well she's been better. Are you her manager?' That explains the hoarse voice then.

'Yes, it's Emily. I just wanted to check she was all right. Myself and another colleague took her home last night,' I explain.

'Ah right, thank you, she says thank you for that.'

'Could I speak to her please?' I ask. There's a pause and some clomping heavy footsteps and then her sister answers again. This time in a hushed husky voice.

'Listen Emily, she's in a right state, she won't be coming in today. I hope that's all right.'

'Okay,' I say slowly while thinking carefully about what to say next. Perhaps now is not the time to recite company policy about phoning in sick, especially to her sister who quite frankly doesn't sound like she'll give a shit.

'Yep, she thinks she's had an allergic reaction to the alcohol.'

I almost laugh but stop myself; an allergic reaction to the *amount* of alcohol, more like.

'She'll be in Monday though, Emily,' her sister offers.

'Okay, thank you, umm?'

'Tracey.'

'Thanks, Tracey. Tell her to get well soon and we'll catch up on Monday.' Tracey is not the one to be having that conversation with, I'll have a chat with Sharon myself. The main thing is she's okay, she's alive, and she hasn't inhaled her own vomit in her sleep.

Everyone is saying how out of character it was of her . . .apart from Karen. She knows exactly what's going on. I get a flash back to the party of Karen mentioning that Sharon had been wronged and may be seeking her revenge. I need to find out what that's about. As I walk back into the office, the team, including Jamie are huddled around Jayden's desk. Karen is practically screaming hysterically, in terror or amusement or both, Jayden's laughing like a hyena and Hayden has his hands over his eyes as he occasionally peers through his fingers to see whatever they are watching. Jamie has his hands on his head, rubbing his temples.

'Urgh God, this is so rank,' moans Hayden through his fingers.

'I can't watch anymore, turn it off,' Karen squawks

yet her eyes stay glued to whatever they are watching on Jayden's phone before letting out another scream.

'You've already seen it, you'll know all the moves off by heart soon,' Jayden teases Karen as she smacks him on the arm. 'The lipstick. Best bit,' he snickers, staring at the screen.

'Really? That's the best bit, have you seen what he has on his feet?' Hayden giggles.

'Yeah, best turn it off mate. He could come in at any minute and then we're busted,' Jamie reminds everyone, not impressed.

'What's going on?' I ask as I walk over to see what all the commotion's about. The team all jump out of their seats, including Jamie.

'Told you it would come out sooner or later,' Karen gloats, folds her arms and sets her mouth in a straight line.

Bingo. The secret is finally out.

'Let's see what all the fuss is about then,' I say to Jayden.

Smirking, he eagerly hands over his phone. My retinas burn.

It's Dirk. In all his (none) glory.

'*I Put a Spell on Youuuuu, Now You're Minneee,*' he mimes into the camera as the music blares out in the background. Dirk's big smarmy face is pushed up close to the screen. The camera slowly pans out to reveal his outfit, or lack thereof.

Apart from a tiny red thong, he's wearing thigh-high, red PVC boots and devil horns. His lips are a glittery bright red and he's clutching a devil's fork. Standing with his legs wide apart, Dirk strenuously tenses his abs to show off his chiselled eight pack. He blows kisses and raises his eyebrows to the camera several times before licking his lips and grinning. His eyes roll back in ecstasy. He has lipstick on his teeth – somebody should have told him.

Using the fork to slowly point to various areas on his body, he takes time to focus on his impressive abs, pointing to each individual ripple. Licking his lips and rolling his eyes, it's pure enjoyment. He's in his element, basking in self-love and appreciation. Dirk's huge bed can be seen in the background, above which hangs a giant canvas of…Dirk.

My toes curl as he slowly turns around, gyrating his hips to the music. He's relishing every minute whilst his boots squeak loudly, continuing to mime to the song with enthusiasm, *'You better stop the things you doooooooo, I tell ya I ain't lying.'*

Dirk stops with his arse facing the screen then violently thrusts, using his fork to spank his buttocks, leaving big, red marks. With a few more energetic thrusts and spanks, he propels himself forward onto his luxurious black silk sheets. He's on all fours, sideways to the camera and arching his back like a cat. His bum pops up then down, up, down, up into the air. He's flexible.

He certainly wasn't this flexible in yoga.

Dirk's portrait grins smugly down on him, grading his performance a ten out of ten. As if it couldn't get any worse, the thong so tiny, very little is left to the imagination. He is clearly aroused by his own dancing. I've seen enough.

'Here, have it back,' I squeal, quickly passing the phone to Jayden.

'So bad,' he smirks.

'Who sent it to you?' I ask.

'Sasha. Someone at his work sent it to him,

apparently it's gone viral,' he says with wide eyes.

'Sharon may have sent it to a few people when she was drunk last night,' Karen joins in, knowing full well there is no *may* about it.

'Yeah, unfortunately I've already seen it,' Jamie adds. 'My flat mate had been sent it as well, he stayed up to show it to me last night,' he says, pulling a face.

'Nice little image for you before bed,' I laugh, winking at him, forgetting myself.

'Yes. I can think of better images.' He grins back at me. The kiss, he's thinking of the kiss.

'What I want to know is why did Sharon have this video and why is she sending it to everyone?' Jayden asks Karen.

'I'll let her explain that,' Karen replies curtly. She isn't giving anything anyway, I guess we'll all just have to wait until Monday.

If Sharon turns up.

Jamie

I'd already seen that video because I caught Tim sniggering over it on his phone when I got home from the Christmas party. When I asked what he was giggling at he waved his phone around and tried to show me, but I was more interested in making myself a sobering cup of coffee and collecting my thoughts after what had happened in the taxi. Thank God Emily's friend was there babysitting her daughter or who knows where it might have led? Who am I kidding? Emily has a boyfriend. It was just a silly drunken kiss.

It meant nothing.

Who am I kidding?

'Here,' Tim called. 'You can see it better now.'

I wandered back into the lounge and was met by

Dirk's rippling eight pack spread across my TV in ultra-high definition as he mimed to *I Put a Spell on You*. I stared in shock and horror.

'I thought we'd get a better view on there,' Tim sniggered.

'Where did you get that from?'

'It's everywhere online.' Tim laughed loudly. 'He's local too. Poor sod. Stupid sod.' More laughter. 'Hey, you don't know him, do you?'

I didn't answer. I couldn't.

'I'll play it again. You missed the beginning.'

'Please don't,' I pleaded, but he did and I watched it. Spellbound.

I almost felt sorry for Dirk. How could he have allowed anyone to film him like that.

Dirk didn't come to work today.

Neither did Sharon.

Everyone is putting two and two together, except Karen who sits tight-lipped and smug, full of secrets and knowledge.

Emily
It's Monday and my meeting with Sharon is imminent, I hope she's okay and has a good explanation for her absence on Friday. Confrontation really isn't my favourite. Smiling is my favourite, I think in true *Elf* style. Well, it is nearly Christmas. Jamie is in early and his head is down and buried in his work as I approach my desk. Wow, he is dedicated. Feeling a prickle of admiration for him my stomach joins in the appreciation by doing continuous somersaults, I wish it would stop doing that.

'Hi, Jamie.' He doesn't look up. 'Hi, Jamie,' I repeat

a little louder. Oh hell, this is so awkward. I feel my face turning red so I try to picture someone slapping the colour out of my cheeks with ice cold hands, I was once told it works and now it's become a habit to use this technique every time I blush. Actually, I think it was Sabrina who told me this trick. I sigh inwardly as I think of my friend. Her message is still unanswered on my phone so I make a mental note to call her later. It's Christmas, I can't stay mad with her forever.

'Oh, hi, Emily. Sorry, I was miles away.' His lovely face looks up at me and as I step a bit closer, I notice his head wasn't buried in work at all but he's sifting through the Argos catalogue. He must see me looking as it's then his turn to turn red. Quite a vibrant shade too.

'Ah, busted.' He grimaces. 'I'm trying to figure out what to get Dad for Christmas, struggling a bit, hence the help of Argos,' he continues. Nothing like leaving it to the last minute, typical man. It makes me smile but I don't comment, no need to embarrass him further.

'What's he into?' I ask, eventually.

'Umm, not much really, he's just a normal guy. I really have no idea.'

Poor Jamie, he looks hopeless, I bet he really wants to spoil his dad too, what with him being on his own.

'Why don't you take him somewhere then, people remember and appreciate experiences way more than things. That's what I try to do with Rosie.'

'You reckon?' he asks, stroking his stubble.

'Yeah, she won't remember all the toys she had when she was five but she may remember going to the cinema with me and eating ice cream until we felt sick. That's not to say I don't buy her toys, because I do, I just try not to spend a fortune on unnecessary junk.' I don't want him thinking I'm a total scrooge.

'That's an amazing idea, I could take him to see his favourite football team play, he'd love that.' Jamie grins, looking up at me with eyes twinkling. He has the most unusual eye colour, they're really quite striking. It was too dark to see in the taxi and before that I'd never noticed, or I suppose, cared. Caught off guard by my own thoughts and conscious of my staring into his eyes like a freak, I look away at my watch.

The meeting with Sharon is soon.

'Result, my work here is done.' I beam and to my horror show all of my gums. It's not my best smile. My stomach then somersaults again, it's really not playing ball.

'Thanks, Em. Rosie is lucky to have you as a mum. I owe you for this, maybe I can buy you a drink sometime to say thanks.' He looks up at me in anticipation, biting his bottom lip.

'Yep, sounds good, I never turn down a drink with a good friend.' Oooh that sounds harsh. I want to immediately take it back but it's too late. Jamie looks crestfallen. Why did I say that?

'Yeah friends, of course,' he murmurs into his coffee without looking at me. I feel like the biggest bitch on the planet. It's time to change the subject.

'Well, I best get on. Sharon will be here soon; do you want to sit in on the meeting?'

'No, best not, it might feel like we're ganging up on her if we're both there. Just fill me in later,' Jamie replies, taking another sip of his coffee and still avoiding eye contact. He starts scrolling with his mouse, staring at his screen, so I take that as my cue to leave.

'Okay, Jamie, see you later.'

'Yep,' he replies without looking up.

Shit. I've really pissed him off.

But we can't be more than friends, I'm with Ben. Maybe in a different time, a different place, things would be...different. My mind starts to wander, imagining what it would be like to be with Jamie. Rosie would like him. Ben still hasn't met Rosie, we should arrange that soon.

Sitting at my desk, I sigh and check my watch, ten minutes until my meeting with Sharon. She must have sneaked in when Jamie and I were chatting as she is now sitting at her desk staring blankly at her screen feigning deep concentration. Bless her, she must be feeling like crap. She sure does look a bit peaky. Her hair is dishevelled and the bags under her eyes are huge, it's not like the Sharon I've got to know and like. She's always so bubbly and well put together. I don't think I've ever seen her without makeup before and she's wearing all black, reflecting her present mood I suspect. I get up and make myself a strong coffee, before heading over to the meeting room. Sharon's already inside by the time I get there, sipping water from a plastic cup. I pull up a seat opposite her.

'Hi, Sharon. I'm so glad you're here. How have you been? Are you okay?'

Sharon looks up glumly and I notice her eyes are red-rimmed. I hope she hasn't cried all weekend.

'Not good. I'm so sorry about Friday I just couldn't face . . .' she begins, then starts sobbing, big sobs. I reach out for her hand to comfort her. 'I just felt so ill, I would have been useless and I just couldn't face . . . seeing everyone, especially him, not now *it's* out there,' she explains and sniffs into her water.

How could I forget?! An image of Dirk in his red thong flashes into my mind and stays there, it won't go away and now it's grinding its hips. YUK!

Sharon continues. 'I'm so sorry you and Jamie had to take me home, what a mess. I'm sure I'm allergic to alcohol, it just doesn't agree with me.'

No Sharon, you're allergic to drinking *three* bottles of wine, plus vodka, but we'll let that slide.

'I know you and Dirk are getting rather close and I probably ruined any chances of romance for you both that night, I'm sorry again. I'm not cross at you, just *him*.' Sharon looks at me all bleary eyed. What did she just say? Me and *Dirk*?! I can't hide my shock.

'Excuse me? What? Me? *And* Dirk?' I ask, horrified.

'Yes, you've been dating, haven't you? He took you for a drink a few weeks back, everyone knows about it. To be honest it was over between us by then anyway.' She sniffs and wipes a tear away with the back of her hand.

'Oh no, no, no, Sharon. There's nothing going on between Dirk and I. *At all.* Aside from the fact he's my boss. He *so* isn't my type and I have a partner, Ben, as you all know,' I explain, hoping I've made it extremely clear that Dirk and I never have been or would be...together. In fact, it was Jamie I kissed that night but never you mind Shazza. God, what must the team think of me, did they think I was cheating on Ben with Dirk all this time? Did Jamie suspect this too?

'Really?' Sharon asks, looking hopeful while she dabs her eyes with a soggy tissue.

'Yes. Really. And after seeing that video, that's enough to put any girl off.' I stick two fingers in my mouth and pretend to heave. Not very professional but the mood needs to be lightened. Sharon lets out a little giggle before putting her hand over her mouth and shaking her head.

'I may have sent it to a few people when I was drunk at the work do. I was angry, he's treated me like rubbish, that man.'

'What's gone on between you two? You can tell me.' I squeeze Sharon's hand, encouraging her to confide in me.

'We'd been flirting for months, then at last year's Christmas party he asked me out and it just went from there. We never really went anywhere though, just either to my house or his. He just used me like a piece of meat and then chucked me away when he'd had enough or saw something better,' Sharon mutters, staring at the floor. 'Towards the end he was calling me lardy arse, said I could never do better than him. I was a five and he was a ten, those were his words. He used to text me abuse all the time, said I had to lose weight if I wanted to stay with him and should consider Botox. I got the Botox, see much better.' She points to her nice, tight forehead, trying and failing to frown. 'I explained it was a thyroid problem with my weight, but he was having none of it,' she continues, still wiping away tears with her disintegrating tissue.

'Oh Sharon, you shouldn't feel like you have to change for him, you're beautiful as you are,' I say reassuringly. Jesus, Dirk is more of a wanker than I thought. An abusive wanker. It seems like he's got his comeuppance with the video, though.

'Thanks, and when you came on the scene he was like a slobbering dog, I called him up on it and he told me not to be so stupid. Said I was imagining it, I definitely wasn't.' Sharon folds her arms and looks away, uncomfortable.

'And the video?' I say gently.

'The video was a bit of fun over Halloween, he told

me he was into dress up and dancing so I filmed him doing it. It was just a bit of a laugh at the time. He fancies himself as a bit of a Magic Mike type, doesn't he?' She huffs, arms still folded, trying and failing to frown again. Of course he does.

'Well everyone is certainly laughing now,' I comment, raising both my eyebrows as the image of Dirk gyrating to *I Put a Spell on You* appears in my mind again. I'm not sure if that image will *ever* completely disappear.

'*Good,*' Sharon blurts out, surprising herself. Her face changes from sad to amused and she bursts out laughing, causing me to do the same. She has an hilarious laugh. Once she really gets going, it's one of those braying donkey sort of laughs that just makes it impossible to stop. And impossible for those around her.

'Stop, stop,' I manage between giggles as Sharon *hee haws* into my face with tears rolling down her cheeks. This time the tears are through laughter.

'No. You stop. *Heee hawwwww.* You're the boss,' she guffaws.

'Have some water.' I push her water closer to her. It just seems to make us laugh more.

'Hee hawwww, oink oink,' Sharon carries on. This time there are snorts and brays accompanied by Sharon banging her fist down hard on the table. The plastic cup of water flips from the pressure splashing Sharon in the face. Now she is silent, laughing and slapping her knee with a wet fringe. Tears of laughter are streaming down my cheeks.

'Have you seen him?' Sharon manages with wide eyes, once she's calmed down.

'No, I haven't, I don't think anyone has yet.'

Jamie

Monday morning and a grey-faced, sombre Sharon is back. Emily had a meeting with her first thing. Swiftly followed by a meeting with me.

So, it seems Dirk and Sharon were an item until Emily joined Genevre. Emily has told me all about it, though I cannot discuss with anyone else, not that I would.

He dumped Sharon when he met Emily, not that anyone even knew Dirk and Sharon got together at last year's Christmas party, except Karen and she only found out when it ended. Even Emily didn't know he felt quite that way about her, she just thought he was a slimy perv. Well, I thought so too. Apparently, he told Sharon he wanted to spend the rest of his life with Emily.

Emily is almost as grey-faced and sombre as Sharon now, although she says they did have a good laugh about it.

It still doesn't excuse Sharon posting that shudder-inducing video online.

There's no Dirk again today and gossip is rife.

Emily

Well that's got to be one of the more unprofessional meetings I've had in my career but at least Sharon is feeling better. I'm not sure what Dirk will do once he knows the video is out there, literally for all the world to see. If it were me, I'd want to crawl into a hole and stay there forever.

The day carries on swiftly with people making constant jokes about Dirk's dancing, Dirk's attire and Dirk's package. Jayden applied some of Sharon's red lipstick and did an impression of Dirk's hip wiggle, it was hysterical and had the whole office howling. Karen was on look out to alert us if anyone saw Dirk coming but the rumour is, he wasn't even in work, however he didn't have his out of office on either, which is unusual for him.

Jamie

Tuesday morning and still no Dirk. His performance is still the main topic of conversation.

I saw Chelle in the gym earlier; we didn't have our usual Monday lunch because she was on leave. She'd seen Dirk's performance over the weekend though.

'You work with him, don't you?' Chelle asked, fighting to suppress a smirk.

'Yeah. Sort of.'

'I feel sorry for him.'

'So do I, sort of.' Part of me does, part of me thinks he's a fucking idiot.

'There but for the grace….' Chelle says before adding, 'It could happen to any of us.'

'I don't think so,' I mutter to her retreating form. I'm not hench enough to parade as Dirk had, much less film it. And I certainly would never have the desire to dress like that.

Or jiggle my dick like he did.

Twenty-one

Emily

It's almost 4.30pm and I'm counting down the minutes to 5pm when I can leave work and get home. Ben's coming over at eight as Rosie is at her dad's. That leaves plenty of time to have a bath, get ready and tidy up the house to make it look like I live in a show home; I wonder how long I can keep it up.

Guilt unexpectedly hits me.

Should I tell him about Jamie? A decent person would. As I ponder over what to do, I become acutely aware that I'm looking directly at Jamie and he's returning my stare. My vibrating phone saves me from continuing the awkward exchange, I grab it to see Sabrina's face pop up. It's a message from her.

I've missed her so much.

Sabrina: *Hey stranger, fancy meeting up for a coffee after work?*

Shit. I still haven't replied to her last message. I should have enough time; the house doesn't need to be immaculate. I'm only human.

Me: *Yes, of course, would love to see you, sorry I've been rubbish. I'll see you at the usual place? xx*

Sabrina: *Yes fab, see you then. xx*

I park up at the shopping centre and run into the coffee shop. It's packed, with people having a break from their last-minute Christmas shopping. I feel a little smug as I think of all my beautifully wrapped presents at home, I'm never normally this organised and this year I even have a full-time job. Looking at the full tables, I groan inwardly, I think we'll be lucky to get a table. Marching up to the door, I scan the window to see if I can see Sabrina, I'm relieved when I spot her sitting in the corner, in the perfect people watching spot. I do a double take as one of the members of staff clears our table, it's the blonde guy from when I was here with Liam.

He looks different.

Oh god, it's his forehead, but now it's looking more like a three/two-head. Perhaps he did get that forehead reduction? My eyes fall to his big pouting duck lips, they stick out so much he must find it difficult to talk. I pinch my hand to stifle a laugh as I catch him checking out his reflection in the compact mirror that Sabrina's left open on the table and make a mental note to tell Rosie how beautiful she is more often.

'Hey you,' I say, smiling with my arms open.

Sabrina stands up to give me a huge hug. It's nice to see my old friend again.

'I got us both a Christmas hot chocolate special, gingerbread and cream. Hope that's okay.' Sabrina grins and her Christmas tree earrings swing from side to side.

'Yes of course. Thanks, Sab.' I take a sip. 'Yummy, lovely. So how have you been? Feels like ages.' It's freezing outside so this hot chocolate is just what I need.

'I've been okay, Dave's been a useless arsehole this Christmas so far, so much to do and I'm doing it all.

He's in the dog house at the moment so he's currently trying to make it up to me and is at home wrapping presents. I'm sick of doing everything. I told him if he doesn't buck his ideas up, I'm going to apply for us to go on *Wife Swap* and then the whole world will see how lazy he is. He said go ahead because he'd quite like a break from me and the kids. Cheeky Bastard,' Sabrina rants, rolling her eyes and shaking her head. Despite what she says she adores her lazy bastard. It's the same every year, even when Dave *does* help Sabrina always ends up redoing whatever job it is because he makes such a mess of it. No doubt the wrapping will be redone by Sabrina. I imagine Dave wrapping with newspaper, using duct tape whilst watching TV and drinking beer. They make me laugh.

'You two, what are you like?'

'Enough about me, it's the same old shit, what about you?' Sabrina asks eagerly. I think she's living vicariously through me at the moment.

'Yeah, good actually, had our work Christmas party, it was pretty messy. Jamie and I had to take one of my colleagues home as she was a little the worse for wear.' I chuckle but feel a tad bad for making fun of Sharon. That reminds me, I must tell Sabrina about Dirk. Oh no, he's dancing for me again. I shut my eyes to focus on my hot chocolate while wishing Dirk's hip thrust away.

'Oh yes, working as a team even after hours hmmm?' Sabrina teases.

'Also, I've been seeing Ben quite a bit, in fact he's coming over later. I think I'm going to introduce him to Rosie soon,' I add, testing the water. She blinks at me and smooths her hair over to one side.

'And how did Jamie look at the Christmas party.

Hot?' she asks, brightly. She could at least try to hide her dislike of Ben.

'Do you have a soft spot for Jamie, Sabrina?' I goad.

'No, no, I just think he seems like a nice man.' A nice man for me she means.

'He looked all right.' I sniff and look to the side. He looked better than all right. Hot.

'You dirty hoe,' bursts Sabrina, with cream on her nose.

'What?' I say guiltily. Wiping the cream from around my mouth.

'You tell me right now,' Sabrina orders.

'You've got cream on your nose,' I try to distract her.

Sabrina eyeballs me as she wipes it away.

'Tell. Me. Now,' she repeats, not breaking eye contact.

'Tell you what?' I squeak incredulously. She knows me better than I know myself. I have to confess, I'm a really *bad* liar. 'Sabrina, keep your voice down,' I whisper, looking around the coffee shop. I lean in. 'I may have kissed him. In the taxi.'

Sabrina's mouth opens in mock shock before she screws up her eyes and squints at me. 'I knew it! Did he come back to yours?'

'No, no. Tiny was babysitting and I wouldn't have done that anyway; I'm with Ben.'

'Ah, your new best friend, Tiny,' Sabrina says, a sting in her words.

'Hardly,' I say before moving on quickly. 'Sabrina, I feel so bad, I don't know what to do, should I tell Ben? I'm ridden with guilt.'

'Well, it might be an idea.' Sabrina drinks the remains of her hot chocolate.

'It was just a mistake, just a little kiss. Is it worth chucking it all away with Ben for that? He could just discard me if he finds out, he's a nice bloke and I know he wouldn't dream of doing anything like that to me. It's awful.' My stomach flips as I think of the kiss with Jamie. *It* clearly doesn't think it was a mistake. What is wrong with me? Sabrina just blinks, looking serious, concerned almost, an expression I don't often see on her gorgeous face.

'Tell him,' she barks.

'What, really?' I laugh, shocked by her response.

'Yes, fucking *tell* him, he deserves everything he gets.' She lifts her chin, her jaw tight.

'That's a bit strong, isn't it? What's he done to you?'

Sabrina sighs. 'I wasn't going to tell you now but I think it's the right time.' This sounds horribly ominous.

'What is it?' I ask.

'Ben is a dick,' she barks and I roll my eyes.

'Sabrina, you just need to get to know him, please. He's actually...'

'No, he actually *is* a dick,' she interrupts. 'Look, I've been doing some research, basically I've stalked him online. Something about him just didn't sit well with me and I needed to act on my instinct.'

'Right,' I say slowly, thinking she's gone a little psycho.

'He's married, I'm sorry Emily.'

I gasp as the words smack me in the face, it hurts.

'How?' I manage, blinking back tears. 'No.' I shake my head.

'I googled his barbers and Ben's Barnet's doesn't exist but Ben's Barbers does. When I found the actual place that he worked at, I had a look on the website and the Facebook page. I had to do some real digging but it

275

was there. A single comment on a Facebook photo from someone. I thought maybe it was his sister at first but when I clicked on to her profile, there were all their wedding pics and tons of family photos with his children. And, he doesn't even own the salon, this is the salon owner.' She shows me a photo of a guy in his fifties, also called Ben.

'Is Ben even his name?' I ask, looking up at Sabrina while fighting back the tears in my eyes. 'He said he didn't use social media,' I croak, feeling stupid.

'Well, his wife certainly does,' Sabrina reveals as I rub my forehead frowning, trying hard not to break down in the coffee shop.

'No, that must be his ex-wife, old photos. Let me see.' I hold out my hand for her phone while she scrolls and taps before handing it over to me. There she is, the alleged wife, *Laura Bond.* Blond, slim and glamorous, not the boring old hag he complained to me about.

'But that's not Ben's surname, it must be her maiden name,' I exclaim, clicking on her Facebook page. Sure enough there are photos of her and Ben, her and Ben with the kids, Ben and the kids. Her profile must be set as public as I can see *everything,* all her photos, all her posts. I gasp again. There it is. A photo of Ben, her and the kids posted just last week, visiting Santa. The kids are standing in front of Santa holding unopened presents whilst Laura and Ben Bond stand either side of Santa beaming back at the camera. Ben had showed me that very same photo but it was just him and the kids. He was winking in that one, probably at his bloody wife whilst she took the photo, I think bitterly.

'Arsehole,' I mutter under my breath. 'Can you find me Ben?' Sabrina takes her phone, scrolls and taps and then hands it back again. 'Ben Bond?' I say out loud.

'That's not his surname. He told me it was Simpson,' I repeat.

'That's so you wouldn't find him I guess; did you ever go on Facebook and search for him?' Sabrina asks.

'No, he said he didn't use Facebook or any social media, so I never looked. I guess I trusted him and never saw a reason to check up on him.' I look up at Sabrina feeling pathetic and sad, hurt and utterly stupid. Suddenly everything clicks into place, all the cancelled plans and the excuses about his kids and brother. The fact he wouldn't let me come to the competition in Dublin as they probably knew his wife. How could I have been so blind? What an arsehole. I can only think of one word. Revenge. And it's best served rather warm.

Jamie

A week has passed and we have still not seen Dirk. The gossip has died down now, everyone is too busy trying to clear out their email inboxes in time for Christmas. I've emailed HR about Dirk, about his work and asked what we should do. I had a terse response saying he was off sick.

Sharon is keeping her head down and says she hasn't seen or heard from him. I bet she hasn't. Poor, stupid Dirk. Karen told Emily that Sharon deeply regrets posting that video. Too late now.

'Hey,' Tim says when he comes home from work. 'Apparently that devil guy works at your place.'

'Devil guy?'

'Yeah. You know. From the video.' He rolls his eyes at me.

'Right. Are you wanting any of this? I'm doing a stir

fry.'

'Do you know him? You must know *of* him.' Tim isn't going to be distracted.

'Yeah.' I cannot lie.

'Whoa. Come on. Details.' He folds his arms and starts to tap his foot.

'Yeah, he works at Genevre. Do you want any of this then?' I wave my spatula at him.

'I already know he works at Genevre, *I* told *you* that. No. I'm going round to Lex's.'

'Okay.'

'So what's devil guy's name?'

'Does it matter?'

'I bet he's got a red face to match his boots now.' He starts to laugh.

'Umm, what is your relationship with Lex, then?' It's none of my business but I don't want to talk about Dirk.

'Well, you know.' He grins.

'Was she seeing someone else that night?'

'What night?'

'The night we went out to celebrate your award nomination. Hey, when do you find out if you've won?' I'm doing a sterling job of distracting him now.

'Ahh, could be months before I find out.' He offers a little, self-deprecating laugh. 'Lex isn't seeing anyone else, she volunteers two nights a month with the Samaritans.'

'What? Really. Wow.'

'Yeah. I've been thinking about doing it. Lot of training of course, but…' his voice trails off. 'What do you think?'

'I don't know what to think. You're well-meaning but…' now my voice trails off.

'What?' he demands.

'A bit tactless sometimes.'

'Like you're not.'

'Yes. No.' In trying to distract him away from Dirk I've opened another can of worms.

He leans over and grabs a chunk of chicken from my stir fry.

'Not cooked yet, don't whinge if you get food poisoning,' I mutter.

'Whatever.' He is walking away when he delivers his parting shot. 'It's that Dirk, isn't it? Devil guy. Dirk the dick.' He doesn't even wait for an answer.

'I never said that,' I shout up the stairs after him.

I wonder if there's anyone in this town who doesn't know the identity of devil guy.

Stupid Dirk.

Emily

Sabrina meets me at mine straight from the coffee shop, fuelled by wine and inspired by Dirk's escapades, we hatch a plan to snare Ben. I'm actually very excited about it, now I know he's married and supposedly happily, according to his wife's Facebook page. I couldn't care less about his feelings, though I feel sorry for his poor wife.

'Are you ready?' Sabrina has her hands on my shoulders as she studies my face.

'Yep, let's do this,' I say confidently.

The doorbell rings. It's Ben. Sabrina positions herself on the sofa and I snicker. I take a deep breath before pasting on my best smile, with no gums, as I open the door.

'Hey, big boy,' I purr as I watch Ben drink me in, his eyes are on stalks, looking me up and down appreciably, licking his lips like a hungry dog. I'm dressed in black suspenders and stockings with a sexy purple bra and knicker set. I must admit I look good and I'm glad this will be his last image of me.

'Wow, is this my present?' he growls, looking thoroughly pleased, grinning from ear to ear like a Cheshire cat. He lunges over to kiss me and I put my hand out to stop him. Don't touch me, creep.

'Some of it,' I purr with my hand on his chest. 'The other half is in the living room,' I tease, raising an eyebrow.

He hurries inside and I take his coat from him before dropping it behind us on the porch floor and kicking it into the corner. It won't be there for long. He follows me into the living room and I step aside for him to take in what he thinks is about to happen.

'Wow!' Ben gawps at Sabrina draped on the sofa. She looks sensational, like some gorgeous airbrushed celebrity off the cover of FHM magazine. 'Well *hello, sexy Sabrinaaaa.*' He drools, winking at her. A double wink. What a prick. 'Just WOW girls.' He can't tear his eyes away from Sabrina to look at me.

'All your Christmases have come at once, Ben,' Sabrina simpers with a girly giggle. 'Now, what I'd like you to do for me is go upstairs and get yourself comfortable. We've laid an outfit out on the bed for you, so please go up and slip into it for us. We'll meet you up there in just a minute.' She winks at him and I pinch my hand hard to stop myself from laughing. She's so good at this.

'No problemo, I'm there,' Ben shouts enthusiastically. He slaps my bum, making me jump and wince at the same time. He starts to run upstairs, then hesitates, looking back to wink at me and Sabrina before thundering up the stairs.

'Do you think he'll wear it?' I giggle hysterically as I hear the bedroom door slam shut. The adrenaline almost hurts as it pumps through my veins, I wouldn't be surprised if I spontaneously combust.

'Oh yeah, he's desperate to wear it.' She sniggers into her wine.

'Good, can't wait.'

'Got the stuff?' Sabrina checks.

'Yep,' I say, holding up a can of squirty cream.

Sabrina and I trot up the stairs and knock on my bedroom door.

'Are you ready, big Ben?' I say in my best, sexy voice.

'I'm more than ready, baby,' he shouts.

Turning the handle, the bedroom door slowly opens. Ben is laid there with a big homemade dunce hat on his head which has "I'm a naughty boy" scrawled along it. He's wearing my old eye mask and is naked apart from some edible knickers that I've had in my cupboard for about ten years. I'm surprised they haven't disintegrated into dust. Sabrina and I giggle.

'Oooooh we can't wait to taste those delightful sweets. I bet there's an even bigger dessert waiting beneath them for us,' Sabrina purrs, her voice low and seductive. I bend over pissing myself laughing, careful to do it silently so as not to cause suspicion.

'But first, let's add some cream into the mix. Everything tastes better with a bit of cream; don't you think Ben?' I say as I walk over to Ben and begin squirting cream onto his torso. I'm not sure what I'll write but then it comes to me. 'Ah perfect,' I purr, standing back to admire my handy work. Sabrina grabs my phone and starts snapping Ben from all angles.

'*Tinky Winky Wanker* has a certain ring to it, don't you think?' I announce, turning to Sabrina.

'Yes, it does, Ems,' Sabrina says. 'You could almost make a song out of it couldn't you. Something like;

Tinky Winky Wanker
Is a very bad man
He lied that he was single
But a wife is what he had
Naughty big Ben
Is really very little
His nuts the size of peanuts
And a penis like a thimble.'

Sabrina is a genius, I must get her to send that to me. To my amazement Ben is still laid there, but with the eye mask pulled up on his dunce hat. He's like a stunned rabbit, rooted to the spot with his hands on his face and staring up at the ceiling.

'Have you got anything to say for yourself then, Ben?' I hear myself say.

'I'm I'm, I've got to go,' he stutters, jumping up, frantically picking up his discarded clothes from the floor.

'Yes, you do that Ben *Bond*,' I say coldly.

Sabrina and I watch with our arms folded as he gets dressed and bolts down the stairs and out of the door. I've never seen anyone move so fast.

Now the excitement is over, I'm left staring into the bottom of my wine glass. Alone. Feeling numbingly empty. Sabrina went home an hour ago as she had to get back to Dave and the kids. Were we too harsh? Sabrina thinks I should have sent the photos to his wife but there'll be no chance of that now as I've deleted them. I'm not going to risk being tempted to *do a*

Sharon, the memory is enough for me and even that has a bitter taste.

We humiliated Ben and I can't help feeling a bit bad about it, I'm certainly not feeling as liberated as I thought I would. But I guess that's inevitable when the man of your dreams turns out to be a lying, cheating bastard.

Again.

The kiss with Jamie keeps playing on my mind too, even more so now. So, I'm not so innocent either. In another world Jamie and I could have been together but not now, it would just seem like a rebound.

Jamie

Emily's looked sad all week. She certainly isn't her normal, bouncy self. I've seen her and Sharon huddled together a couple of times. I know she's been giving Sharon some moral support – God knows she needs it – but I don't think it's that.

'Everything okay?' I ask as she sits back at her desk.

'Yeah. No probs.' She smiles at me but I can tell it's an effort.

'I bet your little girl's excited about Christmas.'

'Oh yeah. Counting the sleeps.' There's a brief moment of pleasure in her eyes and then it dies away. She turns and gets back on with her work.

It's been a little awkward between us since the taxi kissing incident, but fortunately – for us anyway – the Dirk video has been such a dominating topic of conversation that neither of us has mentioned *the kiss.*

Maybe I imagined it.

Anyway, what would we say? It happened (I think), it shouldn't have because Emily has a boyfriend.

It was just a drunken kiss.

Twenty-two

Jamie

The meeting request from Alan's PA pops into our inboxes and makes us both look up and glance at each other. We both guess what it's about. It's decision time.

Me, or Emily.

Only one of us can have the job. Before Dirk's little performance I was pretty sure it was going to be Emily, but now, with Dirk out of the picture – for the time being at least – I'm beginning to think I might, just might, stand a chance. Am I delusional?

I had hoped that Dirk's absence might have postponed the decision. It seems not.

I slope off to the kitchen to pep myself up with caffeine. I've barely put coffee in my mug before Emily appears.

'Bit awks,' she says quietly as she rinses out her mug.

'Yeah.' Does she mean the kiss or the job? Job of course.

'I think it'll be you.' She turns and offers me a sad smile.

'I don't.' That's not entirely true. Now.

'Alan knows how hard you worked on that tricky case.' She laughs, almost to herself. 'I made sure he knew.'

'Thanks. I appreciate it.' I did work hard and it's only fair.

'Only fair.' Is she reading my mind?

'Well, we'll know in an hour.'

'He could have given us more notice.'

'Yeah.' I nod and agree. But it makes no difference. Mentally I've prepared myself for the bad news. Now I'm worrying about what I'm going to do if it's good news, if I get the job. I don't want Emily to lose out. Maybe I should just leave anyway. I'm registered with three agencies, surely they'll find me something in the new year. Will it be easier for me to get another good job than it will be for Emily?

Am I being a condescending macho pig?

Probably, but I can't help worrying about her.

Emily

'Listen, I've been thinking and I'm going to turn down the job when we go into this meeting. What I mean is, I'm going to offer to leave. It's yours,' Jamie announces, frowning. He has one single line down the middle of his forehead, it's perfectly straight. He looks so serious, it doesn't suit him.

'Sorry, what?' I reply, checking my watch, forty-five minutes until the meeting.

'It's yours, you deserve it. It's easier for me. I can soon find another quickly,' he says with a small smile.

'And I can't?' Now it's my turn to frown.

'No, I didn't mean it like that.'

'Well. How do you mean it then?' I dare him, willing him to dig himself out of this freshly dug hole.

'It's harder for you.'

'Why? Because I'm a woman?' I snort with my hands

on my hips.

'Well. Yeah, I guess, sort of,' he mumbles and shifts from side to side, looking at the floor. I can't answer him, in fact right now I can't even bear to look at him. How dare he!

I turn on my heels, walking back to my desk and slowly sit down cradling my coffee, desperately trying not to cry. Because of course, that would be so typical of a woman. A woman not worthy of this job. Who's to say I wouldn't have got the job over him anyway. I'm furious. Furious because he clearly thinks so little of me. Furious because I thought so much more of him.

Jamie

We're sitting in Alan's office, another cup of coffee each, courtesy of his PA and we're waiting. Emily is ashen-faced and looking angry.

'Is everything all right?' I ask again, probably inappropriately.

She opens her mouth to speak then shuts it abruptly as Alan walks in.

He plonks himself at his desk and flashes a brief smile at us.

'Sorry about the short notice and thank you for coming.'

Like we had a choice.

We both mutter incoherent acknowledgement.

'I'll get straight to the point; Dirk has left Genevre.' He watches our faces for a reaction.

'Oh,' Emily says while I say nothing.

'No doubt you know why.'

We both nod.

'It was his decision, though I'm glad to say that he took the dignified way out.'

It's hard not to laugh at the thought of how dignified I *Put a Spell on You* looked and sounded.

'There'll be an announcement by email in the next few days. You can tell the rest of your team today, but ask them to keep quiet until the email. I'd be grateful if you'd discourage any more gossip on the subject. I'm sure I can count on you both.'

'Yes,' we chorus.

'Good. We're treating him well, loyalty and all that, good reference, so no one need worry about him. And we won't be discussing this any further.'

The muscles in Emily's legs tense as she readies herself to stand up, she's obviously as eager to get out of Alan's office as I am.

'About the job,' I start, wondering what the hell I am going to say? Alan glances at me and waits. 'I think Emily would be the best choice, between us. An excellent choice.'

Next to me I see Emily's entire body tense, she's perched on the edge of her seat as though ready to jump up at any minute. She doesn't speak, she doesn't look at me.

'Umm, right. Anyway, everything has changed now,' Alan says, not really responding to my suggestion.

Emily slowly sinks back into her chair.

'I've given this a lot of consideration, discussed it with the CEO, regarding the position and the situation with only one of you being successful.' He offers a forced smile.

I swallow hard and brace myself. Here it comes. Out of the corner of my eye I see Emily's hand shaking. I don't know why she's so worried, I've just offered myself up in favour of her. She should be relieved.

'An arrangement I never really agreed with,' Alan

continues, glancing from my face to Emily's. 'I've decided to use the situation which Dirk's departure has created as an opportunity for a restructure. I'd like you both to stay on for at least six more months and I'd like your input into the restructure.' Now he waits for our reaction.

I open my mouth to speak but Emily beats me to it.

'What happens at the end of the six months? I mean, should I, or Jamie,' she glances at me before continuing, 'Start looking for a new job so we don't suddenly find ourselves unemployed?' She's shaking more now. I want to reach over and comfort her, hold her hand the way she held mine when I told her about my mum's death. But I can't, not in here, not now. Maybe not ever.

'Sorry, I'm not making myself clear.' Alan smiles at us. 'I want you both to stay. The six months is how long I expect our restructure to take. After that, I'm sure, one-hundred percent sure, that there will be suitable positions for you both.' If only to prove his sincerity his smile now fills his face.

Emily

Oh hell. That was a shocker. Both of us get to keep the job. I should be pleased, I should really be ecstatic but I can't see past the angry red mist festering in front of Jamie and if I'm honest, I'm feeling pretty darn miserable. Jamie even had the cheek to offer himself up in the meeting.

I felt myself shaking, my adrenaline rising, but it could have been mixed with a bit of embarrassment and anger. Alan chose to ignore Jamie's patronising, misogynistic offer, thank God. How dare he? It's so insulting. I don't need rescuing, I don't need a man to rescue me when all they have *ever* done is let me down. Liam, Ben and now Jamie. I thought Jamie had my back, thought he respected me. I may not have his experience but I'm an excellent manager.

I deserve to be here.

I deserve this job.

'You okay?' somebody asks, making me jump as I drop my coffee cup into the sink.

'Shit,' I shout, as the fragile mug breaks, its handle coming off in my hand. Rosie made it for me, it has a drawing she did of me and her on it.

'Yes, fine.' I sniff, not turning around to the voice. It's Jamie, I can feel his presence. Smell him. His aroma a combination of toothpaste, earth and apples. Weirdly intoxicating, almost suffocating.

'Listen, I'm sorry, I didn't mean to…' he starts.

'Let's not,' I say holding my hand up before examining the handle of my mug; all it took was one little slip, one slip and it was broken, just like that.

Jamie

I try to apologise to Emily. She cuts me off mid-sentence. She's hiding in the kitchen. She's dropped that odd mug she uses, broke it in the sink. That's probably my fault too.

She actually holds her hand up to silence me but I carry on, not with the apology though. I know when not to flog a dead horse.

'I thought Dirk would brazen it out. Didn't you?'

'Who cares?' She grabs a few paper towels and wraps the broken cup up. Stomps off without another word.

I'm left standing in the kitchen feeling stupid. Why couldn't I just keep my big mouth shut? What the hell is wrong with me? I already knew she wasn't happy with my idea; she made that clear enough before the meeting.

I'm as stupid as Tim.

Emily

I rush off to the toilets to gather my thoughts and try to calm down, I need to get through the rest of the day without screaming at Jamie. I slam the cubicle door shut and plonk myself down on the toilet seat, bringing my hands up to massage my head. I have a tension headache. What the hell is wrong with me? Since when did I become such an emotional wreck? I should be pleased I still work here, it should be a happy day but I can't help being pissed off by Jamie's patronising offer. The toilet door creaks open and someone clip clops in, followed by another woman, this one quieter, lighter on her feet.

'Urgh I'm dying for a piss,' the first woman says; it's Sharon.

'Go and have one then,' Karen replies. I didn't know they came in here for catch ups, it amuses me. I remember doing that in my previous job, I don't blame them, it breaks up the day a bit.

'What do you want to do for lunch today?' Karen asks Sharon.

'I dunno.' Sharon calls out from her cubicle. 'I think I'd rather go out today, the vibe in this place is a bit stale at the moment.'

'Yeah, I know what you mean,' Karen replies.

'Hey what do you think is wrong with Emily today? She has a face like a slapped arse, don't you think?' Sharon calls out loudly and I cringe inwardly. Am I that transparent?

'Yeah, I think her boyfriend dumped her, think she

wanted to get married and he isn't interested.' Karen says matter of fact.

'Who told you that?' Sharon asks.

'Can't remember,' Karen replies.

Sharon flushes the toilet and clip clops out of the cubicle, shortly after the tap turns on as she washes her hands. They chat for a few more minutes about boring work matters until someone else enters the toilet and interrupts their get together. They clip clop off together, little do they know I've been sat here the whole time. My Kalms are still in my handbag and the temptation is almost overwhelming now. I take them out and turn the bottle around and around in my hand, listening to the few left rattling inside. The bottle mimics how I feel, shaken and almost empty.

Jamie

I book a meeting room immediately and Emily rounds the team up, we're going to deliver the news – good or bad, depending on your perspective. We're collaborating on this like true professionals, except I don't think I've behaved very professionally.

The look of relief on Sharon's face when we tell everyone lights up the room, but it's quickly followed by one of horror.

'Oh God, it's all my fault.'

'Not really,' Hayden says. 'Unless you held a gun to his head when he did that dance.' He doesn't even attempt to suppress his sniggering.

Karen rolls her eyes at Hayden, Jayden coughs to hide his own snigger.

'Anyway,' Emily starts, 'Say everything you want to in here, get it out, get it said then, please don't gossip about it anymore.' Her eyes move from face to face until she gets their implicit agreement.

'It's old news anyway,' Karen says. 'I'm sick of hearing about it.'

'I shouldn't have sent that video. What's he going to do? I've lost him his job.' Sharon fights back tears.

'Don't worry about Dirk,' Emily says. 'He'll be fine, Genevre has been generous, recognised his years of loyal service. He's getting a good reference.'

'Yes, but…' Sharon starts, sniffing.

'It's done,' I say. 'It can't be changed. Emily and I will be staying for the foreseeable future. So we all need to carry on being the great team we are and just get on with our work.'

'Yes. But. Poor. Dirk,' Sharon says between sobs.

'He treated you like shit,' Karen snaps. 'Get over it. He had it coming. There are plenty of others who wished they'd done the same.'

I make a mental note never to cross Karen.

'Are there?' Sharon turns to Karen.

'I expect so. Are we done here? I've got something I need to finish before I go home.' Karen stands up and everyone else follows suit.

'What was that about?' I ask Emily when we're the last to leave the meeting. 'You don't think Karen and Dirk…'

'Dunno. Don't care,' she cuts in before stomping off, her ponytail flicking its hostility as she walks.

Twenty-three

Jamie

Emily isn't in the office when the email announcing Dirk's departure arrives. She's taken a few days off to spend time with her daughter in the run up to Christmas. She's had the time booked off for a few weeks. It's a bit of a relief that she's not here. Since my act of stupid and misplaced chivalry, we haven't exchanged a social word, only professional ones. I wish I had kept my mouth shut.

But I'm missing her. I'm missing that bright smile, her infectious bubbliness, even if she has seemed a bit down lately as well as being furious at me.

I've churned over my stupidity a thousand times. I will apologise as soon as she is back. I feel like a right shit. I wouldn't have offered myself up like that if she had been a man. But the truth is I wouldn't have done the same if she had been any other woman. Would I?

The rest of the team refrain from commenting when the email about Dirk arrives. They're all reading it, I can tell from the silence as the clicking of keyboards ceases for a few minutes.

When I see Chelle later she gives me a secret smile and a raised eyebrow. I smile back in my best, noncommittal way.

After Christmas Dirk's folly will be last year's news. I hope.

Emily

It's been good to take some time off and just spend quality time with my daughter. We've been ice skating which wasn't a huge success but fun for Rosie nonetheless. Rosie is a natural born skater with no fear whereas I spent the entire time holding on to the edge, fearful of falling over and slicing off my fingers. Luckily Mum was there to help take her around, she used to be a good skater when she was younger.

I also took her to have breakfast with Santa at the local garden centre, Santa was fabulously magical. He was just wonderful. The acting, quality of his beard and suit were so great that even *I* believed in him again. They didn't have things like that when I was a kid. You just sat on a skinny, dishevelled Santa's knee telling him what you wanted for Christmas as you inhaled the smell of tobacco and fusty old beard wig that had been worn by numerous other Santas. Rosie's face lit up when she told Santa all about what she wanted for Christmas and how she was going to spend her Christmas. I felt a deep pang of sadness when she said she would be having Christmas dinner at her daddy's house. We've done it differently this year, it should be better for Rosie.

But not for me.

We'll see how it goes.

The highlight of our few days was our trip to London to see *The Little Mermaid*. Both Rosie and I sat entranced as we watched it. It was amazing and once home, we've binge watched Disney ever since while eating copious bowls of popcorn. Sadly, once Rosie goes to bed the evenings have stretched long and lonely so I've been re-watching the inevitable romantic Christmas films and pathetically crying buckets.

Jamie has been playing on my mind a lot. I can't help but think that perhaps I overreacted to his proposition. Being tired and stressed has a lot to answer for and now I'm thinking more clearly, I feel guilty for snapping at him. It was unnecessary. Tonight's choice of film is *Just Friends* and it's set me thinking. I'm back at work tomorrow so I should probably clear the air before I return. It's 9pm, is that too late to text a colleague?

No, he's more than that.

Me: *Hey Jamie, how are you keeping? Sorry for being a moody bitch before my time off. I was being a little sensitive and was offended when you offered to let me have the job. I know you were just trying to be sweet but I like to think I can impress by my own merits. I clearly needed a holiday.* I add a smiley face.

An hour and a half creeps by before he finally replies; I've stayed up late waiting for his message and I wonder what he's been doing. He's probably got company, a woman. He deserves someone nice. I feel a wrench of jealousy at the thought of this woman. So silly, I need to get a life, Jamie is off limits surely. He's my colleague, my workmate.

Jamie: *Hi Emily, I'm not bad, how are you? Just out with Tim. Don't be daft, you would have got it over me anyway. Isn't it great that we can both stay! I'm sorry too, sorry for being a pig-headed idiot. J x*

Me: *Not at all, glad we got that sorted, have a good night.*

Jamie: *Me too. Look forward to seeing you tomorrow. J*

Me: *Same x*

'Wow, Mummy, you look like a Christmas unicorn,' Rosie grins with excitement as she touches my

Christmas jumper, rubbing the sequins up and down to reveal the different colours.

I must admit, it is pretty cool.

'Thanks, sweetie. Do you think I'll win the Christmas jumper competition?' I don't think there is a competition but it makes Rosie happy to think there is.

'Yeah you will, nobody can beat this,' she squeaks. I stroke her cheek and give her a kiss, she's so bloody adorable, I feel a lump swell in my throat.

'Right, are you all ready for your dad's? Got everything you want to take? Your bag of clothes is on the side there,' I explain, trying to sound as bright and breezy as possible. She's going to Liam and Tiny's for Christmas this year, I won't see her again until the evening of Christmas Day.

'Yep, I only want to bring bedtime bunny.' Her big brown eyes blink at me.

'Okay, sweetie, don't forget those gifts for Daddy, Tiny and Tiger-Lily then.'

'I won't, Mummy.'

We've made cakes for them and have bought each of them a small gift. This is the first year where we've done presents, previously I always made an excuse not to or avoided the subject hoping Rosie wouldn't notice. Perhaps I've grown up a little now, plus they always make us something or should I say *Tiny* always makes us something.

We arrive at Liam and Tiny's and Tiger-Lily is already there, jumping up and down at the door. The girls run up to one another and hug in the street, still jumping up and down, both squealing with excitement. I can't blame Rosie for being excited, she gets to spend Christmas with her best friend, her sister.

'Hi Emily, the girls are exceptionally hyper I see, to

be expected I guess.' Liam laughs. I notice that he's trimmed his moustache and it doesn't look quite so tosserish anymore.

'Yep, good luck with putting them to bed tonight.' I laugh back. I'm putting on a big, brave face.

'I'll send you some photos in the morning if you like, of Rosie opening her presents,' he offers with a small smile.

'Yeah, that would be nice, thank you.' It's kind of him to suggest that. Tiny comes up behind him, she's wearing a fitted navy-blue polka dot dress with full hair and makeup. She looks like a 1950s movie star.

'Hi Emily, lovely to see you. Aren't the girls sweet?' she says as they come running in past her.

'Yes, it's lovely to see.' I force a smile again. 'Well I best get off or I'll be late for work. Have a good Christmas.' I turn to leave.

'Wait. Before you go, I have something for you.' Tiny shimmies off for a few seconds and returns with a gold bag tied up with a big red ribbon.

'Oh wow,' I say, taken a back. Usually it's the standard homemade Christmas jam.

'Open it.' Tiny's eyes sparkle.

'Honey, she can do it when she gets home. It isn't Christmas yet anyway,' Liam says softly rubbing Tiny's arm.

'That's no fun is it? Go on, open it now.'

I look from Tiny to Liam and begin to untie the bow. The wrapping looks expensive.

'Oh my.' I gasp

'Do you like it?' Tiny winces.

'I don't know what to say,' I reply in shock.

'It's the wrong colour, isn't it? I just thought you might want something a bit different,' Tiny explains, wringing her hands.

'I can't accept this, it's too much,' I mumble, staring at the gorgeous, red Louis Vuitton handbag. Oh hell. We only made cakes and got them a novelty gift each from Primark. I know how much these bags cost, I'd been on the website and snooped when Liam's mum bought me one and that was years ago. This has got to be worth at least a grand. Shit, why did I tell Tiny about my bag-vomit mishap, I bet she told Liam. Cringe.

'Oh, don't worry, silly. It's second hand, it didn't cost as much as you think. Great condition though, isn't it. Try it on,' Tiny insists as she grabs the handbag off me and places it on my arm, over the top of my coat.

'Wow. You look amazing. Like a film star, it even matches your lipstick.' She arranges the handbag on me making it sit better.

'It suits you. Tiny has great taste,' Liam says while twizzling his moustache.

'Yeah, she does. Thanks guys.' I feel so lame for my rubbish presents.

'It's the least we could do,' Tiny whispers in my ear as she gives me a big hug. 'You've made our Christmas.

I kiss Rosie goodbye and tell her to be good for Daddy and Tiny. I can't quite believe my shiny new handbag from my shiny new friend. I message Sabrina a photo of my new bag and she sends back a shocked face and jokes that maybe she should start getting friendlier with Tiny. I tell her she should, but not to expect any handbags or gifts. Tiny is a sweetheart, it's just taken me a long time to realise.

I arrive at the office and everyone is clad in their Christmas jumpers. Jayden makes a fuss of me but I think he might be the one to win any competition with his flashing lights ensemble. The atmosphere is beautifully charged with festive cheer. I spot Jamie and a spasm of nerves stings me from the outside in. Should I have messaged him late last night? Does it not seem desperate?

He looks so attractive in his winter jumper. It's not as garish as mine, it's super cute, homely and non-offensive, just like him.

Jamie

Christmas Eve and Emily is back. She looks a lot happier than she did before her days off. And I think she's forgiven me. I was shocked when I read her text last night, and annoyed that I'd missed it when it arrived. That was down to Tim, who insisted we put up some external Christmas lights. So stupid doing it in the dark, though the house does look festive now, if you like wonky icicles and a blow-up Santa – which he insisted on putting up on the porch roof.

'Is that the best you could do?' Jayden stands before me with his hands on his hips.

'What?'

'That.' He waves his finger at my jumper.

'It's Christmas…y.'

'No, it's more ski…y.'

'Same thing.' I turn away, laughing.

'Now Emily, *that* is a Christmas jumper.' Jayden walks around Emily as she takes off her coat, checking out the back of her glittery top. It's a concoction of every Christmas cliché ever, reindeers, snowmen, Santa, sleighs, even mulled wine and all topped off with a ton of glitter.

'Thank you,' Emily says, laughing and preening and

catching my eye before quickly looking away.

'Dirk never wore one on Christmas Eve either,' Jayden says, turning back to me. 'He said he didn't like dressing up. Now we all know *that* was a lie.' He stomps back to his desk and, as a parting shot, presses a button somewhere to switch on the flashing fairy lights that cover his gaudy garment.

'Cheeky sod,' I call after him, while everyone else laughs.

Today is officially a full working day, but everyone says we'll finish at lunch time. I think every place I've ever worked, except during my student days working in retail, plays this game. If you want the day off you have to book a full day's holiday even though everyone knows we'll only work half a day. If you can call it work.

There's a party atmosphere already. Jayden is giggling, almost manically, Hayden and Karen are laughing at him and even Sharon looks the least miserable I've seen her since the Christmas party. Mince pies and sausage rolls have been delivered to every department as well as a large tin of Cadbury's Roses. These are already open and Jayden has had several coffee creams. That may be why he's so hyper.

'Did you have a nice break?' I ask Emily once she's settled at her desk.

'Yes. Thank you.' There's a shy smile.

'Did you have a good break, Emily,' Sharon calls over.

'I did. Spent some lovely time with Rosie, took her to see Santa and we went to see *The Little Mermaid* in London.'

'Oh my God, oh my God. Was it good? Say it was, say it was.' Jayden is back at Emily's desk.

'It was brilliant.'

'We're going next week. It's Sasha's Christmas present to me. He's coming even though he hates that stuff. I can't wait.' Jayden bounces back to his desk, stopping briefly to pick up another chocolate.

'I bet Rosie loved it,' Sharon says. 'Bless her.'

'She did.' Emily gets that faraway, dreamy look in her eyes. Then her face drops. 'She's gone to her dad's now.'

'Ah, not got her tomorrow? Surely not.' This time it's Karen who asks.

'I'll get her back tomorrow afternoon, then I'll take her round my mum and dad's. Everyone will be there and we'll do presents.' She smiles brightly but I can tell it's an effort. I see her take a deep breath before turning her attention to her work.

Five minutes later and everyone else trundles off to the kitchen to make themselves coffee. Jayden plus more caffeine and sugar, God help us. Suddenly it's just me and Emily alone in the office. It's now or never.

Still sitting on it, I wheel my chair over to her desk and wait for her to look up. She does so, slowly.

'I know we've covered this via text last night, but I just wanted to say it face to face. I'm sorry. I was a fool. I insulted you. I humiliated you. I embarrassed myself. I'm ashamed.' All the words come tumbling out of my stupid mouth and I feel even more stupid. Talk about begging. For fuck's sake.

She looks at me for the longest of times, her face inscrutable, her eyes searching.

The seconds tick away and she doesn't say anything.

God, this is humiliating.

She tilts her head. I think I see the hint of amusement flash across her face.

'Okay,' she says, eventually. 'I overreacted. Let's agree we don't discuss it again, cos it's a bit cringe.'

I smile. I'm not commenting or arguing or even agreeing.

'What are you doing for Christmas?' This time she smiles, properly, eyes and all. I take her cue and speak as though the last few minutes have never happened.

'My dad's. Just the two of us. He's already got the turkey on.' I laugh as though I'm making a joke, but I'm not; he texted me at seven this morning. I whizz my chair back to my desk. 'Are you having lunch with your boyfriend?'

'No. There is no boyfriend.' She grimaces. 'Now.'

'Oh. Um. Would you like a sausage roll?' I ask, jumping up to bring the plate to Emily.

'No. Thanks.'

I sit back down and eat one myself, even though I really don't want it, I have to, just to show that I was getting up for one anyway.

Would you like a sausage roll? What the hell's the matter with me? Mince pie would have been better, well, marginally less crass, anyway.

When the others come back from coffee, the frivolity dies down and some of us actually do some work, even if it is just tidying emails and folders on our computers.

The email from HR telling us what time we can go arrives at 11.30; we can leave at 12.30. After that, the pretence of work stops and everyone closes down their computers and starts tucking into the mince pies and sausage rolls – what's left of them, inadvertently I've eaten six – with gusto. Jayden dances around with the Roses tin attempting to force feed us before he eats them all.

Sharon produces a bottle of prosecco. Emily and I exchange raised eyebrows but say nothing. Fortunately, it doesn't go far between the six of us.

'This is to say thank you for being so supportive,' Sharon says as we huddle round with plastic cups full of fizzy alcohol. 'I'm sorry I caused so much trouble and, well… you know…'

'It's all turned out for the best, some might say.' Jayden nods in mine and Emily's direction then laughs, very loudly.

'How much have you had?' I hear myself ask.

'Do you mean drink? None, 'til this. It's the season, darling. And the sugar.' He's off again with the maniacal laughing. 'And how many sausage rolls have you had? You'll soon be porking up again. Which would be a shame.' He dances away from us with the Roses tin and tries to tempt Sharon.

'You like sausage rolls then?' Emily asks. She's standing right beside me, so close I can smell her perfume.

'Not as much as you'd think by how many I've eaten.'

Emily attempts a light laugh. 'You know we're all expected to go to the pub now,' she says, arching her eyebrows.

'Yeah. I might give that a miss, my dad is already having a turkey crisis.'

'You can't. Jayden's booked a nook.'

'Oh. Are you going?'

'I've got nothing better to do. Come on, let your hair down.'

The prospect of sitting in the pub on Christmas Eve with Emily is so very tempting. And scary.

'It's not that I don't want to…' I start. 'It's,

well…my dad has messaged me five times in the last hour about this bloody turkey. We don't usually cook, he, and me when I've been here, usually go out for Christmas dinner, but this year… He's worried he's going to burn it. Or poison us.'

'How long's it been in? What temperature?'

When I tell her, she smiles.

'Tell him to take it out, cover it in foil and leave it well alone.'

'Okay.' I grab my phone and message my dad. He replies instantly. 'Oh, doesn't need any advice now. Rita from next door has come round and sorted it out. Typical.'

'There you go then. Crisis over. You can come to the pub.'

'Yeah. I suppose I can.'

'Don't sound so freaking enthusiastic,' Jayden says as he prances past balancing the mince pie plate on one hand above his head. 'Have one of these and sweeten yourself up. It'll be all that sausage meat sitting down there that's making you grumpy.' He points to my groin. 'Too greasy, those sausage rolls. Way too greasy.'

'Oh God, what have we let ourselves in for?'

Emily

The morning whizzes by in a hyper, Christmassy, festive blur. I'm surprised to find myself quite excited to spend the afternoon with my colleagues. It's wonderful to be a full-time mum but also nice to be something else. To just be me. I'm missing Rosie dearly but this afternoon is certainly an okay way to pass the time.

I've had one glass of Sharon's fizz and my head's spinning yet I don't think it's because of the alcohol.

Jamie has been so sweet and fell over himself to apologise to me, he needn't have bothered, all was already forgiven. I overreacted. I let my history get the better of me, Jamie is different. My stomach is out of control performing somersaults every time I look at him and I can't help stealing glances. We keep making eye contact a lot more than we should and I'm enjoying it more than I should. The taxi kiss is playing over and over again in my mind and all I can think is how much I want to do it again.

I need to do it again.

Jamie

I find myself sitting next to Emily in the nook that Jayden has booked. I don't know if this is a good idea, I certainly didn't plan it. Maybe we would have been better apart. There's still a stilted, faux friendliness between us.

'Bet you're glad you came now,' Jayden says, nudging me as he sits down.

We've all added money to the kitty and a jug of what looks like sangria appears on the table.

'Sangria?'

'Yes. Christmas sangria.' Jayden reaches over the jug. 'Hot and spicy.' He giggles.

'Not for me, I'm driving.'

'Urgh. Spoilsport. I'll have yours.' Jayden pours us a glass each then moves them both over in front of him.

Pretty soon another jug appears and I manage to get a jug of water brought to the table too.

'This is lovely,' Emily says. 'I bet you wished you hadn't brought your car to work.'

'Yeah.' I'm still wondering if coming was a good idea. I feel awkward.

'You could always get a taxi,' she offers. 'Share one with me.' In my head she winks and nudges me, in reality she blushes. Maybe she's being overfriendly to compensate for overreacting. Who am I kidding?

'I don't want to leave it in the car park overnight.

'No, don't,' Sharon calls over. 'They lock the barrier down. You wouldn't be able to get it until the holidays are over.'

'Jan second,' Jayden says, as if I didn't know. 'And you'll have to get it by six or risk being stuck there anyway.' He laughs again. If Jayden is this merry after two Christmas sangrias and half a tin of Roses, God knows what he's like when he really gets going. I don't remember him being quite so inebriated at the Christmas party, but maybe my memory of that night is full of other things.

'Maybe I should have moved it.' It's already 2pm, and we're only just getting started.

'Oh no. I'll be leaving before then. I can't drink all afternoon. Can't take it.' Emily laughs. It's lovely, her laugh.

Despite myself, I still have a good time. Jayden is outrageously funny, Sharon has brightened up, Karen is sharply quick witted and Hayden watches us all.

The only person missing is Dirk.

'A toast, a toast,' Jayden says, picking up his glass. 'To our new team members, who, it seems, will be staying longer than expected. Hurray, I say. And to… ahem… absent friends. Not that they were always friendly. To us.' He raises his glass as we all chorus his toast.

'Silly Dirk,' Emily whispers in my ear.

I love the feel of her breath on my skin.

I'm so glad I'm not drinking.

Soon everyone's exchanging Christmas plans. Jayden is spending it with Sasha, and goes into great detail about what he has planned for their first Christmas together. Everyone else is happy to get some time with their families.

My dad messages me mid-afternoon to tell me Rita is now joining us tomorrow. Well, I wasn't expecting that.

'Who's Rita again?' Emily asks when I tell her. I don't know why I felt the need to tell her.

'She's a widow and neighbour.' I hear myself sigh. What was that sage advice that Tim imparted? Oh yeah, time to move on.

Emily reaches over and grips my hand, squeezing hard. I smile at her. Now, I feel properly forgiven. Then I remind myself that even if I am not drinking, she is. Oh, to hell with it.

'I wanted to do that to *you*,' I say, hoping that big ears Jayden isn't listening. 'When we were in Alan's office. I could see you shaking. Before I said the stupid thing, I mean…'

'Urgh. I was angry. And scared. I didn't want the sack before Christmas. I just wanted to get out before he could say it.'

'Me too. Funny how it's turned out. I can't say I'm sorry enough…'

'Forget it.' She waves her hand about, batting away my stupidity. I hope. 'Good how it's turned out. Though not for Dirk.'

'Not our fault.' I couldn't give a shit about Dirk, he'll land on his feet in a pot of gold, his sort always does.

'No,' chimes in Jayden. 'We have Sharon to thank for that. Thanks Sharon.' He raises his glass in her direction and smiles, but fortunately she's deep in conversation with Karen and doesn't hear him.

'I think I'd better be going. It's after four.' Emily starts looking round for her coat.

'You'd better get your car,' Hayden says to me. 'They lock the barrier at five.'

'I thought it was six.'

'Oops.' Jayden starts giggling. 'Sorry. My mistake.'

Outside in the cold air, Emily and I head down the street, she in search of a taxi, me for my car.

'Come on, I'll give you a lift.'

'It's out of your way.'

'So what?'

She frowns at me as though she's giving it some thought.

'Anyway, I doubt you'll get one now. A taxi, I mean. It's Christmas Eve.' I wave my hands about in what I hope is a humorous way.

'You sure you haven't been drinking?'

'Course not. Come on.'

She doesn't agree, she doesn't disagree, she just links her arm in mine as we walk to the Genevre campus. It's cold and almost dark and we can see our breath as we increase our pace.

I'm forgiven.

Emily

Jamie opens his car door for me and I step inside, he's old fashioned. I should have guessed. I notice his forest-fresh air freshener hanging from the mirror, it's almost overwhelming, heady but not unpleasant. The smell matches the mood. A passport size photo of what I assume is his mum and dad is placed between the cigarette lighter and the gearstick. Bless him.

He looks like his mum, same eyes.

'That's better, it's so cold,' I say for something to say because we are so close and alone. It's awkward, nice, but awkward. 'Have you heard anymore from your dad about the turkey?' I ask, again for something to say as he's now gone quiet. I think he saw me spy the photo, it must be hard for him and his dad.

'No. Mercifully.' He sighs as he changes gear.

'What will you do, go there now?' I'm talking too much, partly nerves, partly alcohol. He must think he's in an interview. I give him a non-gummy smile to reassure him he's not.

'No. I'll rock up when he's peeling the spuds tomorrow. About ten. He likes to eat his Christmas lunch at lunchtime. That's no later than one.'

'My parents eat at two. Every Christmas. They'll all be there, my brothers, their wives, all the kids.' I feel desperately sad about my imminent lonely Christmas meal for one. It's Marks & Spencer so at least it will be good quality.

'Sounds busy. And fun. You'll have a great time,' he says, just as we're approaching my street. We pull up outside my house. The drive seemed to take no time and I'm left here wanting more. More time with Jamie.

'I'm not going,' I blurt out, then hold my breath. Don't cry.

'I thought you said you were taking your little girl there.' He turns to look at me, frowning.

'For tea. Not lunch. I can't bear to go without her. All the kids will ask where she is. I can't stand it. So I'm dipping out. This is my first Christmas lunch without her. Ever.' The words fall out and a tear escapes, sliding sadly down my cheek. I thought I was fine with this, it hasn't truly hit me until now. Jamie wipes it away with his thumb and his hand stays there, his eyes searching mine.

'Ignore me,' I continue, shaking my head. 'It's a good thing. And I'll still see her on Christmas Day. Just not tonight, or in the morning. But it's only fair.'

'Fair?' he questions. We're holding hands now, I'm not even sure how it happened, who held whose first, but I don't care. It's so comforting, so intimate.

'I wouldn't let her dad see her on Christmas Day before. But we've had a sort of rapprochement, is that the right word? Anyway, we're getting on better,' I reply, hoping I don't sound like a massive, man-hating bitch. I follow this up again with my best non-gummy smile.

'You mean you might get back together? Is that why your boyfriend is no more?'

'God, no.' I smirk, before feeling the need to explain 'No. Liam, my ex, he's remarried. We're just all getting on better. And my boyfriend, well, he's also married. I dumped him when I found out,' I reveal, breaking eye contact to look at the glittery, red festive nails on my free hand.

'Bastard,' Jamie spits.

'It's his wife I feel sorry for.' I sigh.

'Yeah. And you.' He says squeezing my hand and I slyly sniff back another tear. I don't want to let go of his hand.

Oh hell. What the hell.

'Coffee?' I ask quickly, not looking at him, still inspecting my fabulous nails.

'Okay.' He smiles and I smile back, gums and all because, let's face it, he's seen them before. He knows I have a gummy smile. He's my colleague, my workmate, my something else perhaps?

We get out of the car and hold hands again, I turn the key in the lock, letting the front door slam shut behind us and lead him into the kitchen. I flick the switch on the kettle and begin to ask him how he likes his coffee, pretending I don't know.

I know how he likes it.

He takes my face in his hands and we're kissing before the kettle has even boiled.

Heaven.

Jamie

We stop for coffee, we have to, we're both getting carried away.

'I think I should go.' I put my empty cup on the draining board.

'Why?' Emily looks at me with a hurt expression in her doe-brown eyes.

'Why? Whoa.' I so *want* to stay.

'Your dad doesn't need you for turkey duty now, does he?'

We both laugh. Nervous. Embarrassed.

'No. But. You've had too much to drink. And you've just come out of a messy relationship. You're on the rebound. I don't want to take advantage of you.' Oh shit, I sound patronising again. What's wrong with me?

Emily laughs. 'I'm a big girl, in case you hadn't noticed.'

'You're anything but a big girl, but I take your point about being an adult. Even so…' I shake my head.

'You don't like me.'

I breathe so hard through my pursed lips that it comes out like a donkey's bray. We both laugh, perhaps too much.

'I more than like you,' I hear myself say.

311

'Me too.'

'And that's why it's not going to be like this.'

Emily sighs, yanks open the dishwasher door and, with a lot of clattering, puts her coffee cup, followed by mine, inside. 'You're probably right.' Now it's her turn to sigh, but she doesn't bray like I did.

'Come for lunch tomorrow.'

She turns and frowns at me.

'You'd be doing me a favour. Sort of rebalancing.'

'Urgh.' She pulls a face that clearly shows I've said the wrong thing. Again.

'And I'd love to spend Christmas Day lunch with you.'

'Ah.' She takes a step towards me.

'I don't like to think of you on your own.' I take a step towards her.

'Oh.' She takes my hands.

'Please say you'll come. I lift her hands to my mouth. I kiss them and it doesn't seem at all cheesy.

Twenty-four

Emily

The Christmas meal was where it all started for them and where it all ended for us.

Jamie's dad, Richard, greeted us with a huge carving knife in his hand, and wearing a novelty apron that had "Burnt to perfection" written on it in big black letters. Rita had bought it for him as a Christmas present, her sense of humour obvious from the beginning. I liked Rita.

Richard was a lot shorter than Jamie and a lot jollier than I expected him to be. Rita gently took the mickey out of him for his cooking panic and Richard laughed with a twinkle in his eye and a warm crackle in his voice. I caught Jamie rolling his eyes a few times at Richard's poor *dad jokes* but I could tell he was begrudgingly happy for him. It started that day for Richard and Rita, they were inseparable from then on in.

It ended for Jamie and I because it was the day we stopped being just *mates from work* and started being something a whole lot more.

The Christmas lunch was gorgeously, deliciously yummy, a lot tastier than my lonely Marks & Spencer meal for one. I know this because I shared it the very next day with Rosie, padded out with various cheese, breads and crackers on the side. It's amazing the random crap and bizarre mixtures you eat over Christmas that you wouldn't dare touch at any other time of the year. We later had a chocolate selection box for dinner. Bliss.

Rita had brought round honey roasted parsnips and a gammon joint and Richard had prepared chestnut sprouts, runner beans, carrots, roast potatoes, Yorkshire puddings and gravy, not to mention the Turkey with a rescue job from Rita. The conversation seemed to flow exceptionally well between the four of us considering that two of us were strangers. But, by the end of the dinner it was as though I had known Richard and Rita for years and Jamie, all my life.

'So how long have you two been together then? You make a lovely couple if you don't mind me saying,' Rita asked in her friendly northern twang as she ran her fingers through her immaculate grey bob. She blinked at both of us expectantly, waiting for an answer as she played with the stem of her wine glass.

'Umm well…' I stumbled and gave Jamie a sideways glance. Oh hell. I could feel my cheeks burning and the imaginary cold hands immediately came to try and slap the colour out of them. I think they'll always try to come and save me, thanks Sabrina.

'Well, not that long actually,' Jamie said, studying me with his hypotonic, mesmerising eyes. 'It's quite… umm, new?' He looked at me as he questioned what we were.

I held my breath and gazed back at him, lightly squeezing his knee under the table. It's okay Jamie, I thought as I tried to will him with my eyes. Say it. Say we're together.

'But we're very happy, thank you Rita,' he added, grinning back at her. Phew. I felt his hand slide onto my knee before giving it a firm reciprocal squeeze. Blushing again, my ears were also burning and my face was aching. I can only put it down to the fact that I was so sickly happy and it hurt so much from smiling a lot.

So that was it, Rita assumed we were together and we didn't want to make an ass out of her, did we?

Six months later
Jamie
'Did you consult my manual?'

'Yes.'

'The *What to do in a crisis* section?'

'Yes. That's why I'm ringing you. It says to ring you.' I sigh down the phone. I knew this wasn't a good idea.

'Ah, yeah. I didn't really put much in that section, did I?'

'Tim,' I say, really getting annoyed with him now. 'It's hardly a manual, is it? Four Post-it Notes stuck on the back of the tank.

'Mate, how can you have lost her already? I've only been gone a few days.' Now it's Tim's turn to sigh. 'How long has she been missing?'

'She was there when I moved the cage last night, gone this morning. And I really don't have time for this. I've got to get the painting finished in that room by the end of the day.'

'What colour?'

'Lilac.'

'Oh yeah.'

'So, any ideas?'

'Yeah, lilac's good. You having a new carpet?'

'Yes. Tomorrow, hence the urgency. I meant ideas about Delilah, not the décor.'

'Well, if she went missing downstairs try down the side of the cooker. She likes it there. Been there a few times.'

'I remember.' But only the once. 'How many times?'

'Not sure.' In the background Lex calls out to ask Tim if he wants coffee. 'Gotta go, mate. Have fun.' He ends the call. Lex knew what she was doing banning Delilah from *her* house.

I can't see down the side of the cooker, not without a torch. I open the drawer in the kitchen, the one full of batteries and screwdrivers and spy Tim's head torch. It's too handy; I wonder exactly how many times Delilah hid down the side of the cooker.

And there she is, her beady little eyes reflecting the torch's light back at me, her tongue tasting the air.

'Right, you little fucker.'

I'm already armed with the nylon-feather duster and the oven gloves. I poke the duster down behind the gecko and keep a gloved hand ready to catch her.

And it works.

'Get in,' I shout.

Keeping hold of her isn't so easy but I manage, even if that does involve a soft shoe shuffle through the kitchen and into our tiny utility room. I'm clutching her to my chest with both hands but I don't know how the hell I'm going to get the tank door open and get her inside.

'Do you need some help?' an amused voice asks.

I turn to see Emily smirking at me.

'Hello. Yes. Please.'

She slides the door open and together we bundle Delilah back inside her tank.

'How long have you been here?' I ask as I pull Emily to me and kiss her.

'Long enough. I called out when I came in the front door and I thought you answered.'

'Ah. No. I was catching that little f…..'

Emily puts her finger to my lips and smiles.

'I know. I'm working on the swearing. Honestly, I hardly swear, it's that little …Delilah that brings it out in me. I'm really having major doubts about keeping her.'

'Tim can't have her. Lex said no, an emphatic no. She has two cats, so Delilah probably wouldn't have lasted long anyway. If Delilah can get out of the cage then the cats would have no problem getting in. Too cruel.'

'I know.' I really didn't want to be lumbered with Tim's gecko.

'And Rosie loves her.'

'I know she does.' I blame Tim for that. He tempted Rosie, allowed her to play with Delilah, feed her crickets, change her water. It backfired on him though, when Rosie drew the picture of Delilah, a leaving present for him so he wouldn't forget her, he'd cried. Big, blubbering fool.

'Why don't we just get a better cage. One that works.' Emily turns and shimmies past me in the close confines of the utility room. She's wearing leggings with a big shirt over, and a scarf around her head, cleaning gear, she says. God, she looks hot. She'd look hot in a bin bag.

'I suppose.'

'Rosie will enjoy a trip to Pets at Home.'

'Yeah, as long as we don't come back with a bunny or a puppy. No more pets.'

She frowns at me. 'You're grouchy. Have you been out for a run today?'

'No. I wanted to get the painting finished. Still got a bit of woodwork to do, want it to be completely dry before they fit the carpet tomorrow.

'Come here.' She makes a grab for me. I have to fight her off so I can get that painting done. It needs to be done.

'Rosie's so excited about moving in on Friday. She can't wait to see her bedroom, we couldn't decorate at our place because it was rented. This is going to thrill her to bits.'

'Anything for my girls,' I say, and I don't feel even a little bit like a dick.

Emily

It's now June, they say a lot can happen in a year but a lot has happened for me in just six months. For the past two weeks Rosie and I have been living with Jamie in his two-bedroom house. He owns his house so of course it made sense to move there rather than him move in with me. Rosie and Jamie get on so well, when we go out for walks, he often lets her sit on his shoulders and she loves being up so high, she says she feels like he's the BFG. Listening to her giggle like that makes me the happiest mum on the planet. Rosie also has a soft spot for Delilah, Tim's Gecko. She's fascinated by her and especially loves watching her eat live crickets.

Yuk.

As it turns out, Tim couldn't take his Gecko to Lex's. So, much to Rosie's delight if not Jamie's, the Gecko is still here until Tim can find her a new, suitable owner. Jamie says she will probably stay with us forever as Tim won't deem anyone good enough to look after her and he views this house as Delilah's home, Tim says it's all she's ever known. Rosie drew Tim the cutest picture of Delilah so that Tim wouldn't forget her, he was very touched by it and blubbed like a baby. So sweet.

Liam and Tiny took Rosie on holiday for two weeks over the Easter holidays, her first ever holiday abroad. She was so excited, I couldn't help being as pleased as she was, even though a small part of me was disappointed that it wasn't me taking her. For the first time in almost six years, Rosie and I were on our own separate journeys. Jamie and I spent almost every evening at each other's houses, cooking together, going out for walks or going out to the pub. And let's not mention the frisky stuff, I don't want the cold hands to come out and slap me round my red face again.

So, when he asked me to move in, it just felt like the most natural thing in the world. Rosie had met him a lot between Christmas and Easter and we planned to spend lots of time together afterwards so it wasn't like Jamie was a stranger to her. Jamie wasn't introduced as a friend or hidden away for months on end until we were sure it was the right time to introduce him, because we were always sure, right from the start. He was my boyfriend and when it's right you just know, there's no need to slow down. Even all those months ago when we got given the team building assignment at work, the feelings were always there, bubbling under the surface, under the paintballs, just waiting to be discovered.

Jamie

'Good day?' I ask as Emily comes bouncing through the front door with Rosie by her side. They've settled in so well that it feels as though they've always lived here even though it's only been a few weeks.

'How's Delilah? Rosie asks by way of a reply, rushing past me on her way to the utility room.

'Still there when last I looked.'

'Hey, you,' Emily says, stepping into my arms. God, this feels so good.

'How was work?'

Emily smiles her response.

'Yeah, it was good. The novelty's wearing off now and I'm starting to lose some of that imposter syndrome.' Emily's been underwriting department head for six weeks now and she's bloody good at it. The restructure Alan wanted ended up being fairly minor, except that Emily's team is bigger than Dirk's ever was. And I don't work in insurance at all now.

'You're brilliant, you don't ever have to feel like you're not.' I kiss her. I can't help it.

'What about you?'

'Got my first private paying clients today.'

'What? Wow! Tell me more.'

'It's Tim and Lex, to be honest. But they're paying, full whack. And when I've finished with him, Tim has agreed to be my model for *after*. I've taken the *before* pictures and already posted them on the website.

'That's still brilliant. Go you.' She high fives me just as Rosie comes back clutching Delilah.

'Don't let her go,' I say, thinking I'd prefer her to stay in the super expensive cage we've just bought.

'I won't. Don't be silly.' Rosie sits down with the gecko on her shoulder and starts singing Disney songs to her.

'That's nice, darling,' Emily says, smiling.

'I know. Delilah likes it too. She told me it keeps her calm. What's for tea?'

'I've made a lasagne,' I say. 'It's in the oven.' Since Tim moved out and Emily moved in there have been no more takeaways or fry ups.

'Delilah doesn't like lasagne,' Rosie says, stroking the gecko's head.

'There's a nice juicy cricket for her.'

'Would you like to see my bedroom now, Delilah?' Rosie stands up.

'No,' Emily and I chorus and then I leave it to Emily to explain our *no pets upstairs* rule. Again. I have to hand it to Rosie, she is persistent.

Emily

'Helloooooooo, anybody here??'

I jump up from the sofa and bolt to get the door, it's Sabrina shouting through the letter box. I must have dozed off. Shit, where are the keys?

'Hello, my lovely. How are you? I've missed you,' I say as I finally open the door and give her a big hug and a kiss.

'I'm great, my darling.' Sabrina grins at me. 'Wow, this place is so gorgeous, is the décor down to you?' She wanders into Jamie's beautifully decorated living room.

'Yeah, well sort of, we picked it together. Jamie and Tim decorated it all before we moved in. It was a surprise; I didn't see it until it was finished, although I did choose the wallpaper. All I did was rock up for the cleaning at the end.' I beam as Sabrina stares wide-eyed at the duck egg blue walls. She points to the feature wall.

'Laura Ashley?'

'Of course.' I feel slightly smug that he let me have my paisley gold wallpaper. It's not exactly masculine.

'Wow, darling, he's a keeper, Dave would shit all over that. I love him but that man has no taste. That's why we live in the land of magnolia.' She shrugs her shoulders, helpless to Dave's shit taste. 'Can I nose round the rest of the house?' She's already wandering into the kitchen.

'Yeah of course you can. I'll make us both a cuppa.'

'Sounds like a plan, I feel like I'm on *Come Dine with Me*. Don't worry, I won't riffle through your knicker drawer.' She laughs as she trots up the stairs.

'You best not, you'll be jealous of my underwear collection,' I shout after her.

'Collection of old granny knickers you mean,' she calls back.

'Cheeky cow,' I holler, laughing. Letting out a happy sigh, I walk back into the kitchen and switch the kettle on. It's only a small house, she won't be up there long, but it's the right size for us. She's probably nosing at Rosie's princess room now, it's lilac with a hand-painted mural of Ariel from *The Little Mermaid* above her pink princess bed.

I finish making the tea and glide into the living room with the cup. Sabrina's back from her house nosing and is sitting on the sofa again. Crying.

'Sab, are you okay? What's up?' I ask, putting the teas on the coffee table before wrapping an arm around her.

'Yes. Yes. I just think it's wonderful, that he did all this for you. I'm so pleased,' she squeaks, sniffing back tears and wiping her fingers under her eyes to save her immaculate eye makeup.

'You're so sweet mate, wanna know something else?' I nudge her.

'What?' She sniffs, with gusto. It's really not very ladylike.

'That picture of Ariel above Rosie's bed,' I start.

'Yes.'

'Jamie painted that.' I grin.

'Oh my God, Jesus, heavens above.' Sabrina wails, her eyes streaming as more tears run down her cheeks.

'Here.' I offer her the cup of tea. She shoos it away so I give her another cuddle instead.

'I just think it's wonderful,' she blubs into my hair. 'He's perfect for you and you deserve it darling. After everything with that awful shit, Ben and Liam before him, it's your happy ending.'

'Thank you.' I peel her off me to pass her some tissues.

'Let me be your maid of honour,' she blurts out, frantically wiping her face and trying to fix her eye makeup.

'Sab.' I laugh. 'He has to ask me first and we've only been together six months.

'Why not ask him?'

'What? No way.' I'm all for equality but me proposing just scares the living daylights out of me.

'Sorry, darling. It's just amazing to see you with someone decent. And happy. Finally.'

'I know, I've never been happier, and not a Kalm in sight.' We both laugh at that. 'And who knows, we have been discussing the future, buying a bigger house eventually. More room, you know.'

'More room for what exactly? She blinks, her eyes welling up again.

'Yeah, anything could happen.' I wink, patting my

belly and we both roll around giggling.

Never say never.

But not yet.

Jamie

Emily has her friend, Sabrina, coming round. It's the first time she's seen my house, our house, our home. Rosie's at her dad's and I thought I'd give Emily and Sabrina a bit of space for a good old catch up. Sabrina is lovely, but a bit full on for me. She never stops talking and is so dramatic. Emily says it's because she's half-Italian. Dave, her husband, has the patience of a saint.

I guess with us living together I need to get used to stuff like this. It's so very different from when Tim lived with me. Thank God.

I love Emily like I've never loved any woman before, but we both need our own space. Emily has been used to being on her own since her husband ran off, used to making her own decisions. She's having to adapt just as I am. I love that she's independent but also supportive. If it hadn't been for Emily's support, I probably wouldn't be doing what I'm doing now. It was Emily who, together with Chelle, encouraged me to take the leap, to enrol on a fitness instructor course. It was lucky that I still had most of my redundancy money left from Kanes and could afford to live on that while I trained.

I'm running. I like to do 5K every day, just to keep myself fit. I love the freedom to just concentrate on the movement, the feel of my feet as they hit the ground. It relaxes me and energises me at the same time. I enjoy the fresh air, the sights, the sounds of nature all around. I love this exercise shit. Who would have thought it? Not me.

'Hey, Jimbo. Is that you?' A figure clad in a black wifebeater vest and short-shorts steps out in front of me. He's wearing red Man Rox wristbands and a sweat band around his head. He has muscles on top of muscles. Tosser.

'Dirk?' It takes me a moment to recognise him. He's grown his hair long and it's wavy and shiny like a woman's, he also has a full-on beard.

'Hey, Jimbo,' he says again thrusting out a hand to shake mine.

'Jamie,' I correct as I grip his hand just as hard as he grips mine. Really, are we going to have a hand wrestle in the park? He lets go first.

'I hardly recognised you. Chelle has done a good job. Cuel.' His voice is low and gravelly and annoying and I'm finding it hard to banish the image of him singing and prancing around as a horny devil from my mind.

'She started a good job, mostly I did it myself.' I want to go now but it would be just too rude and anyway, I'm curious. 'How are you?' I ask. 'Where are you working now?'

'Hey, I'm good. Cuel actually. Just won my latest comp.' He launches into a muscle-man pose, right in the middle of the park. For God's sake there are children about. 'I'm just doing a bit of light running to run some of this muscle off. Oh, and I landed myself a nice position over at Kanes.'

'Kanes? In town?'

'Yeah. You know it?'

'Yes. I used to work there.' Which you should remember from my interview. Were you even listening? 'They were downsizing.'

Dirk looks at me for a second too long. 'Not since I went there, hey.' He laughs his stupid, deep, manly laugh. 'Enough of me. What happened with you? I hear Emily got the job?' The grin on his face goes from ear to ear.

'She did. And well deserved. Though it wasn't exactly that job, they restructured.'

'Yeah. Cuel. What about you? What did you get?'

'Oh I left before the restructure.'

'Oh?' He frowns, jutting his stupid square jaw out, even his beard is square.

'Yes, I realised that sitting at a desk all the time really wasn't for me. I retrained as a fitness instructor. I work three days a week in Genevre's onsite gym and the rest of the time I'm working with private clients.' He doesn't need to know that my private clients are just Tim and Lex, and possibly Dave, if Sabrina gets her way.

Dirk takes ten seconds or so to take in this information, his stupid, thick eyebrows rising and falling as he thinks, then ignores it.

'I messaged Emily congrats, but she didn't reply. I wonder if I've got the right number for her.' He strokes his beard. 'Do you have her number? I'd like to hook up with her again. Do you ever see her?'

'I see her every day.' I wait for that to sink in before continuing. 'We're together. A couple. We live together.'

Dirk blinks a few times.

'Cuel.' His face doesn't look cool. 'So you have her number?'

Is he for real?

'Yes, of course I do. But you're not having it.'

'Oh. But I thought I might hook up with her.'

'Hook up? If you mean what I think you mean, forget it. She's not interested in *you*. She's marrying *me*.'

He blinks again.

'Cuel. Hey Jimbo, it's been good.' He thrusts his hand out for another shake. I don't reciprocate.

'It's Jamie, Dick. Jamie.' And I run off before he can react.

He's such a dick.

Emily

'You just missed Sabrina. Good run?'

Jamie looks quite red in the face, I hope he isn't overdoing it.

'It was,' he says, running his hands through his hair. 'Until I bumped into Dirk. He wants your number. He wants to hook up with you again.'

'Urgh. No. He messaged me months ago. I just blocked him. He found me on Facebook too, I blocked him there as well. What did you say?' Urgh, the thought of Dirk in those red kinky boots, that thong, those horns. I feel sick.

'I warned him off.'

'Good. I hope you told him I'm with you and that we won't take no shit from him.' I wag my finger and smile as I say it, we're allowed to swear when Rosie isn't with us.

'Yeah, I might have told him we were getting married.' Jamie looks away, not meeting my gaze.

What did he just say? Have I misheard? One look at his earnest face tells me I haven't.

'Is that a proposal?' Oh hell. What have I just said?

Jamie scrabbles around in his pocket and pulls out a coin.

'20p,' he says, smiling. 'Not a ring but a symbol of our first meeting.'

'Don't lick it,' I say, giggling with excitement.

'I know we've not been together long, but I feel like I've known you forever, so yes, I think it is a proposal.' He drops down onto one knee. 'Emily Cod, will you marry me?'

Oh my God. Oh my God.

'Yes, Jamie, I will.'

About the authors

Belle Henderson

Belle Henderson is a lover of books, especially romcoms; she loves a happy ending. People's idiosyncrasies fascinate and occasionally amuse Belle. She loves to home in on these quirks which subsequently help to breathe life into her characters.

Belle has co-written her debut novel with CJ Morrow, but plans to fly solo next time.

Email: **bellehendersonauthor@gmail.com**

Instagram: **instagram.com/bellehendersonauthor/**

Facebook: **facebook.com/bellehendersonauthor/**

CJ Morrow

CJ Morrow writes about everyday life as though viewed side on - she likes to catch the object which moves in the corner of your eye and disappears when you turn. She's fascinated by the ordinary man, or woman, who isn't quite what they seem. She likes to see the magic and mystery in every situation and relationship. Life intrigues her and she finds much of it funny.

Word weaver, lover of things curious, unseen and unexplainable, general wordy person. Always watching. And laughing - mostly at herself.

When she doesn't like what's going on in the world, she writes another one.

Email: **cjmorrowauthor@gmail.com**

Blog: **cjmorrow13.wordpress.com**

Twitter: @cjmorrowauthor

Instagram: **instagram.com/cjmorrowauthor/**

Facebook: **facebook.com/cjmorrowauthor**

Printed in Great Britain
by Amazon